PEACO

Sharon Maas was born in Georgetown, Guyana and studied in England before returning to Guyana where she worked as a journalist. She travelled extensively in South America and spent a number of years living in an Ashram in India, before settling in Germany and training as a social worker. She is married with two children and lives in Germany and England.

To find out more visit www.sharonmaas.com

By the same author

OF MARRIAGEABLE AGE

SHARON MAAS

PEACOCKS
DANCING

HarperCollins*Publishers*

HarperCollins*Publishers*
77–85 Fulham Palace Road,
Hammersmith, London W6 8JB

www.**fire**and**water**.com

First published by HarperCollins*Publishers* 2001
1 3 5 7 9 8 6 4 2

Copyright © Sharon Maas 2000

The Author asserts the moral right to
be identified as the author of this work

A catalogue record for this book
is available from the British Library

ISBN 0 00 711847 3

Set in Aldus

Printed and bound in Great Britain by
Clays Ltd, St Ives plc

ACKNOWLEDGEMENTS

My thanks to Dr Ishwarprasad Gilada, General-Secretary of the People's Health Organisation in Bombay, for his invaluable help during the research for this novel. I wish him the world's support in the struggle against AIDS and child prostitution.

To Rupert Westmaas for the use of his poems. To Mary Norrito-Koller, Henry Baldwin and Timothy Pegler for their advice.

To Sarah Molloy, more than an agent.

And of course to my editor Susan Watt for her insight and encouragement, and for always knowing what is hiding in the shadows.

Mirdad: You must be ever full that you may fill the wanting. You must be ever strong and steady that you may prop the wavering and the weak. You must be ever ready for the storm that you may shelter all the storm-tossed waifs. You must be ever luminous that you may guide the walkers in the dark.

MIKHAIL NAIMY, *The Book of Mirdad*

Dear Diary,

Hello. Now I am six. My name is Rita Maraj. I live at Number Seven, Victoria Street, Georgetown with Daddy and Mildrid. Mildrid is the made.

Daddy gave you to me today. He said You will be my Freind and I can write Things to You. I like the puppy on your cover. I also got a bysicle, its red, I can ride my bysicle almost alredy. I had a party with Polly and Dona and Brian Coolij. I had a cake with six candles and I blew them all out but I didnt let Brian Coolij kiss me. I made a wish. I wont tell you my wish but I'll tell you everything else about me.

I have too dogs and three cats. I fownd them by myself. I like watching ants.

My Mummy ~~dide~~ ~~dyd~~ dyed when I was Born. I had too Grannys but one dyed two last year thats why I came to live with Daddy. I never met that Granny (Daddys mummy). she didnt like me but the other one likes me *a lot* but she lives far away in a Creek. She has a boat and pigs and lots more anamals and I used to live in the Creek with her two (and Anty). I love anamals and Daddy says I can have lots of them. Creek water is black. I like to read.

1

Daddy didnt come home to read my Story for me tonight thats why im writing to You. I learnd to read and write at the Mary Noble Primary School but I still make some speling mistakes but not meny. I like school but Im always getting into truble I cant help it.

Janet Focks said I look like a ragger Mufin so I throo her books out the window. Miss Lee made me leve the room. I wrote my name on the wall. She gave me a letter for Daddy. I ~~read~~ red it and throo it away. She told him to kome my hair before I go to school but Daddy sleeps in the morning so he cant so Mildrid komes it for me. It has two many nots and it hurts when she komes it thats why I bit her hand today but I didnt mean to. I was going to kome it myself but I *entirley* forgot.

Goodbye, Rita

PS I hope you like me I hope we get to be best Freinds.

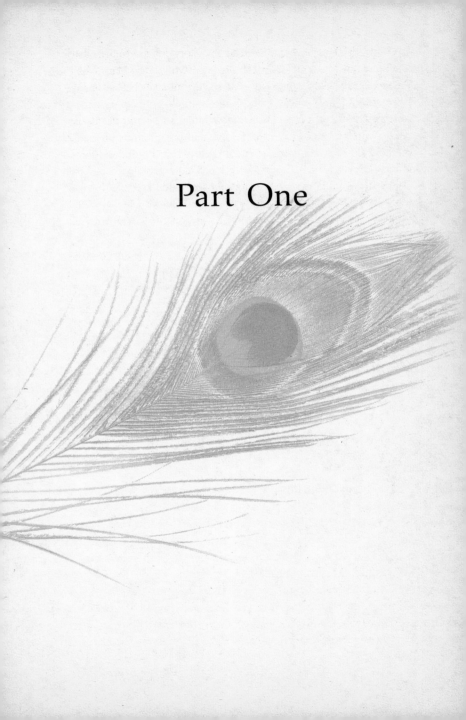

Part One

ONE

A Catastrofee

'Either *they* go,' Marilyn said firmly on her very first day at Number Seven, 'or I.' She laid the silver knife and fork primly together beside the chicken bones on her china plate, daintily lifted the white damask napkin from her lap and pressed it to her crimson lips. The silver and the china and the damask were all her own: they were part of her trousseau, prime weapons in her war against the established disorder at Number Seven. She pushed the plate forward, placed her elbows on the table, rested her chin on clasped hands, and stared at Rita across the table with the narrowed eyes of a cat.

Rita was just about to say, 'Then go,' but Daddy leaned sideways and put his arm around Marilyn and looked at Rita and smiled and winked, and instead of speaking out Rita stared at her plate and bit her top lip and pushed out her bottom lip, and Marilyn said, 'Look at her, she's pouting again! That girl's spoilt silly!'

That evening Daddy came to sit on Rita's bed and explained everything to her. 'Marilyn doesn't like ants,' he said. 'And we need Marilyn. You know why, don't you? I told you. Most people don't like ants, you know, most people don't have ant farms in

5

their homes. So please be a good girl and don't vex her, sweet-heart. Let's keep the peace, OK? Just do what she says.' And he bent down and whispered in Rita's ear, 'My favourite little girl!'

Rita pulled away, sulking. He didn't have any other little girls, and anyway, it wasn't just the ants, it was the dogs and everything else.

'She kicked Frisky, that day when she first came. I saw, I was hiding but I saw. And she called Dolly a dirty old bitch. She's a bitch herself!'

Daddy chuckled. 'Where you learn words like that, eh? Come now, go to sleep. Y'all going to get used to one another. You got a nice new mummy, soon you going to have a little brother, you going to have a real family again!'

'Go *'way*!' Rita flung herself down upon her pillow, twisting in mid-air so her back was turned to Daddy. Serve him right.

The very next day Frisky was dead. The day after Daddy mar-ried her and brought her home, the day after doomsday. Frisky was the first sign of terrible things to come. Frisky had mange and the vet had given Rita something to bathe him in and she had been doing so lovingly each day, but when Rita came back from school the day after doomsday Marilyn said Frisky was no more. 'Put to sleep,' she said. 'That mangy old thing!' And Rita heard Marilyn telling Daddy, 'I'm not going to have any animals in the house and she'll just have to get used to that. You've spoilt that girl completely, she's running wild and I'll have to take her in hand. I'm sure this place is full of fleas. She had that mangy old thing in her *bed*!'

That was the worst thing about stepmothers, Rita concluded after several weeks had passed: they hated animals. Especially stray puppies. And stray kittens. Not to mention ants, tadpoles and caterpillars kept in shoeboxes with lots of green leaves. Daddy should have known that before he married Marilyn. Now it was too late. Take ants, for instance. Rita loved ants. She could watch ants for hours, marching in straight lines along the windowsills, march march march, looking at them through a magnifying glass and wondering just what they were thinking. Did ants think? Or did they just thoughtlessly wordlessly *know*, feeling what they had to do, follow follow follow, sugar sugar sugar? You could put a piece of pink sugarcake on a table with no ants and in no time one would be there sniffing, then two, and then an excited scurrying crowd crying look look look, come come come, sugar sugar sugar, then the marching ants carrying pieces of sugarcake bigger than themselves, march march march, carry carry carry, back to their homes. They marched around the house, up and down the walls and doorframes and table legs, and Rita's eyes followed them, knowing where they came in and where they went out; she kept them in jars filled with sand and watched them marching through labyrinths of underground tunnels, carrying the crumbs she fed them, carry carry carry, waving their antennae, singing their march songs. Rita gave them names but mixed them up. She imagined herself small, ant size, and marching and singing with them. She strained her ears to catch their cries of sugar and their march songs, sure that if she tuned her mind fine enough she could hear. She had been running her successful ant farm for a good three months. Then Marilyn, on her very first day, came pumping a red can of Flit and the ants were gone. For ever.

After that Rita kept her animals in the yard. Under bushes, behind a heap of planks, on the back seat of the Morris wreck. A litter of kittens she found drowning in a trench. A kiskadee with a wounded wing that died. Polly Wong's dog Rover for two weeks when the Wongs were in the Islands. She moved her Animal Clinic to Polly Wong's garden. When she grew up she was going to be a vet, live in a big house and fill it with animals.

The second worst thing about stepmothers was they made you tidy up behind you. Wherever Rita went now, she had to be picking up this and that and putting it here and there. Walking and turning around to pick up whatever she had just dropped. In the good old days of just her and Daddy you could just walk around the place in your panties leaving a nice comfortable trail behind you: sweetie papers, comic books, bits of string you no longer needed, and nobody cared – least of all Daddy, because he did the same. Sometimes Mildred would pick up the things and put them in their proper places but in a house the size of Number Seven there were a whole lot of proper places, and you couldn't find the things again when you most wanted them, so what was the use?

Marilyn put an end to all that. She brought a maid with her when she came and the maid was supposed to clean but Marilyn wouldn't let her clean up after Rita. She made Rita wear clothes and comb her hair. 'That girl needs training,' Rita heard her telling Daddy. 'A real little ragamuffin you got growing up here. Nothin' doin', not in my house. What visitors goin' to think? I didn't become Mrs Maraj to let people call me a slut.'

The third worst thing about stepmothers was that they didn't fret quietly like other people, sucking their teeth and shaking their head. No, they yelled the place down if you did something wrong. Like when Rita made herself a paw-paw milk-shake and not only used one of Marilyn's best heirloom silver spoons to scoop the paw-paw meat into the shaker, but left the spoon in the shaker, switched on the motor which broke the shaker and bent the spoon. Marilyn yelled so loud the whole neighbourhood came running, and Rita ran and hid up the back-yard mango tree till Daddy came home. 'That child better not touch a single *one* of my things again!' Marilyn shrieked at Daddy, and poor Daddy just smiled and said yes, yes, and took her in his arms and she cooled down.

The one good thing about stepmothers was that Daddy was home earlier each day. The trouble was, when he was home he only had eyes for Marilyn, cancelling out her one good point.

In other words, Marilyn was a catastrophe, in capital letters. Rita wrote it in her diary. *Dear Diary*, she wrote, two months after Marilyn came, *Daddy said I'm getting a new mummy but all I've got is a CATASTROFEE.*

TWO

An Enormous Slip-up

There were poison-tongued people in Georgetown who would whisper, behind upheld hands, that Ronnie Maraj himself was a catastrophe, that even the best of wives couldn't settle him down. People who waited eagerly for the next catastrophe, which had to come the way the sun had to rise.

Ronnie had always liked his drink, not a fitting preference for a member of a devout Hindu–Christian family. This predilection was a curse, weaving its way through his life, causing a mishap here and a slip-up there, and little knots along the way, and no one in his family escaped its loops. The slip-ups sometimes had far-reaching consequences: Rita's conception, for instance, had been such a slip-up. But perhaps Ronnie's entire eat, drink and be merry act could be traced back to an enormous slip-up back when he was three, and his mother, father and four siblings were killed by a drunken driver.

Ronnie couldn't be blamed for the accident, of course, but if he'd been a good little boy he'd have been killed too. After all, it was his very *naughtiness* that kept him home from church that Sunday. He liked to pinch the bottoms of the ladies in the pew in front of him or crawl under his own pew to escape into the aisle, and so his parents finally left him at home with Grandma while they all drove off in the grass-green Vauxhall that fatal day.

The two cars slammed into each other at the corner of Vlissengen Road and Lamaha Street and nobody had the remotest chance. Ronnie's father never even had time to brake. Neither did the driver of the other car, packed full of fun-loving, rum-drunk young men on an early-morning sprint. Ronnie's mother lived a few hours in the hospital, and one of the young men survived to swear off drink for the rest of his life. Everyone else died on the spot. It was Georgetown's worst accident that year.

Little orphan Ronnie was left behind to be raised by Grandma and Aunt Amy at Number Seven, Victoria Street, the Dutch colonial green-and-white mansion round the corner from the Canadian Embassy in Kingston. Kingston, one of Georgetown's greenest, breeziest neighbourhoods just a stone's throw from the Sea Wall, wrapped itself protectively around Victoria Street, its hub.

Victoria Street itself was a town-planner's miscalculation in a city of orderly grid-worked streets, for it was a cul-de-sac, jutting into one of the blocks with no other purpose, it seemed, than to lead up to Number Seven. Numbers One to Six, pristine fairy-tale white wooden mansions, stood sedately on stilts, orderly sentries gazing silently at each other across the short street, whispering primly to each other through jalousied windows over fragrant oleanders, reminiscing about the Dutch and French and British colonial lords who'd once lived in their spacious halls, decorously hidden behind well-trimmed hibiscus and oleander hedges. Number Seven stood aloof, displayed in brazen grandeur at the stub-end of Victoria Street, a two-storey misshapen matron with broad hips and several long spindly legs keeping watch over the street, making no attempt to hide behind foliage. An ugly matron at that. A monstrosity of a house, people said, put together higgledy-piggledy, as if the past generations who had lived there had each had different ideas as to how to construct more room for growing families, servants, maiden aunts and old grandmothers.

Rooms sticking out here and there; stairs going up and down, some wood, some wrought iron, some painted, some left in their original state turning silver with age and weather. Many old Georgetown houses had towers, but none quite like Number Seven's, a single ugly tooth jutting from the roof of an upstairs room, with a ladder leading up to a quadrangle just large enough for one thin person to stand upon, doing nothing. Hideous, naked and unashamed, Number Seven glowered in its oversized yard (in no way could this be called a garden). No hedge to cower behind, no neat herbaceous border along her driveway, no false modesty, only an enormous mango tree rising from a tangle of weeds and unkempt bushes on one side of the unkempt drive of sand and weeds, and a cluster of coconut trees on the other. And behind the house a veritable jungle, left to its own designs, with a star-apple tree, a genip tree, and another, smaller, mango tree next to Number Six, which Rita sometimes climbed to peep into James Isaacs's bedroom window and throw things in at him. Grandma and Aunt Amy had both given up on gardening, given up on Ronnie, and, at least in Aunt Amy's case, given up on life itself.

At Number Seven Ronnie enjoyed a carefree, pleasant childhood. The lack of parents and siblings was no handicap, for Ronnie had the gift of making friends and among the boys and girls in Numbers One to Six he was the undisputed king. They were always a wild lot, those Victoria Street children; their loyalty to each other was legendary, their unspoken 'us-against-the-rest-of-the-world' philosophy a fact of nature. But being born to Number Seven was at once a legacy, a responsibility, a challenge and an honour. Ronnie shouldered that duty with good-natured insouciance.

Unlike Ronnie, the children of Numbers One to Six were handicapped. They had parents. Parents who disapproved of insouciance in general and, in particular, of Ronnie and his two-woman Hindu–Christian household, of the doubly inept reins of guardianship held too slackly in the Maraj home, the lack of discipline

11

therein: the lack, in other words, of a man. Disapproved in general of the country's political confusion and the threatened end of colonialism. Disapproved in particular of their children's association with a cooly. The problem was solved in various ways as the children entered puberty and the country gained, at long last, independence from Britain. A few children were sent to boarding school in England. The remaining families did not remain long; they emigrated to England, America, Canada, places collectively known as Abroad, seeking a better life. The Victoria Street Band broke into scattered fragments, leaving Ronnie behind.

The Maraj fortune was too much bound up in the country for them to leave: it lay in sugar. For generations they had owned a huge estate far away on the Corentyne River, an estate nostalgically named Balliol by some former owner, an Englishman. When slavery was abolished and his three-hundred odd slaves deserted him *en masse*, replacement labour had been hard to come by, the poor Englishman found; the plantation went to seed and he had been only too happy to sell it for a song to a certain Mr Maraj, to flee the mosquitoes and the scorching heat and return to the safe world of academia. Balliol Estate was now owned by Grandma, who had never once been there, and managed by a Mr Nath, a very competent manager who could be entirely relied upon to be in sole charge of every aspect of the business. The money flowed; Grandma kept an eye on the books, and was satisfied.

Ronnie had grown up with the benefit of two religions. Grandma was staunchly Hindu; but her two daughters, Rohini and Lakshmi, under the influence of a dedicated English mistress at Bishops' High School, had converted to Christianity at an early age and changed their names to Catherine and Amy. Hinduism and Christianity had been practised with equal fervour in an uneasy yet peaceful coexistence in Number Seven. Both religions – and both of Ronnie's female guardians, Grandma and Amy – were hostile to Ronnie's predilections, but their hostility had absolutely no effect on the growing young man and his tastes.

Ronnie liked his girls, he liked his loud music. He revered Ringo Starr, bought himself a drum-set and for six long months set his sights on becoming the drummer of one of Georgetown's several bands. Number Seven and the whole of Victoria Street boomed and rattled at all hours of the day or night (Georgetowners were a very tolerant people, and nobody ever complained, and Grandma, who only wore her hearing aid when she had to, was oblivious to it all) until, tired of the effort, he gave it up.

When Ronnie was fifteen Aunt Amy died, leaving Ronnie entirely in Grandma's morally upright but to all practical purposes incapable hands. Occasionally she emerged as a dragon from its lair, to lay down the law in no uncertain terms, and at such times Ronnie quaked. Otherwise she held her peace. She hired a string of servants to take care of the boy and retired to her room up in the eaves beneath the tooth-tower, to her prayers and mantras.

13

THREE

Ronnie Tries Fatherhood

If Rita's conception had been an accident, her birth was a calamity. Her mother Lynette, a coloured girl from a poor up-country family, died immediately after the delivery.

Ronnie fell in love with Rita the moment he set eyes on her. He decided to turn over a new leaf.

Ever since leaving school with three O Levels, Ronnie had worked at a variety of short-lived jobs. He had helped out at a garage for three months, loaded and unloaded ships at the dock for five weeks, and for the past four months had been stacking shelves at Quang Hing's Supermarket. Now that Rita was here, though, stacking supermarket shelves was simply not good enough. He wanted to be a worthy father for her, a father of whom she would, later, be proud. He wanted a real, decent, white-collar job. Fate played into his hand: the *Daily Graphic* advertised for trainee reporters. Ronnie applied, took the test and got the job.

And in journalism Ronnie found, at last, his personal professional niche. But he had lost Rita.

The baby had been snatched away from under his eyes by her mother's family and taken to live on the Pomeroon River, behind God's back in the inaccessible Essequibo District.

Ronnie wanted her back but Grandma – though she could easily afford a nanny, and wasn't Rita her own flesh and blood? – would not hear of it. Grandma had been infuriated enough by the scandal of Rita's birth: she refused even to see the bastard half-caste child, a disgrace to the name of Maraj; as far as Grandma was concerned Rita did not exist. But when Rita was five Grandma died, Ronnie battled for Rita in court, and won her. Rita joined Ronnie at Number Seven.

By this time the status quo had changed somewhat. Grandma had not left even half the amount of money Ronnie had been dreaming of, and a good part of what she *had* left was swallowed paying off the worst of Ronnie's outstanding debts, and what remained of the mythical fortune was melting quickly thanks to Ronnie's extravagant lifestyle on the one hand, the country's dismal economic situation on the other, and on top of that the declining demand for cane sugar on the world market. Finally, the Marajs' sugar plantation was nationalized, and the cash flow came to an abrupt end.

Ronnie had to keep his job at the newspaper. They weren't by any means rich, but at least they had the house, that freak of a construction which by now had turned from an architectural monstrosity into an eyesore, the white paint cracking from the walls, the garden a miniature jungle.

When she first moved in Rita proceeded to help peel the paint away from those parts of the wall she could reach, sitting on the front stairs or cross-legged on the veranda, sliding long fingernails under the layer of old paint and pulling so that it fell away in great white flakes. Sometimes she used a knife to scrape it off. She could sit for hours, scratching away at the paint. No one prevented her from doing so; no one cared, not Ronnie, and certainly not Mildred. That was in the first days after moving in. Then she met Polly Wong's dog, and then Polly Wong herself; and after that everything changed.

Numbers One to Six were by now inhabited by a rainbow of *nouveau riche* young up and coming families. The Maraj name alone stood for Tradition, and Old Money, and Establishment, despite Ronnie's reputation as a converted ne'er-do-well, despite the dilapidated state of the house and the chaos of its garden. Rita slid effortlessly into her role at the helm of a new generation of Victoria Street children. It was, after all, her birthright.

FOUR

All Holding the Rope

Rita, some people whispered, shaking their heads and tut-tutting, was a strange child. Taciturn in the extreme, she radiated a mercurial intensity and authority which both challenged the world to ignore her at its peril, while displaying a complete indifference towards that world. She focused her attention exclusively on those living beings she deemed worthy of such single-minded attention, and only a few hand-picked adults were in that privileged circle: her father Ronnie, when he made himself available, their housekeeper Mildred, and Polly Wong's mother. Towards almost all other adults Rita maintained an icy silence, speaking only when she was spoken to (that is, if an answer was required), and then in monosyllables. She hardly ever smiled, and she never laughed if there was any danger of an adult seeing her. And it was good so. Adults deserved no better.

Rita had a natural rapport with children, she was loved and respected by her schoolmates, the children of Victoria Street. But her heart belonged to animals, animals of every variety. Her entire inner being focused on their needs. Her very life revolved around the puppies and kittens she brought home to nurture. With them, she would lose herself, ignoring the rest of the world;

and the world – that is, the boys and girls who had gained admission to her world – would gaze on her in admiration, ask questions which she answered crisply and cleverly, and offer their services. Helpfully, they brought wounded or stray animals to her, sometimes going far out of their way to find such presents: a puppy with a thorn in its paw from Aunt Ida's home all the way across town, or a tailless lizard, victim of some sadistic boy's torture. Rita would douse their wounds in mercurochrome, then wrap them generously in bandages. She had found interesting uses for methylated spirits, witch hazel and calamine lotion. The Dettol bottle on the bathroom shelf seemed to empty itself at breakneck speed. She had found out through trial and error that Band-Aid didn't stick on feathers or fur, and that cats were less patient patients than dogs. And she knew the power of a soothing voice and a caressing hand. Occasionally, Rita would gather her troops and they would all march off to the Police Headquarters, Mounted Branch three blocks away, where Rita would inspect the rows of horses in their stables, whisper in their ears, give them pieces of carrot, stroke their glossy necks. If one was lame concern would crease her forehead, and she would cross-examine Mr Hendricks, the head groom, to make sure the poor creature was well looked after, assuming a proprietorial distress that touched Mr Hendricks's heart and impressed her peers beyond measure. Compassion, not flaunted but unadorned and unassuming, was her expertise, its aura magnetic.

It came to Rita's attention that Madame, the ancient chestnut mare in the loose box, was to be put to sleep for no other reason than old age. She set out to move heaven and hell to prevent such an abomination. Sergeant Peters treated her with amused condescension, flicking a forked tongue and looking at her with warped eyes. Rita stormed out of his office and made her way to Corporal Duarte. Corporal Duarte had no time for a child of six. Rita spoke with the head groom, who was busy picking the bay gelding Valerian's hooves.

'Would you sell Madame to me?' she asked in tears, speaking

to Mr Hendricks's buttocks. Valerian was swinging his foreleg impatiently, and Mr Hendricks needed all his concentration to hold it steady.

'Sell her? She in't wort' nuttin',' said Mr Hendricks absent-mindedly, thrusting vigorously with the hoofpick. 'You could have she for free.'

'For free? True? You not lyin' to me?' Rita's eyes bulged with excitement.

'We would pay yuh to tek she,' said Mr Hendricks with a chuckle, letting go of Valerian's hoof, standing up, and rubbing his side.

Rita ran home in great elation and waited half the night for Ronnie to come home, which he didn't. Finally she fell asleep, but the first thing she did when she woke up next morning was run to his room, pounce on him in his bed, and tickle him, calling out, 'Daddy, Daddy, Daddy, wake up, wake up, is terribly 'portant!'

Ronnie turned over with a grunt and opened one eye.

'What is it, sweetheart? Wha's the time?' He pulled one arm out from under the sheet and looked at his watch. 'Six o'clock only! Why you wake me up so early?'

'Daddy, it's most terribly terribly terribly 'portant!' Rita cried, and the story of Madame, sentenced to a premature and cruel death, poured from her lips, concluding with the heartfelt words, 'Can I, Daddy, can I, can I? Please please please say yes!'

Ronnie, deeply touched and dying to turn over and sleep for a further hour, grunted, 'Yes, of course, darling, whatever you want.' Rita gave a shriek of delight, flung herself forward to plant a loud kiss on his cheek, and fled.

That afternoon, after school, Rita returned to the Mounted Branch with a long rope looped many times around her arm. Word had spread like a forest fire in Victoria Street; the entire collection of children, not only Rita's inner circle of six- and seven-year-olds but also the five-year-olds and even, condescendingly, the eight-to-twelves, gathered around her.

'You can lead her back,' Rita said generously to Polly Wong from next door. 'I'll ride her.'

'Can I help hold the rope too? It's a long rope, Rita!' begged Kalaam Farouk, of Number One. Kalaam was twelve, and felt he had a right to make demands of his own, but, after all, it was Rita's horse.

Dawn deSouza (Number Four) and Christine Knight (Number Two), the ten-year-olds, stood looking on and trying to think of something terribly clever to say, though technically speaking playing with the babies was beneath their dignity.

'Yes! Yes! Let me hold the rope too! Please, please!' cried Dennis Roy (Number Three), Donna deSouza (Dawn's sister) and Faith Isaacs (Number Six), while little Maxine Wong grabbed her big sister Polly's hand and looked imploringly up at her with coal-black almond eyes, knowing she wouldn't have a chance against the bigger children. 'You'll let me hold it with you, won't you?' she whispered to Polly, who fondly stroked her hair and nodded yes.

Christine Knight and Dawn deSouza said nothing but looked at each other – they wouldn't beg, of course, but each knew what the other was thinking. Then Dawn, not wanting to be daunted by a six-year-old, courageously suggested, 'Why can't we *all* hold the rope? It's long enough, isn't it?'

All the ten children stared at Rita, waiting for her answer. Madame was *hers*, and she could choose; Polly Wong was her best friend, and obviously privileged. But the others? Ten children waited for her word, gazing imploringly at her. Rita looked kindly at them all and gave one of her rare smiles.

'That would look silly, all of you leading me back,' she said reasonably. 'But you can all take turns. OK? And Maxine can get up on Madame's back behind me, and ride her home.'

'*Oooh*, can I? Can I really?' cried Maxine, jumping up and down in glee. 'I love you, Rita, I do!'

'Is it *safe*?' asked Polly anxiously, knowing her responsibility.

'It's *perfickly* safe,' said Rita reassuringly. 'I wouldn't let her if it wasn't, would I?'

'And what about me?' cried Brian Coolidge, who was five, like Maxine, and who lived with his mother in the Number Four Bottom House, beneath the deSouzas.

'I'll let you ride her afterwards,' said Rita, 'when we get back. Three of us would be too heavy.'

And with that she turned and marched off purposefully towards the Mounted Branch, and the children flocked behind her, impressed by the wisdom of her words and the valour of her actions. Not one of them would have even dreamed of bringing Madame home to their own back-yards. Not one of them could even dream of daring to approach a parent with such a request. And not one of their parents would even dream of acquiescence. It was a big day, a historical occasion. No more stray puppies, half-drowned kittens, tortured lizards, broken-winged birds. A *horse*, a living, breathing horse, was taking up residence in Victoria Street!

A horse, it seemed to each child, was just what they needed. A horse would put the finishing touch to their perfect little world-in-a-nutshell, to the alliance of mutual understanding and unspoken loyalty that made up their pact against the adult world, that bizarre and prickly and at times completely mad system of domination and subjugation, of tangled associations and rejections, bad-mouthings and bickerings in which their elders operated, right there on Victoria Street. Ronnie Maraj, a Christian–Hindu, for instance, was friends with Shankar Roy, a Hindu, but although both were Indian, they were hated by the Farouks at the corner, who were Indian too, but Muslim. Mr Farouk, on the other hand, was friends with black Mr Knight across the road, even though blacks and Indians were officially enemies, because both had studied 'abroad' – different universities, different disciplines, but still 'abroad' – and were thus above hoi polloi. (They longed for association with Dr Wong, Polly's father, the Cambridge graduate.) Mrs Knight, who was white, was Mrs Wong's best friend, whereas Dr Wong often went with Mr Roy to the race-course and usually betted on the same horse. The Portuguese deSouzas at Number Four kept pretty much to themselves, though Mrs deSouza often visited white Mrs Knight, who, by dint of her pure-blood Englishness, possessed an all-round popularity. Her opinion was second only to the Word of God: though

Mrs deSouza was a lawyer and her husband a High Court magistrate, and Mrs Knight only a housewife and retired secretary and her husband a British Embassy employee (not even Consul), it was quite clear Who was Who in the hierarchy. Miss Coolidge, the single mother who lived in the deSouzas's Bottom House, exchanged many snide observations on Mrs deSouza's uppityness with her next-door neighbour, Mrs Isaacs, for both were coloured – Mrs Isaacs two shades lighter than Miss Coolidge – and carefully cultivated pride set them in a class of their own, in their reverse-racist own eyes far superior to the likes of Knight–deSouza.

They were a thorny lot, the grown-ups. Their offspring took note of the bickering in total incomprehension, and bonded all the more in defence, feeling superior, more mature than their parents. They were a many-hued medley of loose-limbed youths, the colour of their skin ranging from Polly Wong's blanched-almond-cream, through olive-toned Donna deSouza, honey-skinned Christine Knight, to the various shades of gold-brown offered by the Roys, the Farouks, and the Isaacs. Rita was the darkest. If the children of Victoria Street constituted a microcosm of Guyanese society, with representatives or half-representatives of all six races among them, then Rita was the prototype of that microcosm, representing four continents. Ronnie had given her the blood of Asia, but from her mother she had received a perfect blend of African, European and Amerindian stock which, in well-tuned synthesis with her father's contribution, had produced this forest-brownie of a girl, at once ethereal and earthy, with large round pixie eyes of disconcerting night-black clarity, thick black hair heavy with curls bouncing against her back, and a strong and sturdy body that seemed to contain a coiled-up spring barely concealed by tawny skin of dark rich chocolate. Rita's face was not beautiful in the classic sense, not symmetrically perfect as Polly Wong's was, but intriguing as only a face can be which reflects (unadorned, unmasked and unfiltered) the personality of its wearer.

And right now, Rita's face wore determination undiluted by doubt. She was going to get her horse. The king of animals. A horse to crown the sweet bonding of young souls striving for unified strength in a world made weak by the petty partisanship and power-plays of adults. A horse, even an old horse, was strength. With a horse, they would not be simply a herd of children; a horse would turn them into something more: the Goodies against the Baddies. Roy Rogers and Trigger against the outlaws. The other children fed on Rita's determination, watching her for their cues, showering her with questions to dispel their own looming doubt, chattering in excitement as they hurried along trying to keep up with her stride.

'Where will you keep him, Rita?' Dawn asked.

'In the back-yard, of course. Tied to the star-apple tree.'

'How will you feed him?' asked Christine.

'*Her*, not him,' Rita corrected. 'Grass, of course, you don't know horses eat grass?'

'You have enough grass in y'all yard?' asked Christine doubtfully. Christine had always refused to speak the British English of her mother; her Creole was every bit as good as Rita's.

'No, but I could get Persaud to bring some on a donkey-cart. Fresh grass every day. Daddy said he gon' pay for it.'

The children looked suitably impressed, not only by Rita's forethought and organizational talents, but also by the fact that Mr Maraj supported her enterprise both morally and financially.

'But what about his poopy, Rita?' Dennis Roy put forward hesitantly.

'Her, her, *her*,' insisted Rita. 'She's a mare, silly!'

'Yeh, but what about all the poopy she gon' make? What you gon' do with it?'

'Put it in the garden! What else! You don't know poopy is good for flowers?'

'All-you don't have no flowers! My mums say all-you got is weeds an' is a disgrace to Vict–' Kalaam, still struggling with his shame at being the eldest in the group, thought it high time to demonstrate his superiority.

'Shut you mouth, or I gon' bring all the poopy and throw it in *your* garden!' Rita stopped, stared Kalaam down, then stamped her foot and marched off, the five- to eight-year-olds trooping around her, the uppity ten- to twelve-year-olds trailing behind trying to balance condescension with curiosity, sanctimonious contempt with reluctant respect.

The Mounted Branch nestled in the midst of the Police Headquarters at Eve Leary, a mere ten minutes' walk from Victoria Street. The buildings here were of various sizes yet all of the same simple characteristic style: living quarters and offices in squat single storey oblong houses on high stilts with outside stairs alternated with larger, many-storeyed, down-to-earth administrative buildings, all of horizontally planked wood, painted in the same faded and flaking creamy yellow. A half-hearted attempt to beautify the area resulted in several scrawny hibiscus bushes between the buildings and rows of wilting canna lilies lining the driveways.

Madame's loose box was empty. A young groom was spreading fresh straw on its concrete floor. There was no sign of Madame.

'Where's Madame?' Rita asked, looking around as if Madame would suddenly appear from around a corner, neighing with pleasure at the sight of Rita and in anticipation of fresh carrots. The groom, who was new at the Mounted Branch and had not yet learned of Rita's position there, said, 'Oh, she mus' be dead an' gone by now, you got to go to de slaughterhouse to fin' she.'

Rita stared open-mouthed. The groom, noticing her prolonged silence, looked up at her, grinning as he pitched a forkful of straw into a corner. 'Wha' yuh doin' deh, girl, ketchin' flies in your mout'?'

Rita's face crumpled at the words. She turned and ran. The children ran behind her, but brave little Polly Wong stayed long enough to defend her best friend's honour.

'You're a mean, mean, mean, nasty old *murderer* and we all hate, hate, *hate* you!' she shouted at the groom, and it was his turn to stare with open mouth as Polly Wong turned and ran with all her might to catch up with the others, the long black plait at the crown of her silky head flying out behind her.

That night Rita cried herself to sleep, burying her head in her pillow to stifle the sobs. Though it didn't matter anyway, Daddy wasn't home to hear them, and Mildred was down in the kitchen eating crabs with her new boyfriend Cyril.

She had only cried like this once in her life: the day Ronnie Maraj had come to get her, tearing her from Granny's skirts. He had had to hold her all the way back to Charity; with her struggles she had almost capsized the boat.

Two months after the fiasco with Madame Marilyn moved in: the next day Frisky died (was killed!) and Rita cried again.

FIVE

Anihilashun

The first time Ronnie brought Marilyn home, only four weeks before the wedding, Rita hid behind the curtains in the cupboard beneath the stairs and watched and listened. Daddy had called her several times already, shouting down the place, and walked through all the rooms looking for her, but she had not answered.

'I can't think where she is,' Daddy said to Marilyn. 'I told her to be home this afternoon because I was bringing you to meet her. I'll just run over to that Polly Wong next door and see if she's there. Wait here. Mildred! Mildred, I'm just going over to the Wongs to see if Rita's there, please bring some tea and cake for Mistress Prabudial.'

'Why don't you send the servant to get her?' Marilyn grumbled.

'She might need some persuading,' Daddy replied, and walked out of the door.

Rita, holding her breath and peering out from behind a crack just one finger wide, watched Marilyn alone in the drawing room. Luckily, the staircase was placed in a back corner of the living room so that, clutching the two curtains above and below her peephole and turning to follow Marilyn as she moved about the room, Rita had a full view of what went on.

Marilyn started to investigate the set-up, but was interrupted by Frisky, who came bounding through the front door which Daddy had left ajar and enthusiastically began investigating *her*, Marilyn, sniffing up her legs and writhing around in ecstasy, flinging himself in rapture against Marilyn's silky brown calves giving short little yaps of delight. Marilyn yelped herself, but in annoyance, then began shouting, 'You bloody bitch! Get out, you rascal! Go on, get out, get out! Go away!' beating at Frisky with her handbag and kicking at him. Rita was just about to jump out and rescue Frisky, who after all was only living up to his name, when Mildred rushed out of the kitchen shouting 'Out! Out! Out!', grabbed Frisky by the scruff of his neck and flung him out of the door so that Rita could hear the poor thing tumbling down the steps outside. She suppressed the overwhelming desire to rush out and throw Mildred and Marilyn out of the door in turn, vowed to have it out with Mildred later, and commanded her heart to stop pounding so loud, which it did. She watched.

Marilyn was brushing at the hem of her dress with little flicks of her hand, her mouth, or what Rita could see of it, turned down at the corners in an expression of utter disgust.

'That animal has *mange*! Did you see his back! Why you allow that child to . . . Ronnie told me she has a dog but that mangy beast . . . Why didn't he tell me? And I'm sure it's full of fleas, and . . .'

On her way back to the kitchen Mildred said, 'A dog? That girl got at least *four* dogs, las' time I count, an' dis one is de latest, she bring it home the other day because de people want to put it to sleep, an' if you arsk me—'

'Four dogs? And you allow them in the house? But what kind of a place is this? My goodness, he didn't tell me, and *look* at the condition of everything, I thought you were housekeeper here?' But Mildred just sniffed loudly and disappeared behind the curtain of threaded shells that inadequately shielded the drawing room from the kitchen. Marilyn gave herself over to the more rewarding task of continuing her investigation of the drawing room.

She stood on the threadbare carpet in the middle of the room, facing Rita's hiding place, and looked around, frowning, her gaze glancing on and off the sundry pieces of faded furniture and other miscellaneous items arranged haphazardly around the room, her brow gaining a new wrinkle at each station. It lingered on the large oval dining table. Except for the little space at one end where Ronnie took his meals (Rita always ate sitting on the Berbice chair, looking out of the window, a bowl of food in her hand), the table was completely covered with papers, school books, old newspapers, comics, paper clips, a dog collar, an empty bottle of Old Spice, a broken porcelain cat, all the clutter of daily life at Number Seven. In one corner stood a rusty metal dome of fine wire mesh designed to keep the flies off food, but which was especially good for *catching* flies so you could watch them buzzing around excitedly for a while, and then magnanimously set them free. At the moment Priscilla, a bluebottle Rita had caught after lunch and was feeding up for later release, was throwing herself in suicidal despair against the mesh. Marilyn seemed to cringe when she took that in, and her eyes wandered off to the bits of furniture about the room. Rita's pyjama trousers still hung over the back of the Berbice chair where she had hastily flung them that morning in her hurry to dress for school (Mrs Wong had been blowing the horn outside the gate). Inexplicably, one of Daddy's shoes lay sole-up on a windowsill – Rita vaguely remembered using the shoe to try to coax a lizard down from the rafters several weeks ago; she'd placed a juicy living spider in the heel of the shoe hoping the lizard would come for it and she could keep him a few days as a pet – but he hadn't.

Marilyn's gaze lingered longest on Rita's ant farm. That was in a place of honour in a corner of the gallery; Rita had been working on it for several months. Kalaam Farouk had given her his old aquarium, which she had filled with sand and placed in an old plastic blow-up swimming pool. The water wasn't deep, but made an adequate moat around the glass fortress that housed the ants, and within that fortress Rita had constructed for them a complete little world, a paradise, where they could have all the food they wanted without having to go out to look for it. For Rita fed them all the sweetest delicacies she could get her hands on – a piece of this and a crumb of that – and, kneeling before the farm, watched them, march march march, carry carry carry, follow follow follow, and listened to them singing their march songs and their follow songs. She did that for hours. Nobody minded.

Except Marilyn. Rita could tell by the pull of the corners of her mouth. She didn't like Rita's ant farm, just as she didn't like Frisky. So Rita didn't like Marilyn.

Marilyn wore a tight-fitting red dress that stopped at her knees, made of some smooth shiny material flawed by a series of creases in the lap area, caused by sitting. Three spaghetti straps on each shoulder seemed a mite too tight, but matched perfectly the array of straps and spikes on her high-heeled red patent-leather sandals. Gold-brown shoulders, gold-brown ankles, silky gold-brown skin everywhere. Soft gold-brown orbs trying to burst out of the bodice of the dress, and as Marilyn turned round Rita could see the orbs of her buttocks (invisibly gold-brown) contoured against the seat of the dress. She wore gold bangles and a gold chain round her neck and carried a purse of sequinned gold.

The face that topped this vision of red and gold might have been pretty if it hadn't been marred by the down-turned mouth and wrinkled brow and narrowed eyes, and the expression of vexation so clearly written across it. Peering through the curtain, Rita saw Marilyn looking intensely at the floor and then digging at it with the point of her sandal, and wondered what was going on. When Marilyn bent down and scratched at the floor with a long curved red fingernail, she knew: Marilyn had discovered one of the blobs of chewing-gum trodden into the floorboards. There were so many of them in the house Mildred had stopped grumbling and trying to scratch them off and simply left them to merge into the wood, as was proper. Marilyn crouched just two yards before Rita; her red dress slid tightly up her thighs, so that Rita could see the triangle of her panties, and they were red, which somehow gave Rita a comforting feeling of utter disdain.

She shrank back for a moment as the slit of Marilyn's eyes raised suddenly and looked straight at her cubby-hole, not daring to let go of the curtain lest it move and give her away. Had Marilyn seen her eye gleaming? No. Marilyn stood up, having confirmed her suspicion of chewing-gum, wiped the palms of her hands on the hips of her dress, smoothing it down as well as drying them of sweat (Rita could see the damp flecks they left on the material) and stalked, tottering on her heels, over to the cabinet where they kept their crockery and glassware. She glanced over her shoulder, as if aware of being watched, opened the cabinet, removed a glass, and held it up to the light. Rita couldn't see her face, but saw the round black helmet of stiffly-sprayed hair nod, as if confirming another suspicion. The glass was replaced, the cabinet closed, and Marilyn stalked back across the room, directly towards Rita, just as if she had suddenly received information as to Rita's hiding place and was coming to sweep back the curtains with a dramatic flourish. Rita pressed herself flat against the back of the cupboard and held her breath, and just then Mildred walked through the shell curtain, balancing on one hand a tray on which two tall glasses of lime juice wobbled precariously. She placed the tray on the little round purple-heart table next to the Berbice chair, smiled at Marilyn and said, 'Why you don't sit down, madame? It might take some time to find the chile! An' here's some nice cold lime juice!'

Marilyn nodded and sat down on the sofa next to the Berbice chair. She raised one of the glasses to her lips just as Daddy walked in.

'I can't find her anywhere,' said Daddy, and he sounded really disappointed. He plonked himself down on the Berbice chair and took the second glass. 'I went to all the houses and none of the children have seen her. And I *told* her to be at home, I *told* her I was bringing you!'

'Well, if you ask me that's probably the reason *why* she can't be found,' Marilyn said, sipping at her juice. 'You know what people are saying about that child? People are talking, you know, and they warned me several times. My own father said—'

'Yes, I know, dear, you told me, but when you come she going to tame down, I know it, a lovely mother like you! She needs a family life again. Once she got that she'll settle down.'

'Hmmmph! We'll see about that. It's one thing to have your own children but when you take on other people's hard-ears children you got your hands full. What with my own little one coming along soon . . .'

At those words Rita felt a hefty thud inside her chest. *What little one coming along?*

'An angel like you! She might be a little worried and that's why she's not here now but I'm sure when she meets you . . .'

'What exactly does she know about me?'

'Well, not much. I told her I was bringing a friend along. A lady friend.'

'A lady friend? That's all?'

'Well, I didn't want to get her too excited. We should take things slowly.'

'That's what you've been saying the last eighteen months, Ronnie Maraj. Take things slowly. Don't rush things. Let her get used to the idea. Keeping me dangling, dangling, dangling. Look how you broke off the engagement when your grandmother died – "Let's just postpone it a few months till Rita gets used to living with me. We'll take things slowly and get married later." Ha ha ha! Nothing but lines, Ronnie Maraj. And now the wedding's just round the corner and she still don't know?'

'Well, I thought it best to wait as long as possible. I still think that's best. It's a little bit much you know, you and the baby and all.'

'So when you going to tell her about me and when you going to tell her about the baby? When this belly swell up so big she think I'm a rain barrel, or what? I got a good mind to get an abortion and call off the whole thing.'

'But you not going to do that, I know. I know you love me, darling, just like I love you. You always loved me and I always loved you. We were made for each other. Come now, calm down and don't fret so.' He leaned over and Rita knew that he was kissing her. She felt such disgust she squeezed her eyes shut, but

31

opened them on hearing Marilyn's petulant voice. Apparently she had not allowed herself to be kissed.

'Ronnie Maraj, don't think I don't know you. I can see right through you. If it wasn't for the baby . . .'

'Darling, you know I do love you. It's just that Rita—'

'Rita, Rita, Rita is all I hear, that girl got you wrap 'round she little finger.'

'No, no, dear, it's you who got me 'round your little finger.'

'If I didn't know you were rich yourself I would believe you only marrying me for my inheritance.'

'What bosh, darling. You know Grandma left me everything. This house, the fortune . . .' He leaned over towards her again, and she pulled away once more.

'Yes, and you pulled the Maraj name through the mud, you know. Look at how you let the place go to pieces. And yourself too, I might add. It's going to take all my energy to get the house and the yard looking like something to be proud of. I mean, with all your money you could have done something to keep it up. What would the old lady have said! Just look at the place! I never saw such a hotchpotch in my life, and you didn't even make the effort to clean it up for my visit! And look at the yard! Nothing but weeds, and rubbish everywhere; you even have a rusty car under the mango tree! What's it doing there?'

'Oh, you saw that? Yes, that used to be mine. I had an accident with it.'

'Why you don't take it to the scrap-yard?'

'Well, you see, Rita likes to play in it. It's a nice place for a child to play. Our son will like it too, you'll see!'

'Oh no, he won't! The first thing I do when I move in here is get that rust-heap *out*! I telling you, Ronnie Maraj, once you get me as your wife I not taking no nonsense! That old wreck got to go! First thing, you hear?'

'Yeh, right; whatever you say, darling. Whatever you say. First thing.' He leaned over again and third time lucky: this time she let him.

*　　*　　*

32

But the first thing that went was Frisky. The day after doomsday. Along with the ants, eradicated with a mist of Flit, along with the cats, the caterpillars and the tadpoles, unceremoniously carted down to the yard and dumped.

When Marilyn had finished inspecting the house and making her decisions as to what was to be done where, she started on the garden. The bushes, the old wood-heap, the Morris wreck. Out, out, out, said Marilyn, walking around with a scowl and a tight round swelling belly, pointing here and there and creating havoc in Rita's kingdom. She ordered the mango tree cut down.

'Mango trees are for back-yards,' said Marilyn. 'In my front garden I want canna lilies, roses, a hibiscus hedge. Oleander, of course. Croton and fern. That group of palm trees can stay, they'll look lovely growing in an English lawn. Daddy's gardener Doodnath is sending round his cousin with his wife and children. They'll do a good job, we'll soon have this place looking all spick and span.'

Rita bred frogs and fish in an old tyre sunk into the ground. When Marilyn saw that, stepping over the knee-high weeds that protected it from view, she turned up her nose and said, 'That's a breeding place for mosquitoes. Out.'

The palings along the back boundary hadn't been painted for years. The wood was silver with age, crumbly with mould and wood-ants. Marilyn had braved the jungle protecting them from view and found the place where Rita had broken through so as to gain access into the gutter behind, where you could catch as many fish and tadpoles as you wanted. The water there was a little stinky but it was worth it. You could put the baby frogs on pieces of wood and float them downstream right down to the Lamaha Canal.

'This place is an utter disgrace,' said Marilyn to Ronnie, who had trailed shame-facedly behind her. 'I'm going to pull down those palings and build a nice high concrete wall. With barbed wire along the top. You never know what kind of choke-and-rob ruffians might break in. Really, Ronnie, if you had any respect for me you would never have allowed me even to see a disaster

33

area like this. The house was an absolute mess – thank goodness it's looking nice now. We just need some fresh paint on the outside and it will be as good as new, but the yard is a complete shambles. That daughter of yours is trouble with a capital T, she's the next thing I have to take in hand. I'll teach her manners if it's the death of me.'

Rita, hiding up in the far reaches of the jamun tree, her face stained purple from the plump juicy jamuns she was stuffing into her mouth, heard every word. She spit out a jamun stone, carefully aimed, and it hit Marilyn on a tender spot. 'EEEE!' shrieked Marilyn, twisting around to rub her bottom and frowning accusingly at Ronnie. 'Do you have marabuntas in this yard? One just stung me!'

That night, Rita, lying on her tummy on her bed in the room where the walls had been painted pink and where brand-new pink-and-white flowered curtains danced in the salty moonlit breeze drifting in from the Atlantic, chewed her pencil and tried to think of a word terrible enough to fit the Marilyn effect. 'Ruin' was not strong enough; 'Destruction' was worse but still not quite right, and even if you wrote 'Complete' in front of Ruin and Destruction you only proved how weak those words were. She crept down the stairs to the bookcase and pulled out a falling-to-pieces dictionary smelling of wood-ants and residues of Flit, and carted it back to bed with her. She looked up 'ruin', but that wasn't bad enough, though it was certainly true that Marilyn had ruined her life.

She looked up at the large black-and-white photo of Mummy on her wall. 'I *hate* her,' she said to Mummy. 'I wish you were here. Why did you have to leave me! Please punish her for me!'

She chewed her pencil some more, scratched at the scab on her knee, and turned back to the dictionary. Under 'ruin' she had found 'destruction', she looked that up next. And there, under 'destruction', she found just the word she needed. The definition, she saw to her satisfaction, was 'complete destruction of soul and body'. The word stuck for ever in her mind. She closed the dictionary and finished her diary entry. Rita used the dictionary for meanings, not for spellings. The important things about words were what they sounded like and what meanings they held. So she never bothered to copy them from the dictionary; she said a word to herself, and wrote it the way it sounded.

Dear Diary, this woman is a wicked witch. She has brought ANIHILASHUN.

SIX

Going to See the Queen

On the third day after doomsday Rita vanished. Nobody knew when and nobody knew how, and because nobody could remember having seen her since breakfast the length of her absence was a further mystery. Mildred was the first to notice, when the drumstick she had placed on the table for Rita's lunch grew cold and white with coagulated fat. She went over to Polly Wong's but Polly hadn't seen Rita all morning. Mildred shrugged and went on with her work, and it was only when Rita wasn't back by four that any kind of alarm shivered through Number Seven, and Ronnie was telephoned at the *Graphic*, and came home early frowning, and asked Marilyn wherever could she be, and Marilyn shrugged and said she must be gallivanting with her friends, and messages were sent out to Numbers One to Six to ask who last had seen her.

Nobody.

Rita returned just before dusk. Mildred saw her first, from the kitchen window, slipping through the bushes in the background as quiet as a shadow, and raised the alarm. Ronnie was there to meet her as she slunk through the back door, and was just about to sneak upstairs when Ronnie gathered her up into his arms, chuckled out his relief, carried her over to the Berbice chair and pulled her onto his lap, where he teased and tickled her the way he used to do before Marilyn came. But instead of wiggling and giggling she shook her head sullenly, slithered out of his grasp and ran upstairs where she wrote secret things in a diary which she hid in a very secret place. So Ronnie just grinned and shrugged his shoulders and said to Marilyn, 'She was always a bit wild but she's a good girl, she'll settle down and get used to the changes.'

Marilyn was annoyed because she didn't like being outmanoeuvred by a little chit of a girl. She went up to Rita's room and pulled her out by her upper arm and said, 'Where have you been, where have you been?'

'To see the *queen*, to see the *queen*!' yelled Rita, and she squiggled and squirmed, she kicked and pulled, she pinched and bit so that Marilyn had to let go; and Rita in a trice was out of the house and up in the jamun tree and looking down making faces at Marilyn. Marilyn rubbed the place on her arm where Rita had bitten her and she too shrugged her shoulders and said, 'Ronnie, you better lock that minx on a chain. Me, I had enough.'

Rita stayed up in the jamun tree till it was dark. Then she sneaked into the house again – they had left the back door unlocked – and up to her room, unseen. Then Marilyn came up and told her about the boy she was going to have.

'Go and have a talk with her,' Ronnie had pleaded, after Rita ran outside screaming, having bitten Marilyn. 'Just go and try to be nice to her, like a mother. Please, Marilyn.'

Very well. She would talk to the child – when Rita had calmed down. The child must know the facts. No use turning its head with a pack of lies and mushy sentimentalities about a happy family. The child was a barbarian. It was time she faced the facts. So Marilyn told Rita the facts.

'Your father is longing for a son,' Marilyn told Rita when she came down from the jamun tree. She sat on the edge of Rita's bed, rubbing the spot where Rita had bitten her. There was still a circle of tooth marks; Rita had almost drawn blood. Marilyn frowned. And now *she* was supposed to make the first move! Swallow her justified anger and reassure Rita! And Rita had not even *apologized*. The child should at least *apologize* first, before any sort of talk could take place.

'Every man wants a son, and especially Indian men, to pass on the name and the blood. Your blood is anyway mixed; your father is desperate for a boy of pure Indian blood. Did you know that a man without a son is a disgrace to the whole family? He's not really a man. Of course, you couldn't know that, you grew up with coloured people and you never learned Indian ways the way Ronnie and I did. Ronnie doesn't expect anything from you, you're only a girl. Don't be hurt, he is very fond of you, of course, but you know what it's like with men, they're very particular about having a son. And the baby is kicking a lot so it's bound to be a boy. My grandmother knows about these things and she says, the way it's kicking, it's a boy. So don't be hurt when he's born and you get the feeling your father has lost interest in you, it's just that his dearest desire has been fulfilled. I'm telling you this so that you can get accustomed to the idea. You've played first fiddle for a long time, Rita, but you must know it's not natural and it's only because he hasn't got a son. So prepare yourself.'

After that Rita came and went as she pleased, establishing a pattern which nobody bothered to break. Nobody knew where she went to; but as it was still the August holidays it didn't really matter, since sooner or later she always came back. The Victoria Street children felt abandoned; life hadn't half the spirit without her. Not even Polly knew where Rita spent her hours, or if she did, she wasn't telling. The girls played boring things like hopscotch and jacks, and the boys set traps for lizards, and the holidays lazed by without Rita.

Meanwhile, Marilyn was putting the house in order. Initially, she had had something of a shock to find there was hardly a fraction of the Maraj fortune left. She had ranted and raved against Ronnie, threatened to leave, threatened to get her father to sue for breach of contract (what contract? asked Ronnie innocently) and finally faced the reality and used her own fortune for the renovations that needed to be made. It was a matter of saving face: Marilyn had coveted the Maraj home and the Maraj name for years, and she wasn't going to make a fool of herself. She wouldn't have Georgetown society sniggering behind their backs and pointing at her: 'She married a drunk and a pauper.' Ronnie liked his drink but he wasn't a drunk; and as for him being a pauper, she'd see about that. Her father didn't own Georgetown's biggest furniture store for nothing. She wasn't an only child of an only child for nothing. She hadn't been her deceased grandfather's beloved for nothing. Her grandfather hadn't been quarrelling with her father for years on end for nothing. Grandfather Prabudial hadn't left acres and acres of prime Guyana rainforest to her for nothing. Marilyn Prabudial was rich. So the appropriate changes were made, and Number Seven came into its own.

Dealing with Ronnie was easy: he was easy-going to a fault. He caved in to every suggestion she made, so that she soon no longer made suggestions, she gave orders, to which he was obedient. He had slatternly habits, but with the help of her maid Marilyn managed to remake his image so that she could appear at his side at this reception or the other without feeling ashamed. Dressed up in the clothes she chose for him he cut a dashing figure; he was good-natured and likeable and people laughed at his corny jokes, the same sort of jokes that laced the frothy entertainment articles he still produced for the *Graphic*. He tended to drink one too many at parties, but Marilyn had methods of steering him into other directions, if necessary bringing him home and into her bed, before matters got out of hand. So married life would have been quite pleasant if not for the one little fly in the soup: Rita.

Rita slipped through the hole in the palings and followed the trench to the place where it emptied into the Lamaha Canal. She climbed a few more fences and found herself in a place almost like the countryside: patches of gardens tidily laid out in handkerchief-size beds, interspersed with banana trees. She sat down on a patch of grass to think. She did a lot of thinking these days, ever since Marilyn's arrival. There were so many problems to solve. Like what she was going to do about Marilyn. Marilyn had emptied the world of everything worth living for, and there was no getting rid of her. Marilyn was here to stay. Daddy wouldn't listen to *her* any more. Daddy, who had always done everything Rita ever wanted, had lost his mind to that witch. All the animals were gone. Exiled from the house first, then thrown out of the yard. Some things were just too hard to bear. Rita didn't so much mind about the ants and the tadpoles because they were safe, they could go on living in some sort of way, but what had become of the kittens? Frisky was dead. She had almost cured him but Marilyn had killed him. Mildred had taken the other dogs away to be given to friends and relatives in La Penitence. They were watchdogs now, tied on a string and spending their days barking at strangers. The cat and her kittens had been given to Doodnath; nobody knew where they were and nobody cared, except Rita, and nobody cared about Rita either. Nobody in the whole wide world.

'How yuh doin', beti?' Rookmini was waving from the callalloo patch, waving and smiling. Rita waved back but she didn't smile. Rookmini stooped down, bunching her skirt between her spread knees and hacking at the black earth. She had forgotten Rita. Rita stood up and continued on her way.

The East Indian gardeners were all out, working in their tiny plots along the canal, digging and hoeing to coax vegetables from the soil. Rita knew them all by name now. They were her friends. They waved as she went by, calling a greeting as Rookmini had done.

'Come, girl, come, have some dunks,' said Latchman's wife, and Rita went up to her and held out her blouse in a pouch which Latchman's wife poured dunks into.

'Look, chile, look what I got here!' called big fat Mrs Abdul. Rita stepped between the rows of bora-beans and looked into the sack she was holding out.

Her eyes lit up. 'Genips!' she said. 'Where you got them from?'

'Sookdeo bring them down from Buxton this morning!' Mrs Abdul said. 'He take the rest to Bourda market to sell. Sookdeo's nephew Ram comin' to sell these on Water Street. But you could have some. Tek, tek, we got plenty!'

Rita looked down at the dunks she held bunched up in her blouse, then she looked uncertainly at the genips, green, plump and inviting.

'I already got these dunks,' she said hesitantly. 'I don't have any room for genips!'

'You don't have pockets in those shorts? Put the dunks in the pockets, and put the genips in the blouse. Look, I gon't help you.'

Mrs Abdul helped Rita squeeze the dunks into her side pockets which now bulged like great knobs on her skinny hips. Then genips were poured into the pouch, straining the material so that it stretched right down to the tops of her thighs.

'You mummy gon' be too vex, you blouse stain-up bad from them dunks,' said Mrs Abdul. 'An' don' forget genips does stain bad too.'

'It don't matter,' said Rita. 'I don't have a real mummy.'

'You don't have? What? Who does look after you den, beti?' asked Mrs Abdul compassionately, but Rita only shook her head and her eyes filled with tears and she stuttered her thanks for the genips and went on her way.

Ranjeet Singh was loading the donkey-cart with pumpkins.

'You late today,' he said, 'I thought you weren't comin' at all!'

'Course I comin'!' said Rita. She clasped the bunched-up material of her blouse in her left hand and approached the little grey donkey harnessed to the cart. She fondled it behind the ears, the neck, and when it raised its head she kissed the muzzle.

'If you mummy see that she gon' be vex,' said Singh, but Rita wasn't listening, she was running her hands along the donkey's swelling belly.

'I'm *sure* it's coming today, she's much fatter!' she said, turning to Singh with huge pleading eyes. 'You shouldn't take her out today. What if she gets it on the street? Please, please keep her here today!'

Singh only laughed and shook his head. 'An' how you expect me to get dese pumpkins to de market?'

'But . . .'

But Singh wasn't listening, he had gone down to the canal with two rusty buckets and he was dipping them into the tea-brown water.

'Don't worry, Lucky, I'll come with you and help when you get your baby,' Rita whispered into the donkey's ear. She dug her free hand into her pocket and took it out overflowing with dunks, some of them falling to the ground. 'Here, Lucky, do you like dunks? Try them, they're sweet, sweet, sweet!' she said. Lucky pushed her muzzle disdainfully into the handful of dunks and gave a disapproving snort, blowing them all to the ground. Rita laughed and flung her free arm around her neck.

'Oh, Lucky, I love you so!' she said, and buried her face in the soft fur on the donkey's neck, and felt happy.

Rita spent the rest of the day beside Singh, her legs hanging over the front of the donkey-cart. She had to train Singh not to whip Lucky, and Singh allowed himself to be trained. He also allowed Rita to take the reins and drive Lucky, clucking her tongue and calling 'giddy-up, giddy-up' whenever she stopped to pull at the grass on the roadside. They delivered the pumpkins to the market and then they loaded manure on the cart and carried that to somebody's garden, and then they went to the Promenade Gardens and loaded the cart with coconut branches which hung out so far behind the cart they almost swept the road. (Singh tied a red flag to them.) Rita ate the genips as they plodded through the streets, cracking open the stiff green shells and plop-ping the peachy-pale balls of flesh into her mouth. When the stones were sucked dry she spat them on to the road, aiming at the passing cars. She, Singh, and Lucky carried all sorts of loads all over the town, and at lunchtime they had fish-and-rice with Singh's wife at the Stabroek Market (but Rita wasn't very hungry for she was full of genips), and drank mauby, and then they carted some more things here and there, and by the time dusk came and it was time to go home Rita was burned a little browner and felt as exhausted as if she herself had pulled the cart around town. And Lucky hadn't had her baby yet.

Perhaps it would be born tomorrow.

SEVEN

Rita's First Job

Marilyn, Ronnie, and Mildred first realized that the August holidays were over when Mrs Jarvis rang up to ask if Rita was sick, and why wasn't she at school. Rita had missed three days already, and no letter of excuse. Rita knew school had reopened, because Polly Wong had told her, but she didn't tell any of the grown-ups.

'Aren't you coming to school any more?' Polly had called over the palings.

Rita glanced up at the kitchen window. 'Shut up, silly, or they'll hear you.'

'But aren't you going to come? Please come, I miss you. Look, here's some chow-chow, Mummy sent it for you. She saw you from the window and sent me down and she wants to know why you don't come round any more. But tell me if you're coming to school tomorrow, or if you're sick or something.'

'No, I finish with school,' said Rita importantly, scratching a scab off her arm. 'I got a work now.'

'Work? True, Rita? You're working already?' Polly stared at her friend with wide-eyed envy. Then reason got the better of her, for Polly was a sensible child, well grounded in adult thinking. 'No, no, I don't believe you. Chirren don't go to work. Don't dig that scab

– look, it's bleeding now. It never going to heal if you keep digging it off. You should let it dry out and fall off by itself. Otherwise it leaves a nasty scar. Here, you don't want the chow-chow?'

Rita raised her arm and put the bleeding wound in her mouth, sucked, lowered it and looked at the wound. She wiped the spit off with the back of her hand and as an afterthought took the bowl of chow-chow Polly was holding out. With dirt-smeared fingers she shovelled a heap of it into her mouth. It was delicious.

'You don't believe me?' she said between chews. 'Then just go to the market tomorrow morning, you gon' see me sellin' pumpkin and greens! And I get to eat genips all day, for free.'

'And your daddy allows it?'

Rita shovelled two more loads of chow-chow into her mouth before answering. 'Course he does! You don't know my daddy does whatever I tell him? My daddy said if I want the moon he's going to climb up the sky and bring it down for me. He told me.'

'Yes, but . . .'

'You know he does, he always does. I'm my daddy's favourite person, his very favourite, he's always telling me that and I can have whatever I want. And he doesn't want a son, he likes girls better. An' it's true. He don't like boys at all.'

'Rita, don't talk with your mouth full, it's disgusting. You should come to school, you know. I miss you, and all the chirren asking, and Mrs Jarvis, and anyway if you don't go to school you get stupid, and—'

'I finish with school. School is for babies and assholes. I *hate* school. Here, take this.' Rita pushed the empty bowl at Polly and ran away to check on a secret horde of ants, a mini-farm she kept in a guava-jelly jar, hidden from Marilyn's prying eyes on a bottom-house rafter. You could only get to it by climbing up the heap of rotting planks Daddy was storing for the bicycle shed he never got around to building.

A few days later Marilyn had the planks removed, for she was starting work on the yard. And Rita was yanked off to school, which put an end to the days of dunks and donkeys.

*   *   *

45

You can send a girl to school but you can't make her learn.

'She seems *preoccupied*,' said Mrs Jarvis in a confidential telephone call to Ronnie. 'Have there been any changes in her life lately? She's an extremely bright child, one of our brightest, but since this term began she simply refuses to work. She just sits there dreaming. She won't write a word. She doesn't take anything in. It's like trying to teach a stone wall.'

'Well . . . ah, we've been having a little bit of trouble with her lately,' stammered Ronnie. 'She's slightly unsteady at the moment but I'm sure it will pass. No need to worry.'

'Well, I certainly hope it passes soon. It's always such a shame when a child doesn't live up to its talents.'

'Talents? What talents?'

'You must know that Rita has an extraordinary gift for expressing herself in writing,' said Mrs Jarvis, a note of astonishment in her voice. 'I mean, as a writer yourself, you must have taken an interest. You must have seen the exercise books she filled last year. Even when she first started school, we didn't have to teach her, she could write already. I thought *you* had taught her, that you had been encouraging her! And all those little stories she used to bring to show me, they're so good! That story about the Queen Ant and her birthday cake, for instance. Surely you were some kind of a co-author?'

'Well, er, as a matter of fact, no, I wasn't.'

'All the more astonishing, then, and all the more a pity. I can't believe – I mean, I wrote her a glowing school report at the end of last term, so it can't possibly be new to you, Mr Maraj. I think you should come round and we should have a long talk about your daughter. I read in the papers that you married recently, could that be at the root of the matter? Perhaps you'd like to bring your wife, Rita's stepmother, so that we can consider together how to give Rita the support and encouragement she needs?'

Ronnie was silent for so long Mrs Jarvis thought he had hung up.

'Mr Maraj?'

'Yes, I'm still here. Mrs Jarvis, I'll speak to my wife and I'll ring you back in a day or two, is that all right?'

'Very well, I'll be looking forward to that. I'm sure it's just a passing phase, so I wouldn't worry. If we all pull together then we'll soon have her back to normal, I'm quite sure. We should have that talk as soon as possible though, in the next day or two.'

'Yes, yes, of course.'

But Mrs Jarvis never heard from Ronnie Maraj. Ronnie drew encouragement from Mrs Jarvis's words, 'I'm sure it's just a passing phase,' because that was what Ronnie believed too, and if Mrs Jarvis confirmed this belief, then it was better just to let things be. The phase would pass by itself; no use upsetting Rita by making a fuss. And why upset Marilyn? She had enough on her hands already, what with craftsmen and gardeners who failed to turn up, Mildred who refused to cook according to instructions, and all the troublesome side-effects of a swelling belly.

Ronnie was quite enjoying married life. Occasionally Marilyn had a little tantrum but she was easily mollified by a few hugs and a candlelit dinner at Palm Courts. She was happy if he went window shopping with her, her arm hooked into his – though she complained steadily that these days there wasn't anything to *look* at in the windows – and she had quickly accepted the fact that it was her money paying for everything. Ronnie had little more than his own meagre salary, which didn't go very far, but Marilyn not only had shares in Prabudial's furniture store, she actually owned a piece of jungle, and at the moment there was a boom in demand for tropical wood in Europe, and exports in greenheart and purpleheart had soared. Once Ronnie had asked his wife what would happen when all the trees in her piece of forest had been cut down and exported, and if she was thinking of planting new ones, but Marilyn only shook her pretty head.

'What do I know about business matters?' she said. 'I have a manager who takes care of things like that. I trust Mr Pooran one hundred per cent.'

Marilyn was all for leading the kind of agreeable life Ronnie liked. They spent their Saturdays at the Pegasus poolside, sitting with friends old and new at one of the shady tables where Marilyn would sip a Pina Colada and Ronnie enjoyed a rum and coke or two, cracking jokes. Once he had suggested they bring Rita along: she would have fun swimming in the pool with the children of their friends, but Marilyn had wrinkled her nose and told him why that would never work.

'Rita would not enjoy their company,' she said. 'You don't know your own daughter. Rita has a way of talking that would immediately make her unpopular. The other children might tease her and she would feel left out. And anyway, she much prefers running wild in the yard covering herself with dirt or running off wherever she runs off to. It would be wrong to try and tame her. Let her be.'

'We could maybe all go up to Buxton beach next weekend,' Ronnie suggested amiably. 'She always used to like that. The Allicocks have a beach house they let us borrow, we could sleep there Saturday night. She enjoyed watching the crabs, and playing cricket on the beach, and . . .'

But Marilyn wrinkled her nose even more, and shook her head vigorously. 'Ronnie, you know how I hate Guyana sea water. That awful dirty brown water.'

'It's not dirt, it's only mud! People say it's good for the skin,' Ronnie joked. 'It will make you even more beautiful than you are! Maybe we should try putting it in jars and exporting it as the latest beauty potion!' He hastily stopped when he saw Marilyn's expression, and continued in a conciliatory tone, 'But if you don't like the beach, we could go up to Redwater Creek . . . ?'

'That's even worse! Do I look like the sort of wild woman who goes swimming in those bush creeks? You never know what snakes and alligators are going to bite off your toes. Not me, you won't catch me dead up there!' Marilyn rubbed her cheek, frowned, and then smiled, showing two rows of sparkling white teeth. 'Now if you really want to go to the sea we could go and visit Uncle George in St Lucia. What you say to that?'

'Great idea!' Ronnie enthused. 'We could go in the Christmas holidays, Rita would be so excited! She always wanted to travel!'

'Christmas holidays? Are you *mad*? I would be . . . let me see
. . . seven months pregnant by then, I would be enormous, you
don't think I would be seen gallivanting on the beach in that
condition? No, if we go at all we have to go soon, maybe next
month. And we never had a proper honeymoon. October would
be perfect.'

'But then Rita—'

'Rita this, Rita that. Mildred is perfectly capable of looking
after that girl; she does whatever she wants anyway. All she
needs is a bowl of cornflakes in the morning, a chicken leg for
lunch, and half a jar of peanut butter in between. And a bed at
night. That's settled then. I'll write to Uncle George tomorrow.'

All in all, Ronnie thought, he had a very harmonious marriage.
They hardly ever quarrelled; any differences they had were
quickly reconciled for Marilyn always had some very good
suggestion which would more than adequately solve any problem
they had. She was a genius at that. If only Rita would come to
her senses. If only she and Marilyn would make friends. But once
Marilyn had a baby of her own, he said to himself, all her
motherly instincts would surface and everything would turn out
for the best. After all, he had given Rita a proper family at last.
He had developed regular ways, like a proper husband, and he
had stopped hanging out with bachelor friends and coming home
drunk – Marilyn would never stand for that sort of behaviour –
and when his son was born they would finally be like all the
other Victoria Street families: father and mother, boy and girl,
grand house, lovely garden. Grandma, had she lived, would have
been proud of him.

Grandma, Ronnie realized, had brought all this about. Grandma
had suggested Marilyn as a suitable wife. Grandma had known
all along. A pity, though, that Grandma had never acknowledged
Rita. Poor little Rita. But finally, all this was for her sake. Rita
needed a family, and that was what he was giving her. If only
she would settle down.

EIGHT

The Hello-goodbye Plant

Hunkered on the grass verge beside the gutter outside Polly Wong's home, totally immersed in the soul of the hello-goodbye plant, Rita didn't hear the footsteps approaching from behind, and she didn't look up when Mrs Wong crouched down beside her, laying her tennis racquet on the grass. Mrs Wong didn't speak; she only watched. Rita squatted firmly in her favoured position, bare bony brown knees tucked snugly into her armpits. One arm hugged her legs for balance, her left hand cupped one knee, the right held a long stalk of grass which she held forward, slowly moving it from one tiny branch of the hello-goodbye plant to the other. Her lips whispered the words hello, goodbye as she worked through the clump of grass. The hello-goodbye plant was really nothing but a tangle of weeds, consisting of hundreds of tiny branches like miniature palms. Most of the time they were open; but when you touched them, they slipped into motion: the palms moved their branches upwards, reaching up to clasp each other in long tight nodes, refusing to unclasp till the plant was perfectly certain that danger had passed. Rita ran her grass-stalk gently from palm to palm, barely touching them, yet even such slight encounters sent each one into withdrawal.

Absorbed in the spectacle, Rita made not the slightest gesture to acknowledge Mrs Wong's presence by her side, other than to stop whispering her hellos and goodbyes, and only mouthing the words, her lips moving in rhythm: hello, as her stalk approached a new palm, goodbye as it closed up, and on to the next. Mrs Wong watched, saying nothing. Though she had not glanced up, Rita had felt at once when Mrs Wong entered her space, and closed up, drawing an inner cloak around her being. Waiting for the attack. However, when Mrs Wong did nothing, said nothing, but only watched, Rita felt an inner release of tension; and now it seemed certain there was to be no assault she first glanced sideways up at Polly's mother, and then she slightly turned her head. Mrs Wong did not look back, she was as absorbed in the hello-goodbye plant as Rita had been, for now the tiny palms had not been touched for several minutes and they were slowly, hesitantly, opening up again. Mrs Wong pursed her lips and blew gently, touching one branch with her breath, and right away the plant took fright and drew its leaves together. Only then did Mrs Wong chuckle softly, and turn her face towards Rita, who smiled slightly and turned her face away so Mrs Wong wouldn't see.

Mrs Wong spoke then, in almost a whisper. 'Rita,' she said, 'you've been here for hours, I saw you when I went to tennis and you've not moved an inch. If you sit here much longer you'll turn into a plant yourself!'

'I could have gone in the house just after you left and come out again just before you came back, couldn't I?' said Rita.

'That's very true,' Mrs Wong agreed. 'But wouldn't you like to come in for some ice cream? Polly would love to play with you again – she's not home right now, she's at her ballet class and so's Maxine, but you could come in and have some ice cream with me, and then we'll go and pick them up. They'd love to see you. You haven't been over for ages! We all miss you so much!'

'Ice cream makes you fat. That's what *she* says.'

'Who's she? Oh, you mean . . . Well, I wouldn't worry much what she says, Rita, she's a grown-up lady and maybe she worries a lot about her figure. Ladies do that, you know, but someone

51

like you, you're so thin, you can eat as much ice cream as you like! Soursop ice cream, really delicious!'

Rita turned then and looked up into Mrs Wong's eyes, because if there was one thing she loved in the world, it was soursop ice cream. Mrs Wong caught Rita's gaze in her eyes like night and they looked at each other for a whole minute without saying a word, without smiling, though the edges of Mrs Wong's lips twitched once.

Mrs Wong had a lovely face. She had the same skin like creamed cashew that Polly had and her wide-apart eyes were big enough and steady enough to hold you and keep you safe. When she smiled it was like when you watched the sun rising over the Atlantic from your bedroom window, a warm clean feeling. Rita wished she would smile now, so she could get that warm clean feeling, for inside she was crumbling. Last night she had written a poem in her diary, and looking at Mrs Wong the words rose in her mind:

When I think,
it's like sand.
When I feel,
it's much too bland.
When I cry,
it's like stones.
When I laugh
it's made of bones.

Mrs Wong smiled, so Rita smiled back, and said, 'OK.'

She climbed to her feet, stretching her limbs slowly like a cat because they hurt from crouching so long. Mrs Wong got up too, and bent to pick up her racquet. She wore a white blouse and a white pleated skirt that stopped halfway down her thighs, showing bare legs which were creamy like her face and just as smooth.

'Come,' she said cheerfully, and held out a hand, and Rita took it and followed her over the gutter-bridge and through the gate and up into the house.

The Wongs' house wasn't a bit like theirs. At least, not a bit like theirs had been before doomsday. Since doomsday, their own house was changing every day and soon it would look just like the Wongs' inside. The floor was polished to a high dark gloss, and a couch and two armchairs were placed around a square carpet with a low purpleheart table in the middle, and on the table was a purpleheart ashtray and a vase with artificial flowers.

Rita immediately walked over to the aquarium on a table against the far wall; she knew the goldfish well but hadn't been over for such a long time she was surprised by the changes.

'Where's Slippy?' she asked.

'Slippy . . . Who . . . Oh, yes, Slippy died. Didn't Polly tell you?'

'Why did Slippy die? Was she sick? If she was sick, why didn't you call me over? I could have taken care of her and made her well. And you've got two new fish. Do they have names yet?'

Mrs Wong came over to watch the fish. 'No, I don't believe they have names, at least, Polly never told me if they do. Would you like to choose some names? And then if she hasn't given them names already, she might like to use yours!'

She didn't have to ask Rita twice. 'Aaaah . . .' Rita said, her brow creased in concentration. 'That one there with the black stripe, I think he should be called Flush. And the other one, the one that looks like Slippy, she's . . . aaah . . .' She held a finger against the glass and peered closely at the fish in question. 'She's Pinky.' She swung her head around to look up at Mrs Wong with radiant eyes.

'Flush and Pinky. Those are good names. Very good names. I'm sure Polly would like those names,' said Mrs Wong, adding cautiously, 'if she hasn't given them names yet.'

Mrs Wong left Rita looking at the fish and went into the kitchen to get the ice cream. She brought two bowls of it back and together they sat in the gallery on the rattan chairs, in front of the open window where the sea breeze swung through smelling of salt, and in companionable silence they ate. Rita took time to eat hers, savouring the tangy, sweet-sour flavour of the soursop.

There were small bits of slithery soursop flesh mixed up in the ice cream and those were the bits she loved most. Absorbed in the flavour, she spooned tiny pieces of ice cream and fruit into her mouth and felt it melting and becoming part of her, and then she licked the bowl clean with her tongue (Marilyn said you weren't supposed to but Marilyn wasn't here now) and then she looked up and saw Mrs Wong was watching her, but not in the mean old sourpuss way that Marilyn did, but in a nice quiet warm sunrisy way. So she smiled.

'Thank you,' she said simply.

'It's a pleasure,' said Mrs Wong, and then she looked sort of worried, and said, 'Your daddy and . . . and your . . . your . . .'

'Stepmother?' Rita offered.

'Yes, stepmother. They've gone away, haven't they?'

'Oh yes, they went to St Lucia. They're staying in an awful big hotel with a swimming pool. They sent me a postcard. It looks horrible. I'm glad I refused to go.'

'You refused to go?'

'Yes. Daddy really wanted me to come, he begged and begged but I said no. I told him I'm busy, I have things to do. 'Portant things. And I like it here and I hate those places. Broad places.'

'Broad places?'

'Yes, broad. Those broad far-away places. I don't want to go broad.'

'Oh, yes, you mean abroad.'

'Yes, that's what I said. Broad places. So I told Daddy to go with her and he went. He wanted to stay with me when I didn't want to go but I told him no. I want to be here alone. With Mildred, alone.'

'But aren't you . . . just a little bit, sometimes, you know, lonely? I mean, you haven't got any animals any more, and you're not playing with the other children . . . ?'

'No. I like being alone by myself.'

'But what do you do alone by yourself all day?'

'Well, you know, I do some thinking. Sometimes I think about things.'

'What things?'

'*Every*things. Sometimes I think about my thoughts, and sometimes I think about being something else, like a plant or an ant. She killed all the ants in the house, you know, but there are still plenty in the yard.' Rita grinned in a sly way, and whispered, 'I even know where the wood-ants are eating up the house, but I won't tell her, so the house will fall down. And I can climb up in the star-apple tree and think up there. I can pretend I'm a tree and wave my arms like branches and be the sky.'

Now that she had started to speak the words came pouring out of Rita, as if Mrs Wong had pressed a button and a dam of communication had burst open. Mrs Wong sat silently listening, nodding, now and then smiling.

Then she looked at her watch and interrupted Rita's flood of words. 'Rita, it's getting late,' she said. 'I have to go and pick up Polly and Maxine from their ballet class. Would you like to come? It's only around the corner in Lamaha Street, just a short walk.'

Rita hesitated, not knowing what to say. It was a funny thing with friends, sometimes you stopped speaking to them and you didn't say a word even when they came out of the gate with their housekeeper and walked right past you talking to the hello-goodbye plant. You heard them walking by but you didn't turn round and say hi, just pretended they weren't there, and they didn't say hi either. So you weren't friends any more. But you wanted to be friends again and you didn't know how to go about it, and you didn't want to be the first one to start being friends again, but you were the first one to stop being friends, and you had forgotten why exactly, so perhaps it was only just if you were the one to start talking again, and going to pick them up from ballet class?

'Polly doesn't like me any more,' she said.

'Of course she likes you! I told you she's dying to play with you again, and Maxine too. She thinks *you* don't like *her*, she said you stopped talking to her a week ago and you just ignore her at school, and I told her perhaps you're preoccupied.'

'What kind of pie is that?'

'Pre-occ-u-pied. It means lost in thought so much that you don't notice things going on around you.'

'Say it again?'

Mrs Wong did so.

'Pre-occ-u-pied,' Rita repeated. 'Is it one word or more?'

'It's one word,' said Mrs Wong.

'And it means all those things at once?'

'Yes.'

'Pre-occ-u-pied,' Rita said, memorizing it. It was a nice word. A big word with a big meaning, not like all the silly little in-between words the language was full of, words that by themselves meant nothing. Preoccupied held all kinds of little words together and meant them all at once. Rita knew exactly what preoccupied meant, and she resolved to write it in her diary that night and use it as often as she could.

Mrs Wong looked at her watch again and said, 'But, Rita, I really have to go now, so if you're *preoccupied* I'll leave you here to do some more thinking, otherwise let's go!'

When Rita, moving her lips to memorize the wonderful new word preoccupied, didn't make a move, Mrs Wong added craftily, 'We'll take Rover with us. You can hold the leash.'

And she held out her hand and Rita took it, and jumped to her feet, and held Mrs Wong's hand all the way to the ballet school in Lamaha Street, and the end of Rover's leash in the other, and after that she and Polly were friends again.

'Why weren't you friends with me for a whole week?' Polly asked later, for Polly was a frank, outgoing girl who never kept her thoughts to herself like Rita.

'I was pre-occ-u-pied,' said Rita grandly, 'but now I'm not any more. Those two new fishes you have – what are their names?'

'They don't have any names – yet,' said Polly. 'I was thinking we could name them together. You're so good at names, what d'you think?'

'Pinky and Flush,' said Rita immediately.

*　　*　　*

Rita no longer slept in her bedroom. Since Ronnie and Marilyn's departure ten days ago the house had more or less returned to its pre-Marilyn state of comfortable disorder, and Mildred didn't mind in the least when Rita dragged her mattress to the top of the stairs, sat on it, and whooshed down to the bottom like on a flying carpet. Nor did she mind when Rita dragged the mattress to a corner of the drawing room and declared she was going to sleep there from now on, at least till Marilyn came back and raised objections.

'You got de big house all to youself,' said Mildred dismissively. 'For all I concern, you could do what you want. You is de mistress.'

In a way it was nice having the big house all to herself, all alone in all the space. On the other hand, it was a bit spooky if you didn't have someone to talk to. It wouldn't have been so bad with animals around. She knew there was no point starting an ant farm all over again, but she did bring up a jar full of tadpoles, who all died after two days, floating soft-belly-up on the water. Which made it even more spooky, for the tadpole ghosts swam through the rooms at night, trying to talk to Rita, blaming her for their baby deaths.

So the evening after she and Polly started talking again Rita was still awake when she heard the gate creak open. At first she thought it was Cyril, who, since Ronnie and Marilyn had left, had begun to visit Mildred at night sometimes, like he used to do before doomsday. But she hadn't heard Cyril's car so she wondered if it was a ghost, not a tadpole ghost but a people ghost. But no, ghosts didn't need gates. Then she heard a gentle knocking on Mildred's door through the open window, and then voices talking, and it definitely wasn't Cyril's voice, it was another woman's. Funny, Rita thought, and then she fell asleep.

But next morning there was a big surprise waiting for her. She was going to be late for school as usual and was gobbling down her breakfast sitting in the Berbice chair with a flustered Mildred goading her on when Polly burst through the door.

'Rita, Rita!' she shouted. 'Rita, you can come and stay with us!'

Rita's mouth was full of peanut butter and bread so she made some strange gulping noises in the process of trying to get it down.

'Mummy spoke to your daddy last night. She rang him up in his hotel on St Lucia and he said it's fine with him if you want to. Oh, Rita, Rita, please come, wouldn't it be wonderful, you can come and sleep in my room, we have a mattress for you but you can sleep in my bed even!'

Mildred, picking up Rita's pyjamas from the carpet, said laconically, 'Oh, yeh, I forgot to mention it, Rita, Mrs Wong came over to arsk if it would be all right and I give she you daddy's telephone number. So she done telephone already?'

'Yes, yes!' cried Polly. 'She spoke to him last night when we were all sleeping, and he said yes, and you can move in right away! After school! And we're going to have such fun! A whole week!'

And they did. Living with the Wongs was like having all the whole world reach out and say hello, and not say goodbye again, and at the end of the week when Daddy rang from St Lucia Rita prattled on so long Daddy had to shout to get a word in.

'Rita, just be quiet for one minute please. Listen, dear, I'm glad you're happy there, I thought you would be, and Mrs Wong told me she likes having you, that's why I know you won't mind if Marilyn and I stay a week longer, will you?'

'No, no, it's all right, Daddy, I like living here . . . Oh!'

'What?'

'It's my birthday next Thursday!'

'Your . . . Oh, hell, yes, I forgot.'

'You promised!'

'Yes, I know, dear, and we will, we will, I still promise! Just another day, not on Thursday.'

'But then it's not really a birthday treat, if it's another day.'

'Of course it is, dear, we'll go up next weekend. No, not next because we're coming back on Saturday, but the weekend after that – Oh hell, no, that's the Miss Guyana contest, I have to cover it, but . . . I promise, dear, we will do it some time. Soon.'

'But it's not going to be for my birthday. It was to be a birthday trip. It's not the same. I hate you I hate you I hate you and I hate her too.'

And she banged down the receiver.

Mrs Wong found her an hour later, up in the star-apple tree. 'Are you feeling better now, darling?'

Rita nodded.

'Would you like to come down? I've got some soursop ice cream.'

Rita nodded again, and came down.

'Would you like to tell me all about it?'

Rita nodded. 'Daddy promised. He promised on my birthday I would take the day off from school and he would take a day off from work, and we would fly up to Kaieteur Falls, just me and him and not Marilyn, and we would spend the day there, and then we would come down. It was to be my birthday present. He promised me ages and ages ago, even before she came, and now he says we can't. Because of her.'

'Well, dear, we'll just have to see what we can do for your birthday, won't we? We'll have a party for certain, we'll invite the whole street, and maybe we can borrow a pony for pony rides, and . . . I'll think of something.'

Rita nodded. She wasn't really listening. She was preoccupied.

'Happy birthday to you, Happy birthday to you . . .'

Rita sat up, rubbing her eyes. Mrs Wong, Dr Wong, Polly, and Maxine stood in a circle around her bed. And something else, someone else . . . Mrs Wong held a stick in her hand, a stick with a crossbar, and on the crossbar sat a macaw, tied to it with a rope attached to a ring around its left leg.

Dr Wong was grinning from ear to ear, Polly looked as if about to burst, Maxine was jumping up and down.

'What's . . . what's that?' Rita stuttered.

'It's a macaw, silly,' cried Polly. 'A macaw! And he's yours!'

'It's your birthday present,' added Mrs Wong.

'He can *thpeak*,' said Maxine. 'You can teach him to thpeak!'

'But . . . but I won't be allowed . . . Marilyn!'

'To hell with Marilyn!' cried Mrs Wong. 'Of course you can keep him. You can keep him here, in our yard, but he'll be all yours and you have to look after him, feed him, clean his droppings away . . .'

'And teach him to thpeak!'

'His name's Robert, Rita. The man we got him from said all macaws are called Robert.'

'Not this one. His name's Ringo Starr. Mr Starr for short.'

Ronnie and Marilyn returned home quarrelling. Marilyn was furious at Ronnie, Ronnie shamefacedly defending himself. They were quarrelling as they left the taxi, walked up the front stairs, entered the house. When she saw the state of the drawing room Marilyn immediately stopped accusing Ronnie of whatever sin he had committed, and began to berate Rita and Mildred, calling them a pair of sluts – which was unfair, since Rita hadn't been living there for two weeks, so it couldn't be her fault that Mildred hadn't tidied up, Mildred was dismissed on the spot.

It was quite a few days before Rita discovered just what the original quarrel had been about, but gradually the secret came out.

Marilyn had lost her baby. It was all Ronnie's fault, he was a horny bastard, Rita heard Marilyn shouting at him one night when they thought she was asleep (she had had to move her mattress from the drawing room back to its bedstead upstairs, where it belonged).

Rita was puzzled by the use of the word 'horny'. She knew what a 'horn' was, of course. Finally she came to the conclusion that Marilyn had been tossed by a bull with large horns, that Ronnie had been trying to get rid of her in this way. It was an explanation that satisfied her deeply. And she was glad that there would be no little boy coming to Number Seven. Not just yet, anyway.

Part Two

NINE

Kamal Goes Outside

Kamal tried not to breathe; he was sure they'd hear him if he did. He could hear his own breathing and the drumming of his heart, loud and erratic, and it seemed to him the whole world must be listening, watching for him. He crouched lower in the hamper, hugging his knees, curled into a ball with his head tucked in, exactly fitting the circular shape of the basket. For the first time in his life he was glad that he was so small, so supple, like a cat, they said, loose and limber and able to crawl into the smallest spaces and jump from the highest windows, landing like a coiled spring and sprinting off before they could blink twice. That's why they never caught him; that's why when Rani sent them for him he was able to wriggle loose and run, and that's why Rani tried all the more to bind him to herself. But bondage, for Kamal, had the effect of a whiplash, urging him to escape, stimulating his ingenuity so that, short of winding him in thick chains, Rani remained the loser. He smiled to himself, thinking of Rani's rage, and then her panic, when he turned up missing.

He had placed a cloth over himself so that if someone did happen to open the hamper, they wouldn't notice he was there; they'd be deceived into thinking the hamper had been sent back with its contents intact, rejected by the chowkidar. At first he squeezed his eyes together as if in shutting out the world the world would also shut him out – at least the little world of Mahapradesh which he knew so well, every tiny corner and crevice so that he could find his way blindfolded through the labyrinthine passages and staircases, led on by the pungent smells, the sounds, the shape of the cobbles, the smoothness of the stones beneath his bare feet, the texture of tapestries and curtains, the senses of touch and hearing and smelling refined to such perfection he could almost do without the sense of sight.

With the passing of each second his excitement grew. The more time it took to load the cart and coax the bullocks into movement, the more dangerous it would become for him; he had to make sure everything outside was *normal*. Cautiously he opened his eyes to a slit. It was dark inside the hamper but not fully dark: slabs of daylight glinted between the strands of wicker. Curiosity won over caution: carefully he adjusted his position, pushing his face right up to the hamper's side, aligning his right eye with one of those daylight cracks, and peered out.

Everything seemed normal. In the greyness of the first morning light there was the usual courtyard bustle. Punraj, wearing only his kaupina and a turban, trotted across Kamal's limited line of vision, bent slightly forward under the weight of the rice sack he carried on his back. Punraj's body, black as ebony, glistened with sweat although the sun was not yet out; it was a long way to the storeroom at the back of the complex and this was certainly not his first sack. Kamal smiled to himself; he wished he could call out to Punraj, and share his secret; Punraj wouldn't mind and Punraj wouldn't talk. Punraj was a friend, a forbidden friend, one of the many forbidden friends Kamal had made among the palace subordinates.

He couldn't see much through the slit, and after Punraj there were a few seconds when all he could see was the red-brick building at the back of the courtyard. But he could hear the familiar morning noises and knew therefore that he had not yet been missed, that everything was as it should be. A goat ran across the fine strip of courtyard revealed to Kamal, the white nanny goat which Kamal had named, for a reason known only to himself, Wendy. Wendy was being chased by Bibi, another of Kamal's forbidden friends. Bibi wore a long red skirt and she raced zig-zagging behind Wendy, thrusting out grasping arms which the little goat neatly evaded, before she, too, disappeared from sight. Kamal smelled the smoke from fires lit in the kitchen at his back, and his mouth watered as he heard the sizzling of ghee as the cooks began to fry the breakfast puris. He heard the clang of buckets being let into the well to his side, the creaking of the pulley, the gush of water poured into clay vessels. The chatter of a hundred servants; the strident calling of a peacock on a faraway roof.

He felt the first prick of impatience; it was time to get going. Else they would . . . there! The bell for breakfast rang out and Kamal bit his lip in nervousness: he should be long gone because if he didn't come for breakfast it would certainly be noticed. And they would start the search for him while he was still within the palace and certainly find him. He felt his spirits sink – had everything been in vain? Every day for the past week he had watched and waited and every day the bullock cart had left well before breakfast began.

The empty hampers were loaded in the blackness of pre-dawn, which was why it had been easy to slink through the empty corridors, mount the cart and climb into one of them, covering himself carefully before reaching out, groping for the propped-up lid, and closing it over himself. Once hidden all he had to do was wait. Today, though, driver-wallah was taking his time. Kamal knew that on every other day he had sat on the freshly swept earth outside the kitchen drinking tea and sharing gossip with some of the male servants who breakfasted at this time, before the day's work began. They sat in a circle around a small brazier, wrapped in layers of cloth for warmth since the mornings were chilly at this time of year, murmuring to each other, pouring their tea from cup to cup to cool it, raising their chins and opening their mouths to receive the milky brew. On previous days Kamal had watched, hidden, and on every day well before now the men had stood up and shaken out their clothes and dusted themselves before separating to go about their various tasks. Driver-wallah would return to the cart, settle himself on the wooden perch between the rumps of the two bullocks, call out *hey-hey*, prod the slothful animals several times in their backsides, and the cart would rumble off long before the bell for breakfast began its rigorous, joyous pealing. The bullocks would pause at the huge grid of gates let into the palace walls. Watchmen swathed in heavy wraps would draw back the many bolts and turn the many keys and unwind the many chains before heaving the heavy gates slowly inward, letting the bullocks and the cart pass through. The gates would close again, be bolted, chained and locked. The bullocks, the cart, the hampers were Outside.

Kamal, in all of his nine years, had never once been Outside.

He had a cramp in his right foot, bent awkwardly into the curve of the hamper. He adjusted his position slightly, wriggled his toes, and tried to move his foot but couldn't, it seemed stuck into position. Everything was aching by now. And he was cold, and hungry. And worried about being found. Everything was going wrong. Driver-wallah had disappeared from the face of the earth. Today of all days. Why today, of all days? That was the worst of it.

Kamal knew that things only worked out if they were supposed to. You could plan and plot and arrange circumstances as much as you liked but if your plan was not simultaneously Destiny's plan it would definitely go wrong: for, as Teacher always said, man proposes but God disposes. So if today of all days driver-wallah's schedule had changed then Destiny was saying a loud clear unmistakable *no*. And now there was an unfamiliar commotion somewhere up in the West Wing, and Kamal couldn't see but he knew that Lakshmi was up on the balcony outside the servants' room shouting down to somebody in the courtyard. He could hear every word clearly, and he knew his time was almost up; if driver-wallah did not turn up in the next few minutes they'd start a serious search for him.

'Ramanath, have you seen Kamal?'

'Kamal? No, he's not here, why?'

'Well, he's missing, he didn't go to breakfast and the Mistress is frightfully angry, in fact she's furious. He's not in his room either.'

'He's probably in the stables, have you looked there? That dog must have had her pups, you know he watches for them every day. I'm sure he's there.'

'That's a good idea. I'll go and check.'

And then Kamal breathed out in gratitude for the cart swayed to one side with the weight of driver-wallah's ascent, and the bullocks shifted, the cart creaked, and he heard the familiar cry of *hey-hey*, and they were off. He heard the grating of gates opening, and then they were Outside.

TEN

Eyes

Near the chowk, the market-place, the cart came to a halt and
Kamal climbed out unseen. He jumped to the ground and, following his senses, drawn by the noise and smells and whirl of colour,
made his way to the bazaar. What a world! A world teeming
with fruit and vegetables, some of which Kamal had never seen,
much less tasted. His nostrils absorbed a thousand different
aromas at once, some so sweet he stopped simply to look, and
because he was hungry and had had no breakfast his mouth began
to water as he stared at a man cutting open a big round fruit and
pulling it apart into soft, slippery, translucent sections, bright
yellow and luscious.

'What's that?' he asked the vendor, who laughed out loud.

'You don't know what a jack-fruit is? Where are you living,
little boy?'

'In the palace,' said Kamal truthfully and immediately clapped
his hand to his mouth and gazed at the man with petrified eyes;
then he ran down the row of fruit stalls till he came to the flower
vendors. Here the fragrance was intoxicating. Kamal looked right
and left and all he saw were flowers, piles of garlands and baskets
of roses; a girl his age sitting on the ground before a basket of

tuber-rose blossoms threading them expertly with quick, nimble fingers; vendors coming with full baskets and going with empty ones for it was still early, the stalls were still being replenished, and Kamal alone had nothing to do but stare.

Having seen all there was to see in the bazaar he wandered up and down the surrounding lanes, the hunger in his stomach gnawing more and more insistently. He found himself in a narrow alley where the road's tarmac crumbled and the shops on either side all seemed to sell nothing but rusty nails. Another lane was unbearable because here every building was a tea-shop and outside every shop pans of oil sizzled on open fires and golden puris swelled up into crisp balloons emitting the aroma of breakfast which invaded his nostrils and sank into his belly and screamed there for succour.

Kamal's pockets were empty. He had not thought to bring money; even had he thought of it, he would not have known where to get it. He had never handled money, he had no need to. And now, though his clothes were of silk and the chain around his neck and the ring on his finger were of pure gold, he was as poor as the poorest beggar – *those* he had seen everywhere – because he could not eat silk or gold. At this thought something clicked in his mind and boldly he approached the boy – not much older than himself – frying puris outside the next shop. He eased the ring from his finger and held it out.

'Would you accept this ring as payment for breakfast?' he asked hesitantly.

The boy stared at the ring and then at Kamal and called to someone in the black interior of the shop. A man came out, wiping his hands on a grubby cloth, and, looking Kamal up and down, said, 'Where did you get that ring, boy? Is it stolen?'

'No, of course not,' said Kamal angrily, and then remembered that no one knew who he was and so added in a milder tone, 'my grandmother gave it to me. It is mine. I would like to eat but I have no money. Would you accept this ring as payment?'

'Yes, yes, of course,' said the man then and showed Kamal a bench where three other men were sitting at a long table, eating. Kamal slid in and waited to be served.

One of the men, dressed in white pyjamas and a white cap, looked keenly at him and said, 'Are you a fool, or what?'

'Why should I be a fool?'

'To pay for your breakfast with that valuable ring. Look, don't do it. Come with me afterwards and I will show you where you can sell it for a good price. I will pay for your breakfast.'

'Very well,' said Kamal gratefully and ate with more appetite than he had ever done in the palace, for the simple food tasted more delicious than the most sumptuous feast Rani had had prepared for him alone.

The shopkeeper was not happy with this new arrangement. When Kamal and the man got up to go he spoke some sharp words but the man simply left the money on the table and strode off. Kamal running behind him, thanking him profusely.

'It was only my duty,' said the man, brushing off Kamal's gratitude. 'A boy like you must be careful in this town: there are wicked people just waiting to rob you. Look at your fine clothes, your jewellery! Why do you walk around looking like a prince in this place? Where do you come from? What are you doing on the streets at this time, shouldn't you be going to school?'

Kamal felt he could trust this man and told him his name and his story. The man laughed and wished him luck. 'I hope you enjoy your day,' he said. 'Goodbye. It was interesting meeting you.'

'But aren't you going to show me the jeweller's shop? I have to sell my ring and give you back the money!'

'Don't worry about the money,' said the man. 'It was my pleasure to buy you breakfast. Just be careful!'

Kamal found the jeweller's shop anyway. It was on a street with several such shops. He sold his ring for thirty rupees and felt delirious with joy at possessing his own money. When it was time for lunch he paid for his own meal in a dark restaurant where boys younger than himself ran around with pails of water, collecting the dirty plates and wiping the tables after the customers left. He ate with joy and he paid with pride.

After lunch he wandered up and down more streets at random.

He found himself in a part of town where the colours were reduced to black and grey, the streets teeming with human and animal life. There were beggars sitting at the roadside, their clothes black and caked with grime. There were children, infants, with limbs bent backwards and eyes oozing pus and swarming with flies. There was a dog with half its head missing, walking around with its brain hanging out. Pigs in the gutters, eating human waste. A stench of offal pervaded these lanes; Kamal felt on the verge of vomiting yet still he walked on, observing, wondering, asking himself questions that could not be answered. He had never in his life seen sights such as these; he had not imagined such misery could exist in the same world as the palace of Mahapradesh.

It was mid-afternoon when he found himself in a pot-holed street, wider than the others, lined by ramshackle buildings. The strange thing about this street was that there were so many women on it. The women sat or stood outside the open doorways; they sat in the dust or on mats or on sharpais, or they leaned against the doorframes, laughing, chatting with each other. They combed and plaited each other's hair; they gathered around an open tap and walked home carrying full buckets in their hands or on their heads. Some of them held plates of food in their hands and ate; others nursed babies; a few crouched on the ground cooking over an open fire, or washed pots and infants over stinking gutters. They glanced at him as he walked past but quickly went back to whatever they were doing. There were one or two girls among them, some not much older than he himself. There were several small children. But there were no men.

He was mistaken: there was one man. He stormed out of one of the doorways, chasing a screaming girl with long dishevelled hair, a girl about the size and age of Nirmala, Bibi's elder sister who had married last year when she was fourteen.

Just before she reached the street the man caught hold of the girl's arm and pulled her towards him, shouting words Kamal did not understand. A few of the women nearby looked up for a moment but quickly returned to their tasks. The man turned back to the house and shouted one sharp word; an older woman emerged with what looked like a piece of broomstick which she handed to him. To Kamal's utmost horror the man began to rain blows on the girl's back. The girl screamed pitifully, begging for mercy, but still he beat on, shouting all the time, his face almost black with rage.

For two seconds Kamal stood petrified with outrage; then he ran up to the man and began pulling at the beating hand. 'Stop it! Stop it! You're hurting her! Leave her alone!'

For one frozen moment the man stopped, his hand raised. Kamal grabbed the girl and tried to pull her away. The girl looked up at Kamal.

Those eyes! He would never forget them, not in all his life. The look in them! Such terror, such agony, such abject despair! The wretchedness in those eyes wrenched at Kamal's heart, for he had never seen such inner pain nor even a shadow of it; he had not known such anguish could exist on earth, for earth for him was a happy place where people smiled, and even if they felt pain, they hid it behind that smile, unless they were babies and could not yet tuck away their hurt. This girl's pain lay naked in her eyes, in the mouth pulled down at the corners. Her wretched-ness was in the wet smudged cheeks, the lacklustre hair; it was in the body twitching away from Kamal's grasp, the shrill scream she now let out as the moment unfroze and the man's hand whisked down. The stick met her arching, writhing back with a dull thud.

Fury grabbed Kamal. He pummelled the man's forearm, sunk his teeth into it, but the man was tall and strong and Kamal slight, and with only a flick of annoyance the man flung him away. Kamal landed on hands and knees in the middle of the street, like a cat, and scrambled to his feet again. He was about to hurl himself once more at the man but he felt strong hands on his arms pulling him back. He looked up; a woman, obviously a neighbour, was holding him back and speaking.

'Don't interfere, boy, that's her uncle and she's been a bad girl. She has to be punished.'

'But he's hurting her!'

'He's only hurting her so she'll obey him next time. We all have to learn to obey; that's life. You have to obey your mother too, don't you? And your father? So she has to obey her uncle.' She cackled with foul laughter.

Another woman approached them. 'What are you doing here? You're only a child; go away. You have no business on this street.'

'I only want to—'

'Go away. Don't come back here. You must be mad, to mix yourself up in what does not concern you.'

'But that girl . . .' Kamal turned back to the man and the girl but they were gone.

'She'll be fine, don't worry about her. Her uncle will take care of her. Now you go away and don't come back here.'

'Not till you're grown up,' added the first woman, and laughed again. Kamal stared at her; she was not like any of the palace servants. Her face was small and pockmarked. There were loose black-ringed holes in the sides of her nose and in the lobes of her ears but she wore no jewellery save a cluster of plastic bangles rattling on a bony wrist. Her teeth, those that remained, were yellow. She wore a threadbare faded sari of an indistinguishable colour. She smelt of rancid coconut oil and stale sweat and perfume gone sour.

'Yes; *then* you can come back,' said the other woman. 'With all your silks and your fine jewellery!'

Both the women roared with laughter at a joke Kamal could not understand. What he *did* understand was that they were right: he had to go. He did not like this street; he did not like these women; he could not help the girl. Some instinct told him he was out of his depth. It was time to go home.

Finding his way back to the palace was no problem. Everyone knew the way; he was directed back, from street to street, until, in the early evening, he found himself outside the gates and the sentries called out in relieved astonishment, and, it seemed to him, the entire palace household came running out into the courtyard, calling out to him how much he had been missed and where had he been, and what a naughty boy he was, and how angry Rani would be.

'She's angry with me, too, Kamal,' his friend Hanoman, Teacher's son, whispered. 'She thinks I helped you out. Look!' He opened his hands and showed Kamal the thick red welts across his palms. 'She beat me to tell her the truth. But I didn't know! I didn't know anything!'

Kamal's filthy clothes were peeled from him by clucking servants. He was bathed and perfumed and bedded for the night.

'Rani says she will see you tomorrow,' came the message just before he fell asleep.

ELEVEN

Rani

Rani was having a foot massage, reclining on her cloud-cushion of puffed purple velvet, exclusively designed to enclose her enormous bulk, its invisible steel skeleton taking over the work of her atrophied muscles, buried as they were in mounds of flesh. Her legs were spread open before her, her sari drawn up beyond her knees and bunched up between them. Her feet rested on matching purple poufs while two crouching sylphine maidens kneaded her puffy soles and massaged her swollen toes.

Her right hand lay languidly on a plate of milk-sweets, occasionally conveying one to her mouth. Her other hand loosely held a fan of peacock feathers and lay now on her extensive bosom. Her eyes were heavy-lidded, half-closed, and a less knowledgeable visitor might think she was asleep. Kamal knew better. He knew that behind those sluggishly drooping eyelids lurked a mind as sharp as a two-edged sword, and that Rani's outward appearance of sloth, the inertia of her fat, indolent body, was his grandmother's best disguise, one which only a mind of her cunning could have divined. And Kamal had not the slightest doubt that she wore this disguise not of necessity but of design. Obesity had not crept up on Rani from behind; she had seen the advantages of wrapping keenness of wit in layers of fleshy languor, and concealing daggers of guile within a mound of innocuous jelly. It was part of her master plan.

He approached from the garden. The white floor-to-ceiling louvred door-flaps were folded back, opening on to the terrace and the cupid-fountain (imported from France), so that the Surya Hall, where Rani spent the greater part of her life, extended in one unbroken expanse of grey marbled flagstones to the emerald green lawn. Rani sat in a shadowed recess at the back of the hall, for she could not bear the sunshine, yet liked to look out on her domain, occasionally dozing off, usually just sitting, watching, waiting, motionless except for the one hand moving from plate to mouth and the other hand now and then rising, fanning, and sinking again.

Beyond the reach of sunlight lay a scattering of plush carpets. Kamal felt Rani's concentrated perusal as he drew nearer; he saw the instant's pause as her hand drew near to her lips; he knew that the eyes had narrowed to a slit barely visible between folds of fat, and that the very air surrounding her vibrated with venom.

With a barely perceptible motion of her fingers Rani dismissed the two maidens. They stood up, namasted and bowed with a graceful bend of knee, stepped backwards and vanished on silently tripping feet. They left in their stead a vague perfume of jasmine and rose which Rani briskly eliminated with a sonorous passing of wind, slightly raising one side of her body to allow the reek to escape, falling back into position with a thud and a wobble of flesh. Kamal held his breath, namasted, smiled and lowered himself to the carpet before her, sitting back on his heels.

Her lips moved. 'Come nearer!' she commanded, and Kamal edged his knees forward a fraction. He took a trial sniff but abruptly cut it short: the stench was foul. But Rani must be appeased so he smiled, and gestured, still without breathing, to the rosewood incense holder next to the tray of sweets, bobbing his head with the question which, he hoped, he would not have to utter – not yet. Rani grunted and gave a slight nod of assent. Thankfully, Kamal reached for the incense holder and the silver box of matches next to it, struck a match and lit four sticks of incense. He removed them from the holder and waved them in circular figures, as if he were worshipping Rani, so that she might not guess at his true purpose. The mingling of scents was only a slight improvement, but Kamal was desperate for air and slowly breathed in, smiling all the time so she would not guess at his disgust, and wishing he could make a quick dash to the garden and fill his lungs with sunlit space. Here at the back of the hall no air could penetrate; odours accumulated, and what remained was a stagnant sour mustiness which only Rani could tolerate for any length of time – Rani, and those she condemned to share her time such as the massaging maidens.

Rani grunted and shifted position again, and Kamal feared another blast of exhaust fumes, but all she did was lean forward to bring her face slightly nearer to his.

'Yesterday you left the palace,' she said.

Kamal shrugged.

It was done, it was over, he was back, and there was no way Rani could erase what had happened. No punishment would make the day undone; it was there, impressed upon his consciousness, senses stirred awake and fed but not nourished, doors and windows opened that would never again be closed.

'I have forbidden you to leave the palace, and yet you left,' Rani continued. She spoke slowly, her voice low and without the least emotion: stating a fact. It was the voice she used when the anger was boiling within her, boiling with such violence that all her strength was involved in holding it back. Those who were in daily contact with Rani knew that voice well, for a thousand little things drove her to anger: a carpet with an untidy fringe, a stray dove relieving itself on the terrace, a sesame seed lodged in a back tooth. Summoned into Rani's presence, the evil-doer (the maid who had not brushed the carpet fringe, the gardener who had not chased away the dove, the cook who had made the sesame sweet) would stand quaking before her while first she stated the bare facts in this voice, crouching low like a leopard before a deadly lunge.

Kamal, ever since he was a small child, had wondered at Rani's ability to inspire fear. He had seen countless hand-wringing servants stand or kneel before her, sweating with terror, their eyes pleading for pity, sometimes clasping their hands, kneeling and begging for mercy. What was it about Rani that evoked such naked terror? Even when Rani's inner dam burst and she shouted at someone, it might not be pleasant, but she didn't actually hurt anyone with her noise. Why didn't they just shout back? Kamal used to think. Or simply turn their backs and walk away, the way he did when she yelled too long or too loud?

Kamal himself had never known fear. Neither fear of Rani, nor fear of any living thing within the walls of the palace. He had *heard* the word fear, of course, and had feared vicariously with many of the heroes in the adventure books he loved to read, so that he did have second-hand knowledge of what it was to sense danger, the obliteration of all things dear and familiar, the loss of life itself. But here there was nothing to fear. Here he was safe. Here there was nothing to hurt him. Rani had made it so. Rani had created this safe soft perfect world, this world of golden platters overflowing with ambrosial eatables, of silk garments and emerald lawns and bowls filled with jewels you could plunge your hands into, cup and raise up, letting them ripple through your fingers like water. A world where peacocks strutted across brilliant lawns, their tails fanned out in glory. Rani had created this world and kept it perfect for him, which was why he did not, could not, fear Rani. Rani, who reigned with absolute jurisdiction within the far-flung walls of her empire.

'This is the world,' she had told Kamal when he was a little boy. 'This is the only world you need to know.'

And he knew there was a world outside, a bigger world, but he had no idea of what big meant; how big was big, and how much bigger could it be than Mahapradesh?

Mahapradesh was enormous.

'I have created this world for you,' Rani had told him again and again. 'It contains all that you will ever need. It is enough for you. I have provided for you; here there is everything you want; and if you want more, you only have to ask.'

'But what is outside the wall?' Kamal had asked, for he had walked all around the perimeter of Mahapradesh and looked up along the high stone wall, topped by bits of spiky broken glass set in concrete. And there were sentries posted along the wall; and a huge iron gate let into it, and at all times of the day people left and entered, but never Kamal, and never Rani.

'Bad things. There is poverty and dirt and bad people who will hurt you and who will want to take away the things you have. Do not even think about the world out there; you do not need it.'

She had smiled then, and held out her arms, and Kamal, not knowing better, for Rani was mother and father and all people for him, ran into her arms and she lifted him onto her knee. She pointed out beyond the terrace. 'Look! Look at that beautiful lawn! See how it gently slopes away to the garden! Look at that peacock, strutting across! Soon he will lift his tail and open his wheel, and then he will dance for the peahens, and for me! The peacock dances because he is aware of his beauty; only beauty must exist in the world. I want you to know only beauty, Kamal. I am sorry I have lost the use of my legs, else I would take you by the hand and walk with you through those beautiful flower groves and tell you the names of all the roses. When I was a young girl, Kamal, I loved the roses and tended them myself. Now it is all done by gardeners. But they are the best gardeners in all of India. I have instructed them to make of Mahapradesh a paradise; and this paradise is for you. For you, Kamal, are a prince and you must have the best.'

And she told him for the billionth time the story of the family, a line of kings dating back further than it was possible to think.

'Mahapradesh was bigger then. Bigger than what you know now – Mahapradesh was vast, spreading in all the four directions, as far as the eye could see, a real kingdom. There were no walls around it, for its lands reached out among the rolling hills. It contained villages, towns even, and all the people worshipped us and paid us tribute. But, Kamal – and this was the fate of all the great kingdoms, not just Mahapradesh – there came conquerors from abroad, white men with weapons, white men who wanted it all for themselves, and those white men reduced us to what we are now. So we built the wall to keep what we had, and this is what you see today. It is smaller than it was, true, but it is still big enough to call a kingdom, and one day it will all be yours.'

'And we owe it all to the worms!' Kamal declared proudly.

'The worms?'

'Yes. The silkworms. The silkworms that work for us.'

'Who told you about the silkworms?'

'Hanoman did. He says we have an army of silkworms in the hill district working for us and making us a fortune and if it weren't for the silkworms you and me would be poor like the rats in the bazaar.'

'Hanoman told you that? Hanoman knows nothing.'

'Hanoman is my friend. He knows a lot and he tells me a lot.'

'Hanoman cannot be your friend. Hanoman is only Teacher's son and you are a prince.'

'No, I'm not. Hanoman says the English conquered the kings and there is no royalty in India any more so I'm not really a prince. And Hanoman has been Outside. He knows about all the things Outside and he tells me.'

'Then I forbid you to talk to Hanoman!'

'You cannot, Mataji! He is my friend, the only friend I have! Hanoman and me, we are like brothers even . . .'

'You are of royal blood, Kamal! You are a Ksatriya, you cannot be the brother of a teacher's son.'

'Oh, but I can, we are! He tells me so much and I need to know about everything, about Outside and the silkworms and everything.'

'You do not need to know about the silkworms. That is not your business. They do their work, you do yours – every creature on earth has its allotted place. I have paid servants who care about the silkworms and look after them and make sure they are doing their work. I have servants to collect the silk and turn it into wealth so that you may live like the prince you were born to be. Because one day India will return to her former glory and you will sit in the Surya Hall and rule. It is Destiny. Nobody, least of all the English, can outsmart Destiny. The Wheel of Time turns slowly but one day she returns to recapture all that was lost; and all that was lost returns to its rightful owner. That is you. That is why I am preserving everything for when that time comes. I am the only one left who believes in the old ways, who knows that the old ways were good and that the old ways must return. Did not Swami Subramaniananda . . . oh, never mind.

'I am the guardian of your fate, Kamal. Do not sully your mind with matters which do not concern you. You must have the attitude of a king: you must rule, and command, and delegate, and demand obedience. You must show your subordinates that you are their head, that your word is the word of God.'

Kamal was seven when Rani told him this. His mind was sharp as a razor and picked up details the adults slid over, which is why, at the next opportunity, he had run to Teacher and asked, 'Teacher, who is Swami Subramaniananda?'

Teacher had looked down at him and raised his brows and said, 'Where did you hear that name?'

'Oh, I just heard someone say it.'

'Well, forget it. It means nothing.'

His curiosity fanned, Kamal asked others.

'Who is Swami Subramaniananda?' he asked his favourite counsellor, Jairam, who only shrugged and raised his shoulders and shook his head. Challu had smiled secretly and turned away.

Only Gaindha Dwarka, Rani's Chief Counsellor, had hinted at more. 'You must not speak that name,' he whispered to Kamal. 'Never mention it again. It is better for you.'

'But why?' Kamal insisted.

Gaindha Dwarka had looked right and left before whispering, 'He is the one who knows who you really are, and what will become of you if you leave Mahapradesh. More I cannot say.' And he had placed a finger on his lips and slid behind the curtain leading to the Indra Hall, and Kamal had never been able to unseal his lips again.

So Kamal had been left to smoulder, not understanding. All he knew was this: Mahapradesh was Rani's creation, and she had tried to make it perfect, for him. Rani was queen here; Rani ruled with an iron hand; Rani's word was law. And for some reason known only to herself and a mysterious Swami Subramanian-anda, Rani would not allow Kamal, her only grandson, her only relative, the only living human she cared about, to pass beyond those walls. And now he had done so without her permission, and there would be trouble.

Kamal had known this from the start. He had taken the risk, knowing full well that there would be consequences. But he had also known that Rani's power to punish him was limited – she would not have him whipped, as she had the servants whipped; the worst punishment she could mete out was, in fact, the status quo he lived with from day to day – confinement inside the palace walls.

So now he knelt in silence before her and watched her and waited for her to speak. She would have him locked in his room for the evening, perhaps. Or for several evenings in a row. It had not been fear of punishment that had kept Kamal from escaping a long time ago, but lack of opportunity: the walls were so high, the sentries so diligent, that it had been near impossible to find a way out. It had taken wiles to get out; and he had done it. He would do it again, he knew, and he knelt waiting for his punishment.

'How did you get out?' Rani's voice was now little more than a whisper, and the lower her voice, the more dangerous her mood. Yet still Kamal was calm, lulled by the faith in his own invulnerability.

'You will not speak? You won't tell me how you got out? Very well, then I will take my own appropriate measures. Obviously the sentries were negligent. You must have bribed one or other of them – there is no way out without the help of a sentry. If you will not tell me which one then I will have all of them punished. Every one of them.'

Kamal froze at those words; he had never expected this. His eyes opened wide in horror, for now he understood why her last words had been so soft as to be almost indiscernible, hardly stirring the heavy space between them.

'Tell me.'

But Kamal could not speak. His tongue seemed stuck to the bottom of his mouth, his jaw locked, and for the first time in his life he knew fear. Fear, not for himself, but for others. And now he knew, with a flare of insight, why it was that, no matter how he had begged and pleaded, none of the servants, not one of his friends, not even those who would walk through fire for him, had ever agreed to help him leave the palace walls. Why he had been forced to make his own plan, and escape with no one's help. He knew then that he was not invulnerable. He knew that Rani, with a word, with a nod of her head even, could punish him by punishing others. He knew now that Rani knew him better than he had assumed; she knew that he *cared*.

He had never even tried to hide from her that he cared. Rani's instructions, to treat the servants with the contempt due them by reason of their position, he ignored, and blatantly did the opposite: he courted them as his equals. The only friend his own age was Hanoman, who had his own duties to attend to, and so he had found other friends among the servants: Munsami, Gangadin, Ali Yusuf; he knew them all by name. He knew their children's names, and their children's ages. He knew when their wives were ailing and the children were sent to an aunt. He knew when an eldest son won a place in a better school, and when a daughter's betrothal turned a father's hair grey. It was easy to make friends with the servants, for Rani was immobile and her eyes could not see around corners. Confined as she was to the Surya Hall, what did it matter what she ordered? True, she had her spies. Kamal knew whom he could trust, and whom not.

Soondath was a snake, and Ramsaywack was a rat. They and their underdogs: Kamal avoided them; those were the ones sent to catch him when he disappeared, who clawed his upper arm and dragged him through the corridors and into Rani's presence where they immediately turned slimy as snails and released their grip – for Kamal was not to be hurt – and pasted simpering smirks of deference on their faces. They were the ones who would betray him, whenever there was something to betray. But up to now there had been no transgression so serious that the blame could be placed on anyone but he himself. Up to now it had been fun and games: a little boy being a boy. Leaving the palace was another matter. Kamal had always known that that was the one sin which would never be forgiven. It was the one sin for which the punishment, when it came, would be dire. And since there was no punishment that could touch him, Kamal, others would be penalized for him.

Kamal knew that servants who transgressed were whipped. He knew, but avoided the matter neatly by making himself absent during such times, removing himself to the farthest point of the Surya Hall. Once he had seen a fellow afterwards, bent and broken, dragged across the courtyard, the gates flung open and the man kicked out, never to be seen again. Kamal had turned and fled and pushed the incident to the back of his mind. Today there was no avoidance. Kamal was made to sit beside his grandmother as one by one the guards were brought forward, stripped to the waist, flogged across the backs until they were unable to stand, and booted out of the presence.

Kamal tried to plead with Rani. He begged and coaxed and swore by his life that not one of them had helped him escape. He told her the whole story of his escape, in all its details; he beseeched her not to hurt the guards, to whip *him* instead, for *he* was at fault and no one else. He wept his apologies; he knelt before her imploring her to accept his remorse; he promised on his life never to do it again: all to no avail.

Rani made Soondath and Ramsaywack hold Kamal, one on each side, and though he writhed and wriggled he could not escape their iron grip. Soondath grasped him under his chin and held it up so he was forced to watch, and he cried aloud and squeezed his eyes shut but the tears escaped and flowed down his cheeks, and still he could hear the buzz of the whip as it slashed the air and the dull thwack as it cut across a bare back, and the agonized cries of the guards. He heard them beg for mercy and he recognized their voices: Mahadai and Challu and Basdeo were among them, men who had smiled and joked and laughed with him, men who were his friends, and punished without guilt for his foolishness.

Even before it was over Kamal fainted for he could not bear the pain; it was as if every whiplash landed on his own back. His cries were louder than those of the guards, for he cried not only for them but for the girl in the street of women, and Ramsaywack tied a cloth through his mouth to gag him. That was when he mercifully fainted, for it was all too much for him.

When he came to, he found himself lying on the carpet at Rani's feet, the hall emptied except for Hiraman, sitting naked to the waist in a far corner and playing on his tabla. The hollow rattling of the tabla had replaced the screams. A soft tranquillity now filled the hall, the reverent hush that heralded the evening.

Rani sat in her usual position, eating. At first Kamal simply watched her out of half-closed eyes, without moving, and knew that she watched him too. He moved then, and so did she, signalling for Hiraman to leave.

When they were alone, Rani gestured for him to come nearer.

'The next time the punishment will be worse,' said Rani. 'So I am hoping for your peace of mind there will not be a next time. I have not dismissed those guards. They have been returned to their positions with their backs stinging and bleeding, and now they will be more vigilant than ever.'

Kamal never tried to go Outside again. He accepted his confinement, knowing that one day it would come to an end. Somehow, he no longer minded. Outside, he knew now, was too much for him to bear.

TWELVE

Asphyxiation

Kamal was now twelve, tall for his age and handsome. But he was ill. He was dying. Rani sent for the best doctors; doctors from Bombay and Delhi, and they all said the same: Kamal was dying.

'What does he have?' Rani cried. She would have had the doctors whipped for incompetence and almost wept in frustration.

The doctors shrugged and packed their bags. 'We don't know. We can't help him. He has decided to die and he will die.'

Rani sent for doctors from abroad but they could not cure Kamal either. 'The disease is mental. He needs a psychiatrist,' these foreign doctors said, so Rani sent for a psychiatrist, the best available in all the country. The psychiatrist sat next to Kamal's bed with a notepad in his hands and tried to talk to Kamal but Kamal did not answer. He stared at him with vacant eyes, or turned his head away.

Finally – and Kamal heard the words clearly through the mists that veiled his mind – Rani spoke the magic formula that would lead to healing.

'Send for Swami Subramaniananda!!'

*   *   *

Though his eyes were closed Kamal knew it the moment Swami Subramaniananda entered his room. He felt a cool hand on his scalding forehead and light filter through his soul. He heard the soft words whispered: 'Come out of the night, Kamal. Come out of the night. Come into the sunshine. All will be well.'

He opened his eyes.

Swami Subramaniananda had a shaven head, shining like honey, and eyes that saw through him and knew him. When Kamal looked into those eyes he no longer wanted to die. He felt life stir within him and he felt the certain knowledge that it was not his time to die. He felt Grace like a glorious dawn within him, and he returned the Swami's smile.

'All will be well, my son,' said Swami again. 'You will leave the palace.'

From that day on Kamal recovered rapidly, but he never saw Swami again to thank him. There was so much to thank him for: soon, very soon, he was leaving, going to board at the Kodaikanal International School in the Palini Hills of Tamil Nadu. Rani herself had given the order, it was said – it had to be so – and she had done so on Swami's advice.

It was Kamal's friend, the counsellor Jairam, who told him the truth. 'He told her you were dying of inner asphyxiation of the soul. He said if you remain here you will surely die. He told her she had abused his words; that she had lived against his injunctions; that she herself was killing you. Only for your sake he returned: to save you, he said. It is her one last chance.'

'Swami Subramaniananda,' Kamal mused. 'I have heard that name before, when I was a boy. There was some mystery surrounding it, some kind of taboo attached to it. Do you know . . . ?'

Jairam laughed. 'Everybody knows,' he said. 'Everybody knows except you. We were forbidden to tell you when you were a boy. Now, what does it matter? Now, you are leaving anyway. So I'll tell you. When you were a baby – you were not a year old, and your parents had just been killed in a riot – Swami was in the palace. Rani had sent for him in her grief and her anguish, not knowing which way to turn, alone with you, the only heir. She needed his guidance in that situation. He was Rani's guru, you know, who came from his hermitage in the Himalayas once a year until he spoke the words that made her send him away – for ever.'

'What did he say?'

'Well, Rani had great plans for you. You would become a great statesman. You would grow wealthy in the silk industry. You would receive the best education the world has to offer. You would be rich, famous, powerful – you would be India's Leader, bringing back royalty, restoring all the kingdoms to their rightful heirs. You would turn back the clock of Time. Oh, she had so many ideas, so many plans, some of them far-fetched, impossible, and you were at the centre of them. Swami took one look at you and said: "This is a child of God. He is not made for worldly matters. He will renounce women and gold – he will be a monk."

'Rani flew into a rage, tried to make him take back those words – she believed whatever Swami said would inevitably come true – but he refused to recant. That's when she banned him from ever setting foot in the palace again. She ordained that his name should never be spoken again. She went so far as to banish our religion from being practised anywhere in your presence – she turned against God himself, as if that could prevent what God himself had ordained! She hardened her heart. You were to be trained by worldly, private teachers, and reared expressly for the role she had set for you. You were not to go outside – she knew the story of the Buddha, she knew how the sight of poverty and suffering could inspire a man to turn to God. So you were not to know poverty and suffering. You were to be kept a prisoner in a golden cage – like the Prince Gautama. But Prince Gautama escaped, and became the Buddha, and you, too, escaped, in your own way. When you were dying Rani knew she had lost the battle – for the time being. She would never have sent for Swami had she not truly feared for your life, and known that her rejection of her guru was responsible for your illness, and that only he could heal you. She genuinely loves you, you see.'

'So now she will let me go?'

'Yes. Swami said you should go out into the world and get an education. Rani is still Rani – ambitious as ever, and she will never give up on her dreams for you, the only heir. But she has modified them somewhat, and besides, she may be a dreamer, but she is a realistic dreamer. She knows to be a statesman you will need an education, the best India can offer. She also now believes that in letting you go she can hold you all the better. When you see the suffering outside, she believes, you will want to take up the reins of power she is forging for you. She's sending you to a Christian school: the Christian ethic, she believes, is kinder and more tolerant towards worldly ambitions and temporal affairs than the Hindu. So now it's up to you.'

Kamal shrugged. 'What do I know about power? What do I care? I'm glad I didn't die, and I'm glad I'm leaving the palace. I look forward to Kodaikanal. But what the future holds – what is written in my destiny – who knows?'

'Possibly only Swami Subramaniananda.'

THIRTEEN

Completely Ga-ga

Kamal's years at Kodaikanal flew by as happy times always do. He had found friends and freedom; he was the brightest student of his class, and could take his pick of the best universities in the world. He wanted to go as far away from Rani as possible. He chose Harvard.

Rani, of course, had been strictly against his going abroad. There had been a hot discussion, with her extolling the virtues of the Indian universities. But since his illness a subtle change in the balance of power had taken place, and Rani knew now that there was nothing she or anyone in the world could do when Kamal had made up his mind. She accepted defeat on this issue with something very much like grace.

Besides, she told Dwarka, there was absolutely no sign of Kamal fulfilling Swami's prophecy. Kamal might be intense and strong-willed, but definitely not religious: there was no danger of him taking sannyas. He had chosen engineering. She had pleaded with him to at least let it be *textile* engineering, which would come in useful when he took over the silk business, but no, stubborn as usual, Kamal had set his mind on *civil* engineering. And, he told her, he had absolutely no intention of going into the silk business.

Rani shrugged. It was a pity; but, after all, the business ran itself. She had placed good and trustworthy men in charge, and with only a minimum of supervision the profits, especially from the export market, had only increased in the last few years. People would always want silk; women would always want to wrap themselves in fine garments. The future was rosy.

Kamal met Caroline in his fourth year at Harvard. He first met her at a Thanksgiving party in the Cambridge home of a friend; she was the friend of that friend's girlfriend and he had spent the evening answering all her avid questions about India, for she had been fascinated by India since she was a little girl, and, in fact, was an anthropology student majoring in Tamil language and family traditions. She would be going to India in a year's time, she told Kamal, to do the field work necessary for her thesis. She hoped he could give her some tips, maybe some addresses?

She looked up at him with pale blue eyes that somehow touched him with their cool blend of naïvety and intelligence. That naïvety came from a pre-knowledge of India that was entirely intellectual and totally clichéd, picked up from a thousand books and articles written from a Western viewpoint and brimful of Western prejudices and Western condescension of which she herself was not in the least aware.

He found himself in the position of India's defender, coaxing her gently into a position where she could see the same issues from a different perspective. They were so thoroughly engaged in the discussion they did not notice the passing of time, and had to be gently levered out of their wicker chairs on the wrap-around porch at two in the morning. Kamal lived with some friends only a few blocks away, but Caroline lived with her parents in Brookline and had parked her car near the university. Kamal walked her to the car.

They talked all the way down to Harvard Square. Then Kamal felt her hand in his, and stopped speaking in mid-sentence. They walked the next few paces in silence. Then Caroline said, 'There's my car,' and pointed with her other hand, and Kamal squeezed the hand in his.

'I hope . . .'

'Kamal, it was . . .'

They spoke simultaneously; both stopped and looked at each other and laughed. Then Kamal said, 'Go ahead, you first.'

Caroline took his other hand and clasped them both between her smaller ones. 'I just wanted to say . . . I haven't had such a stimulating evening for . . . oh, my God. I don't think I've *ever* had such a stimulating evening in my whole life! It was just great talking with you, Kamal, and I think we're going to be great friends . . .'

Caroline's words were prophetic. They not only became the best of friends, they became lovers. From that first evening Kamal had known that this was the woman he was going to marry. She was so different from him, and not only physically, with her long blonde hair and pale heart-shaped face. She was the stranger he longed to embrace because she represented the half of him he did not yet know, that missing part of him which, once united with him, would make him whole. She was intellectual and warm at the same time; genuinely interested – no, interested was too weak, *enchanted* by India and all things Indian – touchingly ingenuous, sometimes brittle, but the brittleness was only superficial and easy to melt. They could talk for hours, and be silent for hours; when the first snow fell she drove him out to the countryside and they walked through the whiteness without speaking a single word, arms slung around each other in a silent intimacy over-flowing with warmth, and though the bitter cold stung his bare cheeks Kamal felt the winter must melt before them, like the snowflakes melting on his lashes. He opened his lips and caught the snow on his tongue and laughed out loud. Caroline, her face small and white in the soft maroon shawl wrapped around her head, glowed with inner joy. She pressed an icy-cold, snow-encrusted glove against his cheek and said, 'Kamal Maharaj, if you don't promise to marry me I swear I'm going to lie down right there in that snowbank and let the snow drift over me and cover me till I look like the Abominable Snowman and just wait there until you do!'

Kamal chuckled and moved her hand from his cheek. He pulled off her glove and flung it away on to the snow, and replaced the warm hand on his warm cheek.

'That's more like it. Now, Caroline Baxter, what do you want me to do? Go down on my knees and propose officially?'

'No. Just say it. Say it. Say you want to marry me. Say you want to be mine for ever and ever.'

'You know it already.'

'But I want to hear it. I want you to say it out loud. I can't stand this deep Indian silent communication. Go on, just say it.'

'You don't know me properly yet, you know. Wait till I get you back to India. I will turn into the tyrannical Indian patriarch of your worst nightmares! I will ravage you as my wife and keep another four in my harem just for good measure. I will keep you well under my foot, forbid you to step outside the walls of our marital abode unless you walk four paces behind me. You will occupy yourself with raising five fine sons to follow in my revered footsteps. You will refer to me exclusively as "Father of my Sons" and bow your head, hiding your face in the folds of your sari, when I enter the room. You will humbly serve me delicious meals you have cooked with devotion on golden platters and only take food yourself when I and all our sons have been sated. When I die you will—'

'I'll stuff this snow down your damned *throat* if you don't look out!' cried Caroline, then made good on her threat. Kamal wrenched himself out of her grasp and ran stumbling through the snow. Caroline bent down and picked up a handful of snow, pressed it into a huge snowball, and pelted him with it, screaming, 'You asked for it! You *jerk*!' It hit him square on the back of his head.

'OK, it's WAR!' cried Kamal, and bent over for his own snowball.

They fought fiercely, hysterically, for a good half-hour and then, suddenly, Kamal threw up his arms and said, 'OK, OK, you win. I admit my defeat. I surrender unequivocally. I will fulfil each and every one of your demands.'

She flung herself at him so that they both lay in the snow. 'Marry me. That's all I want. Say it out loud.'

'Marry me,' he whispered, and the words came out on a breath like smoke, fading into the crisp cold air.

'Louder. I can't hear you.'

'Marry me, Caroline.'

'Sorry? What was that?'

'I refuse to shout. I'm not going to shout. Come here.' He drew her head close to his, her ear to his lips, and there he spoke the words again, clearly and gently. 'Will you marry me?'

She smiled, put her arms around him and rested her cheek on his. 'Yes,' she sighed.

The path to marriage was, for Kamal and Caroline, rough. Caroline took Kamal to meet her parents and they received him with a civil but icy reserve which caused him to fear the worst.

'You see, they belong to the old Boston aristocracy. Old money, real old. Very Anglo-Saxon, very white, very Protestant. They have a precise idea of the kind of man they want me to marry and – well, Kamal, you just don't fit the cookie-cutter.'

'They haven't even *tried* to get to know me.'

'Getting to know you isn't the issue. *Who* you are doesn't count; it's *what* you are.'

'What I am? Come on, I'm not exactly the plumber! I'm a Harvard student, for goodness' sake. All right, I realize a medical or a law student might be more up their street but . . .'

Caroline cut in. 'That's not the point, Kamal. Even if you were going to be a doctor they'd be against you. It's where you come from, how you look.'

'In other words, they're racist.'

Caroline hung her head. 'I'm sorry, Kamal. That's just the way they are. They can't jump over their shadows. I *warned* you they'd be this way.'

'Look, I don't give a damn about *them*. The question for me is, can *you* jump over their shadows?'

'Oh Kamal, why do you even *ask*?'

'So you'll go against them? Marry me, even if they don't agree? Come with me to India?'

'Kamal, I've *always* known I'd end up in India. Ever since I read *The Jungle Book* as a child I've known it – it's a pull I can't explain and for me it's only logical that I should marry an Indian and go there with him and there's nothing in the world my parents can do about it. They can't hold me back. But anyway,' she smiled, 'sooner or later they'll have to give in because they love me. And when they hold my first baby in their arms, they'll be just like grandparents anywhere. They'll go completely ga-ga.'

Kamal took Caroline to India and married her there. Caroline was writing a thesis on Tamil family structure. For this she wanted actually to live in a Tamil family, in a traditional village far away from modern influences. So the newly-weds travelled around Tamil Nadu for a while, looking for just the right village, just the right family; the plan was for Kamal to help her get settled, and go off and look for an engineering job not too far away – he had in mind a hydroelectric dam project, fairly central. It would mean separating during the week and only seeing each other at the weekend but it would only be for a while – their love was strong enough, it would only be nourished by the pain of parting.

Caroline found her place. The Iyengars lived in a village on the outskirts of Gingee, a small town a few hours' drive from Chennai, Madras. It was perfect: a traditional Hindu family, mother, father, two children. But best of all the father was well educated, with a degree; he was a secondary school headmaster, and spoke perfect English, and took a personal interest in Caroline's thesis. He was able to explain to her everything she wanted to know, and an hour a day he taught her Tamil. And Kamal got the job he wanted.

They hadn't planned a baby just yet – but these things happen.

They were delighted. They made plans to build a nice house near the dam, she would write her thesis, have the baby: perfect. Who needed the Baxters of Brookline, who needed the Rani of Mahapradesh? Not Kamal and Caroline Maharaj.

But they were forced to delay their plans for a while. They hadn't built their house yet, for there wasn't enough money, and both refused, for obvious reasons, to ask their families for help. Then Kamal received a lucrative offer to go and work on another dam project in North India – just for a year. He'd earn well and improve the family finances; they could have their home sooner. After the year he'd come home, get back his old job but with a better salary – his present employers certainly didn't want to lose him – and build their home. The set-up with the Iyengars was so ideal it would have been nonsense for Caroline to accompany Kamal to North India. She was happy with her Tamil family; Sundari, the mother, had become her close friend. Their third child was a girl, just a year old.

Caroline's was also a girl. They named her Asha.

Kamal could not come down for the birth, which was sad for both of them, but, after all, Caroline was in good hands and the future lay before them, round and glowing. Soon they'd have their own home and watch their daughter grow. Caroline took hundreds of photographs of Asha and sent them to Kamal accompanied by expansive, euphoric letters.

From afar Kamal adored his daughter. He was working six days a week and it just wasn't practical to fly down and back in the space of a day and a half – and expensive, of course. And as for Caroline visiting him with the baby, or even coming up and their renting a home nearby so they could live together for that year – they simply decided to save the money. It was so convenient, her living with the Iyengars. She had a built-in babysitter as well as a companion in Sundari, and could continue to work on her thesis.

Then, at Christmas, at Caroline's insistence, Kamal finally came home. Asha was three months old.

*　　*　　*

At Madras airport he saw her right away, behind the wall of dark Indians waving their signs behind the barrier. Caroline stood aloof, beyond the fray, just as she was in that sacred place he held her in his mind. She wore sparkling white cotton trousers and a long, soft blouse batiked in various shades of blue. Her blonde hair, cut short now, was like a sleek, polished cap framing a tanned face, glinting in the midday sunlight; she held one hand as a visor above her eyes as she scanned the line of passengers pushing their rust-brown trolleys out of the airport building. At the moment of recognition her face lit up, as at the sudden emergence of the sun from behind a cloud; her hand shot upwards, waving furiously. She ran forward and into his arms.

When they separated again Caroline took his hand and led him to a waiting taxi.

'You didn't bring her?' Kamal said, peering into the back window of the taxi. He felt a twinge of disappointment. Time was so short; their minutes together were precious. She should have brought Asha.

'Oh, no, I left her with Sundari,' said Caroline. 'It's a three-hour drive in this hot sun; it would just have been a hassle. You know, with nursing and all that.'

'So you had to leave her for six hours? Is that all right? I mean – doesn't she have to be fed?'

'Oh, that's fine. I can express pump milk, you know, and leave it in the fridge for Sundari to give to her. No, you don't know. Oh, there's so much you don't know. You're the father of the most beautiful little girl in the world and you don't know it! Anyway, when we get back you can feed her yourself!'

The drive home was interminable. But then they were there, the taxi bouncing slowly down the unpaved street to the little white house at the end, meandering around the pot-holes. Children swarmed around the car – for motor vehicles were rarities in this village – running backwards before it or skipping along beside it, slapping its bonnet, grinning in through the open window, calling out to Caroline and Kamal. One little boy in ragged blue shorts threw himself across the bonnet and sprawled there waving, another hooked his elbow in through the open window, two others jumped on to the back bumper and clung to the hind parts of the car like stick insects glued to a window.

Kamal, with wise prescience, had brought several packets of sweets. He opened one with his teeth and held it out of the window, emptying the lemon and orange sweets onto the dusty road. Immediately the children dropped away from the car and fell on them, scrambling on the ground and grappling frantically. Kamal looked out of the rear window, then turned to Caroline.

'Some things never change,' he said.

'And some things do,' she replied. 'Look in front of you!'

Kamal turned around. They had arrived at the Iyengar home; the taxi had halted. Mrs Iyengar, who had either heard the commotion or the hum of the car or been warned of their coming through the swifter-than-light grapevine, stood in front of the door, a broad smile on her lips and a bundle of Asha in her arms.

A tiny hand waved clumsily above the bundle. Two small legs hung below it. The rest of Asha was concealed by a thin cotton cloth, but now Sundari changed the position of her arms and held the baby upright in the crook of her arms, one hand bracing her, so that the cloth dropped away from the little bare chest and the child sat as in a comfortable chair, facing her father.

Kamal stared, suddenly silent. Slowly he left the car, not bothering to close the door, and crossed the short stretch of sand to approach his daughter, coming to a stop immediately in front of Sundari. He wanted to speak, to reach for the child, but the words caught in his throat and his arms felt crippled – he could not move them. Even his breath stopped, it seemed, and his mouth was dry, and his ears had lost their hearing for all the world was silent around him, and even his thoughts had raced headlong into a wall and ceased. But then his eyes were suddenly, involuntarily moist, his arms moving upwards to receive the child that in the same moment Sundari was holding out towards him. He took Asha as if he had held her a thousand times before, clasped her to his chest and covered her with his crossed forearms and moved away, walking towards the fence and away from the others so that no one could see his face – or his tears.

Caroline had tried her best. She had bought a plastic Christmas tree and decorations in Madras. She had arranged cotton-wool as snow around the base of the tree, and hung the cheap plastic baubles in glaring red and gold along its branches, and draped long strips of glittering tinsel around it, all in an attempt to reproduce the spirit of Christmas as she remembered it. It didn't work. Not even the fat candle glowing on its polished brass stand could make her believe it was truly Christmas.

'Look at this angel,' she said, handing him a tinny white thing that had fallen from one of the branches. 'Isn't she unbelievably tacky? But I couldn't find anything else. And believe me, I really scoured the stores. I guess Christmas isn't a big thing here.'

'It isn't,' Kamal said. He looked down at Asha, who was wearing a bright red dress which set off perfectly the jet black of her hair and her sparkling eyes, now fixed on the bright angel. Kamal, as he had done so often, marvelled at the perfect little features.

'Christmas is something we read about in books. I'm sorry.'

'Well, could we at least sing some carols?'

'I'm not so good at carols,' Kamal admitted. 'Remember, I never even heard "Jingle Bells" till I got to America. So I don't know if . . . Hey, what's the matter? Caro, Caro, why're you crying?'

Caroline wiped away a tear with her bare forearm. 'It's nothing . . . I guess. Well, no. It's just that . . . it's just that . . . that . . .'

Kamal gently laid Asha on her blanket on the floor, and leaned towards his wife. Her face was turned away from him, and huge tears were rolling down her cheeks. He placed his hand on her chin and gently turned her face up, towards him.

'Tell me. Please tell me what's bothering you. You know you can tell me everything. Here.' He gave her a clean square of cloth, one of several used for Asha to burp on, and wiped her cheeks with it. 'Can't you tell me what's the matter?'

'I . . . I suppose it's just Christmas,' Caroline admitted. 'A bit

of homesickness. Nostalgia and all that. I feel so . . . so sentimental
. . . I sort of miss . . . my parents and stuff. And snow. And
church. Santa Claus. All that soppy stuff. Family stuff, I guess.
And Christmas dinner. The turkey! Oh, Kamal, what I wouldn't
give for a turkey! And apple pie. When . . . when I was a kid I
used to be in the church choir and we used to walk around town
singing carols and collecting for charity. I had this muff and a
coat with a furry bonnet and it was all so warm and snugly . . .
and oh, Kamal, it's just so damned *hot* here! All year round!
And all my friends and everything. I can't even call them to wish
them a merry Christmas. And presents – books! I had to leave
all my favourite books behind and I miss them so. And music.
I should have brought my violin. Why didn't I think of that.
And . . .'

But she couldn't speak because her face was buried in Kamal's
warm shoulder. Kamal patted her back and held her close. She
let the sobs come and they broke from her in stifled, breathless
gulps. Finally she moved so that her lips were free and she could
speak.

'I want to go home! I want to go home, Kamal, I can't stand
it here a day longer. I haven't done any work since Asha was
born. Sundari is an angel, she's a good mother and I'm a terrible
mother. Sometimes I can't even stand to see Asha. Sometimes I
wish she'd never been born. I shouldn't be telling you this. I hate
myself. Sometimes I even hate you but you're all I have. I wrote
to Mom and Dad and they didn't write back! I don't have anybody
but you . . . and . . . and Asha. I'm so alone here! Asha doesn't
even like me very much, she prefers Sundari. I don't know how
to love her. I'm such a bad mother and I'm so ashamed to admit
it. I thought it would all be perfect but it isn't!'

Kamal held her all the time, rubbing her back. Caroline spoke
on and on, repeating herself, sometimes breaking down and crying, sometimes silent for a length of time, only to start again.

When it was over Kamal spoke.

'Caro, Caro, what have I done to you? I shouldn't have brought
you here. I shouldn't have left you here all by yourself. I can't

bear to see you unhappy. Listen – it doesn't have to be for ever. I don't really mind where I live. It doesn't have to be India. It was you who wanted to come here. It was you who had work to do here. I tell you what. We'll go back. Back to America. You finish your thesis, and as soon as that's over we'll go back. You'll make it up with your parents. They'll love Asha. And even if they still don't like me it doesn't matter. I don't have to visit them. You can spend next Christmas with them. I don't mind – Christmas means nothing to me, you see, so I won't feel left out. Anything you want. I can work anywhere. You can do what you want to do. You can go to work. We'll find a way.'

'But – what about Asha?'

'We'll find a way,' Kamal repeated. 'We'll work it out. Look, just hold on for a while. Six months more! Let me work out my contract. She'll be getting on for a year when we get back. You can get a job; I'll look after her. Whatever you want.'

'Oh, Kamal,' Caroline's voice broke, because she was laughing. 'What did I ever do to deserve someone like you? I swear, I'm the luckiest girl in the whole world. My girlfriends should be green with envy. I'm sorry I broke down, truly. I'm so lucky. So very very lucky. I think we must be the happiest family in the world.'

'Even if things aren't so perfect right now. But they will be, I promise. We'll make them perfect.'

'As long as we love each other, Kamal, everything *is* perfect.'

'Then let's hold onto this perfect moment. If we can just remember how it is now, nothing can ever go wrong.' He chuckled. 'Even if the Christmas tree is, well, to put it tactfully, best Indian quality.'

Caroline laughed with him. 'And even if you can't sing "Silent Night".'

'And even if I've got to leave you again, the day after tomorrow. But now at least I know *her*.'

They both gazed in silent wonder at Asha, who had fallen asleep on her blanket. In the steady light of the candle's flame her skin glowed softly golden. Long black lashes touched her cheek. Her chest rose and sank to the rhythm of her breathing.

'She's so, so, so . . .' Caroline whispered, and paused, searching for the right word.

'Sssh,' said Kamal, and placed a finger on her lips. 'I know.'

Perfect moments come and go, and not long after Kamal returned to the North, Caroline's homesickness returned with a vengeance. She missed everything. Her music, her books, her friends, her parents, the winter, the trees, the spring, the food.

Most of all, the food. The food seemed to stand in for everything that was inherently wrong about her present life. Not that it was bad – Sundari was a superb cook. Caroline simply missed Western, American, food. It became almost an obsession for her. She had always been quite particular about what she ate, something of a health-food fanatic. She liked fresh vegetables, salads, seafood, home-made casseroles and never, ever ate out of a tin. She'd been an on-and-off vegetarian. But during her pregnancy she had developed a craving for meat, which had not receded since the baby was born; and you couldn't get meat – not much of it. There were one or two butchers in Gingee, but just seeing the conditions in those shops – the meat lying in the open, the flies, the blood, the unwashed knives, the dirt – put her off. Sometimes she had a chicken specially slaughtered, and she watched over it and made sure it was all done quickly, no flies, clean knives, everything. However, cooking a chicken was a bit difficult in the Iyengar household – Sundari wouldn't touch it, and she didn't really even like Caroline doing it herself, and sullying her cooking utensils with the carcass.

When Asha was seven months old Caroline discovered a supermarket in Gingee hidden away in a back street where one could actually buy food from the city – butter, cheese, spaghetti, soy sauce, and so on. She asked them if they could get tinned corned beef, sausages and spam. They could. She ate it and enjoyed. She went back and asked for more. The shopkeeper was delighted to oblige. The next time she went there he showed her a real treasure: tinned ravioli! The tin was old, dusty, and slightly dented, but Caroline couldn't care less. She couldn't wait to get home, open it, warm it up and eat it.

The next thing Kamal knew was a telegram calling him home immediately. Caroline was seriously ill: it was Botulism, food poisoning, caused by eating infected food from a damaged can. By the time he arrived home it was too late. Caroline was dead.

Kamal held the bottle to Asha's lips but she pushed angrily against it with her little clenched fist. She kicked and wriggled, and twisted around so that her head was bent almost backwards. Kamal tried to put his arms around her, to hold her in the crook of his arms to try again with the bottle but she lashed it away again and frowned, squawking in fury. She twisted around again; she had heard sounds in the kitchen and she knew who was making them. Kamal gave up and put her on the floor. Immediately Asha was crawling at full speed towards the source of sound. She disappeared into the kitchen. A moment later Sundari reappeared, Asha in her arms.

'She ran away again,' she said smilingly, and held the child out to her father. Kamal reached for her but Asha kicked his hands away, squirming and struggling, refusing to be handed over.

Sundari frowned. 'She never used to behave this way,' she said apologetically. 'She used to be such a quiet, well-behaved child. The thing is, she's teething. It will pass.'

'And her mom just died,' Kamal reminded her.

'Yes, that is true. But to tell you the truth, I don't know if she even noticed that. Caroline was having some problems in the last few months. Asha thinks I am her mother.'

'I noticed that,' said Kamal.

'Well, what was I to do? Whenever the child cried Caroline panicked. She gave her to me and Asha was quiet. Should I have refused to take her? And now it's the same thing. She doesn't know you're her father. She won't even let you feed her.'

Sundari bent over and picked up the bottle that was lying on the ground, wiped the teat with a corner of her sari and handed the bottle to Asha, who was already reaching for it, gurgling with anticipation.

'The thing is,' Kamal said slowly, 'what do we do now? I have to start work again in two days. They don't believe in compassionate leave up there. I'm sure I can find someone to take her during the day but—'

'You're not thinking of taking her with you?' Sundari drew back with a gasp, moving Asha slightly to the side, away from Kamal. Asha lay luxuriously in the curve of her arm, sucking at her bottle with eyes half closed in bliss. She looked as if she belonged there, would always belong there.

'Well, of course, what else?'

'Are you out of your mind? You would take this child, who thinks you are just some stranger always bothering her, and take her up to the North, and let another stranger look after her?'

'It would only be in the daytime, while I'm at work. I know it's not the best solution but I . . .' He stopped, for his voice was breaking. 'I mean, I've tried to think of . . . another . . .' He stopped again. He stood up and turned away so that Sundari would not see the tears gathering in his eyes. 'All I want is her happiness, but now . . .'

'Her happiness must come first,' Sundari said firmly. 'You cannot think of yourself at this time. You have lost your wife and your mental state is one of deep anguish. The child feels this and, added to the fact that she does not know you, it makes her yet more wary of you. Whatever actions you take on behalf of the child at this point will have the deepest consequences. You cannot drag her away and give her to a strange woman to look after. Even if you were to look after her yourself she would not be happy. Who would ever think of taking a seven-month-old baby away from its mother and happy surroundings? As far as this child knows, I am her mother. Look how secure she is.'

Kamal looked, and saw.

'You see how she is wary of you. That is normal at this age. In fact, the first three years are most crucial in the life of a child. A child needs stability. Familiar faces. A steady home. You cannot just tear a child from one home and put it in another. That would be most selfish. And apart from that, what do you know about babies?'

Kamal rubbed his temple tiredly. He had asked himself this question several times in the last two days. 'Nothing whatsoever. And anyway, you are at work all day so you would be obliged to give her into strange hands. You would pay someone to keep your daughter! Why go to all that trouble when she has a good home here already?'

'Sundari, I've thought of all this myself. I've asked myself if it wouldn't be better to leave her here, with you . . .'

'Better? Of course it's better. How could there be any other alternative? I love this child as much as any of my own children. You must see that.'

'But just until my contract runs out. Then I'll move here and try to get to know her, and be a proper father.'

'Still the child will need a mother. You realize that, don't you?'

Kamal nodded. 'I know I can never be father *and* mother to her.'

'So you will have to marry again. Very quickly.'

Kamal shook his head vigorously. 'No. I won't marry again. Caroline was the love of my life. I can never replace her.'

Sundari smiled knowingly. Asha smiled too, gazing up at Sundari and hooking her forefinger into the woman's bottom lip. She threw the empty bottle to the ground, where it rolled into a corner. Startled by the noise, Asha twisted around in Sundari's arms, saw the bottle, and struggled to be put down. Sundari placed her on the floor, and she darted off to retrieve the bottle.

'Ah, that's what you say now. However, once the grief has faded, you will start searching once more – you will try to fill the emptiness. You will start looking for a new bride. If you like, I will help. My husband has some excellent connections, you know. It is always better to have a go-between in these matters.'

105

Kamal shook his head as if to repulse the very suggestion. 'No, no, I won't remarry. I'm certain of that.'

'How will you look after Asha, then? It's not as if you have a mother who would take her.'

'Other men have raised children alone.'

'Maybe in those foreign countries, not here, not in India. Perhaps when she is older, but as long as she is young she should stay with me. I will be her mother. I don't mind in the least. In fact, I would be very happy. And Asha too.'

Asha, meanwhile, had clenched the rubber teat expertly between four tiny teeth and, the bottle swinging gaily before her, returned to Sundari's feet where she pulled herself upright and made the appropriate noises. Sundari bent over and picked her up. Asha pulled the palu of Sundari's sari over her face and tried to engage her in a game of hide and seek. She ignored Kamal.

Kamal felt despair wash over him like a cold and final wave. All his senses were still reeling from Caroline's abrupt death; he felt incapable of making a single decision. Just the day before Caroline's eldest brother had arrived in Gingee and retrieved the body without so much as a by-your-leave. Kamal, who had been planning to have the body cremated, signed the appropriate papers without a murmur. He didn't want Caroline's dead body. He wanted Caroline! He ached for her. Where she had been was a huge black gaping hole inside him, and he stood precariously at its precipice, tottering, tottering, bracing himself against a fall. It was the thought of Asha that held him back. He looked at the child in Sundari's arms in despair; Asha was now twirling a curl of her thick mop of silky hair around a fat finger, gazing up adoringly at the woman she would one day call Amma.

She will never call me Appa, Kamal thought. I can love her enough for that love to fill the emptiness in me – but where do I begin? To take her away would be heartless, egoistic; it would be serving my own purpose, using her. She is happiest here. Sundari is right – her happiness must come first. I must love her enough to lose her. True love is letting go. I can love her as well from a distance as by her side, with a love not bound by time or space.

Two days later Kamal left Gingee. He did not return for three years. And when he came back he wore the saffron robe of a monk.

Part Three

FOURTEEN

The Abyss

Marilyn lost two more babies over the next few years. But now she had done it. A boy was on its way. She had passed the danger mark, and was following Dr Jagdeo's instructions to the letter: no work, no strain, just lying in bed and giving orders. And even Rita had settled down.

Rita was now ten. The annihilation she had predicted had come to pass. The world she had created at Number Seven had been eradicated; now there was not one fly too many in the house and not one lizard too many in the yard.

The house had been painted, parts of it taken down, other parts built up, brought into harmony with the bulk of the building. The ugly spindly legs on which it stood had been disguised by a latticework enclosing the Bottom House, and a garage built in. Giant bougainvillaea climbed up the latticework, almost reaching into the gallery windows, and, to the right, had been coaxed higher to enclose a shady porch. The gardener, his wife, and his brood of five children, ranging in age from five to fourteen, had created a miracle of growth and colour. The flowerbeds had been dug and redug and cartfuls of manure poured into the hungry earth, seeds strewn, seedlings planted, water poured, weeds pulled.

There had been prunings of roses and tyings of vines; what had once been a tangle of overgrown weeds and wild bushes was now a luscious spreading park of emerald green lawns artistically sliced by beds of rich brown earth bearing an abundance of flora; luxuriant brilliance spilled from green foliage in a sumptuous riot of colour, hibiscus petals of shocking pink in joyful contrast with shrill orange cannas. In a Garden City this was the crowning glory; people made pilgrimages to Victoria Street to stand before the immaculate palings and peer through the hedge to the lushness beyond. 'Lovely,' they said. 'That woman has worked miracles. She has style.'

'Nice, but a bit overdone,' said the envious grudgingly.

And as the jungle had been tamed, so had Rita, the jungle princess. She had recognized defeat, and, hiding behind a veneer of sullen acquiescence, found new friends in books, the books she devoured in the privacy of her own room or in the branches of the star-apple tree (which Marilyn, miraculously, had left standing). 'You've got such a nice home now!' people exclaimed.

'It's OK,' Rita replied. She missed the tadpoles, all the same. She and Polly Wong were still the best of friends; Mrs Wong had tided her over the worst times, Polly's animals had received a double portion of love. Ringo Starr held a place of honour next door; Rita had loved and tended him as a mother her baby, yet all her efforts at teaching him to speak had failed. All he ever said, sidling back and forth on his stick, was 'Robert!' And all he ever answered to was Robert; so Robert became, finally, his nickname. Robert was free. He flapped around in Polly Wong's yard, great clumsy wings batting the wind gracelessly; climbed the trees the girls could not, pulling himself from branch to branch with beak and claws; but when they called, he came.

'She's settled down nicely,' said Ronnie to Marilyn. 'She's like a real daughter now, she don't give no trouble no more.'

'I told you all she needed was a tight rein,' said Marilyn.

Rita crossed out the word 'hole' in her diary entry, and chewed the end of her pencil. She stood up, fetched her dictionary from the shelf, looked up first the word 'hole', followed by 'cave', 'hollow', 'cavity', and, finally, 'pit'. Under 'pit' she found 'abyss', and that was exactly right.

She licked the lead of her pencil and wrote in her neat round script:

Between the thoughts there is something and not nothing. The thoughts are covering it up and shielding it like a curtain and it is in my middle and if I stop thinking it will swallow me up. It is a hole an abyss.

FIFTEEN

Ole Year's Nite

Dear Diary,

It wasn't a brother after all, it was a sister, and I'm so glad because that was what I was wanting. But I haven't seen her yet because of Ole Year's Nite. I'll tell you how it happened.

Her Royal Majesty was peeved all day and didn't let me go out and I was fretting all day because I'd promised Polly and Donna I'd come around and we'd go liming on the Sea Wall but forget it. I had to ring them up and tell them to go without me. And then I had to run behind Her Royal Majesty . . . well, not really run behind her, because Her Majesty never left her royal chamber all day. But run all the same.

Rita, my back is hurting, bring me some cushions from the settee downstairs. Rita, run quick and tell Hyacinth to serve me lunch in bed. Rita, the noise is terrible, my head is killing me, go and get some aspirin and close the louvres. The sunlight is terrible! And the *noise*! Turn off that radio! No, turn it on again but not too loud, I forgot my story is coming in a minute. No, Rita, please stay home today, I may need you, I feel so unsettled and my head is killing me.

Anyway, after lunch she fell asleep and I took a deep breath and I went over to Polly but she was still at the Sea Wall. So I spent the

114

whole afternoon staring out the window till she woke up again and began bossing me around again.

Daddy didn't come home all afternoon. And he didn't come home all evening and he didn't come home all night. And when she began screaming in the middle of the night he wasn't home either. Only me and Hyacinth.

And what was dear Mr Maraj doing all this time? Of course: Ole Year's Nite, all kinds of big parties going on, so Mr Ronnie Maraj was working, going to this party and that and seeing how all the big shots are celebrating. And of course you couldn't telephone him anywhere.

So when I hear her screaming I run to get Hyacinth from downstairs and then Hyacinth get up to see what she's screaming about. But of course we know. So Hyacinth burst out of her room and yell at me to ring Daddy and ring the doctor because 'de baby comin''.

So how'm I supposed to ring Daddy? Daddy gallivanting around town working hard at reporting on the parties. So I ring the hospital instead and they say Dr Cameron is off duty and they say to send Her Majesty over in a taxi. So I call for a taxi and they said, no taxis right now, we'll send one over as soon as one is free.

And Marilyn screaming screaming screaming.

So anyway, we wait half an hour and nobody comes so I ring back and taxi service engaged, and engaged all the next half-hour. And then when I ring back again, nobody answers. So I ring hospital, and they say, big accident on Regent Street, drunk driver or something, no ambulance available.

Meanwhile Hyacinth still up there with her and between calls I run up to tell her what happening, and to see what going on, if baby come or what.

Hyacinth holding on to her and wiping her forehead, and she breathing heavy like, and hissing at me whenever I poked my head round the door.

Where is that man? (Meaning Daddy.)

When is that man coming? (Meaning Dr Cameron.)

Why's he taking so long? (Meaning the taxi driver.)

And all I had was bad news, and she wanting to kill me for it.

An hour passes, and she get real vex. She throw a tantrum and yell the place down about bloody doctor and bloody taxi driver and bloody baby and bloody everything else, except she didn't say bloody. Lord, I feel sorry for Hyacinth! Then Hyacinth say, all calm and sensible, 'Girl, run over to Mrs Wong and ask if she would drive her to hospital.'

And I do that, but of course Mrs Wong not home, at some fête, no car, only a babysitter.

Same in all the houses. Nobody home except servants and baby-sitters and housekeepers, nobody with a car. Plenty of bicycles, but no car.

'Bloody Ole Year's Nite!' she scream.

Then Hyacinth say I should boil some pots of water and I know things are getting serious, because in all the books the first thing you do when a baby born is boil water.

And then she really start screaming; till now it was just shouting. After that the screaming don't stop. You'd think she was being mur-dered, and all she was doing was having a baby! Well, right there and then I swear that if I ever get a baby I not going to scream like that.

OK, so now I got four big pots of water on all the four burners boiling away and I run up the stairs and knock on the door to tell Hyacinth. Nobody answer my knock and all quiet so I open the door just a crack and poke my head in, and I see her lying on the bed in a naked sweat and then she see me and scream, 'Get out of here, you stupid idiiieeeeeaaaagh!'

I slam the door and stand there trembling in the corridor for ages, listening to the screams, and then one real long loud scream, and then a wail, and then Hyacinth poke her head round the door and say, 'Well, dear, you have a sister, and is the hot water ready?'

So, dear Diary, that's how my sister was born. Aren't you as pleased as me? That she didn't get a boy, like she wanted?

'Rita, what are you doing?'

Daddy never knocked at Rita's door, but she didn't mind so much with him. Marilyn never knocked either, but there she *did* mind, though she never said so. This time Daddy came in with a wide grin all over his face. Rita hastily shut her diary and shoved it under her pillow. She sat up on her bed.

'Writing your diary, are you?' Daddy said. 'Well, at last you've got something to say, haven't you? What do you think of her?'

'Oh, well, she's – well, she's so, so – isn't she?'

'Like a little doll. That's what new-born babies are like, girl, that's what you were like too, you know! So what you think?'

Rita simply stared at him. She wasn't going to let on. She had seen her sister before breakfast, before anything. Marilyn had sent for her. She had waited at Marilyn's door hardly daring to go in because Marilyn might snap off her head, and then she had knocked, and Marilyn had called out languidly, 'Come in.' So she had gone in, and stood before the crib next to the bed, and seen her sister for the first time.

Staring at the baby Rita had known all sorts of things all at once. Something gripped her. From inside. From out of the abyss. Rita had no words for what it was; she had never felt like that before, but it was a bit like when you found a kitten half-drowned in a sack in a gutter, and you took it up and it meowed, and you wanted to press it to you and keep it for ever and ever and let it know that everything was all right. That's how she had felt.

She couldn't take her eyes off the little scrap of humanity sleeping in silent serenity on the pillow, soft and creamy rosepetal skin, perfect little hands with upturned palms in a gesture of complete surrender on either side of a little head capped in black silk. Minuscule fingers too fragile to be true, a face of ineffable innocence, perfection so complete that a lump rose in Rita's throat. She gulped to swallow it down.

It was love at first sight. From the moment she set eyes on her sister Rita loved her with an embracing love that was all things at once: reverence and protection; a love too sweeping for a ten-year-old to bear.

'A girl,' said Marilyn. 'It's only a girl. So much trouble for a girl. Rita, I expect you to pull your weight and help Hyacinth look after it. If you want you can take it away. I think it's hungry.'

117

Rita stared. Take it away? Touch that fragile wonderful living being, that looked as if it might break? How could she ever?

'Go on, pick it up. Just pick it up and take it away. It's only sleeping because it screeched itself into a coma. It's been squalling all night, I didn't get a moment of shut-eye ... Hyacinth is making some milk down in the kitchen, take it down and feed it. Just leave me in peace. When your Daddy gets home, if he ever does, tell him not to bother to wake me.' And she yawned and turned away from Rita, pulling the sheet over her shoulders.

There was no way Rita could share that, and all that happened afterwards, the picking up and the holding and the carrying downstairs and the feeding and the tiny lips moving, sucking, and the spellbound awe of beholding, with her father. He didn't deserve it. She looked up at Ronnie now, rolled her pencil in her palms in impatience, and said, to get rid of him, 'Oh, well, I suppose she's OK,' pulled her diary out from under her pillow and ostentatiously began to leaf through its pages. Ronnie took the hint. He shrugged and turned to leave.

It would be the longest, most important entry she had ever made in her life. When Ronnie left the room she got up, walked over and latched the door, and before returning to her bed fetched the dictionary, for there were a zillion feelings in her she had no words for.

SIXTEEN

A Different Drummer

Isabelle was born under a lucky star; born a star. Born to shine, eclipsing her big sister who didn't mind in the least; for Rita, from the very first moment, belonged to Isabelle as she had never belonged to any human being till then. Loving animals had been an apprenticeship; this was the real thing. And over the next year she watched with great wonderment as the tiny little thing, no bigger than Polly Wong's favourite doll (Rita herself perfectly *despised* dolls), grew under her very eyes, from day to day gained size and movement and perception, and she who had raised countless puppies and kittens up from scratch promoted herself to sole guardian of what must surely be creation's crowning glory. Isabelle.

Who could resist Isabelle? Her father, certainly, couldn't; she thoroughly usurped Rita's place in Ronnie's generous heart, for she was helpless and cute and soft, needing Daddy's protection, whereas Rita was tough and caustic and bristling with self-preservation. And as for Marilyn . . .

'Ronnie, are you never going to be ready? My goodness, where is that man, I suppose he's under the bonnet of the car again.

Ronnie! . . . Ronnie, there you are, I told you to change out of that old greasy shirt ages ago. Look at the time, it's almost ten-fifteen, I told Mrs D'Aguiar I'd be there at eleven, you know how she's particular about time, did you bring roses from Tulsiram, no, I'm sure you forgot, you expect me to go with my two long empty hands or what? Come on, haul your backside upstairs and get changed right *now*, oh *gawd*, husbands, why did I ever marry, people say women take so long to get dressed, they don't know you, man, and please go and bathe, I know you, putting your best clothes on stinking skin, and where is that girl, *Rita*! There you are, have you got the baby dressed yet? Then go and bring her, oh there's my little cushy-pushy, Isabelle, come to Mummy, darling, come on, who's a little birthday girl? Come into my arms like a bundle of charms, mmmm, you smell so good, darling, you're one year old and a big little girl, but your *hair*! Rita, what a mess, why didn't you brush this child's hair, you know I don't like it when the curls fall over her forehead like a puppy! Run and bring me the hairbrush and that new pink ribbon I bought yesterday. Come, darling, sit still on Mummy's lap now, no, don't grab the hairbrush, Mummy needs it to style your little curly-wurlies, and I'm going to tie this lovely ribbon on the very top, we're going for a lovely birthday walky-walky in the Botanic Gardens, just you and Mummy and Daddy, isn't that nice, on a lovely Sunday morning, and your little friend Suzie is going to be there, you can play in the sand with her, and this afternoon we'll have a lovely party. Look, hold the ribbon but don't put it in your mouth, it will get all soppy, there we go, now give Mummy the ribbon, come on, give, let go, darling, no, I said *not* in your mouth, open your teeth, if you bite it like that it's going to tear, the lovely pretty ribbon Mummy bought for your hair, come, open up now, open up, like a dear girl . . . Oh, gawd, Rita, come and see if you can get her to let go, baby, darling, open your hands and give Mummy the ribbon, Rita, are you deaf? She's going to bite that ribbon to shreds, come and help me. Stop fighting up like that, Isabelle, sit still, sit still and stop wriggling I tell you and give me the ribbon right now. Rita, if I hold her wrist you can prise open her fingers . . . there! Isabelle, darling, open your mouth and let go of that ribbon, Mummy's going to smack you in one minute and then you're going to cry, there! You see! And next time it's going to hurt. Take this bawling child, Rita, at least she let go of the ribbon now, just look at the way she crumpled up my dress, I'm going to have to change, just take her away and get her quiet, she ruined that ribbon, look at it! Just look at it! And it was so expensive, it's full of *spit*! Take her away, take her away, I can't stand that bawling, take her away and get her quiet, put on her sunbonnet and go into the yard with her and wait there till I come down, but careful and don't get burrs on her clothes, oh that child is a headache I tell you, why did I ever think of becoming a mother? Ronnie, oh there you are, that was quick, did you bathe in that short time, are you sure? Look, I have to go and change my dress, it's all crumpled up and my make-up is a mess, I need a quarter of an hour, what's the time? *What*! Oh Lordy, we're going to be late, I'll just rush upstairs, go down to the car and wait for me but don't start messing around in the engine again, you hear? I hate going places with my two long empty hands, why did you put on that shirt, it's not starched, I put a shirt for you on the bed, are you blind or what? And you know I hate white socks. Oh Ronnie, when are you going to learn? Go and see if the baby is quiet yet, she was bawling her head off and you know how . . . That damned telephone, it always rings at the wrong time, get it will you? I'm going upstairs, if it's Cheryl tell her not now, later, I haven't got a minute's time now . . .'

Down at the bottom of the garden Isabelle and Rita inspected the tadpole pond. Isabelle had stopped crying; she had done so the minute they were out of Marilyn's sight, and it was with a cool smug feeling of satisfaction that Rita had carried her down the stairs into the garden, taken her by her two little hands and held her up as she stumbled forward along the sandy path between the cannas. As they moved along, Isabelle hobbling from left foot to right in the vee of Rita's legs, Rita spoke soothingly to her sister.

'She hit you, didn't she? She's an old meanie. Don't bother with her. I would never hit you, would I? She's a silly old lady, isn't she? Cretinous. Trying to tie that stupid old ribbon in your hair! You would have looked horrible. She thinks you're a little dolly to dress up and tie up in ribbons but you're not, you were right not to let her! Anyway, you know just what to do when she's silly, don't you? Just start bawling! She can't stand it when you bawl. She likes you all smiley and silly like some cretinous baby in *Woman's Own* but you hate that, don't you? Here we are. Careful you don't slip, it's a bit muddy round the edges 'cause it rained early this morning – better take off your shoes so they don't get dirty or she's going to start screaming again. There.'

Rita threw Isabelle's little white shoes and white frilly socks back towards the house; they landed on the path. She settled Isabelle on the edge of the pond. It was a home-made pond, Rita's invention, an old car-tyre sunk into the earth, the circle at its bottom laid out with a plastic sheet to hold the water, carefully hidden from Marilyn in a bushy corner of the back-yard she never deigned to inspect, way beyond the compost heap and the gardener's precious manure pile, a secret shared with the gardener who fully approved of the rearing of frogs. Behind the bushes. You couldn't see it from the house. That was the main thing.

Rita was well aware of the danger of Isabelle's frock getting dirty. Such a cretinous pink frock, with white frills all the way down the front and around the hem, and a wide white satin sash around the waist; Rita rumpled her nose in disdain as she pulled the hem up and tucked it into the sash so that it wouldn't dangle in the water by mistake. Isabelle wore matching panties, the backside frilled, and Rita, responsible as ever, pulled these off so that Isabelle could sit in safety on the tyre-rim in her plastic pants all puffed out from the nappy they enclosed. Rita gave her a twig and happily Isabelle, gurgling and exclaiming in glee, stirred the water with it and tried to touch the tadpoles flitting about beneath the surface. Rita watched her, and as she watched she talked.

'Don't let her get you,' she told Isabelle. 'You're mine. She's a silly old frog and she thinks she can make you into some cretinous dolly she's dreamed up. But you're not a dolly, are you? You're Isabelle. Say it. Isabelle. Is-a-belle.'

'Bell,' Isabelle agreed.

'That's right. Bell. Is-a-belle. Say it again, Is-a-belle.'

'A-bell.'

'Right. Your name is Isabelle. Want to know a secret? I gave you that name. I chose it. Because she didn't want you when you were born. She didn't like you at all, she didn't even want to see you and she hadn't got a name for a girl. Only a name for a boy. Sebastian! Imagine that! A boy called Sebastian. Sebastian Maraj. She said it was an elegant name, and a boy with that name would go far, just imagine! So she hadn't got a girl's name and Daddy had to have a name for the birth certificate and he knew I was good at names so he asked me, but I told him I'd do it only if he promised not to tell *her* it was from me, and he promised so I said Isabelle, and he told her he had thought it up so it was OK. It's a lovely name. Come on, try again. Is-a-belle.'

'A-belle. A-belle. A-belle.'

'That's right. And my name? What's my name?' She pointed to her chest. Isabelle smiled up at her and pointed too.

'Ita.'

'Almost, Rrr-ita. And . . . Oh Lord, she's calling, come quick, we've got to go.'

Rita stood Isabelle on the rim of the tyre, stripped off her T-shirt and wiped off the muddy streaks from the plastic pants. She carried her over to the path, bending to pick up the frilled underpants as she went, pulling them on over the plastic ones, drying Isabelle's kicking feet. At the path she hurriedly pulled on the child's shoes and socks.

Marilyn wrenched Isabelle out of Rita's arms. 'Where on earth have you been? What have you been doing? Look at this child, she looks as if you've dragged her through a bush!' She pulled the hem of the dress out of the sash. 'My word, Rita, can't I even leave you one minute alone with this child? And how often do

I have to tell you not to run around half-naked, at your age? You look like a servant's child, no wonder . . . Oh hell, she's starting up again, Ronnie, take her quick.' She thrust the whimpering baby at Ronnie's chest, and he, taken by surprise, grabbed her a little too heftily and a little too late, digging his fingers in under her arms by mistake. Isabelle began to scream.

Marilyn stamped her feet. 'Oh no, you idiot, why can't you . . . Give her to Rita, quick quick, Rita, take her, oh Lord what are we to do, we're so late already and you know those D'Aguiars. Rita, you'll have to come with us for goodness' sake but keep your mouth shut, do you hear? Run upstairs, give me the baby, no, take her with you, grab some clothes, the yellow dress you wore at the May Day parade, don't put it on, there's no time, you can do that in the car, and bring a hairbrush, your hair's a mess, loosen the plaits and brush it out, quick time now, *run*!'

Rita flew up the stairs, Isabelle, no longer screaming, dangling under one arm.

It was only later, after a hasty back-seat change and a slapdash brush of hair, two corners before the D'Aguiars' home, that Rita realized she was still barefoot. Barefoot, in a cretinous yellow satin dress chosen by Marilyn. Toes stained with mud. She smiled in deep satisfaction, leaned into the back seat, and jiggled Isabelle on her knees. It wasn't *her* problem. Not at all.

By the time Isabelle was three she and Rita were a team – closer than twins. It was hard to tell who adored whom more: on the one hand, Isabelle had Rita on a string, dancing to the tunes she played from the moment she woke up in her sun-splashed room, all through the day to evening, when she laid her silky mop of black curls on a white frilly pillow and rubbed her charming little fists into eyes heavy with sleep, yawning, stretching up those darling arms to pull doting big sister down for a final kiss.

On the other hand, Rita was the centre of Isabelle's universe. Rita held sway over Isabelle's moods – with a few words, Rita could calm a tantrum before it even broke out. It was Rita who toilet trained Isabelle. Rita who got her into bed at night with the promise of a goodnight story. Rita she respected and – to a certain degree – obeyed. If Rita said be still, then Isabelle, somehow, was still. When Rita said sing, Isabelle! then Isabelle sang. She sang 'Twinkle Twinkle Little Star' and 'Frosty the Snowman' in the purest baby voice, and everybody clapped and said how sweet she was. Isabelle wouldn't sing for any other person in the world.

Rita was as proud as any mother. And if Marilyn was responsible for the initial *forming* of Isabelle's body, then surely Rita was responsible for the *thriving* of the same, for its care and nourishment and general well-being. And if she wasn't jealous of the attention Isabelle earned by the mere fact of being, she certainly *was* jealous of anyone who dared to intrude by taking on any of the little essential tasks she considered hers, and hers alone. Only she should feed Isabelle. Only she should bathe her, cuddle her, kiss her, take her by the hand as she learned her first steps, help her repeat her first words. She made faces at the nursemaid who came at eight to replace her during school hours; but the moment she pranced into the house after school, Isabelle was all hers.

Till tragedy struck.

SEVENTEEN

Brain Damage

Dear Diary,

Today was the worst day in my entire life. I killed Isabelle. At least, I probably did, but she's not quite dead yet. She's in hospital now and I'm not allowed to see her and everybody hates me. I don't know what to do and I don't know if I can live through this night. Help me, please, please! I can't sleep and I know when I wake up tomorrow she'll be dead and what if they put me in prison?

I can't believe I killed my own sister. And she's only four, still a baby almost. The sweetest prettiest child in the world, and I killed her.

This is what happened.

Marilyn took me and Isabelle to Bookers for Christmas shopping. Well, it was she doing most of the shopping, she had to get new clothes and shoes and stuff for Isabelle. All I wanted was a book for Polly. Marilyn went off to do her shopping and left Isabelle with me like she always does, and I went to look for a nice book. I took Isabelle with me and I bought her an ice-cream cone and told her to sit down at the bottom of that column just in front of the book department and eat her cone. I've done it before and she doesn't mind. I know she doesn't. She never got up to wander off before!

126

Never ever. She doesn't go anywhere without me. Normally she just sits still and waits for me! How was I to *know*!

Anyway . . . I was looking for this book and I found one that looked interesting, and then I began looking through the comics and got kind of absorbed – you know me, I got pulled in. I don't know how long for, I sort of got lost. Next thing I knew Marilyn was there screaming at me to come and when I looked for Isabelle sitting on the floor where I left her *she wasn't there.*

Just empty space. I sort of stared at Marilyn for a moment and then I dashed back into the book department, because maybe she had gone to look at the picture books, but she wasn't there either. Marilyn realized I didn't know where Isabelle was and began yelling at me to find her. We both dashed off to look for her and it was then we heard the siren outside and we almost collided at the door, trying to get out into the street. There was a whole crowd of people blocking the street and staring at something and that's when I knew. I just *knew*. Marilyn knew too, she started screaming and sort of elbowing herself through the crowd to get to the front and I followed her, and then we were standing at the roadside and looking down at poor little Isabelle in a pool of blood and my own blood froze. I just can't tell you how I felt when I saw her lying there so still in her yellow shoes with all these people in white coats around her, doctors, I suppose, because there was an ambulance there. I couldn't say or do a thing, everything in me was like a stone and in my head I was just thinking no, no, no, no, and even praying, 'Don't let her be dead, don't let her be dead.' And Marilyn was having hysterics and people were holding her back and then a policeman came up to her and a doctor, and people coming and going and everything in chaos. I think I nearly fainted but I didn't.

Then Isabelle was on a stretcher and they were shoving her into the ambulance, and Marilyn was getting in with her.

Before they closed the door Marilyn shot me this look full of hate and I think she wanted to spit at me, but instead she just spat the words: 'You little devil! If you've killed my baby I'll . . . I'll . . .' but she couldn't finish her sentence because they shut the door and the ambulance raced off with the siren screeching.

I stood there for a few minutes longer, I was so shocked I didn't know what to do or what to think. I wanted to cry but I couldn't and there was nobody there to talk to, because everybody was so excited and babbling away about things. But gradually I began to understand what people were saying. There was this market woman just behind me who had seen everything and she kept saying: 'De chile run after Santa Claus, Ah see it wid me own eyes . . . Santa Claus ringin' he bell walk out a Bookers and walk across de street an' de chile run behin' and straight into a car . . . Ah see it wid me own two eyes, Ah tell ya, de pore li'l chile chasin' after Santa. Ah call out, stop, chile, a car comin' but she no hear, she run straight into de car. Oh Lordy, Ah see it wid me own two eyes, an' me sittin' here on de pavement sellin' me genips, de chile run straight into de street not lookin'. Ah see wid me own two eyes . . .'

Then a policeman came up and spoke to the woman and she began the story all over again from the beginning, with the police taking notes, and then somebody said, 'Is de li'l Maraj gal, Ah know she fadder good. De lady is he wife, is dey only chile.'

And that's when I thought of Daddy for the first time so I ran away to Daddy's office to tell him.

Well, Daddy dropped what he was doing and raced downstairs to his car and just left me there at his office, so I went home. Daddy didn't even think of me. All he did was telephone home from the hospital later and speak to Hyacinth and tell her what happened, and that's how I know that Isabelle is dying and it's all my fault.

She might be dead by the morning!

I don't want her to die, Diary! Oh, please don't let her die!

Dear Diary, this was the worst day in my whole life and it's going to be the worst night. I wish I was dead. I wish the car had got *me* and not Isabelle. It's all my fault and when she dies everybody will hate me and call me a murderer, and then I'm going to kill myself. Marilyn will make sure I go to prison, I know she will. And I know what that prison is like, because Daddy once took me and pointed up to those dark holes which were windows with iron bars and showed me the hands sticking out of them and waving, and Daddy said those hands belonged to men living in hell and he knew one or two of them, and that's where I'm going to end up, for killing Isabelle.

Dear Diary,

It's been two days now and Isabelle still hasn't woken up. Marilyn says she's probably going to die. Or else she won't ever wake up again. Anything can happen. Marilyn is frantic and furious with me but this time I don't blame her; she's right and I'm really good for nothing like she always says, it's true and *I'm sorry*!!!!!!!

I'm so sorry but it's too late to be sorry. I wish I was dead or I could die instead of Isabelle; nobody would miss me. How can I live if she dies? Please make her live. Please make her live. Let her live but not in a coma, let her come back!

I'll do anything you want if you only let her live and come back. *Anything.* I'm sorry I'm always dreaming and not paying attention. I'll change. I'll be different. I'll stop dreaming and reading so much. I'll pay attention in school and always put my hand up. I'll be so good you won't recognize me. And one thing I promise with all my heart: I'll always look after Isabelle. I'll take care of her and love her always and I won't mind when she gets on my nerves. I'll take her everywhere with me and do everything she wants me to, I promise, I swear. And I'll never get angry with her. I'll always be nice to her.

But if she dies I'll kill myself because how can I live?

Dear Diary,

Thank you, oh thank you for answering my prayer!

Isabelle is going to live! She has a big wound on her head and she has twelve stitches but she's going to live! But . . . she might have brain damage, Marilyn said. A serious trauma. That means she won't ever be the same again. So it's almost as bad as dying. Is she going to be mad, or what?

I'm glad she's going to live but if she turns mad I don't know what I'm going to do, because I'll be the one who made her turn mad. Why didn't I watch over her? Why did I just leave her there? Why did I start reading those stupid comics? Marilyn is right, I'm always lost in a dream and that's what almost killed Isabelle, and now she's going to be mad. Anyway if she's mad I'll look after her. I promise you, Diary, I'll always look after her if she's mad. I won't let them put her in the Berbice Mad House. She'll have me to take care of her and hold her down if she starts behaving mad. But how do mad people behave? There's that mad man who walks up and down Water Street talking nonsense but that's the only mad person I ever saw. Sometimes they get violent, like Mr Rochester's wife, and then she'll have to be locked into a room but I'll take care of her, they need someone to take care of them and I'll do it for Isabelle because it'll be my fault if she goes mad. I'll learn how to restrain her and calm her down. I'll be loving and kind to her and help her not to be violent, breaking things and attacking people and such. I hope they don't have to lock her away. But if they do I'll be with her all the time, taking care of her. I'll make up for what I did! I'm glad I won't have to go to prison — thank you, Diary, that's your doing, I know. You saved her life but you might let her be mad because I know I have to bear the consequences of letting her go off by herself, when I was supposed to be watching over her. I realize that. And I promise to take care of my sister for ever, *no matter what.*

EIGHTEEN

Matilda

Dear Diary,
 Isabelle has a tummy-ache again. It's the third one this week.
They're really bad, she says, and Marilyn sends her to bed and gives
her medicine but nothing helps.
 Dr Singh couldn't find anything at all wrong with her. He says
she's making it up to get attention. But she cries so pitifully when
she's got a tummy-ache I can't believe she's making it up.

A pebble landed on Rita's floor. She laid down her pen, scraped
back her chair and slowly walked over to the window, practising
what she would say, manoeuvring her lips into a false grin. She
looked down.

'Hi, Poll! What's up?'

Polly Wong stood behind the palings, her face turned up. Even
from this height Rita could see the lines of annoyance across her
forehead. Could Polly read the guilt in her own eyes? Rita thought
not. She hoped not. And why should she feel guilty? She had
been looking forward to this afternoon as much as Polly and was
just as disappointed that it had all gone wrong.

'Rita, why didn't you come? You *promised*! I was so

disappointed. I waited and waited for you outside the Playhouse and then I had to go in and I thought you'd come late but you didn't. What happened? I thought something terrible must have happened, like an accident or something, and I rushed home but Hyacinth just told me *nothing* happened, all you did was go bloody shopping in Water Street!' Polly stamped her foot in annoyance.

'Well, you see . . .'

'Look, I don't feel like standing here talking to you at the top of my voice, I'm coming over, OK?'

Polly didn't wait for an answer. She dashed to her front gate, quickly breached the few yards' distance between their homes, and moments later Rita heard the gong of the front door. Hyacinth would get it; Rita left the window thoughtfully and plonked herself down on her bed, biting nervously on her nails. They were chewed down to the quick by now; whenever she caught herself at it she'd pull her fingers from her mouth and sit on them, but sometimes a force beyond her command took possession of her, pushed her hands – sometimes one, sometimes both – up to her teeth, and it started again, the restless, nervous gnawing. Chewing her nails was so comforting, resistance just too exhausting. Easier to give in. Let it take over. Let *her* take over. The little she-devil of her own creation. Because sometimes that's how Rita thought of Isabelle. Sometimes, when by herself, she could no longer put the brakes on the resentment rising involuntarily from deep within, which she knew was wrong, wrong, because after all she did love Isabelle, and how could she resent a cute little child with the face of an angel? And she knew why Isabelle was like that. It was the trauma, and the trauma was her fault. But sometimes she said yes when she ought to say no, and those were the times when the gnawing began. Inside, and out. And the inside gnawing was worse.

The door flew open and Polly burst into the room.

'So, you'd better have a good excuse but I know you haven't, you moron. I bet I know what happened. I bet it was that sister of yours. It was, wasn't it? It always is! And stop biting your nails, you're gonna have stumps for fingers before you're finished! Now tell me, it was, wasn't it?'

With supreme effort Rita, stung by Polly's words, pulled her hand from her mouth. The fingers so cruelly abandoned began to pick at the threads in the purple counterpane. Rita nodded glumly, not looking at Polly. The hurt and accusation in her friend's eyes, she knew by instinct, would be too much to bear.

Polly flung herself on to the bed behind Rita. She formed her hands into fists and pummelled the other girl's back; and Rita let her, knowing she deserved it. This was to have been the chance of her life. Acting. The leading role in the play *The Taming of Matilda* by the renowned Guyanese playwright Andrew Hinds; the wild young thing Matilda from the Interior, coming to Town and turning the heads of all young men married and unmarried . . . Rita had flung herself into the part, practised in secret, learned her lines by heart. Polly had heard her time and time again; she was perfect. She dreamed of Matilda at night; she WAS Matilda. Matilda was a new beginning. Rita was going to be an actress. A brilliant actress. First she'd make her mark in Guyana, then she'd go abroad. England. America. Broadway. Hollywood! Escape! Release! Escape, release, from what? She knew very well; but it was hard to admit it even to herself. And certainly she'd never confess to Polly.

Isabelle. Always Isabelle. Isabelle needed her; but she needed to escape, to get away from being needed. Yet – she had promised. She had sworn; she had made a covenant with herself, the breaking of which would surely bring down hell's fury. Isabelle needed her. That's why she knew she couldn't be an actress. She couldn't go off to the stage. Isabelle came first. That was her duty, her promise, her sacred calling.

It had been a relief to find out that Isabelle didn't have brain damage after all. But she had *something* – she was changed. Since the accident everything, in fact, was changed. The balance between her and Isabelle was lopsided: Isabelle up, she down, her authority diminished. She loved Isabelle as much as ever: but more and more she realized she didn't *like* her very much.

Isabelle, in fact, was a brat. Sometimes she felt like slapping her, but didn't. Because how could she *know*? How could anybody know? Was brattyness a form of brain damage? That was the question. Maybe poor Isabelle couldn't help it. Maybe the shock had been too much for her. And though she was only four Isabelle *knew* – she knew that the accident had been all Rita's fault because that's what Marilyn said several times a day, reminding everyone, and whenever one of Isabelle's headaches or tummy aches came on – and they came with astounding frequency, any time, it seemed, that Isabelle wanted something she couldn't have – Marilyn said, 'Oh, you poor dear, that's because of the accident,' and Isabelle got what she wanted.

Isabelle had a long scar at the side of her head; you couldn't see it because mercifully her thick black curls fell over it, but Isabelle was proud of it and showed it to everyone who hadn't seen it yet, even perfect strangers, saying, 'Have you seen my scar?' then lifting the curtain of hair, and everyone would gasp and say, 'Oh, you poor child, what a nasty scar, how did that happen?' And then Isabelle would say, 'My sister didn't look after me properly and I ran onto the street and a car knocked me over. I didn't die but I've got this big scar now and I've got it for life though you can't see it because of my hair!' And she said it in such a sweet, pretty way that everyone oohed and aahed in sympathy and gave her a kiss and maybe a sweetie to make up for the dreadful scar. Isabelle's scar story was irresistible.

Dear Diary,

Marilyn took her to another doctor. He's just come back from America and knows all the latest methods. He says it's all pschosomat-isch. That means she isn't imagining it at all, she really does have tummy-aches but they have no physical cause, it's all mental. He advised Marilyn to put her in therapy.

Sometimes Isabelle would bend over double and then everyone would know it was coming on. 'Ooow,' she would say, 'my tummy hurts so badly!' And Marilyn would pick her up and kiss her all over and comfort her with gifts and special treats, and if Rita was nearby throw her a nasty look, and Rita would slink away and try to deal with mean thoughts such as: That nasty little brat! That old bitch! How I wish . . . I wish . . . I wish . . .

But Rita never managed to wish anything through to its end because sooner or later a loud stern voice at the back of her mind would outshout the wishing and say, shut up, *you're* the brat because it's *all your fault* . . .

'Her head is always in the clouds,' Marilyn said to anyone who would listen, referring to Rita. Her anger had never abated; justified anger, Rita knew.

She'd vowed to turn over a new leaf if Isabelle survived but such a vow was far beyond her capabilities – dreaming had become a mode of being, a strategy for existence in a cold, inhospitable, accusatory world, and a welcome escape from that world. She could no more stop dreaming than she could stop breathing. At school she sat staring out of the window till reprimanded by the teacher. She forgot facts. Figures sailed through her mind without making the least impression. The only thing she cared about were words; words that bubbled up in an uncontrolled stream from her depths, words that danced and words that sang, words that gave some order to the confusion whirling around inside her. She found communication hard; the small talk people engaged in bored her to tears. She tried to listen, but her mind wandered off along paths of its own making. *That* she could do all day; it wasn't boring, nor was it laden with guilt.

Since the accident, her interior life had been partitioned into separate rooms named 'Before' and 'After'. *Before*, the world of imagination had been a kaleidoscope whose borders constantly changed; life in that world had a scintillating edge, its content sharp and sparkling and witty. *After*, those edges lost their contours, the content became vague, fuzzy, smudged with grey.

She had to do something, go somewhere. Somewhere where the coldness and the guilt and the recriminations couldn't reach her, some place where she was free, free of the past and of her own deficiencies. Throw herself into some ideal, into some dream that would become reality and not just a play of light and shadow within the confines of her mind. That would fill up the ugly hollows inside, which were so full of demons that threatened and poked and reminded her of her failings. Books delighted her, and films, and theatre: stories that came to life, stories one could enter and lose oneself in, stories where she herself was the heroine and good and brave and worthy, where no one would point a finger and call her names and where she wasn't a near-murderer but a saviour. And now there was the chance of actually taking part in such a story, becoming this Matilda, wayward and unorthodox but who finally found redemption through the healing powers of true love.

But it wasn't working that way. Here now was Polly Wong, arms akimbo, stamping a foot and flinging her pigtails off her shoulders in anger. 'Why, why, why? Oh, Rita, you were so looking forward to the auditions and I know, I just KNOW they'd have given you the role of Matilda! You were just made for it, true! And now guess who got it! Guess?'

Rita half-turned towards Polly. 'Who?'

'Belinda Moore!'

'Belinda Moore! That awful stuck-up—'

'Yes! And it's all your fault, you idiot, because if you'd come like you promised I just know you'd have been much, much better. She can't act to save her life and she's not funny or anything, she's just tall and big-mouthed and her daddy at the Ministry must have bribed the committee. I bet he did! How else did she get the role? She's not even funny and you *have* to be funny to play Matilda else it won't work, and I'm Sweetie Pie and have to play alongside her and I'll just hate it. I know I will! Oh, Rita, I could kill you, I just could kill you for not turning up, 'cause now Belinda's gonna gloat like anything, and she was stuck-up enough to begin with. Why didn't you? I thought wild horses couldn't keep you away!'

Wild horses perhaps not, but a pint-sized brat, thought Rita.

'Well, you see, it was Isabelle.'

'Isabelle, Isabelle, Isabelle. I wish that little rascal had never been born, truly! It's just getting worse and worse. It used to be OK before the accident, she was so sweet, but now she's just a spoilt little, a spoilt little . . .' Polly searched for the right word.

'Brat,' Rita offered.

'Yeah, a spoilt little brat. She knows exactly what she's doing. She's ob— ob—'

'Obnoxious.'

'Obnoxious. I bet she had one of her tantrums again, didn't she?'

Rita nodded.

'And what was it about this time? Some dress or the other?'

Rita shook her head, and pulling a thread out of the counterpane, began looping it around a forefinger. 'Uh-uh. It's this doll, you see. Her friend Suzie D'Aguiar got this new dolly for her birthday, it's got a hole to wee-wee out of and it says Mama, and they have it in Fogarty's. And Isabelle wanted it.'

'Well, why didn't her mummy go and buy it for her?'

'She wanted to go to the store to pick it out, and she didn't want to go with Marilyn, she wanted *me* to go with her.'

'Well, she could have waited till tomorrow, couldn't she?'

'Well, in theory yes but you know Isabelle. Like you said she threw a tantrum and when she does that she gets so worked up that she stops breathing even and starts turning blue and everybody thinks she's going to die, so we try to humour her before it gets that bad. And then she gets a headache and you have to sit next to her with ice and cloths to lay across her forehead.'

'So everybody runs to do what she wants. She's really got you all running circles around her. That rascal! And she knew very well you had the auditions, didn't she?'

'No, of course not, don't be silly. I mean, I told her I had to go to the Playhouse but she couldn't know it was so important, could she? She's only four! And I did try to reason with her, but she didn't really understand . . . you see, it's really this trauma she got from the accident . . .'

'Oh, shut up, Rita, you make me *sick*! Trauma, my foot! She's no fool, she understands everything perfectly well and she's using that accident to twist you round her little finger. Believe me, she knows *perfectly* well. She understands! She just didn't want to let you go, that's the trouble! And it's about time you realized what's going on, Rita – she's tying you up in knots and one day when you really need to get free you'll find you can't! Don't say I didn't warn you!'

'But . . .'

'No buts about it! You know very well I'm right, Rita, and if you don't pull yourself out of it . . . I don't know – you've stopped being *you*! Remember what you used to be like? You used to be fun, the life and soul of the street. Since that imp had her accident all you do is hang around waiting for her beck and call. She's like some queen and you're the lady-in-waiting. Dammit! I want you back, you were the best friend I ever had and I can't stand it one day longer, and of all things you missed being Matilda and I could just kill somebody! Preferably you!'

But Polly was much too well behaved to kill her friend. Instead, she flung herself at Rita, pummelled her around the head and shoulders, wrestled silently with her on the bed for a good five minutes, and only when Rita hollered surrender did she let up.

'And now,' she said, 'you're coming over to MY house *without* that obnoxious little rascal.'

Dear Diary,

Dr Singh persuaded Marilyn to take Isabelle to see this psychiatrist. The psychiatrist says she's emotionally disturbed and that's why she has those tantrums and headaches and tummy-aches. He wants to find out the cause and Marilyn told him I was the cause and made me go to speak to him myself. I had to go but they couldn't force me to speak so I just sat there and didn't say anything for half an hour and then he sent me away. He told Marilyn I'm also seriously disturbed emotionally and he doesn't doubt I have something to do with the tummy-aches. And the tantrums and headaches.

NINETEEN

A Busty Lass

Rita was nearly fifteen when she discovered that Archie Foot was the most evil-looking (*evil* that year being synonymous with out-of-this-world gorgeous) boy she had ever seen and the only one she'd ever love in all her life. The Foot family had moved into Number Two last July. There had been no logical reason not to integrate Archie into the Victoria Street Gang; but with a name like that you had to make some extra effort to prove you weren't a drip and Archie hadn't done so. And it wasn't just the ridiculous name; rumour had it that the Feet were Returnees from England, Archie's father having been offered a position as Professor of History at the University of Guyana. Whoever returned from *London* to Georgetown! Only drips and creeps did that, failures, people with names like Foot. Professor Foot! *Real* people left and never came back! Didn't that prove the Foot boys were unworthy of Victoria Street?

Isabelle alone had proven less superficial in her judgement of the Feet. Soon after their arrival she had seen Archie's two younger brothers climbing over the roof of the house and had declared them her heroes. Isabelle took to standing at the Foot gate and peering into the yard, waiting for a glimpse of one of the younger Foot boys. If one of them appeared he would stick out his tongue and make rude remarks and shooing gestures, but Isabelle was undaunted, and she was tough. She would not be shooed away. She just stood staring in, biding her time.

At the start of the new school year, Bishops' High School, St Rose's, St Stanislaus and Queen's College had all simultaneously turned co-educational, which meant that boys were admitted to Bishops' and St Rose's, and girls to Queen's and Saint's. Polly's father insisted that the Saint's science department was obviously better than Bishops', and made her change schools. And all of a sudden Archie was one of three new boys in Rita's class, the only boy from Victoria Street at Bishops', the classical girls' school. Yet another reason for Archie to prove himself . . .

Girls can be unmerciful. Archie's female classmates shot paper pellets at him with rubber bands. They hid his books. They put a frog in his desk during break. It was as if he had leprosy; in the classroom, girls cringed away from him, giggling and tittering behind raised hands. The other two boys, ignored by the girls, were Chinese identical twins who had eyes only for each other, so Archie was on his own, friendless and isolated, sitting on his own at a desk directly in front of Rita.

In a way, Rita felt sorry for him; but in another way the fun was too much to resist. She watched, and never said a word, never joined in the verbal needling, keeping a straight face when all the other girls giggled and spluttered. So passive she was in the harassment of Archie that he possibly even thought her a friend; now and then she caught him glancing at her, a half-smile on his lips, and she smiled back kindly and innocently, keeping her betrayal to herself.

For, in fact, Rita was the worst of the lot. Her contribution to the molestation of Archie was silent, and Archie had no inkling of her perfidy. He never saw the notes she scribbled hastily during lessons and at break time, rhyming couplets she passed around the class so that everyone could share the joke. When the note had been read by the whole class – excepting, of course, the Chan boys who shared a desk in glorious isolation at the front – it returned to Rita who carefully destroyed it. Over the weeks the poems had grown bolder as Rita's imagination took wing. Today's was a masterpiece.

Rita grinned to herself as she folded the paper. She glanced up; when Miss Humphries's back was turned she leaned over, past Archie, and passed the note to the girl sitting diagonally across from her, next to Archie. At that moment Miss Humphries turned, Rita dropped the note, Archie picked it up, all in the space of an indrawn breath.

'Archibald Foot, bring me that note!'

'What note, Miss?'

'Don't play the fool with me, I saw you pick up a note that girl passed you, now please bring it up here straight away!'

Archie looked genuinely nonplussed. He shuffled his books around as if looking for a note and, finding nothing, looked at Miss Humphries innocently and shrugged his shoulders. 'I don't know anything about a note, Miss.'

Miss Humphries marched forward and stood above Archie, arms akimbo, glaring down at him from her vantage point several feet above. Miss Humphries was enormous at the best of times; fury multiplied her bulk. Her torso was as thick and solid as a sack of flour, with a sharp indentation around the middle of the sack (or, in this case, a polka-dotted cotton dress) where a thin belt hinted at a waistline. Miss Humphries had pale skin. People called her 'white', but in fact it was a well-known fact that she was seven-eighths Portuguese, the name Humphries deriving from an English paternal great-grandfather. That single drop of English blood, however, lent her an authority far exceeding that of all the other teachers put together. Especially when she looked at you like that. Rita quaked.

Archie Foot, however, looked up at the thundercloud looming above him and said in all confidence, 'You must be mistaken, ma'am, nobody passed me a note.'

Miss Humphries exploded. 'You dare lie to me! *You dare!* Stand up, you, boy!'

Archie Foot stood up.

'Now quick march forward to the blackboard. Go and stand there facing the room. Chop-chop!'

Archie did as he was told.

Miss Humphries, her face set in determined lines, picked up each of Archie's books one by one and shook them out. No note fluttered to the floor. She opened his desk; he could, after all, have slipped the note quickly under the flap. But no note lay inside the desk.

To give up now would be an admission of defeat and Miss Humphries never succumbed to defeat. She tramped to the front of the class, grabbed Archie by one ear, pulled him forward and systematically searched him. She began innocently enough, emptying the contents of his trouser pockets and turning them inside out. Nothing there. She peered into his shirt pocket. Nothing there. She made him pull up his cuffs and searched his socks and take off his shoes. Nothing there.

'Take your shirt out of your pants,' she commanded.

Archie did so.

'Now unbuckle your belt!'

At those words a petrified murmur hummed through the classroom. One girl whispered a little too loud, so that everyone heard. 'She's going to make him strip *naked*!' Some girls opened their desks and hid behind the uptilted lids; others buried their faces in their hands and peeped through their fingers. They shuffled their feet, tittered in embarrassment and glanced nervously at each other. Rita kept her eyes riveted to the tips of her shoes.

But Miss Humphries did not need to strip Archie after all, for the note was tucked inside of his trousers, and as he opened his belt Miss Humphries saw the telltale white edge of paper. Triumphantly she stuck her fingers into Archie's waistband and pulled it out. 'You see! You can't fool me!' she cried in triumph and let out a laugh that positively vibrated with sadism. No one laughed with her.

Miss Humphries opened the note and read it. Slowly she turned to glare at Rita. 'Rita Maraj, stand up!' Her voice contained a deadly chill. She raised a hand, fist upwards, and in slow motion uncurled her forefinger so that it pointed towards Rita, and then curled it back into the fist. 'Come here, you,' she said slowly in time to the curling finger. Rita, still sitting, bit her lip and stared.

'Are you deaf? Stand up!' Rita's chair scraped backwards and she rose to her feet. Her knees trembled; Miss Humphries was renowned for draconian punishments.

'All right. Come here.'

Rita's legs felt too weak even to take one step forward, let alone to carry her to the front of the room. She stood immobile, as if nailed to the floor.

'Are you deaf, child? I said go to the front of the class! Do I have to drag you? Go on, move!' Miss Humphries herself moved her enormous frame and stood menacingly in front of Rita's aisle. Rita could not move. She was frozen. And besides, she would have to squeeze past Miss Humphries who blocked the narrow aisle with her huge frame, and who seemed not the least inclined to budge. But no, she was coming, moving slowly down the aisle towards Rita, and gave her shoulder a light shove. Rita hastily stumbled backwards. Fearing further manhandling she scrambled to her feet, almost ran to the end of the aisle and then back up the side of the room to take a position next to Archie.

Rita stepped forward hesitantly. Miss Humphries handed her the note.

'Now read that aloud.'

Rita's voice was thin as she began to read.

> 'Of all the girls who're in my class
> I'm Rita Maraj, the busty lass . . .'

Somebody snorted at the word 'busty' and Rita stopped reading.

'Continue!' barked Miss Humphries. Rita swallowed audibly, scratched her head and rattled off, without stopping for breath, her voice almost squeaky with suppressed panic:

> 'I notice how the lonely boy
> Archie peeks, but he's very coy.

I wicked felt to make stealthy trips,
plant on his cheek my cherry lips
or with my nice reputed...'

Rita stopped for a deep breath and the last word shot out much
too loud:

'...BUST...'

More snorts, more laughter, Rita longed to look up but did
not dare. She looked at Miss Humphries. Surely that was enough?
Hadn't everyone got the gist of it? But Miss Humphries was
merciless.

'Quiet!' she boomed at the class and lashed the desk with her
ruler. 'Well? I'm waiting! Repeat that last line and continue!'

'...or with my nice reputed bust
nudge his head with a gentle thrust,
but before that derring-do I can,
I share with the girls my daring plan...'

A faint titter of anticipation rippled through the class. Someone
smothered a snicker. Rita faltered and looked up at Miss Humphries pleadingly.

'Please, Miss, I can't!' she squeaked.

'*Continue!*'

Rita read on, her voice now barely audible.

'Then as they watched I trepid went...'

She stopped. She couldn't help it, the laughter swelled within
her and if she spoke one more word she would burst.

'GO ON!' Miss Humphries boomed.

'...my bust I thrust, my cherry lips I vent...'

The last word went unheard. The entire room exploded. Girls were falling from their desks, rolling on the floor, hugging each other, shaking with resounding laughter. Rita had dropped the note and stood with her head bowed into her hands and quivering soundlessly from head to foot. Archie faced the blackboard and quivered with sobs or with laughter. The Chan brothers stared uncomprehendingly. Miss Humphries hammered on the desk for silence.

'DETENTION!' she finally cried. 'Three hours' detention for the whole class except Ronnie and Donny Chan. As for you, Miss Maraj, I will speak to the headmistress about you. And *you*, Mr Foot . . .' As if for emphasis Miss Humphries stamped her own foot at this last word, engendering a whole new cascade of laughter so that she never finished her sentence. The class ended in chaos.

By coincidence, Donna deSouza's fifteenth birthday party was that weekend. Archie had not been invited, but the grapevine rippled with stories of Archie's and Rita's budding love affair and everyone – except Rita – insisted that a last-minute invitation be extended to him.

He came.

The jukebox blared like at any other party and they all flung themselves about at the fast music, laughing just like always, and then somebody requested 'Stand By Me' and somebody else turned off the overhead light and without knowing how it had happened Rita was in Archie Foot's arms, dancing slowly, slowly, ever so slowly, almost not moving, and so embarrassed she thought she'd die, because she had been worse than all the other girls in the harassment of Archie Foot, and the poem, just the thought of it now, made her quiver with abashment. How would she ever live it down? Ever look him in the eye? But here he was, dancing with her. How had that happened? Had he asked her? Had someone pushed them together? She couldn't remember. And now, stealing a sideways upwards glance at him, she saw in the faint rainbow glow of the fairy-lights that he was tall and slim and ever so good-looking, with just a trace of soft dark fuzz along his upper lip. Why hadn't she seen those things before?

Archie hadn't said a word to her since the drama. In the classroom he had avoided her as much as she did him, and apart from the fact that he was holding her in his arms that was the situation for the rest of the evening. He simply danced with her till the party was over, not even letting go of her between songs; and she wanted it that way, she had no need of speech or looks. Because she knew she was in love. She dreamed as she danced, dreamed of her and Archie and being a couple and then getting married and living happily ever after, and she buried her nose in his shoulder and closed her eyes and smelled the faint scent of his cologne mingled with sweat, and knew at last what they were all about, those songs and books and films. And plays. This was the real thing! The grown-up thing. Not that stupid Matilda. Not her name in lights on Broadway. No, Love, with a capital L. Oh, she was made for Love. Born for Love. Love was the summit of all things human, the Treasure at the end of the rainbow. Nothing else would ever be boring, once she had Love. And Archie. And Archie would love her too . . . She dreamed away as they danced, picturing herself in Archie's arms for ever and a day, running barefoot with him along a Caribbean beach, he swinging her up into the rolling white surf, her arms around his neck, laughing, laughing, laughing; then stillness, his arms holding her close, outlined against a golden sunset . . . She dreamed on, a slight smile curling her lips, eyes closed the better to see.

She imagined a meaningful exchange at the end of the party, but to her chagrin Archie spoke not a word as he took his leave. He simply squeezed her hand and disappeared with the other guests streaming out of the gate, without even a by-your-leave. Immediately, Rita panicked. He hates me! she thought.

In the days following the party the Victoria Street youth rearranged themselves. Archie Foot had passed the initiation test. He was one of them. And anyway, he had a wonderful new ping-pong table under the house, and a group of discarded armchairs and a sofa around a scratched wooden table where you could sit and edge closer to each other and be hugely silly all afternoon. So the Foot residence became the new hangout.

Without Rita's approval. Rita simply refused to join the gang. She felt the ball was in his court; he must acknowledge her in some way, take the first step. Can't let him think I'm after him, she reasoned, and after all I'm sure he hates me. What if I turn up there and he ignores me, like he did at the party? Her heart pounded in panic at the very thought. If he hates me then I hate him too.

Had she made a false move at the party? She went through every step once more. Replayed all the songs in her mind, relived every tender feeling, but it only made things worse. *He should have said goodbye. He should have pecked me on the cheek. He should have phoned!* But he hadn't. Rita's world was crumbling . . .

TWENTY

Green Sponges

Dear Diary,

    Isabelle has been in therapy for six months and the doctor says he isn't making any headway. He says she must have had a traumatic experience in her early childhood. Of course he's always known about the accident – it was the first thing Marilyn told him – and he says, yes, but that's not it. So he wants her to go to another specialist who's a hypnotist.

    Marilyn threw a fit and said she's had enough of therapy, the poor child isn't a nut case, she's just under bad influence (me) and I'm the source of all her (Isabelle's) problems. She says she's had enough of therapy. Therapee, therapo, she said, they're all quacks. So no more psychiatrics for Isabelle. But she still has her tummy-aches and head-aches and tantrums.

    And as for Archie Foot – I've decided to renounce him, and all men, for ever. I'm going to be a hermit when I grow up.

'Little sisters. They're the pits,' said Polly and kicked a stone into the gutter.

'She's not doing any harm, though,' Rita maintained. 'She just wants to tag along.' She stretched out her hand to Isabelle, who had stopped outside Number Six to make a face at Carol Coolidge, who was sitting cross-legged on the gutter-bridge playing jacks with a girl from round the corner.

'She's a pest. Always has been. Always hanging on like a leech. She does it on purpose, you know. She knows it annoys us and she likes it. She's a pain in the ass. Why can't she make her own friends like any other kid on the block? That Carol Coolidge for instance, they're the same age, aren't they? But no, Madame Isabelle is much too high and mighty, she has to be with the teenagers. I ask you.'

'Archie won't mind.'

'Who says he won't mind? And even if he doesn't everybody else does. I don't know why you can't just tell her to buzz off. Nobody else has their little brothers and sisters hanging on their shirt tails, only you.'

'It's only for today. I promise. The thing is, she likes his brothers and wants to make friends with them and if she does then I'll have her off my back. For ever. You know she doesn't like playing with girls.'

'You're all besotted with those bloody Feet, every last one of you.'

Rita lurched towards Polly and covered her mouth with her hand. 'Shhh, not so loud, you idiot, he might *hear*! We're right outside his *house*!'

Polly laughed, pulling the hand away. 'Well, it's true, and don't glare at me like that. Hi!'

Polly turned off the road and onto the bridge outside Archie Foot's home. She waved and called to someone she must have glimpsed in the shadows under the house, and then that person emerged and Rita felt her knees turning to jelly and her heart started to race like crazy, because it was Archie. It had been Polly who had somehow sensed the drama building up in Victoria Street and correctly interpreted the break in communications between the two main actors, and wheedled a half-confession from Archie.

'He doesn't hate you, stupid! He *loves* you, he told me so – well almost, he just doesn't know how to face you and if you don't come I'm going to tie a rope round your feet and *drag* you there! You're such a moron. He's only a boy, for goodness' sake. Remember how you used to torment him? You weren't scared of him then; how come you suddenly got so shy? That's not like you at all. I don't know what's getting into you these days, all moody and moronic. It's that little pest of a sister . . . *Ow*! She kicked me, the little . . . !'

Isabelle scooted round to the other side of Rita, clinging to her legs and hiding her face. 'I didn't mean to,' she squeaked, 'I sort of tumbled!'

'You very well did mean to, don't think I—'

'Hi, how are you?'

He was just two feet away on the other side of the gate; she could smell him, she'd recognize his scent a mile away. Lifting the latch to open the gate, she didn't dare meet his eyes so she bent down to tie Isabelle's shoelaces so she wouldn't have to say hello. Anyway, he'd said hello to *Polly*, not to *her*; he'd deliberately ignored her, surely it must be Polly he loved? The two of them were chattering away now like old friends (well, since they'd had their little tête-à-tête they *were* old friends after all!) ignoring her! She should never have come, she just *knew* he hated her, he'd only danced with her to make Polly jealous because Polly was in love with Bobby Fung of Fung's Funeral Parlour, the mathematical genius in her class (a still unsettled love story. The only progress they had made till now was to ring up the Fung home, ask for Bobby, and in bursts of giggles order a coffin. They did this several times a week). All of a sudden Rita knew the whole bitter truth and felt like yelling out loud, like kicking herself; why had she come? Why had she let Polly drag her here just so her heart would break? Look, there were all the others, Donna and Dawn deSouza and Christine Knight and James (Cats) Isaacs, Brian Coolidge and Dennis Roy and even Archie's younger brothers Patrick and Robert, and nobody even cared about her. She felt like turning on her heel and running away but that would be too moronic for words. Heavens, only last week she'd been joshing and joking with the others and now she was just a

150

moron on the bridge tying Isabelle's laces in slow motion, and Isabelle was stamping in impatience, and finally running in to join the group under the house, and now she, Rita, had no choice but to stand up slowly and walk over and pretend she wasn't disintegrating inside, smiling and saying hi to everyone except to Archie, *never* to Archie, no, he had to say hi first, she would never descend to the level of a man-chasing floozy. She'd pretend she hated him just as much as he hated her, just look at the way he was talking to Polly, it was a disgrace, and right in front of Cats, who everyone knew had a crush on her! Well, she'd just show them! *But oh, how it aches inside!*

Rita spread a grin wide across her face and walked over to where Cats sat on the armrest of the old discarded sofa Archie had taken over for his friends, along with an odd selection of chairs with broken backrests and unsightly garden furniture. She plonked herself next to Cats, slapped his thigh, looked up at him with batting eyelashes, and asked him about his brother's motorbike which, occasionally, he was allowed to borrow. She need say no more; Cats was off coasting on a waterfall of words, and all Rita had to do was pretend to listen, nodding now and again, keeping her head tilted in such a way that she could see exactly what Polly and Archie were up to, and yet keeping it turned away towards Cats in an interested sort of way, nonchalant and cool as a cucumber, laughing out loud at all the right places so no one, no one at all, least of all those two traitors Polly and Archie, could ever suspect her heart was slowly breaking.

Isabelle ran over to join Patrick and Robert Foot, who were climbing up the latticework at the other side of the house. Having reached the top they carefully reached out for a rafter, caught hold of it, swung a few times to-and-fro, and jumped to the ground, only to swarm back up the latticework for another swing. Patrick was eight, Robert six, disdainful of girls and especially of Isabelle, who nevertheless craved their recognition and friendship. Seeming not to realize how privileged they were – the only children in Victoria Street Isabelle deigned to acknowledge – these two scathingly ignored her cries of 'I can do that too!'

Isabelle stood pouting, watching, longing to join in yet lacking the courage to do so unassisted. 'Let me come up too!' she cried, and stamped a little foot. Patrick and Robert pretended not to hear; they were counting the number of times they could swing before having to let go. Patrick managed seven, Robert only four. 'I can do that better than you!' Isabelle called at the top of her voice. 'I can swing *ten* times, I can too, I can too!' And she grabbed hold of the latticework and began to climb up.

'Oh, get lost, little brat,' said Patrick as he jumped to the ground. 'And don't you dare climb up there!'

'I can, I can, I'm going to show you!'

Isabelle was scrambling up with remarkable speed.

'Come *down*, you little idiot!'

'I'll get her!' called Robert, who was up at the top. He climbed down a little way and fought Isabelle's hands with his feet; whenever the girl tried to get hold of a lath, Robert kicked her fingers away. At the same time, Patrick pulled on her legs from below, but neither he nor his brother had reckoned with Isabelle's stubbornness and need to conquer. The more they fought her the more she struggled; her hands were quick, they clung to the wood with the tenacity and sheer power of a monkey to a branch, and kicked at Patrick with a viciousness he had not expected. She caught him in the eye with her heel; he cried out and briefly let go, then returned with a vengeance, this time swarming up the latticework himself and catching hold of her around the waist.

The teenagers across the way couldn't help but notice the commotion; and as Patrick and Isabelle fell to the ground, intertwined and squirming, Rita and Archie both dashed across to intervene.

'Isabelle, it serves you right, you should have left them alone!' Rita scolded, giving her bawling sister a hand and pulling her to her feet. She wasn't hurt; Patrick had broken her fall, and her cries were cries of rage and not of pain. Rita knew the difference, knew how to recognize the peeved screeching of wounded conceit, knew that if it wasn't quickly soothed it would burst all boundaries and the result would be a tantrum. She couldn't face a tantrum now. So when Isabelle flung her arms around her waist and buried her face in her belly and sobbed bitterly, Rita stroked her black curls and said, as gently genuine as she could make her voice, 'It's all right, dear, calm down, Patrick didn't mean to hurt you. Don't cry, darling, it's all right.'

Archie, meanwhile, was dealing with his brother. 'How could you pull that little girl down like that! The poor child could have hurt herself badly. What's the matter with you? And you too, Robert, if you want to fight why don't you pick on boys your own age!' He swung out and gave each boy a slap across the face.

Patrick shouted back at him, 'She's just a little pesky brat, always hanging around here an' trying to barge in! What's she doing here at all? She should find friends her own age. Why do we have to play with a baby like that? Who invited her to come here? We don't play with girls and we don't play with babies!'

Robert yelled, 'She's always hanging around at the gate peeping in and we hate her and we weren't fighting her, but she can't climb up with us, girls can't do that and she tried to climb up and it's dangerous for girls!'

At those words Isabelle yelled: 'I can, I can too, I can climb up there and swing, I've done it a hundred million billion times and I hate you I hate you I hate you! I want to go home, Rita, take me home, I hate those boys and I'm never coming back here, I hate all of you, nasty mean bloody Feet, and my mummy says your mother is an old bag, she's all fat and ugly and her bum wobbles when she walks and her bosom looks as if she filled it with two buckets of jello, so there!'

Rita gasped aloud, and before she could stop herself looked up at Archie. She met his eyes, saw her own mortification reflected there in the second before they both looked away. Rita knew she couldn't possibly let that pass; she leaned over and landed Isabelle a hot slap on her cheek. Isabelle wailed. She threw herself onto the concrete ground and yelled for all she was worth, squirming with rage, kicking and squirming so that her dress twisted up around her waist.

For a moment Rita stood staring at her hand. She'd never

done that before, never slapped Isabelle, though she'd often been tempted. The old familiar guilt swept through her but there was no time to deal with guilt right now for Isabelle was ranting.

At times like this Rita knew, she simply knew, that Isabelle suffered from severe brain damage; and it was all her fault. But at the same time it had to be dealt with.

Rita bent over and picked her sister up. She knew exactly how and where to hold the squirming, squealing Isabelle. She'd be black and blue from the kicks by the time she got home, there'd be a few scratches on arms and face, but enough was enough. She couldn't afford to have Isabelle throw a tantrum here, on the Foot property.

'Come,' she said firmly, 'let's go home.'

'I don't want to go home, I want to climb, I want to stay *here*!'

'You can't, we're going home.' Arms tightly around the struggling child, Rita turned towards the gate.

'I hate you I hate you I hate you and you're an old bag too, and I saw you stuffing your bra full of green sponges, I did, I did, and I'll show everyone, and . . .'

Before Rita could stop her Isabelle had torn open her blouse and pulled the green sponges out of her bra. There they lay, scattered on the concrete for everyone to see. Green sponges. Some of them painstakingly cut to fit the contours of the bra she had so carefully chosen with Polly at Fogarty's lingerie department just a week ago, her very first bra, giving her the bust she was so proud of, the very bust which had inspired her poem to Archie Foot. And now the green sponge filling lay as an offering at Archie's feet.

Rita didn't wait to hear them all laugh. She let go of Isabelle's waist, grabbed her by the wrist, and dragged her towards the gate. She opened the gate and hauled Isabelle out into the street. Isabelle screamed and pulled and twisted but Rita's grasp was like iron. Rita lugged her all the way home, and only when they were safely inside the gate of Number Seven, safely out of hearing and out of sight of Archie, Polly, Cats and everyone else; only then did Rita turn on her sister.

'How dare you, how dare you!' Her voice was icy cold, the words pressed out between teeth gritted together in the effort not to explode. A primitive rage screamed inside her. She balled her fists, fighting the urge to pummel the child from top to bottom.

'You're a wicked, wicked little devil!' She growled the words in a low, slow voice, dangerously toneless, for she could not trust what would come out if she once let go. 'I'll never take you anywhere again! That's the last time, the very last time. You're a devil, devil, devil and you've ruined my whole life!'

A wild desperation came into her eyes. She looked around her as if for a weapon, a stick, a cricket bat, a twig, anything. Finding nothing, she raised her right hand, her left one still holding the petrified child as in a vice, fingers digging into her skinny upper arm. The right hand hovered above Isabelle's head, gathering force and momentum for a swift and painful descent, for the second blow of the day.

Isabelle, who till now had been frozen stiff by the chill of Rita's voice and the unaccustomed finality of her words, looked up at the hand hovering above her, opened her mouth and let out a piercing scream, the scream of a torture victim before the final onslaught, squirming to free herself from Rita's grasp.

Marilyn came clattering down the front stairs. 'Isabelle, Isabelle, what happened? Oh my baby, my poor baby, did she hit you? Did that bad girl hit you? Come to Mummy, darling, come, oh baby darling, don't cry. Mummy's darling girl. Heavens, look at your face, what did she do to you? That's a bad bad girl, remember how she almost killed you? Come to Mummy . . .'

Rita stood watching. She had let go of Isabelle the moment Marilyn appeared, and the passion that had filled her a moment ago with the urge to strike, to hurt, to maim, left her as quickly as it had risen. She simply stood and stared as Isabelle ran to her mother and buried her face in her skirt, blubbering indistinguishable words between the desperate sobs. Marilyn crouched down to enfold the girl in her arms, stroking the curly-mopped head and the heaving back. She raised her head for a moment to throw

Rita a stare in which threat, accusation, antipathy and triumph mingled and fought for ascendancy.

Rita bowed her head and walked away. The primitive rage had evaporated. All that remained was guilt, and the shreds of a broken promise.

That evening when Rita went to bed she found it already occupied.

'Isabelle!'

Isabelle looked up at her, huge sleepy eyes blinking. 'Can I sleep here with you?'

'Why don't you go to your mother?'

'Don't like Mummy, she's mean. Rita!'

Rita had turned away to undress, and didn't answer. She was still burning inside with shame and anger; now she'd never in her whole life be able to face Archie again, nor any of her friends. Her whole life was ruined.

'Rita!' Isabelle's voice was soft and coaxing. Grudgingly, Rita turned around to look at the little girl, who had drawn the sheet up beneath her chin. She hugged a tattered teddy bear. Her features were soft and languid with sleepiness, and her smile was innocent and apologetic and heartbreakingly sweet. When Rita looked at her she stretched up her little arms, and wiggled her fingers in impatience.

'Rita, I'm sorry, I'm so sorry I behaved badly and I pulled out your green sponges. Please, please don't be vex with me. I can't bear it when you get vex with me, Rita, I love you so much. Please let's be friends again. It hurts so bad when you don't like me and you didn't give me a goodnight kiss and I couldn't sleep and I can't never sleep again if you don't give me a kiss.'

Rita looked sternly down at the little girl, unsmiling, ignoring the wiggling fingers and the outstretched arms.

'What you did was just terrible.'

'I know, Rita, and I'm so sorry and if you like I'll go over there tomorrow an' 'pologize. Promise. An' I'm goin' to be good for ever and ever after, I promise, Rita, please don't hate me!'

'I don't hate you.'

'But you vex with me! Oh Rita, please don't be vex with me any more, otherwise I goin' to cry!'

And sure enough, the big black eyes moistened, looking like glimmering pools above the smooth honey-golden cheeks. The child gazed up at Rita with such abject misery she couldn't bear to look into them. So she turned away and busied herself with the bookshelf.

'I don't care if you cry, just don't do it here. Go back to your room and cry there or go to your mummy and cry on her lap.'

Her back still turned, she took her time selecting a book. Isabelle did not speak again, so Rita walked over to the window, a book in her hand, and drew the curtains. She glanced at the bed. Isabelle had drawn the sheet up over her head. The tiny white hump quivered. Rita strode over to the bed and whipped the sheet away.

'Come on now, none of that. Get out, go over to your own room.'

Isabelle lay on her stomach, her face buried in Rita's pillow. Her back heaved with repressed sobs, which at Rita's callous words now burst their boundaries and escaped in a blustering, blubbering fountain.

Rita sat on the edge of the bed. Tentatively, she stretched out a hand and placed it on the mop of silky curls.

'OK, Isabelle, that's enough. Now calm down and go back to bed.' She tried to keep her voice dispassionate. The sobs increased.

'Isabelle, that's enough! Come on, I want to go to bed and you're tired too. Stop that bawling and go to bed!'

But Isabelle could not hear above the din of her own sobs, and besides, Rita's words were unconvincing even to herself, and it was her fingers, now gently massaging the back of Isabelle's head, which told the truth, and to which Isabelle now responded. In one hefty motion she flung herself from her prone and helpless position across the bed and into Rita's lap, her arms flailing out and locking behind Rita's neck. The sobs, loud up to now but nevertheless muffled by the pillow, were a clamouring barrage of snivelling howls.

Isabelle was the best apologizer in the world. She could break a sister's heart with contrition. But there had never been a tiff as bad as this. This was serious; Rita's whole life lay in splinters under Archie Foot's house. Green sponges! The more she tried not to think of them the more they loomed into her consciousness. Even now her cheeks burned at the memory; and yet Isabelle's sobbing was irresistible.

Involuntarily, Rita's arms closed around the little girl's body, giving reluctant comfort even as her inner voice argued with a better knowledge.

She's only a child. Only a baby. She doesn't know any better. She doesn't understand, can't understand. She didn't do it on purpose. She didn't mean to embarrass you in front of Archie, she doesn't even know you love him. She's your baby, she loves you, she needs you. She can't help it if she has problems, after all she's been through. You have to forgive her. Poor thing. Poor little baby, who does she have but you? You've got to love her even when she does those bad things, because you caused her to be that way. She needs you. Look at the way she's crying, poor little thing. If you don't love her, who else will? Come on, don't be heartless.

And so Rita's arms grew tighter and her hands spoke in gentle caresses to the little girl, and she fell back on to the bed and drew the sheet up over both of them, and Isabelle sobbed herself to sleep in Rita's arms without another word spoken.

Isabelle kept her promise. The next day she went to Archie's house, all by herself, and apologized sweetly to him, charming him with her big black eyes and a bunch of white roses stolen from Marilyn's favourite bush.

And then it was Rita's turn. For a whole week, Isabelle spoiled her. Every day when Rita returned from school there was a bunch of flowers in a jar on her desk. There were cute little paintings on the pillow. Isabelle danced attendance on her; she brought Rita glasses of juice, squares of fudge (stolen from the biscuit tin). She peeled tangerines and split them into segments, laid them out prettily on a plate which she presented to Rita with smiles and curtseys. She polished Rita's bicycle until it glowed. She sat Rita down on a chair and danced for her to the favourite tape, twirling and swirling and leaping on her toes so that Rita couldn't help but smile.

Rita wouldn't so much as glance at Archie. She walked past his house with her head turned away. In the classroom she changed desks so that she was at the other side of the classroom. Whenever she saw Archie coming she turned and walked in the other direction. She vowed never to look at him or speak a word to him in her whole life. She contemplated running away from Victoria Street.

Then it was Archie's turn. Out of the blue he rang Rita and asked her to see a rerun of *My Fair Lady*, now on at the Metropole. Rita said yes. Archie picked her up punctually at three and side by side in embarrassed silence they rode their bicycles into town. They still hadn't spoken when they took their seats in the cool dark balcony. Rita was so busy thinking about green sponges she couldn't follow the film; she still had not so much as glanced at Archie.

In the middle of the film Archie reached over, grabbed Rita's hand, and held it for the rest of the film. Rita felt his hand around hers, stared at the cinema screen, and saw only bosoms filled with green sponges.

Her own bosom was as flat as it was before the green sponge episode. She hoped it would always stay that way. She loved Archie. She hated him. She would never, ever live this down. Green sponges would haunt her all her life.

When Archie brought her safely home again he gave her a quick peck on the cheek and said, 'Thanks, er, it was lovely.'

'Yes, thanks, er, it was very nice.'

'You really enjoyed it?'

'Um, er, yes, thanks a lot.'

'Um, would you, I mean, I thought . . . well, if you like we could – um – ride to school together?'

Rita nodded, without looking at him, of course. On Monday morning he was waiting for her. They spoke in monosyllables, then in three-word sentences. Finally they were a couple.

Then the term was over and Archie's parents sent him to England, to boarding school. Archie left as suddenly as he had appeared. Rita was devastated for exactly three days. And then she fell in love with an Older Man.

TWENTY-ONE

An Older Man

The Older Man was an American. Three Americans had moved into Number Six when the Isaacs moved out the previous month, next door to Rita, and opposite Polly. But would an Older Man ever notice fifteen-year-old Rita? He was at least twenty-five, which made him, on the attainability scale, the equivalent of Mount Everest.

The Americans were single, and, as all the Victoria Street girls squealed, absolutely *evil*. Eee-*vil*, they giggled to each other. Oh Lord, the absolute height in evility! And American! Imagine what marrying one of those would do to your future! They were computer consultants, the grapevine said, and they were helping to bring Guyana into the Electronic Age. They would be here for half a year.

Rita liked the dark one best and that was the one she fell in love with. Polly preferred the redhead, while Donna deSouza was desperate for the blond. But life was difficult when you're only fifteen and in love with Older Men. You had to use your wiles.

So when Polly's parents were out they gathered behind lowered shades with a splendid view of the house across the road, which had a gallery fronted by an unbroken row of curtainless windows, all of which stood open, so you could see clear across the gallery and the living room and into the inner recesses of the house, and you could see exactly what the men were doing at all times. Right now they were eating supper, but the telephone rang and one of them – Polly's redhead – got up to answer it.

Across the road at Number Five there was a minor scuffle as Polly and Rita fought for the telephone receiver, but luckily Rita's hand, wet with the sweat of excitement, was firmly clasped over the mouthpiece so the redhead couldn't hear the squeals and giggles. Rita won the fight and turned away from Donna and Polly the better to keep her face – and even more important, her vocal cords – frozen into seriousness.

'Hello? Who is this speaking?' she said, her voice soft and sultry.

'This is Tom, who's that?' said the voice at the other end.

'Oh, *Tom* . . . Well, Tom, I must tell you that a friend of mine is quite smitten by you. And she's wondering . . . aaam . . . Well, as a matter of fact, I'm a great admirer of yours too, you know . . . Where we saw you? Oh, we saw you at the bank the other day, we both work at the bank you know . . . We saw you fellows there and . . .'

Rita felt a poke in her ribs and made an impatient gesture with her free hand, not looking. Another poke, and then Polly's face appeared before her, mouthing excited words and pointing behind her back. Rita turned and peered through the laths of the venetian blinds. The other two men had left the table and now all three were gathered around the telephone – just like the three of them.

Rita cleared her throat and put on her most expensive voice.

'Ahem . . . well, Tom, we saw all three of you fellows and we think you're just our types. Only thing is, we don't know which of you is which. Or rather, who is who. So tell me now: who is that tall dark handsome one? . . . Oh, *Russell*. Now listen, Russell is the one *I* like best. Could you give me Russell, please? . . . Hi, is that Russell? May I call you Russ? My name is . . . is . . . Julia. I saw you the other day at the Chase Manhattan Bank and I was really admiring you. I'm sure you saw me. You couldn't have missed me. I'm tall and dark and very beautiful, if I do say so myself. My lips are like wild cherries. Everybody says so. Even now they twitch to touch yours . . . Hey, what are you laughing about? This is *serious*. Now, listen, Russ, you have a nice blond friend there, don't you? . . . Bill, is it? Of course we know about him. We know all about you guys. We have our spies. Anyway, my friend, who is an evil busty Indian lady, is just dying to talk to him. Here she is, so let her talk to Bill, all right? Bye, Russ, see you soon . . .'

Donna grabbed the receiver from Rita but instead of talking she pressed the mouthpiece to her breast and, bent over double, exploded in helpless giggles. Polly, too, seemed incapable of speaking a serious word. So Rita took back the receiver.

'Sorry about that, Russ . . . Oh, sorry, Bill. Well, Bill, my friend Genevieve really adores you but she can't speak right now, she's too full of emotion. Anyway, we're three really lovely lonely girls and we're dying to meet you fellows soon. How about it? . . . Where? Well, let me think a moment, where would be a good place. Let me ask my friends.'

Polly was again desperately mouthing some message. Rita looked at her, understood, and spoke into the receiver: 'Listen, Bill, what about the Atlanta Hotel? It's great there. We'll meet at the bar, OK? Saturday afternoon? Four o'clock? Oh, wonderful. Fantastic. I'm really looking forward to it. Don't forget our names: ask for Julia, Genevieve, and . . . and . . . Carmen. See you then. Saturday. Give my love to the boys. Bye!' Rita made some final kissing sounds and replaced the receiver.

'On second thoughts,' said Rita, wiping the palms of her hands down her blouse to dry the sweat, 'I don't think the Atlanta Hotel was a good idea. It would have been nice to send one of us to watch the fun, but who wants to go to the Atlanta on Saturday? Not me!'

The Atlanta Hotel, on the East Coast a mile outside of Georgetown, was the country's most notorious brothel.

*   *   *

163

It was Isabelle who finally brought Rita and Russell together. Isabelle, riding her bicycle up and down Victoria Street, swerved when a cat ran across the road and fell, hurting her knee. She dropped her little bike and ran screaming into the house, where the knee was tended by rather too many concerned adults. Isabelle recovered quickly from the shock and the pain and disappeared into her room to listen to a cassette on her Stereo, forgetting the bike.

Rita was on the phone with Polly – though they lived next door it was much more agreeable to spend hours chatting on the phone than actually seeing each other – when the doorbell rang. She hung up and went to open it and nearly dropped dead when she stood facing a sheep-faced Russell.

Shocked speechless, she could only stare, but Russell was too apologetic to notice her confusion.

'Look, I'm real sorry but – well, look what I've done!' he said, and held up a twisted knot of metal. Rita recognized Isabelle's bike and pulled herself together. Russell had not come to confront her, had not come to force her into admitting that she was the mysterious Julia who had been calling him up with seductive messages every single day for the past week. Who had apologized profusely for the misunderstanding concerning the Atlanta Hotel ('The moment we saw it was *that* kind of a hotel we of course went straight home – we aren't *that* type of girl') and since then had been entertaining him every afternoon with anecdotes and jokes and invariably reducing him to tears of laughter. Depending on the circumstances – no adults around – she called sometimes from her own home, sometimes from Polly's, where she could peer through the blinds and watch his reactions. She knew she had the power to make him laugh – but she knew that meeting him would be the end of it. And now, here he was, face to face with her on her doorstep.

She gulped and tried to pay attention to what he was saying.

'. . . I didn't look, you see. It was lying on the road behind my car and I just got in and reversed into the road and the next thing I knew there was this crunching sound and . . . it was this thing.

I've seen that kid, she's your sister, isn't she? . . . I thought so. Couldn't be quite sure, so many kids on this road . . . Anyway, of course I'll buy her a new one, no question. You got to be careful on a road like this with so many kids, always look behind you, lucky there wasn't a kid *sitting* on it at the time . . .'

'It's all right,' Rita's voice emerged as a squeak in the attempt to disguise it. And then Isabelle came prancing down the stairs and saw the bike and promptly burst into tears.

'It's all right, it's OK, sweetie, I'll buy you another, I'm sorry, look, you'll get a real nice bike, OK?'

'*When?*'

Russell's eyes met Rita's above Isabelle's curly mop.

'Well, how about . . . now?'

Before she knew it they were heading into town. Isabelle bouncing about in the back. Rita in the passenger seat next to Russell, not daring to say a word *just in case* he recognized the voice. She needn't have bothered.

'Rita knows another boy called Russell,' Isabelle piped up.

'Is that true?' said Russell, and turned to grin at Rita. 'It's not such a common name over here, is it?'

'He's her boyfriend. She's in love with him and she draws hearts all over her exercise book and writes his name and hers in it. And sometimes she talks to him on the phone and puts on this stupid drooly voice. "Russell, dahlin' . . . Oooh, Russ, sweetheart." I heard her myself.'

Rita wasn't sure which magical power she would rather have: the power to shoot Isabelle off to the moon never to return, or the power to evaporate and never return herself. *Both* would be better.

All the way to Persaud's Bicycles she kept her burning face turned towards the window, her body slouched back into the seat as if willing itself to melt into the upholstery. Russell did not speak for five minutes but she felt his glance scorching through the back of her head. She felt his anger – in a minute he'd stop the car and throw her and Isabelle out head first and then she'd *really* kill Isabelle.

So when she heard the first chuckle she didn't quite trust her ears. The second chuckle was louder and longer, more in the nature of a small explosion, and she glanced suspiciously out of the corner of her eyes, but all she could see was Russell's profile with a wide grin spread all over it. And then, suddenly, Russell swerved to the roadside, stopped the car, slumped forward over the steering wheel, and collapsed in an avalanche of helpless, uncontrolled laughter. Rita, still paralysed by embarrassment, considered opening the passenger door and making good her escape. But then Russell stretched out one long bronzed arm, turned to her with a lobster-red, tear-streaked face, twisted her around to face him, and held her in his arms, burying his face in her shoulder till at last she, too, collapsed with mirth and let the laughter peal out.

'What are you laughing *about*?' cried Isabelle, bouncing furiously in the back seat. 'What's the *joke*! Tell me! And what about my *bike*! I want my new *bike*! Stop laughing I tell you and go and get my *bike*!'

But for once nobody obeyed her.

TWENTY-TWO

Outrageous Things

Dear Diary,

I wish I was five years older and looked like — well, I don't know what kind of woman he likes but I just wish I didn't look like *me*. I just hate being me. My legs are too long and straight and that stupid gap between my front teeth and my mouth is too big. I want to be graceful and elegant and have a soft purring voice. And wear slinky black dresses and high heels. And be all curvy and slithery and bat my eyelashes and wiggle my bum because that's what grown-up men like Russ like. I can't imagine why but that's what everyone knows — after all, it's the way Marilyn is and she got my daddy, didn't she?

It's all right having him for a friend but he treats me just like a little sister and that's even worse than nothing. Like when I first went over there and he introduced me to the others, 'This is my little sister Rita.' Vomit vomit. They all treat me like I was five years old.

And sometimes I just blurt things out and they all start laughing. They think I'm some kind of a clown, there for their entertainment, and that's just the way I feel. Why can't I keep my big mouth shut?

If only he could see me the way I really am. All the love in my heart. But the moment I'm in his company I start that stupid act again and he thinks I'm so funny . . . At least he notices me but not the way I want him to. If he could see what I am inside ... But he wouldn't love me then. He wouldn't notice me because I'd be so shy and tongue-tied and just look at him with mooning eyes. I bet he'd run five miles if he knew.

I love him I love him I love him. I adore him. If I was just two years older it would make all the difference. Why can't I just jump over sixteen? Seventeen-year-olds know all about catching older men.

Dear Diary,

But he does know some good jokes. He likes to tell 'movie jokes' about things you didn't know if you didn't go to the movies. For instance:

All foreigners such as Yanomamo Indians, Nazi sadists, and Russian spies speak perfect English.

All bombs are fitted with electronic timing devices with large red readouts so you can know exactly when they're going to go off.

It doesn't matter when you get to a ticking bomb, because even if you have never defused one before you will automatically know what to do and you will always succeed just one second before it is timed to explode.

Guns are like disposable razors – if you run out of bullets, just throw the gun away. You can always buy a new one.

When you turn on a TV it comes on at the start of the news story you need to hear, not at the end or during a commercial.

I told him I'm sure I can think up some new ones and he said to write them down when I do, 'cause he collects them.

Dear Diary,

Isabelle has started ballet lessons and really loves it. Her ballet teacher says she's a natural. And now all she does is put on that silly little skirt and twirl around the place. She even came over to Russ's when I was there and started showing off, spinning on her toes and kicking up her legs and even flirting with him. I tell you. At five years old!

And he even noticed her and was impressed by her. 'She's going to be a real looker, that little sister of yours,' he said to me. 'She'll have the guys beating a path to your door in a few years.' Vomit vomit.

Dear Diary,

I just discovered that his bedroom is next to the mango tree. I climbed the tree and looked in. He doesn't have any curtains at the window and I saw him without his shirt on. He had his back to me, standing at the mirror, but once he turned around and walked over to get something and I saw he has a hairy chest. He was shaving and I watched him for a long time and then I climbed back down again. If he knew I could climb trees he'd be even less impressed. Big women don't climb trees. Gosh, I wish I was a big woman at last and didn't climb trees and stuff like that.

Dear Diary,

I wish I was dead.

They had a party last night and hundreds of all sorts of people turned up. I didn't even know they knew so many people, in the short time they've been here. And *women*! Grown-up women! How do they know so many women? Russ told me about it and he didn't even dream I would want to come — he didn't even apologize for not inviting me. What could I expect anyway? I'm just a child to him.

And they were loud and drinking rum. I hid in the garden and watched for a long time but I didn't see Russ even once. I was beginning to think he wasn't there, maybe he doesn't like parties, maybe he refused to come because he actually prefers *me* secretly, but I was mistaken BAD.

Because I saw a light go on in his room so I climbed up the tree and he was there with this woman. And I saw the most disgusting thing in the world. The most sickening, revolting, nauseating, repellent, off-putting, unpalatable, foul, nasty, obnoxious, vulgar, shameless, shocking, gross, vile, and utterly outrageous thing in the whole world. Vomit vomit vomit. Don't expect me to go into the details, dear Diary, because I won't; even *thinking* of it makes me vomit and I won't sully your precious pages with such filth. It was obvious what kind of woman that was. I would never have thought it of him. Then they turned out the light so I climbed back down the tree and went to bed.

One thing's for certain, I'm never going to love again and I'm never going to marry. I've made up my mind on that and that's settled.

Men don't like me anyway. I'm too quirky. I think it's probably a good thing.

Dear Diary,

I managed not to see him for a whole week. He might think it odd I don't come round any more but I don't give a fart. Serve him right. He'll just have to do without my delectable company for a while.

Dear Diary,

Aunty Doreen's in town. My mother's sister, in case you've forgotten. I only ever saw her twice in my life, at least in the life I can remember, but I knew her when I was small (of course). She lives in the back of beyond in a place called Charity on the Pomeroon River. She's nice. She used to look after me when I was little but I don't remember. Daddy had to go to court to get me away from her and my grandparents (my mother's parents) and probably he should have left me with her. She says I should come up and visit them: her and her husband and their children and my grandparents. I've never even seen my grandparents! At least not in a way I can remember. I used to live with them long ago before Daddy brought me to Victoria Street (I think I told you this before long ago but maybe you forgot so you won't mind me telling you again) but I can't remember a thing about them because I never saw them again and it was so long ago. They live so far away and it just never happened because I never went back there and they never come to town. Now Aunty Doreen is here because of some trouble with her heart and had to see a specialist and she wants me to go back up with her. For the Easter Holidays. I think I'll go.

First: if I'm not so nearby maybe Russ will realize how much he misses me.

Second: if I go maybe I can get my mind off Russ.

Third: I'm really curious about my mother's family. I lived all my life without grandparents and it's about time I got in touch.

TWENTY-THREE

Car-chase Jokes

'You can't just go with your two long empty hands,' said Marilyn. 'So you better take this with you.'

Rita looked sceptically at the box on the kitchen table. She had seen it before. It was the electric mixer Marilyn had been sent two Christmasses ago from her aunt in the USA. Marilyn had sucked her teeth at the time and said: 'What's she thinking of? She thinks we're so backward here, or what? She don't know I got one of these things already? I tell you, she's just showing off because she lives in America. Anyway, I suppose I could pass it on – save me having to buy somebody a present.'

She had passed it on to a cousin, who had promptly returned it. 'It don't work,' the cousin said. 'You better take it back to the shop and get it repaired. You must have a guarantee?'

But Marilyn didn't have a guarantee and so the box had sat there on top of a kitchen cupboard for two years.

'It doesn't work, I thought,' said Rita now.

'Yes, but it's the *thought* that counts,' said Marilyn. 'You can't go with your two long empty hands, you got to bring something from Town. Something they wouldn't have up there. I thought a nice modern electric gadget would be perfect; you can't get those up there. At least it's new. When they find out it doesn't work you can apologize and offer to have it fixed. But they'll say don't trouble yourself, it's the thought that counts. You think they'll bother to send it down to Town and back? When they hardly ever come to Town anyway?'

'Why don't we just buy something *new*? Something that works?'

'You think we made of money, or what? What you're complaining about? They'll be *glad* to have a thing like this up there! I bet they're the only people to have one! I bet they never even see one of these before, up there in the bush! Look, here's a bag, let's see if it fits inside – yes, perfect.'

'But . . .'

'But but but. Child, you made up of buts. Every other word you say is but. If you go through life like that you going to turn into a goat!'

Marilyn zippered up the bag and lifted it up by the handles, testing its weight.

'And it's not too heavy. You haven't got too much luggage anyway so you can easily carry it. And don't forget—'

'Mummy, let me go with Rita. Please let me go!'

'No, darling, of course you can't go. Rita is going to see her granny and granpa and you wouldn't be happy there.'

'But I don't want Rita to go! I want her to stay with *me*! Who's going to tell me stories at night!'

'I will, darling, I'm your mummy, after all!'

'But you can't make up nice stories like Rita can, all you can do is read those boring ones from a book! I want to go with Rita! Rita, please let me go! Please please please!'

Isabelle flung herself at Rita and clung to her, looking up with eyes brimming with unshed tears, eyes in whose depths a dangerous gleam hovered in anticipation of refusal. Rita recognized that gleam. A tantrum was brewing. And the last thing she wanted to deal with on the eve of her journey was a tantrum.

'Darling, I'd love to take you but think of your ballet classes.

173

You'd miss three whole weeks of ballet. You wouldn't like that, would you?'

Isabelle stopped sobbing for a moment and frowned; Rita could clearly see the little mind working behind the ruffled brow, thrusting out for a new ploy. 'Let me come' was thwarted – wild horses couldn't keep Isabelle from her ballet – but 'you stay with me' would certainly come next.

'I've got a fantastic new story for you,' said Rita quickly. 'It's just waiting to jump out at you. You'd better run upstairs quickly and hop into bed before I lose it!'

Isabelle's face lit up with a broad beam, slyness evaporated, and all she was was a child filled with delight. 'A *scary* story?'

'So scary all your hair will drop out and your skin will turn green and your teeth will start to quiver!'

'IIIEEEEEEE!' yelled Isabelle and scampered off. Rita breathed again.

The house was fast asleep when Aunty Doreen came to collect Rita in a taxi early next morning, so all further debate with Isabelle was averted. Her packed bag was waiting for her by the front door, and next to it Marilyn had placed the black plastic bag containing the box with the mixer. Rita considered simply leaving it there. Why should she insult her grandparents by bringing them a broken, if brand-new, mixer? But then she shrugged, picked it up, and slipped out the front door. She'd hand it over dutifully and then explain it was broken, apologize for the insult, and let that be an example of how despicable Marilyn was.

Rita had met Aunty Doreen several times in the past week and in that time had grown to love both her and the grandparents she could no longer remember. In fact, Doreen was more like a big sister than an aunt and Rita could do with a big sister right now. And if she was a big sister then Granny and Granpa were parents, and Rita could do with a new set of parents too.

It was to be a long trip. The taxi took them to the Stabroek Market where they squeezed themselves into a packed minibus, their luggage shoved between the rows of seats so that there was no room for their feet. They sat perched with their feet on top of their bags. Aunty Doreen said it was always this way. 'We gon't be lucky to get to Charity alive,' she warned.

The bus was driven by a large black man with a multicoloured cap of knitted synthetic yarn, pulled down over an enormous pile of dreadlocked hair. Reggae blared from the loudspeakers, deafening music that condemned the passengers, a more or less equal mixture of Indian and African men and women, to silence for the entire journey.

The minibus raced off, swerved through Georgetown's early morning traffic as if hell-bent, and through the outskirts of Town up the Demerara River. The swaying pontoon bridge over the river forced the driver into a more sedate pace; but once across the river he sped off again at an even more breakneck speed. Rita smiled to herself. Like in a movie car-chase, she thought, which reminded her of Russell's movie jokes and her promise to make up new ones. She was still angry at Russell but . . . she had to do something with her mind over the next few hours. She took out her notebook, a pencil, nibbled on its end a few moments, and began to write.

Everybody will be involved in a wild car-chase at least once in his/her life.

She chewed some more on the end of her pencil, gazed out of the window, watched the action for a while, and continued.

If during a car-chase you see somebody crossing the street just plough straight into them, because they can do perfect back-flips and will land on the pavement unscathed.

Most cars are already running when you get in. If you must start the car it will most likely either fail to ignite or explode.

If you are being pursued in a car-chase, at some point you will fly off a bridge and land on all four wheels. You will never ever have an accident.

If your pursuer tries to shoot you during a car-chase just relax – the bullet will certainly hit the car behind you causing an enormous pile-up so you can escape easily.

By the time they reached Parika hours later in a cloud of dust and a screech of brakes Rita was out of love with Russell. He was, after all, a brother; someone to share movie jokes and clown around with. She had a long list of self-made jokes in her note-book and couldn't wait to share them with him. She had chuckled to herself all the way here and laughter, it seemed, was really the best medicine. The pain in her heart had, miraculously, healed. She didn't want to be Russell's, or anyone's, woman – yet. She wanted to be a child again, with a big sister and a mother and father. This was going to be her chance.

She arrived at Parika more or less in one piece, even if that piece was stiff and aching. She looked around in a daze; it seemed to her that some kind of a riot or maybe a revolution was going on but Aunty Doreen seemed calm enough about it. 'Come, dear,' she said simply, picked up her own bag and one of Rita's – the black plastic one with the mixer – and ploughed into the chaos. Rita gripped her bag, slung the strap around her shoulder, and followed. Aunty Doreen led her to a wharf jutting out onto the Essequibo River.

At the wharf there were several long boats waiting for passengers. The boatmen and their agents on the wharf were furiously screaming at each other, a few of them seemed about to lunge at each other's necks. The moment they saw Aunty Doreen they called to her: 'Come here, lady, room for two, room for two. Just get it. Come, come, sit here. I got room for you. Just come, come on . . .' and surrounded her like yelping dogs. One tried to grab her bags away, but she swung her handbag at him and then at them all, clearing a space for her and Rita . . .

Aunty Doreen screwed her face into a disdainful sneer and cast her eyes contemptuously over the boats and their drivers. 'Where's Errol? I want to go with Errol.'

'Errol not here, madam, he over in Supenaam.'

'Then Harold . . . I'll go with Harold.'

'Harold not here either,' said one of the loudest men, a giant in red shorts. 'Come with me, I nearly full, just need two people and then we're off.'

His boat was indeed almost full. There were at least twenty passengers sitting quietly side by side on the rows of seats, bright orange life-jackets covering their upper bodies, their features fixed into expressions of stoic indifference.

'Well, we not going with you for sure. You full up already. You lucky if you don't sink with that load of passengers. Hey, you – YOU!'

She pointed to a thin Indian man in the next boat, whose back was turned. Hearing her shouts he looked over his shoulder and then came towards her, grinning broadly. 'Yes, ma'am, you want go Supenaam?'

'Yes. Two ah we. Here, take this bag. And let the girl go in first. Come, darlin', step in carefully. Give she a hand – there. Good.'

Aunty Doreen got in after Rita and handed her a life-jacket. This boat was almost empty, but filling up quickly. Only minutes later they were on the river, the boat's bow pointed to the tree-lined horizon on the far bank, the scrawny boatman at the helm tending to the motor. The boat gathered speed; its bow rose high above the water's surface. Soon it seemed as if they were out at sea; to their right, in fact, the brown Atlantic spread out into the neverending East, while straight ahead the line of trees at the horizon seemed as distant as ever. The water beneath them swelled and sank, sometimes rising to meet the boat's bow, sometimes falling away in a trough, the bow falling into it with a sickening thud.

'You not frightened, chile?' asked Aunty Doreen as Rita took her hand.

'I didn't know the Essequibo was so *big*,' Rita admitted. She pointed to the land visible in the distance. 'It looks so far – how long will it take?'

'Oh, those are only islands,' said Aunty Doreen smugly. 'In the middle of the river. Supenaam is about three hours in a speedboat from Parika. The Essequibo is twenty-one miles across here at the mouth. That island there – it's bigger than Barbados. But don't worry, chile, it's perfectly safe. They hardly ever have accidents, only when there's a storm. And anyway, you got your life-jacket. You can swim?'

Rita nodded, blanching.

At Supenaam a crowd of taxi-drivers fought over the disembarking passengers. Aunty Doreen ignored them all, beating them away impatiently as if they were flies. She walked over to one of the waiting cars, plunked the black plastic bag on the back seat, and gestured for Rita to get in. The driver pushed his head in through the open door. His round face gleamed with sweat like polished mahogany.

'To Charity,' said Aunty Doreen curtly. And to Rita: 'Is not far now. Only a couple more hours.'

TWENTY-FOUR

Blood Mixtures

Granny was delighted with the mixer. She placed it proudly on the sideboard, moving a vase of artificial flowers and a faded wedding-photo in a plastic frame aside to make room for it.

'Thank you, darling, it's lovely!'

'Well – it's not from me. It's from Marilyn actually. And it doesn't work . . . I told her to . . .'

'It don't matter if it don't work, we don't have electric current anyway. But it look so nice and new. We don't get too many new things like that up here. It look so nice up there on the sideboard.'

'But . . . I could take it back, you know. She only did it to insult you.'

'How you could say such bad things about your stepmother, girl? It's a very kind, generous gift. I have to write her a thank-you letter. You must help me, my spelling in't so good, you know. I not used to writing letters. That's why I didn't write you all these years.'

'But you shouldn't . . .' Rita stopped. Her grandmother had taken the mixer into her arms and was looking down at it in admiration, stroking it and, it seemed, almost cooing to it.

On her face was an expression of tenderness. She looked up at Rita.

'It's the thought that counts,' she said.

Rita had seen a similar expression of tenderness an hour ago, when she had first arrived and clambered up from the boat onto the jetty and found her grandmother waiting for her with open arms. Granny had cried with emotion. 'Oh, me baby, me little baby girl,' she said over and over again, and her wizened little face, the skin like soft pale leather laid in tiny folds, had been wet with tears and her eyes had shone with love. Rita had never known anything like it in all her life.

Granny was small and wiry and, it turned out as she sprinted up the steep staircase leading to the house's front door, agile as a monkey. Her hair was black, shiny, long and dead straight, caught at the nape of her neck in a plastic clasp and hanging down her back in wispy tendrils. Rita was completely taken by surprise by the dun colour of her skin. Aunty Doreen was dark – sapodilla-brown, as it was called here – and, as she knew from the photos she had of her mother, so had Lynette been.

The darkness, she then discovered, came from Granpa, whom she had found in a rocking chair in the gallery upstairs.

'He can't walk no more,' Granny explained. 'Arthritis too bad.'

'Come here, chile, let me look at you,' Granpa said. Rita kneeled beside the chair and the old black man with the white hair tilted up her face at the chin and stroked her cheek and ran his fingers through her hair. To her utmost embarrassment he placed his palms on her cheeks and drew her face up to his and kissed it all over, weeping profusely. He moved his hands to her back and drew her closer, hugging her so tightly she could hardly breathe. Finally he covered his own face with his hands and wept some more, sobbing loudly and shedding tears which Granny mopped away with a corner of her apron. Granny had wept too and so did Aunty Doreen, and Rita joined in.

It was the first time in her life she had ever been the focus of emotion of this kind. It *was* embarrassing. But so good. Delicious.

Weightless. As if a layer of cloud covering the sky with greyness was slowly drawing back.

'You is all we got left of Lynette,' Granpa kept saying. 'So long, so long. Why you didn't come back to see you old granny and granpa? Why you daddy keep you in Town, why you didn't write we no letters?'

'I . . . I didn't know . . . nobody ever—' Rita began but Granny interrupted.

'Hush, George, don't be so rude to the child, is not she fault, she didn't *know* . . .'

'She was a difficult child,' Aunty Doreen added. 'She never used to talk to me when I went to visit. She would hide under the table until I left again. You change,' she added, turning to Rita. 'You get much better. Must be the growing up.'

'She look just like she mother, eh?' said Granny to Granpa.

'Yeh, but the cooly blood does show. Look at that *hair*!' Granpa replied, taking hold of Rita's huge heavy mane of hair and swinging it back and forth with relish.

'*Half* cooly,' said Aunty Doreen. She frowned, trying to work out the remaining fractions. 'You is half-English, half-Amerindian,' she said to her mother. 'So me and Lynette is quarter-white, quarter-Amerindian. And she is eighth-white, eighth-Amerindian.'

'And eighth-African and eighth-Portuguese,' said Granpa proudly. 'From *me*. Me mummy was a pure Putagee,' he said, turning back to Rita, still twirling her hair through his fingers. 'Me daddy was almost pure black, slave blood. Not quite pure. Some white blood: Vandermeer – good Dutch family. Plantation Den Haag, West Coast Essequibo.'

'So she got English, Dutch, Putagee, Amerindian, African and cooly blood,' said Aunty Doreen, still counting off on her fingers.

'But the half is cooly. So dat's the strongest. Look at dat hair! But here around the edges you see the black blood coming through. Frizz!' Granny ran her hand over Rita's hairline, stroking the line of baby curls. Then she, too, gripped the mass of hair and examined it, weighed it, closed her hands around it. 'And look how it a lil' *stiff* – dem curls too wiry for a cooly. Is de African blood showin' through. An' the lips, and the eyelashes. She got a fine nose, though. Mus' be from the daddy. You all is Hindu or Muslim?'

'Um, Christian,' said Rita. She was used to conversations of this kind – Guyanese loved nothing more than to explain and explore the extraordinary racial intermingling that made each one ethnically unique. It was a form of identity-search, a way of finding one's own place in the web of society, but up to now she had never bothered, never cared, to participate. Knowing only her father, and knowing him to be East Indian, and that perfectly pure, the rest had not interested her. Now it seemed that to be pure-blooded was absolutely boring – what a much more fascinating ancestry her mother had bequeathed to her!

'Christian! True!'

'Yes, well. Not practising. I think my father was baptised Christian. But his grandmother was Hindu.'

'And you is baptised Christian. Good.'

'No ... not as far as I know. We aren't churchgoers. And Marilyn is definitely Hindu. But not practising. It's all a bit mixed up.'

'Mixed up is not good,' said Granny sternly. 'Mixed-up blood is fine. Mixed-up religion, no. God don't like that. You got to decide what you is and where you goin' and how you gon' get there. You can't go in a mosque one day and a church the next and a temple the next. God don't like that sorta thing at all. He give each body a path to travel upon. All paths is different, but all paths lead back to Him. If you go on three different paths at the same time you gon't end up dancin' on one spot. It disturb de soul. You got to decide for youself, child, an' go you path wit' all you mind an' all you soul ... An' if you arsk me, Lynette—'

'Now, Mummy, don't get into that. She's too tired for a lecture and it's not her fault her mummy was wayward and run off with a cooly man. She's hungry and tired. Let me see what food we have for her, and then she can lie down and have a rest and afterwards we can show her the place. And you can meet your cousins, Rita. Fred, George and Pete. They comin' home from school any minute now.'

And Rita had gone up the stairs to the top floor of the big rambling house. She had lain down on the bed Aunty Doreen had shown her, and in less than a minute she had been asleep.

That had been this afternoon. Now the evening was fast approaching; she had done her duty and presented Granny with the mixer, and been somewhat shocked by Granny's reaction. Now she felt like going out.

'Come and I'll show you the place,' said Aunty Doreen on cue, and thankfully Rita turned her back on the strange sight of Granny lovingly, reluctantly, replacing the mixer in its place of honour on the sideboard, and left the house.

The house stood on tall, thin stilts on a creek that flowed into the Pomeroon River. Rita had been surprised when, arriving at Charity, they had not come here by taxi but had taken another, smaller, speedboat from the wharf and down the river, towards the river's mouth. Granny's house had been up the Akinawa Creek on the river's far side, about a mile from Charity. The only way to get there was by boat. There were no neighbours. No electricity. No telephone. Just a long thin jetty into the river, a wooden landing, and a sandy path inwards towards the house.

She had caught a glimpse of trees on her arrival. Of course, there were trees everywhere anyway – the river itself snaked through the jungle, and mangroves lined its banks, long snaky tendrils reaching down into the water's depths. The jungle had, however, been cleared for the plot of farmland on which her grandparents' house stood, and the trees she had seen on arrival were the familiar fruit trees she recognized from Town – citrus, paw-paw, avocado, banana, and, in the background, tall waving coconut palms and a giant mango.

The sand spread over the front yard was pink. Even from a distance – the height of Rita's head – she could tell that it was made up of ground shells, flaky, like Quaker Oats, but hard and crunchy under her feet. She was to learn it had been brought here in boatloads from Shell Beach on the Atlantic Coast. Later, she herself would be taken by boat to Shell Beach; she herself would stand in silence in the dusk and the dark with her cousins George and Pete, waiting for the great leatherback turtles to crawl out of the sea and lay their eggs. For the moment, though, the dogs claimed all of her attention. They appeared from nowhere, two nondescript mongrels, one black, one brown, throwing themselves at her with yelps of delight, jumping up at her with long tongues hanging out, aiming at her face, beside themselves with adoration; she grinning, patting, soothing, stroking, bending low to greet them, finally kneeling on the pink shells. She offered her face to be licked. She placed her arms around them and drew them close, and they were quiet.

She felt her eyes mist over. And once again the clouds inside her parted. She felt their warm bodies and their beating hearts; she felt their aliveness and their joy and she realized that at this moment she was really, truly happy, and that she hadn't been this happy for years: not since she was a little girl mending birds' wings in the back-yard of Number Seven.

That night before she went to bed Granny came into her room.

'I just brought you something, a present,' she said. 'Let me get in with you.' And she lifted the mosquito net and climbed into the bed and she and Rita sat cross-legged facing each other, like two schoolgirls in a tent.

Granny held out a fist and let something drop into Rita's open hand. It was a small golden heart, as big as a thumb-tip, on a chain. Rita turned it over; it was not flat, but slightly swelling, and around its edge was a pattern of intertwined flowers.

'Oh,' said Rita. 'This is for me?'

'Yes,' said Granny. 'When I was your age my daddy – you know he was an Englishman! – took me and my brother to England to meet my grandmother, his mother. She gave me this at that time; it's a family heirloom, passed from grandmother to granddaughter. Let me show you . . .'

She took the locket back from Rita, fumbled at the shoulder of her dress and removed a safety pin, with which she pricked one of the flowers at the tip of the heart. The two sides of the locket sprung open like the covers of a book. In one of the halves was a tiny portrait. Rita took the open heart back and held it up to the weak light of the gas lamp burning at the side of the bed.

'Oh,' she said, 'it's my mother!'

'Yes,' said Granny. 'You can put any picture you want in here but if you wear this one she will protect you. It will bring you luck like it brought me. When I came back home with it that's when I met my sweetheart, your granpa.'

'I'll wear it always,' said Rita, and leaned forward to hug Granny.

TWENTY-FIVE

'Is Not Your Fault'

The more Rita saw of Granny the more her admiration grew. Granny seemed to be the axis on whom the whole household turned; she was the dynamo in its centre, from whom everyone else drew their energy and found their sense of direction. She was up before dawn, sweeping the yard, feeding the chickens, lighting the wooden fire in the kitchen, fighting with the smoke it emitted, fetching bucketfuls of water from the river. Aunty Doreen and the boys – and on the second day, Rita – helped, but it was perfectly clear that Granny was the earth in whom they were all solidly planted; the sun around whom their lives revolved.

At Rita's first breakfast Granny slipped a plate with two bakes and pumpkin stew in front of her with the words 'Eat up, darlin'!' and from that moment on Rita felt as if she was attached to some invisible powerhouse that over the next three weeks was imperceptibly and constantly filling an underground battery of Rita's with nourishment and strength. Granny's little wizened elfin face, sometimes frowning, sometimes laughing, sometimes stubborn, sometimes pensive, drew her like a magnet. When Granny spoke, everyone listened; what she said seemed sometimes as naïve as the utterings of a child and yet her every word possessed a basic truth. Granny got to the heart of things, and what at first appeared naïve turned out, finally, to have a wisdom of its own.

The matter of the mixer, for instance, which still irked Rita. She could not bear to leave Granny in her self-deception; she could not bear for her to be Marilyn's dupe.

'You should send it back,' she told Granny again. 'Marilyn was just being stingy and she thinks you people up here are too stupid to know the difference. If you keep it she'll just crow over you.'

'No,' said Granny. 'I gon' keep it. And I want you to help me write a thank-you letter tellin' her how much I 'ppreciate her kind thoughts.'

'But her thoughts *aren't* kind!' Rita cried out. 'She's a mean old bitch! She hates me and she's arrogant and spoilt and vain!'

'Chile, I don't like to hear you usin' them words for a grown-up lady. An' what you say is uncharitable and unchristian. You shouldn't be saying such bad things about your own stepmother.'

'But it's true! And what use is it to you when it doesn't work anyway!'

'I think it look good up there on the sideboard. Everything in the house so old and shabby. Is nice to have something new. And it's the thought that counts.'

'But her thoughts about you are *bad*!'

Rita felt she had to put everything into a simple, childlike language for Granny, to help her to understand. Granny didn't seem able to grasp any of the psychological complexities at work here. She was a simple farm woman, straightforward in her thinking; she knew nothing of guile and intrigue, the underhand ploys of a Marilyn were beyond her understanding.

'All the more reason for me to have good thoughts about her,' Granny reasoned now. 'If she got bad thoughts 'bout me and I got bad thoughts 'bout her, then we both like sponges. We draw in the bad thoughts of the other and the thoughts get worse and worse and we both feel badder and badder. But if she got bad thoughts 'bout me and I got *good* thoughts 'bout her, then when her bad thoughts arrive at me doorstep they can't get in. They can't hurt me. My good thoughts is like a shield around me soul, you see. And when those bad thoughts start coming they bounce they heads on that shield and they fall down stunned. And for a moment they don't know what happen. And then they get up and rub they heads and say, "Wha'? Wha'? Wha'?" And they rush back to the sender and say, "We can't get in there, we bruise we head." And whoever send those bad thoughts start to think. And she realize how much her own bad thoughts hurting. And hurting and hurting because they all come back with bruised heads. And it hurt and it hurt and it hurt. And finally she realize her bad thoughts only hurting herself. And then she start to have good thoughts. And then everybody happy.'

On the third day Rita complained about Isabelle. She hadn't planned to do so. She and Granny were in the canoe, and Granny was rowing downriver to the grocery to get some staples. At first there had been no conversation, only silence; not a thick, uncomfortable silence but a deep peacefulness enfolding river, forest, and sky. Granny herself was a part of that silence as she briskly plunged her paddle into the water, which parted silently to let the little boat whisk by.

And then suddenly, without warning, on their way home, the words had broken out of Rita and she had not been able to stop them. It was as if the silence had pierced through the membrane that kept the thoughts at bay, and not only the thoughts but the feelings that clung like parasites to them, bad, dark feelings, feelings of resentment and anger and hate, all directed at Isabelle who was her sister and her child and the one she loved most in the world. They poured out of Rita and Granny listened in silence. The forest listened, and the river and the sky, and they echoed in the silence. Rita felt terrible, as if all around her was beauty and peace and harmony and only she was a misfit, an ugly vicious insect unworthy of this place with its silence, unworthy of Granny. But there was no way to stop the words from coming.

Granny only listened, letting the words come without commenting on them. Finally Rita stopped talking for the flow of words had run dry. All that was left was her own ugliness, like a lump of faeces on a pristine white beach.

And then Granny said, 'She like that because she feel small and bad. She only want to be centre of the world because she feel so small and so bad. Somebody who feel real big inside, big like this river and the sky and the earth, somebody like that don't have to behave bad and don't need attention because they know they is *good* inside. Only somebody who feel *bad* inside need people outside tellin' them they is good and beautiful and important. You is much, much bigger and much, much richer than her so you must have patience. But you got to educate her so that she learn. So that she find things inside herself to make her happy. Because she very, very miserable. But listen, Rita, you can't allow her to get her own way with you. You got to be firm with her, even when she cry. If you let her walk over you, you not educatin' her, you makin' her worse, and you yourself feel bad. You got to know you is bigger than her, you got to love her, give her a hand so she can get to her feet and feel good about herself, but still you got to say no when she's bad and educate her.'

By this time they had returned to the house. Granny clambered up the little ladder leading from the jetty into the water, and Rita handed her the bags of shopping and scrambled up behind her. Granny sat down on the jetty and patted the space beside her, and Rita sat down too. She hadn't finished. The worst was to come.

'The thing is, I always think it's my fault when she starts screaming and throwing a tantrum! That I made her that way and then I want to make up for it and do whatever she wants.'

'Why you think it's your fault?'

And then the whole story came out, Rita's negligence of Isabelle that day so long ago, Isabelle wandering off and ending up under a car. And then the spectre of brain damage that never completely went away, reappearing every time Isabelle stuck her fingers into her ears and opened her mouth wide and screamed as if the end of the world was nigh. Reappearing every time Isabelle's face resumed that pained expression, when she complained that her head was hurting, retired to her bed and lay there motionless because every movement hurt, the blinds drawn because she couldn't stand the light, the folded cloth soaked through with Limacol, moist and cool, pressed against her little forehead.

'It's all my fault,' sobbed Rita. 'I should have taken care of her. It's all my fault!' Even as she spoke she felt something warm pressing against her arm, and it was Bruno the brown dog's head. She let his squirming body edge in between herself and Granny; she pressed her cheek against his brown fur; she felt Granny's arm around her shoulder, drawing her near, and she cried.

She cried until she couldn't cry any more, and Granny offered no wise words of advice but only let her weep. Bruno licked her tears dry and Rex, the black one, laid his head on her knees and looked up at her with huge soulful eyes while Rita sobbed until her grief was spent. And Granny sat with her into the dusk, letting her cry. By the time the night insects tuned in for their evening chorus, Rita could cry no more, but only sit there with Granny and the dogs listening to the silence behind the curtain of sound, and it was good.

Granny, always so busy, had all the time in the world this evening. She sat with Rita until the full moon was high in the sky and the black river caught it and waved it on a million minute ripples, till someone behind them lit the house lanterns and finally Aunty Doreen came out to call them in for supper.

The night before Rita was to return home Granny came into her room and sat on her bed in the darkness. Behind the mosquito net she looked ghostlike, ephemeral. Rita sat up, raised the net and sat beside Granny on the edge of the bed. In the darkness she saw little more than Granny's dark profile, and the gleaming whites of her eyes. But Granny's features were imprinted on her mind and she knew with her heart that those eyes would be like open windows, and closing her own eyes she felt, without looking, the strong love shining there.

'Listen,' Granny said. 'Is not your fault.'

Rita had completely forgotten the conversation on the river. She had spent so many happy days here on the creek. Every day her cousins had taken her up the Akinawa Creek in a dug-out canoe, teaching her to paddle it herself. She had learned to love the all-enveloping silence all around her, a silence somehow unbroken by the occasional gurgle of Pete's oar in the water, the squawk of a parrot or the crashing of its wings as it plunged through the rainforest. Every day she had swum with her cousins in the pure, black, clear waters of the Akinawa, and every day she had drawn a little closer to the truth of what she really was. There were no more tears, for a pure innocence filled her that was happiness itself, and in it there was no room for guilt; she was liberated to be who she really was, healed and joyous.

So when Granny spoke of fault she was taken by surprise.

'My fault? What?'

Granny smiled. 'See? You healed already. But anyway – is not your fault. About the accident. And the screaming. And the headaches. And the brain damage.'

'It *was* my fault, Granny. I was responsible for her and I have to live with that for the rest of my life.'

Granny shook her head. 'No. Is not your fault. The child has a mother – she bears the responsibility.'

'But I was in *charge*. I was looking after her. I should have had my eye on her. I shouldn't have . . .'

Granny stood up and bent low and kissed Rita's forehead. 'No matter. Is not your fault. Remember that.'

And then Granny took her hand and pressed something into it, a little thing that was hard and soft at once. Rita opened her hand and looked at the thing in the darkness but all she saw was a shadow; she felt it, and her fingers told her it was leather wrapped around something hard. Granny chuckled softly.

'What is it?' Rita whispered.

Granny chuckled again and picked it up and fumbled with what looked like a drawstring, and Rita made out a little bag which Granny was turning upside down to empty its contents into her waiting palms. Something hard fell out.

Rita stared through the darkness – she couldn't see, but from the feel of them all she held were a few ordinary pebbles.

'Diamonds,' said Granny. 'Raw diamonds. You know George was a porkknocker. And he daddy too before him. We got plenty, plenty diamonds.'

'But – why don't you sell them? You could get so much money for them, and—'

'What I want with money?' Granny's voice was scornful. 'Don't I got all I want here? De river and de sky. Me chickens and me corn and me coconut trees. We put it aside for de grand-children. I give you your share tonight because *is not your fault* what happen wid' Isabelle. An' because God send you in de world to do a job and one day you gon' need money.'

TWENTY-SIX

Jaws of Death

Rita scraped her way through school. Generally a mediocre pupil, she spent much of her time staring through the window. She hated facts; numbers even more. She forgot history dates and no matter how often she hammered the words 'seventy-two' into her brain, eight times nine remained an inaccessible enigma. The droning of her teachers bored her; certain key-words were all it took to set her off floating in a fantasy of her own. Learning by rote was torture; she felt herself pressed into a mould from which the only escape was dreaming. She nevertheless had her way with words: her gift for language – her own and foreign ones – carried her through the important exams.

The time spent with Granny had healed one side of her soul, but opened the other to a chasm of self-enquiry. Can this be *all*? Isn't there, somehow, *more*?

She had a reputation for being 'difficult'. She was so quiet in the classroom she lived her life there almost unnoticed; some teachers had the impression she slept through classes, upright and with open eyes but asleep nevertheless. Turned off. The work she handed in was uninspired; she repaid dull teachers with dull homework; work so dull, in fact, some teachers had the impression she was mocking them. There was a cleverness to Rita's dullness that bordered on the cynical and some teachers found themselves frowning and wondering if they had missed something, under-rated Rita, overlooked some essential key to the quirks in her character. Her quirkiness was unpredictable. It emerged at the most unexpected opportunities, when they were least expecting it, in forms which contradicted everything they knew, or thought they knew, about her. She didn't fit in anywhere, couldn't be pressed into a stencil outline.

Rita, they said, was not quite . . . well, you know. Not quite 'there'. And they rolled their eyes upwards and smiled knowingly, slyly, to each other.

For there were days when she would suddenly snap into life and start writing furiously, stopping only for seconds to chew her pen, scratch her head, before scribbling away again. And even then, the work she turned in was dull, substandard, ridden with spelling mistakes. She's doing it on purpose, some people com-plained.

It was Miss King who finally found the red exercise book. It was filled with poems, dedicated to her teachers.

Our Miss Norse should change her name,
how her pupils twist it is a shame,
as walking fast she's in a canter,
'cause pupils laugh in horsey banter.

When Mr Baichoo he did sneeze,
he made a loud and awful breeze
that rolled the chalk onto the floor,
which had us laughing all the more.

Mrs McIntyre we all love,
she's overinflated waist above.
Fun-wondered if with pin I stick,
will she deflate by simple prick?

Mr Currie is a friendly fellow
but vex him and he starts to bellow.
Homework we do fear to mention:
quickly puts you in detention.

Rita was called to the headmistress who berated her for wasting precious talent on silly poems, and suspended her from school for a week, to bring her to her senses. She spent that week in the Pomeroon with Granny, as she did all of her holidays.

Those visits were the only weeks in her life that seemed to make sense. Always at the end of them she felt like simply staying – for ever. But always, Granny sent her away. To live your life, Granny said.

When she protested, Granny only smiled and said, 'Life is waiting fo' you to wake up and find the job you came here for. Someway, somehow, somewhere. Some peoples have their jobs given to them right from the start. Like me – my job is here on the farm. Some peoples got to look for their job. Like you. Because they job is special, different. You is different, because God made you different because he want you that way for your job. One day you gon' find that job. An' you not gon' be happy till you find it.'

But meanwhile, Rita dealt with discontent through the farcical.

Life is a farce, true bliss is sparse, she wrote on a white sheet of paper and hung it up on the wall of her room, and did her best, outside the classroom, to live up to this motto. She had always been popular with her peers and even now, or especially now, she retained a certain unspoken authority which made her a sought-after companion for after-school fun. When things got dull, Rita always had some outlandish idea, and with only a few words she had young people scrambling with excitement to set some new scheme into motion, a party, or an outing, or a prank, or worse.

But Rita truly went down in the annals of Georgetown's history with the Week of the Hearse.

She and Polly found the hearse gathering dust in a corner of

Fung's Funeral Parlour. Polly was finally going steady with Bobby Fung and some afternoons she and Rita dropped by to visit Bobby and his gang. Seeing the hearse – a wooden thing shaped like an elongated coach, with running-boards along the sides and an elevated box for the driver and his mate at the front – Rita stopped and stared. She walked silently around it, her imagination working full time. It seemed perfectly in order – just old and dusty, and, of course, hopelessly, wonderfully, old fashioned. It had a mystique to it: Rita imagined it trundling down Georgetown's shaded avenues, a coachman in livery with his whip held high sitting in glory on the box; he would be wearing a black wide-brimmed hat, and black knickerbockers, and a black coat and long black socks and black shoes and black gloves, but he would be white and the dead man in the coffin in the hearse would be white, and the black horse between the shafts would be kept to a slow, mournful gait and all the mourners – the man's widow and his children and grandchildren – would walk behind dressed in Victorian garb, holding black parasols aloft and weeping into black handkerchiefs. All this Rita saw as vividly as a film passing before her eyes.

'Can I buy this?' she said to Bobby Fung.

'You can have it for free,' Bobby Fung replied.

There was no question of bringing the hearse home to Number Seven, but Donna deSouza's mother didn't mind having it in the yard and the Victoria Street Gang set to work restoring it to life. First it had to be brought there, no easy task. They already had a horse, of course – Maxine Wong had been into ponies since she had first ridden bareback on Madame so many years ago, and now had her own which was kept at the Pony Club. To make things perfect, Bolívar was black, and Maxine was more than delighted to lend him to the project.

Rita had no lack of helpers. There were six young people from the old Gang on Victoria Street, plus Bobby Fung's gang, plus schoolmates of those and various stragglers and strays who had heard of the project and were curious to see it take wing – or rather wheel.

Nobody from Fung's Funeral Parlour knew a thing about hearses of this type – it was a relic from a time long past, kept only because nobody could be bothered to throw it out. Now, two employees went so far as to sweep a few layers of dust from it and drag it out into the courtyard. All the rest was left to Rita's imagination. So among many excited calls and curses Bolívar was backed into the shafts, harnessed in a trial-by-error style, and then coaxed into dragging the contraption the several blocks to Victoria Street. The easiest thing to do, Rita decided, was to lead him; she didn't want the hearse driven until it was perfectly ready. So she and Maxine walked at either side of Bolívar's head, each holding a rein, leading him through the streets and past the turned heads of astonished pedestrians, almost causing several cars to collide and several bicyclists to glide into the gutters, while everyone else trooped obediently behind. Thus the hearse arrived in triumph at Number Four, Victoria Street.

They painted it shocking pink with lime-green touches: the shafts, the window frames, the wheels. The harness was old and stiff but otherwise perfectly usable. It was cleaned and oiled and polished till it was the colour of burnished mahogany.

After a week the hearse was ready. It was baptised Jaws of Death with a bottle of XM rum stolen from Ronnie Maraj's bar. It was ready for its inaugural drive.

Bolívar was once again brought forward and harnessed to the Jaws of Death. The youngsters, who had all been instructed by Rita to appear in period costume, piled in. Most of them had moth-eaten church-bonnets, bowler hats, panamas, or somebody's old pith helmet. They wore their father's best grey trousers, tied with ribbons at the knee, and their mothers' worst evening dress, padded at the bosom. They had begged and borrowed jackets (extremely rare and hard to come by in the post-colonial era); somebody had found a fur-lined coat which their mother had brought back from a UK winter visit. A lot of feathers had been found and stuck into hatbands and hairnets.

They were ready.

'Can I come too, Rita?'

Isabelle's pitiful squeak was hard to resist. All week long Isabelle had watched the goings-on with hardly a comment. Sometimes she had wielded a paintbrush; she had asked questions. It had been obvious where it was all leading to. Rita was thus prepared for this moment.

'No, Isabelle, you can't.'

The misting over of dark, soulful eyes. 'Please, Rita, please let me. Let me sit up in the front with you, driving the horse! Please!'

'No, Isabelle. I just *said* you can't!'

'But *why* not!' A foot stamped at the 'why', a frown, two clenched fists. Rita knew the signs. She turned her back on Jaws of Death, went down on one knee, picked up Isabelle's little fists and unclenched the fingers, which she held between her own. She smiled her kindest, most loving smile, and put on her firmest, most resolute, defy-me-if-you-dare voice.

'*Because I say you can't!*'

'But I *want* to! I want to come with you!'

Isabelle's pretty features slid here and there, transforming themselves into a mask of petulance: bottom lip jutting out, nose screwed up, eyes buried in angry red lines. She pulled her hands out of Rita's grasp and held them up with clawed fingers. Rita remained unmoved.

'Very well then, we'll vote on it. Everybody who wants Isabelle to come, raise your hands.'

Isabelle's own hand shot up. Every other hand stayed conspicuously down.

'You see, Isabelle! It's like I said. You can't come. This isn't for little children. And it might be dangerous.'

Isabelle's face screwed up in one of its recognizable signs.

'If you scream,' Rita said calmly, 'if you start one of your tantrums now, you'll be sorry. You see, horses don't like little girls who scream. This particular horse hates them. He eats children who scream for breakfast! Really!'

Isabelle's eyes widened in horror; she glanced at Bolívar, burst into tears, and ran screaming out of the gate, taking the time to stop and latch it carefully behind her before continuing home. Long after the anticipated danger was barred Isabelle's screams could be heard ringing from the windows of Number Seven. Rita shrugged.

'She'll probably get a headache now,' she said. 'But it's not my fault. She just didn't get the hint.'

She led Bolívar out into Victoria Street and climbed up onto the box. Maxine and Polly followed to take their positions of honour next to Rita. Everybody piled in behind her. They were ready.

Dramatically, Rita flicked the end of the reins on Bolívar's gleaming black haunches, and they were off.

It was a Saturday morning; they had the whole day in front of them. Through the streets of Georgetown they roved; up Water Street and into the main shopping area, where entire pavements of people froze into gaping immobility. Down Regent Street, leaving behind them the crowds and entering the quieter, more residential areas. Wherever they appeared, the swaying coach trundling majestically along behind the rather bemused but obedient Bolívar, people stopped what they were doing to stare. Faces appeared at the windows of the houses; there seemed to be an invisible grapevine in operation, because people would be waiting at their garden gates several houses ahead, waving and calling as they creaked past. Rita, Maxine and Polly looked straight ahead, as befitted a funeral procession. The others in the coach, however, were less disciplined. They giggled and tittered and scrambled for places at the windows, where they looked out at the passers-by and waved back. People greeted them as if they were royalty, or celebrities, cheering and calling as they passed by. Sometimes, a camera was held up. Now and then, a young person would run out of a house and shout, 'Hi, can I come too?' And Jaws of Death would stop, its door open majestically, and admit a new crew member.

But then, out of the blue, Rita drew up Bolívar.

'What's the matter?' Polly asked.

'We have to stop now. I'm sending everybody home.'

'Why . . .' but Rita was gone.

She opened the door to the coach. 'Everybody out,' she commanded. 'Everybody go home.'

'But why?'

'Oh, Rita!'

'The fun's just beginning!'

'Rita! Don't be a spoilsport!'

But Rita was adamant. 'You all have to go home! Right now!'

'But why?'

'Because Bolívar's tired, that's why. How would you like to tear around the streets all morning pulling a coach with a pile of hysterical nuts around town?'

'But you said . . .'

'We worked so hard . . .'

'We're having such a ball . . .'

'Ball's over. For today.'

'And tomorrow?'

Rita considered, then she jabbed her finger, five times. 'You, you, you, you and you. Tomorrow at four, we can go out for an hour. And you, you, you and you on Monday. We have to ration this.' And that was that.

On Monday there was a huge photograph of Jaws of Death in the *Graphic*. Ronnie was proud (he had written the caption), Marilyn belligerent, Isabelle pouting and silent.

'That girl always manages to steal the limelight,' said Marilyn.

Jaws of Death lived for a week, and almost lived up to its name.

Driving along the Sea Wall Road some bad little boy pelted a stone at Bolívar, hitting him in the flank. Bolívar shied. His hoof landed in the foot-deep empty gutter lining the street. He stumbled to his knees, got up again, stumbled again. Jaws of Death swerved to the left. A wheel slid into the gutter, then the second wheel. Bolívar was pulled back; Jaws toppled. Its passengers were thrown screaming against its side, causing it to topple even more. Then it was on its side. Bolívar, still caught in the shaft, was pulled over to lie on *his* side. Rita and Polly (Maxine had not come out today) found themselves flying from the driver's seat to earth.

Cars and motorcycles stopped, the police and an ambulance were sent for, but nobody, miraculously, had more than a scratch. Bolívar was lame for a week. Jaws of Death's wheels were irreparably broken. Life returned to normal.

When Rita turned eighteen Marilyn began nagging her to get a job and Contribute. The idea of a job, any kind of a job, was almost as bad as the idea of university, which she had rejected from the start. Sitting at a desk all day, filling out forms or whatever those working girls did in the insurance companies and in the Ministries! It seemed she was good for nothing but dreaming; yet dreaming was not enough. Not enough for the world, which demanded unmercifully that you got businesslike and earned your living, and not enough for her. She longed for some concrete task, a dream she could fulfil.

'I thought you wanted to be a vet,' said Ronnie helpfully at lunch.

'Oh, *Ronnie!*' Marilyn touched her lips with her napkin and shook her head in pity at her husband's naïvety. 'Haven't you been following this child's magnificent school career? Do you think that with her mathematics she'll get a place in a university? And anyway, do you think we can afford to send her away? Why can't you be realistic?'

Rita slammed down her cutlery so that it clattered on the table and bounced to the floor.

Dear Diary,

Why am I walking the face of this earth? There must be some reason. Some great mission, some me-shaped niche I can pour myself into, but what? And where?

Granny keeps talking about the job I have to do. But I don't see it, I don't feel it.

What am I to do? I'm eighteen and have no idea where I'm going. All the other girls are dreaming about husbands. But me? I'm not that sort of a person. Nobody would want me anyway, I'm too quirky. Men don't like quirky girls, they like soft feminine creatures like Cherry Greer.

Can't I just be normal and ordinary and contented like all the rest? All marching in two-two time? But I hear this other drum and need to run and dance and turn somersaults. If I do they'll put me in the Berbice Mad House. Maybe I *am* mad. Dear Diary, tell me if I'm mad, or everybody else is!

And everybody who's anybody is leaving. Everyone! All off to Canada, America, England and leaving me behind. Even Polly!

Polly has a normal mind, not a mixed-up one like mine. A brilliant mind that gets As like that and now she's off studying microbiology in America. Microbiology! I don't even know what that is!

Why don't I go away too? But where? And what do I do once I get there?

Daddy is coaxing me to go into journalism. But I wouldn't like that. You have to write what they tell you to write. I know, because that's what he always says himself!

I'm of no practical use whatsoever. I'm not good for anything. A waste of a human being. An oversight. A huge error walking on earth. No use to any other living thing, except Isabelle, and look how she's turned out. A spoilt brat of a little sister who thinks she can walk all over you. If ever there was a waste of time and effort, that's Isabelle.

Granny's the only one who makes me feel normal. She says I *am* normal. She says don't worry, there's a job for me and the whole universe is just waiting for me to find that job and do what I came here to do. It makes sense when I'm with Granny on the Pomeroon and the river and the sky and the forest confirm every word she says, but here? It just sounds like so much nonsense.

Why don't I get married, said Donna the other day. It's what people DO at my age, after school. She's marrying some chap from Guyson's Engineering Ltd. A bore. But who would I marry? Archibald Foot?

Rita finally chose a career. She would be a poet. This decision came after she won first prize in the National Youth Poetry

Competition. The theme this year had been animals, which was quite up her street; Rita's winning entry was named 'Dogwit'.

> Have you heard the tale of a dog they said
> who fleas so bad did his body invade?
> He scratched and scratched but could not free
> his body of a single pesky flea:
> So he thought and sought a suitable twig
> which in his mouth he used as a rig
> and this is what he craft'ly did,
> to trick those fleas from his body rid.
> With twig in mouth into the sea he went
> till the panicking fleas from paws relent.
> From belly and tail they sucking stop,
> as slowly into the sea he walked,
> all the flustered fleas in terror gawked,
> rushed to his back to be high on top;
> along neck and head and over his nose
> raced the scurrying fleas as the tide it rose.
> Aboard the twig there was barely room
> and the blood-laden fleas they sensed their doom.
> He released their raft into the salty waves
> and sent them to their watery graves.
> Back to shore with a vigorous shake, he headed home
> to his master's care with brush and comb.

Rita enjoyed a few days of celebrity and her hopes ran high; she saw herself bent over her desk, scribbling poems from dawn to dusk, which would be published in a series of thin volumes. She would be the country's Poet Laureate. That was the job Granny kept talking about. Why hadn't she seen it before?

She would live in an open-sided Amerindian hut in the Pomeroon district, writing poems. And people would come from far and wide to get a glimpse of her but she would chase them away with a broomstick. They'd say she was eccentric: poets were allowed to be eccentric. In fact, slightly mad. Head-tapping mad, but brilliant. Her madness would be part of her image, part of the aura of poetic genius that surrounded her in a benevolently glowing haze. She could wear her hair loose, let it float around her head in a thick black cloud of crinkles; she would wear odd, sometimes torn, long flowing robes; she would chew pencils and ride a rusty old bicycle around Town (when she happened to float down to Town from the Pomeroon, to collect prizes and give interviews and things like that) and people would point as she floated past: Look, there's . . .

But fame deflates quickly, as Rita found out after a week of it, and she was back at the same nagging question of What To Do With Her Life. She had to Earn a Living, Marilyn said; they couldn't keep a grown girl all their lives. She had to Pay Her Way. Buy Her Own Clothes. She had to Get Responsible. And Stop Daydreaming. And Ronnie was no support; Ronnie, who might have understood her finer ambitions, only shrugged his shoulders when Marilyn nagged, grinned sheepishly, and said, 'You see, me girl, that's life.'

She briefly considered moving out; but where would she go to? Who in that whole country would rent a room to a single unemployed eighteen-year-old? Rita didn't care much about her reputation, yet she knew that other people did, and having a bad reputation – which living alone, even if such a thing was remotely possible, would certainly give her – would just make life more difficult than it already was. As always in times of need, she went to visit Granny. Granny built her up for three weeks, then sent her packing.

TWENTY-SEVEN

Women's Page

Finally it was Ronnie who found Rita a job at the *Georgetown Guardian*, the rival newspaper to the *Graphic* where he himself was now editor. He and Mr Maugham, the *Guardian*'s editor, were old school friends, and there was a friendly rivalry between the two papers. Mr Maugham was more than willing to give Rita a chance. Rita felt a stirring of excitement; she hadn't thought of journalism but here was, perhaps, a beginning. All she needed now was something to write *about*. Something engrossing. Something that would shake the world or, at least, the placid Guyanese society that was slowly, slowly stifling her to death.

She began, just as Ronnie had, as trainee junior reporter, quickly advancing to feature writer for the Women's Page. She hated the Women's Page.

'But I'm no *good* at all that!' she complained to Mr Maugham. 'I don't know a thing about cosmetics and fashion!'

'Nonsense,' said Mr Maugham, leaning over Rita's desk and smiling in that supercilious, fawning way of his. 'All women know about those things. You expect us to put a man on the Women's Page?'

'Why not Angela Crawford? She's just the right one, she knows about it all. She *enjoys* that kind of stuff.'

'One, Angela Crawford doesn't write as well as you, and two, you have a *name*. Maraj, that says something to people. They know your father, they know your stepmother, and there's a woman who knows about fashion and the social whirl. You have access to everybody who is anybody. And by the way' – his eyes narrowed and he moved a step closer to Rita – 'by the way, I expect you to be loyal to us, you know. If you hear any tips at home, don't let me hear that the *Graphic* got there first. Like when Dr Glen got married to the Ramdehall girl – how come the *Graphic* came out with that story before anybody else got a whiff of it? That's the kind of thing I expect you to chase. And don't tell me your stepmother didn't whisper in your father's ear – Mrs Maraj is the girl's aunt! What I want is for you to get those stories first.'

'But I'm not *interested* in things like that! And anyway, she'd never tell me, she avoids me like the plague, and . . .'

But Mr Maugham had turned away. Rita felt her fists tighten; then she sighed and began to hammer away at her typewriter.

Have you picked up the latest whisper? Geraldine Hinds has been snapped up by Omai Gold Mines Ltd as their candidate for the Miss Guyana Contest, and as everyone who ever stole a rare glimpse of Geraldine knows . . .

Almost automatically, she rattled out the story, but as her fingers moved her mind balked, wayward, recalcitrant and insubordinate as ever. Inside she rebelled against the sheer *boredom* of it all. A drum heard differently – that was the crux of the matter. The drummer she listened to played to a different rhythm; he had spoilt her for the rhythm of the world. She longed to march to that stirring beat, see where it took her, but she couldn't, she was tied, shackled, like one of those prisoners who walked around with iron balls chained to their ankles. She couldn't understand it, it was beyond her – how could people, other people, everyone else except her, it seemed, how could they not *feel* it? Ennui, like a plastic bag drawn over her head, robbing her of breath, robbing her of life? Am I crazy? Neurotic? She went to press conferences held by the Opposition Party and listened to their Party Leader droning on and on and had to fight to keep from yawning; at the end of it all she couldn't remember a word she heard; the reports she wrote were reproductions, cleverly paraphrased, of the press releases issued to all members of the media. Other reporters asked brilliant questions; she kept her mouth shut, not knowing what to ask. She supposed she was just plain stupid; yet the things spoken of with such animation seemed stupid to her, banal, trivial. Nothing to do with the real, big, important question, the question, it seemed to Rita, that demanded solutions NOW, immediately. The huge question written across the sky, the clouds drifting apart and forming the letters that Rita alone could read: *Why do you walk the earth? Why are you here? Where are you going to? Why? Why? Why?*

There was a huge piece missing from her life but she could neither define nor name it. Just a huge big piece of Nothing. A Nothing like a piece pulled from the sky. Nebulous, vague, and yet a Something so essential she was starving for the lack of it. There was a barrage of Nothing within her, and behind that barrage a need to break out, to rise up in arms, swelled to giant proportions. Mutiny! Revolution! It steamed within her. But her fingers tapped away obediently at her little old typewriter.

The best part of her job was the Dear Dianne column. At first it had been boring because almost all the letters fell into one of four categories: young girl abandoned by young boy, wife abandoned by husband, girl in love with boy going steady with someone else, single (or married) woman in love with married man. Then Rita began making up her own letters, and the answers to them, and the sparks began to fly.

Shortly after these innovations began, Mr Maugham called her into his office. 'Sit down and listen,' he said, and began to read aloud from a typewritten page:

'Dear Dianne,

My husband has four wives, me and three others. I was the first and the only real one. He spends one week of the month with each woman and he has a total of seven children with us. This has been going on for eleven years. I can no longer stand the situation but he says I must be tolerant if I truly love him. One of my rivals phones me up morning, noon and night and I am convinced she is using obeah against me – now I am getting bad pelvis pains and can no longer sleep with my husband. I think she is possessed by Satan. I fear for my life – I am sure she has cursed me. What shall I do?

                                                                 Cursed

Dear Cursed,

You must do one of two things:

1. Send him packing. I am sure you can find a more faithful husband.

2. If you cannot do this then there is one simple way to stop this woman's persecutions. Get a good girlfriend to visit this woman and make friends with her. Let your friend pretend to hate you and let the two of them gossip about you. She should mention just by the way that you regularly visit an obeah-man, the most powerful one in the country, and that *your* obeah-man has been known to wither his rivals to death. That will surely stop her in her dirty tracks – and put an end to her dirty tricks!'

'Could you tell me what is the meaning of this?'
Rita shrugged nonchalantly. 'Why not? It's interesting. It's different.'
'And it's pure *rubbish*! Every word of it! Rita, these letters are getting more and more outlandish from week to week. It can't go on this way. As of this week, Angela Crawford is Dianne and you can take over Pen Pals.'
Rita shrugged again and turned to walk out. When she was at the door Mr Maugham called out, 'Rita!'
She stopped and looked at him.

208

'Don't take this personally, all right? I still think you're a good writer but we have our limits and our policies. Do you understand?'

But Rita couldn't help it. Everything she wrote had a spark of controversy to it. Again and again she was summoned to Mr Maugham's office.

'We can't print this, Rita: *Government selling off Rainforest to Foreign Companies* ... Lord, Rita, don't you understand, this newspaper IS the government?'

'Yes, all right, but I also mentioned the private companies selling off to the big logging firms. Would *that* be all right?'

Mr Maugham clapped his forehead. 'And the private company you mention is your own stepmother's. Prabudial. Don't you have any sense of loyalty?'

Rita shook her head. 'No. Of course not.'

'Well, I do. Your father might work for a rival newspaper but he's still my friend. Forget it, Rita. Write about something safe that everybody can agree with. Look, I've been thinking – what about St Ann's Orphanage? A nice tear-jerking story would be perfect for the Women's Page. You're at your best with human interest stories, and everybody can sympathize with orphans. Do that for next Sunday. All right?'

Do I have a choice? Rita asked herself as she nodded, and left the office without a word.

TWENTY-EIGHT

Suitors

Ronnie Maraj, by now, had grown fat and complacent, and so had Marilyn. The good life had settled comfortably on their bones and on their souls. The rest of the population scraped by on ever emptier supermarket shelves and dwindling cash in their pockets; Ronnie and Marilyn had it made, for they could fall back on a fat inheritance and ongoing exports of tropical wood to affluent First World customers with more money to spend than useful things to spend it on. Ronnie and Marilyn spent as if they, too, lived in a never-never land where the good things in life had only to be plucked from the trees.

Marilyn had finally given up on her body and let it fill up in whichever way it pleased. She had got her man and her house; she hadn't got a son, but she did have a daughter as beautiful as the day, and growing more beautiful by the day, with an effervescent, winsome character to match (if one ignored the occasional temper tantrums). Isabelle's ballet lessons had given her a grace in motion that locked (mostly masculine) gazes; her every gesture was a joy to behold, every smile to be treasured. She had come near to winning a few ballet prizes, but Isabelle really didn't have the discipline and capacity for hard work that a fully-fledged

career as a professional ballerina would have entailed. And anyway, who needed a prima ballerina in Georgetown, when the
economy was slumped and the country as a whole was sinking
into quicksand? But ballet was never supposed to be a career
move anyway: simply a means to an end. Isabelle would get a
first-rate husband, that was certain; a foreigner it had to be, a
white man. Of course, the choice was limited, but Ronnie as
editor of the major newspaper was in the best position to know
exactly who might be coming, and when, and for how long,
and where he was staying. Ronnie knew when the Canadian
Ambassador was visited by his younger, single, brother. He knew
when a team of American civil engineers came over to consider
building a pontoon bridge across the Demerara; he knew when a
world-famous, young, single, British ornithologist came to study
and write a book on the habits of the Harpy Eagle. (Though here
Marilyn turned up her nose. Ornithologists, she said, were by
definition poor; and she didn't want to send Isabelle tramping
through the jungle behind a bird-obsessed husband.)

Isabelle met them all. Guyanese, after all, were famous most
of all for their hospitality, and Marilyn felt a sacred duty to
ensure that every single *worthy* foreign gentleman who set foot
in the country was invited to some sort of a party, reception, or
function in his honour: the Press invited, his picture in the papers,
and a radiant Isabelle introduced to him. Marilyn trained Isabelle.
She showed her how to bat long silky eyelashes, looking up
mysteriously, adoringly, from beneath them; to smile provocatively; to stand with style, one perfectly modelled leg slightly in
front of the other; to walk with grace, not wobbling on high
heels, but with elegant hip-swaying sensuality. Men liked that
kind of thing. True, Isabelle was only fifteen, but it was never
too young to start, to sow the seeds that might one day bear
fruit. An early marriage was envisaged for Isabelle, an early
marriage to an older, experienced man, a connoisseur, a man who
would take her away and give her all the good things in life she
deserved. For one thing was certain, there was no future for
Isabelle in her own country. Anyone who was anyone had already

left; she must set her sights abroad, and invest all she had into the serious matter of husband-catching.

To Marilyn's chagrin the tactics weren't working.

Isabelle at seventeen was as single as ever before. Isabelle was experienced in the art of flirting, expert in the art of small talk, the cadence to her voice perfect, the lift of her chin exquisite, the angle of her eyebrows when she lifted them to ask a pertinent question utterly charming – and yet manless. Isabelle was sweetness and grace personified; she knew exactly how to circle in on a victim and ensnare him in the web of her wiles but with the innocence of a child. And still she was manless. Either they were too clever for her, escaping while their wits were still about them, or she was simply too young. Her mother concluded the latter was the case. Their tactics changed. They changed their goal. Not an older, experienced man, but a younger one, a boy, maybe the *son* of such an older experienced man. A bright-eyed, promising Harvard student or some such thing, Marilyn mused vaguely. The best thing would be, of course, to send Isabelle away to university, where she would be sure to meet such candidates, but with her less than mediocre school record, there was no chance of that. One thing was certain – she had to go abroad.

'What about modelling school?' Isabelle asked. 'Perhaps in London?'

'Or waitressing,' Rita added. 'In Cambridge. I can just see those fellows forgetting all their theorems and what-not and queuing up just to get a glimpse of Isabelle sashaying across the restaurant with a tray of mush, making goo-goo eyes at them.'

Marilyn pointedly ignored Rita. To Isabelle she said, 'Modelling? I don't too much like the idea, it's so, so *cheap* somehow.'

'Those top models make a fortune!'

'Yes, but first you have to get to the top and that's not so easy. You'd be competing against all the loveliest white girls. Whereas here you're a princess, a lovely Indian princess, and that's the card you have to play, it's the card you play best. I don't want you among the riff-raff. Aspiring models are all riff-raff. You're special, and if you're to win you have to stay special.'

'I'd love to be a model. Just imagine, my face on the cover of *Vogue*!'

'Isabelle! That's not the point at all. You've got to have a long-term plan, and that can never be modelling.'

Marilyn had been trying all this time to avoid Rita's eye but when she now looked away from Isabelle she couldn't help it: Rita's gaze caught hers like a fish on a hook.

You and I, we know the truth, don't we? that gaze said.

At first, Rita didn't know what had awakened her. She rubbed her eyes, then turned on her bedside lamp to check the time. Three a.m. She switched off the lamp and rolled over to sleep again. Then she heard it. A piercing whistle that she knew all too well. She groaned. Isabelle. Again.

Walking over to the open window she felt the pebbles under her bare feet. Isabelle must have thrown several handfuls in before waking her up; the floor was strewn with grit. She leaned out of the window and looked down.

'Rita! It's me; come down quick!'

No point arguing from this distance. Rita silently pattered down the stairs and opened the front door. She pointedly looked at her watch. 'Isabelle, it's three o'clock! Are you out of your mind? What on earth . . . And oh my God, *look* at you!'

'Let me in!' Isabelle muttered. She pushed Rita aside and entered the house.

'You're drunk, and you've been smoking, and your dress, that good expensive dress, you've only worn it twice and look at it! Torn right down the front! Are you hurt?'

Isabelle bent over to tear off her sling-back high heels. She hooked them on an index finger, placed her fist on her hip and stood akimbo, glaring Rita down. Just barely visible in the dim glow of the streetlight shining through the gallery window, Isabelle bristled with a tawdry voluptuousness Rita *felt* more than she could see; in one glance she had taken in the rip across the bodice of Isabelle's dress (the one that till tonight had been her favourite), noticed the smudged lipstick and the black lines of mascara-stained tears, the mussed hairdo. There was a reek of rum on the girl's breath, the stench of stale smoke emitted by clothes, hair, and skin. Another smell, vague, yet pungent, unknown to Rita, a smell which was at the same time a feeling, an uneasy, sordid feeling. She felt her spirit sucked down, muddied by Isabelle's presence.

'Isabelle,' she whispered, genuinely shocked. 'Where have you been? Who've you been with? Hell, you look a fright, better not let Marilyn see you like that!'

'Marilyn c-c-can l-l-l-ick m-m-my ass!' stuttered Isabelle, and took a step towards the staircase. She stumbled.

'Come, let me help you.' Rita offered her an arm, which Isabelle gratefully took.

'R-r-r-ita, d-don't tell nobody, you hear? You promish? That jackass Terry Quail . . .'

'Ssh, don't talk now, you'll wake up the whole house. You better get into bed, it's a good thing tomorrow is Sunday, you can sleep late, Lord, Isabelle, you *stink*!'

'Everybody shtinks. The whole world shtinks. Terry Quail shtinks. Rita, he throw me out the car, he make me walk home once he finished with me!'

'Yes, but why you go out with people like that rat I don't know. Marilyn would have a fit if she knew . . . But quiet now, can you tip-toe?'

Isabelle couldn't. She stumbled along the darkened upstairs corridor, an arm slung across Rita's shoulder, and somehow managed to reach her own room. The door creaked when Rita opened it, and Isabelle giggled loudly.

'Sssh!' admonished Rita. She dragged her sister across the carpet and practically threw her onto the bed. She returned to the door, closed it gently, and switched on the overhead lamp. Isabelle was asleep already, spreadeagled on the bed and snoring, her shoes still hooked onto an index finger now relaxed in sleep. Rita sighed. She walked over to the bed, rolled Isabelle onto her side, unzipped the dress which would find its way into the rubbish bin tomorrow, and pulled it down over Isabelle's hips. She pulled the top sheet out from under the prone body and covered her sister with it. For several minutes she stood still, silently regarding Isabelle's face and pondering the changes the younger girl was going through. Now that sleep had relaxed the girl's face it had lost the expression of cunning sensuality, cheap in its very artificiality, vulgar in its very flagrancy, that was beginning to mould itself permanently into Isabelle's features. Isabelle, in her sustained effort to be irresistible, was banishing that very essence of beauty she had been born with, the artless grace which had needed no help in order to radiate, but which, once tampered with, had lost its soul and hardened into this lifeless mask. Now, in the innocence of sleep, it shimmered through; not even the mess of Isabelle's smudged make-up could camouflage it. Rita walked to the washbasin, dampened a rag, and carefully wiped away the caked remains of lipstick, foundation, eye-shadow and mascara. That was better. Beneath the make-up Isabelle's skin was perfect, brown and smooth and glowing like polished wood.

Poor Isabelle. Poor spoilt Isabelle.

Sometimes, Rita was convinced that *Isabelle* was the job in life that Granny so often talked about. That she owed Isabelle a debt she could never repay; that she would spend her life protecting, defending, forgiving, and educating her sister, but never healing her. Sometimes she felt that, though she could not take care of herself, though she herself often floundered as if on a stormy ocean, not knowing where to go or how to get there, Isabelle played the part of an anchor. Isabelle kept her earthbound. If it were not for Isabelle, and the fact that Isabelle needed her, she felt she would float up to the sky and lose herself in the clouds.

Tomorrow, Rita vowed, she would have a long talk with Isabelle. For the umpteenth time. She'd warn her, as she had before. Isabelle would laugh gaily, Rita knew it already. Tonight's humiliation long forgotten, she would first look at Rita with huge innocent eyes, apologize profusely, shed a few tears of contrition, beg for forgiveness. And when Rita had forgiven her she would toss her black curls behind her shoulder in a practised gesture, fling one perfect leg over the other, draw her feet up in a pose she

knew was, at least to men, irresistibly seductive, and yawn nonchalantly, stretching her arms lasciviously and saying, 'Boys, oh
boys. Rita, you're right. Boys are the pits. You don't have to tell
me about boys, I know more about them by now than you. I
know what they're after.' Then she would giggle and preen herself
and, wearing her cutest mask, say, 'They're after me, girl, me!
They adore me! And I'm taking my time in making my choice.
And as for that jackass Terence Quail . . .'

Rita had heard it all before. She sighed, turned off the light
and left the room, closing the door gently on the volley of coarse
snores that followed her into the corridor. Isabelle snored like a
dock labourer after a hard day's toil.

TWENTY-NINE

Goody Two Shoes

'Rita! Rita, come quick!' Isabelle, bursting through the door, flung her satchel in a corner and took the hall stairway in bounding leaps, loosening her tie on the way, hauling the noose over her head and throwing that over the banisters. She flung open the door to Rita's room and for the first moment since entering the house stood still, panting, getting her breath back, grinning from cheek to cheek.

Rita, bent over her desk in the corner next to the window, swivelled her chair around and looked at her sister. 'What?' she said, slightly peeved because now she wouldn't be able to finish today's entry in her diary; she could tell by Isabelle's bright-eyed, almost hysterical expression that for the rest of the day, her little sister would entwine her in the web of her latest intrigue, asking for advice, begging for encouragement, wheedling for flattery, hungry for applause. She clapped the diary shut and stood up. Isabelle, like a hunting dog suddenly released by its master, plunged forward and clasped her in her arms, swinging her around in a clumsy polka.

'Rita, guess what, guess what? Oh, you'll never guess. It's too great to be true. You can't imagine. But guess, go on, just guess!'

217

Isabelle pulled her down to the bed, squeezing both her hands as if to press a response from her sister. Rita couldn't help laughing; Isabelle's gushing was, of course, a sign that once again the girl was heading for a precipice, but nevertheless she couldn't help but be infected by such innocent enthusiasm.

'Well, let me see,' Rita said slowly. 'Terry Quail has made you an offer of marriage! At long last!'

Isabelle pouted. 'You're such a spoilsport, Rita. I was just dying to talk to you about what's happened but if you don't care, then I'll just go and . . . and . . . I'll go and tell Mum! She'll listen! I wanted to tell *you* first but . . .' She stood up and made as if to leave but, as she knew would happen, Rita pulled her down.

'OK, you know I'm just teasing, don't pretend you're offended because I can see you just can't wait. Out with it!'

Isabelle, who had been waiting for such an invitation, sprang to her feet and paraded to the centre of the carpet, where she struck a pose, threw her hair over her shoulder, tipped her chin to look coyly down at her sister, and announced: 'I'll have you know, sister, that you're looking at a candidate for the next . . . Miss Guyana! Tan-ta-ta!' At these last words she flung out her arms in dramatic triumph. Her face lit up as suddenly and as clearly as at the turning of a switch.

'Ohmygod,' said Rita at this performance, burying her head in the crook of her elbow.

Isabelle dropped her pose, scowled and glared at her sister. 'Is that all you have to say?'

'What more is there to say? When did you dream up *that* gimmick? Or did Miss Norse tell you that's your best career option?'

Isabelle flung herself on to the mattress, pouting. 'You *never* take me seriously! One of these days you'll *see*, you just wait! And then you'll be sorry!'

'You take yourself *too* seriously, Izzy, that's the trouble. You need me to keep you on the floor, else you'll just spread your wings and float out the window.'

'So you don't think I could be Miss Guyana? Is that it? I'm

not beautiful enough?' Both hands rose self-consciously to her hair, rumpled from the mad dash home, patting and primping it back into place.

Rita snorted and got up to return to her desk. 'Beautiful? Who *cares*? And what if?'

'Oh, you! You're just envious because you're—' Isabelle stopped in mid-sentence.

'Go on. I'm what?'

'Nothing?'

'Were you going to say I'm *ugly*?'

'No, I wasn't. You're not *ugly*, but you're just, well, you know. A little bit out of proportion.' Isabelle chuckled coyly. 'I mean, you've got an interesting face but no one would ask *you* to try for Miss Guyana, would they?'

'And somebody asked you? Who?'

'Yes, that's exactly what I wanted to tell you! You see, after school I went to Fogarty's to buy some . . . well, never mind, anyway, when I was there Mr Behari came out of his office and saw me and came to talk to me – you know what he's like! Chattin' me up like always, that big fat old man! He must be about forty, and he's got a wife and children, though I heard his wife left him, but she came back – anyway, he was chatting me up and then he said Fogarty's is looking for a girl to sponsor for Miss Guyana and I'd be perfect, would I like to enter! And I didn't even have to *think* about it, Rita, I just said yes right away!'

'You said yes? Did you sign anything?'

'Well . . . not exactly. He said come with him into his office so I went and he told me some more about it and then he asked me how old I was and when I said seventeen, he said Daddy would have to agree, but I told him that won't be a problem.'

'Oh, I see,' said Rita.

Isabelle flew into an artificial rage. 'What d'you mean, "I see"? I know your "I see's". I know exactly what you're thinking. You want to spoil everything for me, you're just a jealous boring ol' tight-assed stupid ol' . . . ol' . . .' She stopped, searching for the right word. 'Ol' Goody Two Shoes,' she finished lamely.

'I didn't say a word,' said Rita calmly. Isabelle gratefully accepted Rita's calmness as a measure of neutrality and pending support. She stored her rage in a corner of her mind for future use if necessary, and, adopting a supplicating tone, plunged onward with her plea.

'But, Rita, you *have* to support me, you just have to. Think about it – it's the best break I ever had! And what if I actually *won*! Then I get to go to London and I can try for *Miss World*! And imagine if I won *that*! And it's all so easy, all I have to do is look beautiful and I know how to do that, you know I've got a chance!'

'But what's it got to do with me? *You're* the one who's going to be beautiful and win, not me! I can't be beautiful for you, can I!'

'No, but listen, I can't do it all on my own, can I? I'll need you for advice and things, and to drive me to rehearsals and staying out late and stuff like that. I'm going to need a real snazzy bathing suit and an evening gown. I'm going to design one myself – I'm going to be a knockout, I tell you! I was thinking of green sequins and a really low neck-line. I can just see myself . . .' She jumped up from the bed and practised elegant strides and flamboyant twists, explaining all the time her goals and ambitions, and every third word was 'I'; she looked at Rita with eyes that did not see, and her words did not meet their mark, and she floated off in a bubble of self-adoration. Rita watched her silently. So silently that Isabelle finally noticed and stopped to glare.

'Why you watching me like that?'

'Like what?'

'Like you know what. Like you think I'm off my head. You don't believe me, do you? You don't think I've got a chance of winning.'

'Of course you have, a very good chance. I just don't think it'll do you any good.'

'You're just *jealous*. How couldn't it do me any good? It's every girl's dream, but of course most ordinary girls don't have the remotest chance. Just think of the prize! A car, and entrance in Miss World, and if I was to win that, just think of it! And even if I didn't win, think of the model agencies that'd come knocking at my door, and maybe even Hollywood! Think of me being a film star, Rita! I can just see myself up on screen, and . . . Rita, what are you thinking? Why are you grinning like that, as if I'm talking nonsense?'

Rita stood up. She looked at her watch and turned to Isabelle, smiling affably.

'I was just wondering,' Rita said, 'how many eligible young film star bachelors are floating around Hollywood these days, because of course you'll want to marry one of them, won't you?'

THIRTY

Mr Hanoman

Rita was alone at home when the stranger came. It was a Saturday morning. Isabelle was with her mother at a photo session, and Ronnie was at work. Rita was up in her room, reading, when she heard the ring of the doorbell, once, and, when no one answered it, twice. Reluctantly, she rose to her feet and, using her finger as a bookmark, went downstairs and opened the front door. She saw at once that he was different, though on the surface he looked like any other Indian man. Tall, middle-aged, thick-set, black hair oiled and slicked back from a face with remarkably smooth, almost childlike skin. What was it that made him look foreign? She couldn't place a finger on it. Everything about him was ordinary, and yet the moment she set eyes on him, she knew he was different; she felt a quickening within her, as if the silent drummer had surreptitiously quickened his rhythm, changed the beat, ordered a new step. She looked at him, and knew.

The man stood smiling, and neither spoke, as if both were waiting for a word of recognition, but finally it was Rita who broke the spell, saying, 'Good morning, can I . . . ?'

The man seemed to give himself an inner shake, and then he said, 'This is the Maraj household, I presume?'

The moment he spoke Rita's instinct was confirmed, for the accent was foreign. It was one she had never heard before: neither English, nor American, certainly not Guyanese, Trinidadian, or anything West Indian.

'Yes, yes it is. Who do you want to see? My father isn't in right now, he's at work.'

The man smiled enigmatically and said only, 'May I come in?'

Rita was nonplussed. Should she let him in or not? A stranger, and she not knowing his business, and he unwilling to state it? And yet, again, instinct acted. 'Of course, but I don't know how I can . . .'

Still smiling, the man bent over, unbuckled the straps of his leather sandals, and removed them. Barefoot now, he took a step nearer and Rita found herself stepping aside to allow him to enter the house. This wouldn't do.

'Excuse me, I don't know your name!' she said, and her voice sounded loud, too loud.

The man only chuckled. 'Hanoman,' he said, 'Dilip Hanoman,' and instead of giving her his hand to shake he placed the palms of his hands together. Rita was more confused than ever; she had no idea how to react, what to say, and so she led the way to the group of chairs in the gallery where Marilyn received visitors and waved at an armchair, signalling him to take a seat, which he did.

'Mr Hanoman, I . . . er . . . can I offer you a drink?'

'Just a glass of water, if you please,' he replied.

While Rita was getting the water her thoughts raced. Something strange was going on but for the life of her she couldn't imagine what. The man behaved as if he knew her, and she knew him, as if it were perfectly normal to knock on someone's door and come in and sit down and ask for a glass of water, without even hinting at what business had brought you. Why hadn't he explained himself on the doorstep? Why did he seem to expect her to ask him in, and why had she done so, as if under a spell?

She couldn't explain it, and so, she reasoned as she brought him his water, she would simply pull herself together and ask.

'Mr Hanoman, who did you come to see? As I said, my father is at work, and—'

'Oh, so Mr Maraj, Mr Ronald Maraj, is your father, is he?'

'Yes, of course, but—'

'And how many brothers do you have?'

'Brothers? None. There's just me and my sister.'

The man's smile seemed to fade just a fraction. 'Only you and your sister? But then you have cousins of course. Male cousins. Don't you?'

'Cousins? Yes, I do have male cousins, three, but they're not here, they're on the Pomeroon with my aunt, their mother. My mother's sister.'

The man was shaking his head vigorously. 'No, no, not on your mother's side. On your father's side. Maraj cousins. You must have some, don't you? Male cousins? Second cousins, third cousins?'

'Mr Hanoman, I don't understand a thing. What's going on? Why are you asking all these questions? Why are you here? Who are you? Where are you from?'

The man leaned forward, and almost whispered, 'I am here on a very urgent mission!'

Rita frowned. The man must be off his head, behaving like some kind of a secret agent in a cheap spy novel. She ought to show him the door, but somehow she couldn't. Instead, she felt herself sinking into the Morris chair next to Mr Hanoman, and simply staring. She said nothing, and Mr Hanoman seemed to understand the gap in the conversation perfectly. At any rate, it brought forth a new explanation. He slightly lifted one hip, reached into the pocket of his trousers, and took out a bulging wallet. This he opened, removed several cards from one of its pockets, chose one, and handed it to her.

'I am the Special Envoy of the ex-Maharani of Mahapradesh,' he said grandly. 'Her Majesty has asked me to come here to meet the Maharaj family.'

'We are the *Maraj* family,' said Rita.

'No. The name Maraj is a bastardization of Maharaj, a royal name. The original name of your family is Maharaj.'

'How do you know all this?'

'I have made my investigations. These last few days I have been enquiring in the Register Office and looking at the various records of births and deaths. I have been attempting to find the offspring of the late Maharaj Mokesh.'

'I've never heard of—'

'Your great-grandfather. He is the last of your family to keep the family ties alive. The last information he sent was at the birth of his fourth child. Since then we have heard nothing. Nothing at all. Maharaj Mokesh had no brothers or sisters; his father sadly contracted mumps after his birth and was rendered sterile by the disease. Maharaj Mokesh promised to father several children in order to revitalize the Maharaj line. Maharaj Mokesh married a certain Sati Bholanauth and she gave birth to two sons and two daughters. I have been trying to trace these children but all I have found is this Mr Ronald Maraj, who is apparently your father. There are several other Marajs in the country and I assume some of them must be related to your father. I am enquiring specifically into the birth of *male* offspring.'

Rita shook her head. 'As far as I know we don't have any relatives. My father doesn't have any brothers and sisters.'

'Ah, but surely aunts and uncles? Cousins? The children and grandchildren of Maharaj Mokesh. He had four children. I am making a list of their offspring. There must be several offspring. My calculations are on the stingy side. I estimate two children for each of those four, that would make at least eight grandchildren including your father. And if those eight grandchildren had an average of only two children – I am calculating on the stingy side, as you can see – then there must be surely sixteen great-grandchildren of Maharaj Mokesh. Including you and your sister. At least sixteen. Averaged out, sixteen children in your generation. That is being conservative. If we are fortunate, there could be several more. Assuming for instance that each of Mokesh's children and grandchildren had not two but an average of three children, then – I have already made my calculations, you see – then we would have thirty-six great-grandchildren which would be more usual. But if we are to remain conservative, then I am expecting at least sixteen great-grandchildren. Including yourself. But I am only looking for the males. Of those sixteen, we can assume that half would be males. So I am expecting to find *at least* eight males in your generation of Maharaj descendants. And if we are fortunate, perhaps several of those sixteen already have male offspring. You for instance. Are you married?'

'Married? No, of course not.' Rita was offended by the bluntness of his question, and generally disconcerted by the authority with which he had recited his speech – as if rehearsed, she thought, and certainly he knew his figures off by heart.

'How old are you?'

'I'm twenty-seven. Why?'

'Twenty-seven, and not married? That is highly unfortunate, your father is being very negligent. Why has he not found a husband for you as yet?'

'Mr Hanoman, people here don't find husbands and wives for their children, this isn't India. We stopped that long ago. We are free to find our own partners.'

'Then it's your own fault. If you had been married you could very well have been the mother of sons, and it would have been my delight to enter those sons on my list!'

'Mr Hanoman, please, I don't understand a thing! What list? Why are you making a list? What are you doing here? Why are you looking for male Marajs?'

Mr Hanoman looked at his watch. 'As I told you, I am the Special Envoy of Her Highness the ex-Maharani of Mahapradesh. She has sent me to make a list of male descendants. The purpose is no secret: these males are heirs to the Mahapradesh fortune. I have to find them most urgently. If it is true that your father has only two daughters, then I must find the rest of the family, the males. I must speak to your father – when will he be home? Where can I find him?'

'He'll be at his office right now, at the *Graphic*.'

'Then I am hurrying there to meet him and extract the names of his relatives. It is unfortunate that he has no sons or grandsons of his own but what to do? What to do?' As he spoke Mr Hanoman rose to his feet; treading lightly, rolling forward on the balls of his feet, he reached the door, stepped outside, bent over and put on his sandals. Then he stood up, and offered Rita the same enigmatic gesture of hands placed together at the chest, as if in prayer. He smiled, nodded, and was gone.

THIRTY-ONE

Heiress to the Throne

'But, Daddy,' Isabelle pleaded, 'think, just think. He *must* have said where he was staying. He must have!' She stamped a foot in frustration, glared at her father, and shook her head in amazed frustration (Men! They're so *ignorant*!). She marched to the fridge, tore open the door, scanned the bottles of drinks, grabbed a Fizz-ee Lime, and slammed the fridge door.

'If he did I don't remember!' Ronnie spoke mildly, soothingly, but Isabelle would not be placated.

'And you just let him go like that!' She snapped her fingers. 'You let him walk out! You must be mad, Daddy!'

She rummaged in a cabinet drawer for a bottle opener. The Fizz-ee cap flew right across the room. Ronnie lifted a hand and caught it easily.

'Well, I couldn't very well tie him down, could I?'

'You could have invited him over! For dinner!' Marilyn was as furious as Isabelle. 'I mean, hell's bells, Ronnie, don't you ever think of your daughter? An opportunity like that, and you just let it—'

'Daddy, tell me again what he said. Exactly what he said.'

'I can't remember the exact words.'

'Well then, the gist of it. Right from the beginning. Everything's so garbled nobody really understands what's going on.'

'Well, he spoke in a garbled way, but as far as I can understand, he's some sort of emissary of some kind of an Indian Maharani or something, and they've got a fortune and are looking for an heir, and apparently we're their distant relatives.'

'But how did he *know*? How did he find us?'

'Some ancestor of ours wrote to them a long time ago and said he had four children. They must have assumed the family has multiplied and there's a host of eligible heirs by now. And all we have are two daughters.'

A grim silence descended on the gathering. Rita broke it. 'But, Dad, how did that happen? Why are we the only ones left? What happened to everyone else?'

Ronnie shook his head. 'I don't know. The only people I really remember are Granma and Aunt Amy, Granma's sister.'

'And your parents?'

'They're like shadows. All I know is that they died in a car crash along with my four elder brothers and sisters. On their way to church. I've seen their graves; I was three at the time.'

'And your granma never told you what happened to the rest of the family?'

'Well, apparently somebody died in the Water Street fire, before I was born. A cousin or something. Or an uncle. I don't know, it's all sort of vague, and a long time ago. I've no idea what really happened to everyone. I expect they all died off somehow, or never had children. You just pick up snippets here and there. I remember some talk of a fever outbreak where some relative died but that must have been when I was a very small boy. I never bothered to get the details.'

'And the details don't matter. Fact is, we don't have any other Maraj relatives. Right?'

'Right. Not in Guyana.'

'And all the other people called Maraj in Georgetown?'

'No relation. It's a common-enough name. The fellow said that we were originally called Maharaj. In fact, Granma's name was

Maharaj. So that means my father must have changed his name to Maraj. It's easier to pronounce, I suppose. But we're the only ones in that line. No connection to the others.'

'But that means *I'm* the rightful heir!' cried Isabelle.

'You, or Rita. Rita, I suppose, seeing she's the elder.'

Marilyn glanced disdainfully at Rita. 'Oh, Rita doesn't count. These people are Indians, they won't want a half-breed. And apart from that she's illegitimate. You know what these Indians are like. Very strict.'

'They're also strict about things like keeping the faith. You can't exactly claim that for Isabelle.'

'Oh, well, she may have been baptised a Christian but you know what they say, once a Hindu always a Hindu. It's the blood-line that matters and no one can say we've been dabbling in any other paintbox. My family always married Hindu blood even if we did convert to Christianity. Not a drop of Muslim blood anywhere and certainly not a touch of the tarbrush.' She glanced at Rita again.

'But anyway, he said clearly he's looking for *male* heirs. Not an heiress. He just wasn't interested in Isabelle. There was no question of her being the heiress.'

'Who's the heir, then?'

'Apparently – I didn't get the whole story, but this is what I gathered – there *is* an heir already, in India, but he's behaving badly and they want to disinherit him. Or at least threaten to disinherit him. Perhaps that's all they want to do, threaten him, so that he behaves himself and then he'll inherit as planned. Look, Isabelle, I don't know exactly. It was a muddled story and he told it back to front. What do I know? All I can say is you don't stand a chance. He made that quite clear.'

'But you should have at least brought him here to meet Isabelle. And me. We could have found out more. And even if she's not the heiress it would have been important to find out about these relatives in India. Royalty! Imagine, Isabelle, you're descended from a family of maharajas! You're a princess!'

Isabelle perked up, but only for an instant. 'A lot of good it does me. At the moment there's only one title that's any use to me, and that's the Miss Guyana one. I've *got* to win, Mummy, I've got to! I can't stand it here any longer, everybody who's anybody is leaving. Why can't we leave too? All my friends have fathers who somehow manage to get them out of the country. And Daddy just sits around . . .'

'Isabelle, we've been through this a hundred times. Emigrating to any of those countries means you've got to have close blood relatives already living there to sponsor you. And we haven't got anyone. Nobody. Or else you have to have some sort of a profession they need and who needs a newspaper editor over there? I don't hear the *New York Times* beating a path to my door! Or else you have to have a fortune and we don't.'

'I thought we did! Mummy always said that Prabudial Enterprises was a gold mine, and—'

'That was then, Isabelle,' said Ronnie. 'The way you and your mother have been spending money . . .'

'Don't say you're blaming me!' Marilyn cried. 'And what about you and your cars! Who are you to talk! I have to keep the girl looking good, don't I? How is she going to meet the right people if she runs around in rags! And look at how the Government is squeezing us these days, and the price of goods, and what with inflation and all that, a decent person can't survive at all in this asshole country any more, and if you'd had any sense you'd have sold out long ago, Ronnie Maraj, and left the country. Our only asset now is Isabelle and her looks. And, darling, don't worry, you're bound to win. That Rose McGuire is no match for you. And once you're in London at the Miss World you're bound to get noticed. All those contestants end up with modelling contracts, and remember Shakira Baksh!'

Could anyone forget Shakira Baksh? An ordinary but beautiful Guyanese-Indian girl, going on to become Miss Guyana, coming third in Miss World, and marrying Michael Caine! A legend in herself.

Isabelle had nothing to say to that. Perhaps some tinge of modesty forbade her from speaking her dreams aloud, but Rita knew her sister inside out and recognized the faraway expression in her eyes, the half-smile flickering on her lips. Isabelle was, again, going through her list of favourite film stars. One of them, perhaps, might jump to the bait . . .

The Maharaj family fortune was forgotten. Other goals seemed nearer, more attainable, more desirable.

The day after Marilyn signed Isabelle's sponsorship contract with Fogarty's, Ronnie Maraj, driving home gaily at two a.m. from a function after one glass of rum and coke too many, drove into a minibus at the corner of Vlissingen Road and Lamaha Street.

Both drivers were at fault, the police said afterwards. Both drivers were also dead.

The question arose as to whether or not Isabelle should continue as a Miss Guyana candidate. Rita, herself devastated, put the question to Marilyn and Isabelle, who both pouted.

The contest, after all, was in four months' time. Ronnie would have wanted life to continue as always. It was Isabelle's last chance, especially with Ronnie dead, and unable to do things (what things? Rita asked herself) for her. It was imperative for her to find her footing somewhere. To keep her career options open, Marilyn said. This contest was too crucial for Isabelle's future to be dropped just because . . . well, they couldn't bring poor Ronnie back by withdrawing and, as always, the show must go on.

Isabelle swung her hair over her shoulder and shrugged.

'It's what he would have *wanted*,' Marilyn said for the seventh time. 'And, Rita, life goes on. Life must go on. What if we stopped life whenever somebody died? And considering the state of affairs we're going to be left in, financially I mean, it's all the more urgent that Isabelle wins. What is going to become of us otherwise? She has no prospects in this country, no future, none of us have. Just getting to the Miss World will be a great step forward, even if she doesn't make it to the finals. She will be seen by all and sundry all over the world and I'm sure some important media people or someone else will take note.'

'Think of Shakira Baksh,' Isabelle put in.

'We just have to go through with it. By the time the competition starts to get serious Isabelle will have overcome her grief; she'll be able to smile again. We can't spoil her chances through this tragedy. It's also a financial consideration. We are going to be left almost destitute. The life insurance policy he made out is a joke, nobody could ever live off that. And Prabudial is not bringing in any hard cash at all these days, I don't know what's going on. Who is going to provide for us?'

'Well, you and Isabelle could start working!'

'Working? At what, may I ask? Can you see me typing up reports in somebody's office? Not me, girl. And as for Isabelle . . .'

But Isabelle could speak for herself.

'Rita, you just don't know what it's like to have a life-dream. To know you have a future waiting for you, a great future, you can just reach out and grasp it and then—'

'And then Daddy has to go and spoil everything by getting killed, is that it? And dying on us at exactly the wrong moment, so that precious little you can't go sailing off in glory. Is that it?'

'Oh, Rita, you make it sound so mean, but I'm only being realistic. I can't make Daddy alive again by withdrawing from the contest, you know that.'

'No, but it's just bad taste. It's as if you don't *care* . . .'

'But I *do* care, Rita, you know I care. I loved Daddy more than anyone in the world. We were always so close and I'm *devastated* by the thought . . .' Isabelle lowered her head. When she looked up again her eyes were moist with emotion, the corners of her mouth turned downwards in grief. 'I can't bear the thought of poor Daddy being dead. I'm trying so hard not to think about it. If I didn't have the contest to help distract me and take my mind off everything I would go mad with agony, Rita, really I would.'

Rita shrugged. Probably Isabelle was right. People got on with their lives, even when other people died. Granny had not missed a day of farm work when Granpa had died two years previously.

She herself was overly sentimental, overly emotional. Her nerves were too near the surface. She felt things too deeply; that was no way to live in this raw, hard world.

That's what Mr Maugham kept saying. She shouldn't let things *get* to her the way she did. It was one thing to chase a scandal and dig up the dirty stuff as a journalist; to get so *upset* by matters, to put yourself on the line emotionally, to let things get under your skin the way she did, that was looking for trouble. And why did Rita have to get so upset by such . . . well, by such *unpopular* matters? Time and time again, Rita had thrown herself into some cause, discussed it with Mr Maugham, begged, cajoled, fought for permission to pursue the issue, written what she thought was a brilliant treatise, only to have it finally rejected outright.

'Listen, Rita, people don't *care* about prison conditions,' Mr Maugham said. 'I'm not going to publish *Hell behind the Prison Bars*.'

'But those poor men live like *animals*!' Rita almost wept at the thought. 'They lie in their own filth, in darkness! They have to sleep on their backs with their arms by their side and don't even get to go to the toilet. Their food is fit only for pigs. They have nothing to occupy their minds with, they live in stinking holes – it's a scandal!'

'Yes, yes, I know, you have it all in here.' Mr Maugham tapped the sheaf of papers on the desk in front of him. 'But it's a scandal the ordinary citizen just isn't *concerned* about! This might be brilliantly researched and beautifully written but it just isn't *printable*! For the ordinary citizen these are despicable criminals who deserve all they get. You know how the crime rate is soaring – everybody knows somebody who was robbed or burgled or raped or murdered. They want these men locked away for good, and the worse the conditions, the better!'

'But . . .'

'Look what happened when you wrote about the Berbice Mad House last year! You thought it would cause a revolution but all I got was a sackload of readers' letters saying it was good to have them put away instead of walking the streets – you can't tell with mad people, half of them are dangerous, was the basic tenet.'

'Still, I have to—'

'Rita, you have a good heart but you can't mix compassion with business, and I have a business to run. I can't afford a loose cannon running around complaining about anything that offends her sense of humanity. I didn't take you off the Women's Page to have you mooning over poor dear murderers. You're a good writer but maybe you should have been a poet. Or a philosopher. Or a nurse. Write about conditions at the Public Hospital. Things are just as bad there but people *care* about that because it touches their own lives – anybody can get ill and have to be hospitalized. But spare me *this* drivel.'

He slapped the article on prison conditions into Rita's hand. Rita bit her lip; a rude retort was itching on her tongue but she swallowed it down, turned up her nose, and walked out of Mr Maugham's office.

A week later a giant rat bit off a newborn baby's little finger at the Public Hospital and Rita had her hook for *Hell in the Hospital Wards*.

THIRTY-TWO

The Return

It took Rita a moment to recognize him. The past twelve years hadn't been particularly kind to him: he had put on weight, and the boyish grin had become a sort of embarrassed smirk. But the eyes were the same; blue eyes were rare here anyway, she hadn't seen more than one pair of them in her whole life, and the brilliance of *these* blue eyes would be unforgettable even in a pure Caucasian society.

'*Russell!*'

'Hi, Rita! You haven't forgotten me!'

Rita's grin was so wide her cheeks hurt. 'No! No, of course not! Come in! What are you doing here? Are you on business again? What—?'

'Hold it, hold it, I'll tell you everything but slow down . . . I tell you what, you've *grown*!'

Rita was almost dancing with joy. 'Come in, sit down! What can I get you? Lime juice? Or tea? Coffee? A Coke . . . oh, we haven't got any Coke. But biscuits. And—'

Russell took a seat in one of the gallery rattan chairs. 'Nothing, nothing at all. I just want to see you . . . You know, of all the people I met in Guyana, you're the one I remember the best?

The one I was looking forward the most to meeting again? In fact, you're the first person I came to visit. How about that? My little sister from next door! C'mon over here, let me look at you . . . Wow, you've changed – you're a real woman now, not a little girl any more! You look good, real good. How are you? Tell me what you've been doing with yourself. I was almost sure I wouldn't find you. Don't kid yourself, Russ, I said, see, she's gone. Emigrated like everybody else, to England or Canada or somewhere. Or else married. To some fellow from the Chase Manhattan. Hey, you're *not* married, are you?'

He grabbed her left hand and looked at it in jest. Rita felt herself flush hot. She looked away before he could see her embarrassment, and pulled her hand away. During the course of Russell's speech she had stopped her childish dancing, banished her foolish grin and struggled for a grown-up, womanly stance . . .

'No, I'm not married, of course not.'

'Why of course not! I'd say I'm lucky. And damned relieved. Because I don't want any jealous husbands in the background when I take you out to dinner tonight at the Pegasus. Or boyfriends . . . Oh shit. You've got a boyfriend. I bet you've got a boyfriend. What's that heart around your neck? I bet some guy gave it to you. I bet it's that guy you told me about from down the street – what's his name? Somebody Foot.'

'Archie . . . No, Archie's left the country, he's in England right now. My granny gave me this heart.' She touched it, held it between her fingers, played with it. Perhaps *it* had brought Russell back to her. Her first love.

'And nobody else? No boyfriend in the shadows?'

'No.'

'Whew.' Russell waved his hand in front of his face in a fanning gesture and let out a long breath, as if in relief. 'You really had me sweating for a moment. So tonight then, at eight, I'll come pick you up. Now let's catch up . . .'

Rita answered Russell's questions about her present life mostly with monosyllables. She had never, ever felt so ridiculous. She didn't know what to say, what to do, where to look. Russell was *flirting* and he hadn't done that back then – then, he'd been the big brother, she the little sister. The awkwardness (oh, those stupid phone calls!) of their first meeting had been quickly converted to laughter, and since then it had been one long game – their age difference had been such a chasm between them, Rita's youth so obvious, so protective, that the potential fire with which she had played had been doused at the very first spark. Her romantic flights of fancy had been cleverly disguised, and even while languishing for his love she'd known, even relished, its futility. Loving in vain had been part of the charade she'd played. So wonderful to love with one's entire heart, and suffer the agonies of love unrequited! It had been a fairy-tale romance, conducted entirely in her own imagination, easy to hide from him by playing the part of the brash tomboy. It had all been completely safe.

Now, nothing was safe.

He was flirting with her. It wasn't fair. He had broken the rules and left her floundering.

She wasn't used to this. She wasn't the kind of woman men flirted with. As a young girl she'd decided no boy would ever find her attractive; males didn't like quirky eccentrics, they liked soft pussycats, and *that* she definitely was not. She had accepted that fact with stoicism and relief; and having once accepted it, developed her quirkiness in the presence of men to make sure the theory held up. You could steal horses with Rita but you didn't go mushy with her – that was the established order, and all the Georgetown males knew it and played by the rules.

Now she was a twenty-seven-year-old virgin and this Russell was kicking down the barriers, dark-haired, blue-eyed, hairy-chested Russell, the prince of her girlhood dreams. Russell, who unknowingly had opened her heart to a deluge of love, Russell with whom she had soared in celestial spheres, Russell who again unknowingly had kicked her from a mango tree into a crash landing so severe she would never recover, never again let a fledgling of love stir her heart.

Archie Foot. Russell. Those two she had loved. No one else.

Now Russell was back, larger than life, looking at her with eyes that were not only brilliantly blue but sparkling with something she had never yet seen aimed at herself and never imagined she would see and never *wanted* to see, because what was she to do now?

She felt as gauche as a goat in a ballet class.

Russell either didn't notice, or didn't mind. He interrogated Rita about her present life, and went on to talk, unasked, about his own life. Russell had been married, divorced, moved to California, done some more training, built up his career, and had recently been asked to set up an internet service provider in Georgetown, as well as found a Training Centre for computer and internet courses. That's what he was here for now. While Russell expounded about Guyana's entry into the Internet Age and bandied technical terms back and forth with himself, Rita was fighting a battle for life.

She might be inexperienced but she had a perfectly healthy instinct and that instinct right now was flashing red lights. Sooner or later Russell would be back to his flirting routine and she couldn't continue with yes–no answers. Not if she was going to eat with him at the Pegasus that night and not if she wanted to see him again. Did she want to go to the Pegasus that night? Did she want to see him again? Would she respond to that teasing glint in his eyes, would she let the fire with which Russell practically *glowed* (even while he droned on about browsers and a host of other terms Rita had never even heard before) ignite in her own heart? *Yes yes yes, of course*, cried a long-forgotten love condemned to a dark prison somewhere in the depths of her soul and now battering for release.

And *no no no, never*, cried another voice, the voice of reason, perhaps, or the voice of habit, or the voice of a little girl who had never been loved by man and never ever *could* be loved by man.

Before he left he called her honey. He touched her hair, picking up a strand that fell forward over her cheek and pushed it back behind her ear. He said, 'You've grown into a lovely woman,' and his voice was gentle and no man had ever spoken that way to her before. And when she hung her head at those words he put a finger under her chin and raised her face so that she could not help looking straight at him, and he chuckled and said, 'You weren't this bashful as a little girl, you know. I like you this way.'

'Well, I'm not a little girl. Not any more.'

He chuckled again. 'You don't need to tell me *that*. I see it plain enough.'

Rita smiled and looked down again.

'Rita, lovely Rita. Something tells me coming here was the best decision I made in a long time.'

He looked at his watch then, and said, 'Uh-oh, gotta go. But I'll be back. Quarter to eight? OK?'

She wanted to say no, but a yes came out in a whisper and she nodded without thinking, and Russell grinned a lopsided, boyish grin that made him twenty-five again and brought back all the heartache and agony of a young girl's yearning for love. He kissed her on her forehead and was gone.

Rita had to admit it: Isabelle looked delectable. If only she wouldn't squirm.

She stood, now, between Rita and the wardrobe mirror in her full-length red-sequinned clinging ball dress, twisting and turning, adjusting her hips, raising a hand to place it behind her uptilted head. For a moment she frowned, fidgeted with her neckline and her bosom, peered anxiously at the mirror, then smiled again, glanced provocatively over her shoulder at Rita, pouted, blew kisses at an imaginary crowd, waved coyly at the mirror, lifted her hair with both hands, held it in a fountain above her head, and let it fall swirling around her shoulders in bouncing black waves.

With a dramatic flourish she posed facing Rita, her face lit up by a smile so dazzling the sunlight drew back in shame.

'Well?' she demanded after a while, withdrawing the smile.

'Well, what?'

'Don't you like me? Aren't I good?'

'Isabelle, you shouldn't be asking me and you know it. I'm not the expert, your mother is. Or those fellows from Fogarty's.'

'Oh, Rita, you know they always say I'm wonderful. What I want is some honest criticism. I want you to tell me the *truth*. That's why I asked you here because I know you won't lie to me. What do you think?'

'Delectable. If only you wouldn't squirm so much.'

THIRTY-THREE

Isabelle Strikes Again

Two weeks later Rita was waiting for Russell outside the Pegasus.

'Sorry I'm late,' he said, and pecked her on the cheek. Rita smiled up at him.

'It doesn't matter, they're sure to start late. Guyanese time. I've reserved seats for us, near the front. Come on . . .'

She took his hand and squeezed it. 'I'm really sorry about this,' she whispered as they walked into the ballroom where the contest was to take place. 'Normally I wouldn't be seen dead at the Miss Guyana contest but you know how it is. Sisters!'

They eased into a row of chairs near the front, and sat down on the two Rita had reserved with programmes. The room buzzed with excitement, alive with expectation. Rita and Russell spoke in louder than normal voices to be heard above the feverish chatter.

'I've got three myself – sisters, I mean.' Russell grinned. 'So I know.'

Rita pulled a face, then gestured in dismissal. 'She depends on me for some good sense. Wish she didn't but there you are. And my paper expects me to cover the show.'

'Aren't they afraid you might be biased? If your own sister's a contestant . . .'

'Well, I can't help her win, can I? And if she does, well, I've got the inside story. My editor's hoping she *will* win, for that reason.'

'So she has a good chance of winning?'

'She's the favourite. She probably will, and then I dread living under the same roof as her. She's vain enough as it is. Unbearable. It'd be better for her *character* if she loses. But then she'll be even more unbearable. The thing is, she's not *really* vain. Deep down inside she's just a poor little empty-headed waif with not a whit of self-confidence. I suppose that's why she needs this.' Rita waved towards the stage. 'She's got this obsession about becoming a star. Like if she could say "I'm a star, I'm a star, I'm a star" a million times she can convince herself it's true. I mean, OK, she *is* beautiful, it's true, and she gets a lot of admiration but there's nothing behind it. Nothing. Hot air. She's sailing up in a hot-air balloon and I can only hope it doesn't burst tonight.'

'You sound as if you're sorry for her.'

'I am. You see – Isabelle's wounded inside. She's . . . well, not quite *whole*. If you know what I mean?' Rita hesitated. One day she'd tell Russell the entire story but this was neither the time nor the place. 'There are times I can't stand her, when she's so conceited and full of herself but then she shows her real face and all she is is a poor little girl who needs to be loved. And when she was a baby I was just about all she had. I sort of feel . . . responsible for her – a bit like a mother. She's just so *shallow*, so obsessed with her looks and turning men on and getting admired. I just wish—'

Russell touched her hand and pointed. 'Sssh, Rita, it's about to begin.'

Rita nodded and turned her eyes to the stage. The buzz of chatter died away, the President of the Lion's Club made his speech, the audience clapped enthusiastically, there was movement on the stage and some more speeches, and the first contestant walked on. The stage had been extended by a short catwalk jutting into the audience; the girl in her bathing suit walked forward, turned, posed, and smiled, presenting herself, her dazzling smile and her delectable limbs to be inspected, admired, applauded. Rita turned to Russell to make a snide comment in the 'cattle market' category, but Russell's eyes were riveted to the ravishing piece of femininity parading before his eyes, so she clapped her mouth shut before a word could slip out, and turned to watch the contestant with eyes more narrowed, a mind more sharply critical. She felt herself involuntarily sinking into a slough of disappointment. A mute cry of affront rose up in her. He actually *likes* this! She felt betrayed, and cut off from the man she loved by that betrayal. Yes, loved. She could finally admit it. She loved Russell. It wasn't just physical attraction, though that was there too. No, it was a union of minds, an unspoken complicity, a joining of souls; so how could he be staring at this piece of female flesh as if he wanted to gobble it up? How could he fall into the ancient trap? How could he be such a *fool*?

Her fight against falling for him hadn't been a fight after all. She should have known it; if she had been more experienced she *would* have known it. Russell had won her over with the very first twinkle in his eye at that initial meeting, with the very first lowering of his voice into a cadence that to her innocent ears had been like honey to a prisoner surviving on bread and water.

Everything about that first meeting seemed engraved on her soul. Russell saying with something like worry in his voice, 'Hey, you're not married, are you?' Russell fanning himself and grinning with relief. Russell calling her lovely. Russell raising her face so that she had had to look into his eyes. Russell brushing her hair away from her face. Kissing her on the forehead. Looking back, it seemed almost pre-programmed.

Of course she would go with him to the Pegasus.

Of course she would go with him to his room after dinner.

Of course she would give herself to him, mind, body and soul.

Of course she would love again, tentatively at first, but then with a surging onrush of feeling which took her by surprise but which she didn't bother to curb. Let it come! Let it only come! This is it!

After that the shyness had evaporated and she was his lover and his friend, and she was so happy, so very very happy, she wanted to shout it from the mountaintop, sing and dance down the streets, let the entire world know that she was his and he was hers.

But she didn't. She kept her love as a secret for the time being, especially from those nearest to her, from her sister and her stepmother, jealously guarding that secret as if letting them know would somehow sully her love. She wished nostalgically that Ronnie was still alive, that she could share her joy with him; that Polly was still next door, a friend to exchange intimate girl-secrets with and giggle and gush. But Ronnie and Polly were gone. All she had was a diary, which listened patiently, absorbed all, but gravely abstained from comment.

For the time being, Isabelle and Marilyn were not to know. It was too special, too sudden. Yesterday, however, she had changed her mind. Isabelle, in one of the nervous attacks that had been more and more frequent as the day of the contest approached, had been particularly bitter and nasty.

Rita had switched off inwardly and thought of Russell and smiled dreamily. Isabelle took that smile as a personal affront.

'What are you smirking about?' she said cuttingly to Rita. 'At least I'm taking *part* – you wouldn't even get near to being a candidate! You can't even get a *man*!'

And Rita thought, I'll show her!

Now, wounded by Russell's evident enjoyment, she crossed her arms and leaned back in her chair. *Men! When you come down to it they're all the same.* The voice of Reason, silent these past two weeks, tucked neatly into a far dark corner of Rita's soul, sneaked into the foreground and sneered. *Shut up*, yelled Love in defence. *He can't help it. It's human nature.*

The next contestant was Rose McGuire, a sultry black girl with endless ebony legs. She flashed a last brilliant smile at the panel of judges, waved to the audience, and disappeared behind the red velvet curtains. The audience burst into enthusiastic clapping; Russell's applause was no less impassioned.

'She was good,' he said, turning to Rita. 'If your sister can match her she must be really great.'

'She can,' Rita said sulkily. Russell didn't notice the sulk. His eyes were glued to the next contestant, a creamy-skinned girl (Rita guessed she had a good dollop of Chinese blood) who, despite her obvious charm, was considerably shorter than her predecessors and, for that reason, less impressive. The applause was accordingly less clamorous, and Russell's praise less warm.

'She's OK, but no comparison with the last one,' he whispered to Rita. When she didn't reply he looked at her again. 'Rita? Are you all right?'

'I'm fine,' Rita said curtly.

'Nervous, huh?' Russell chuckled. 'I'd be too, if it was my sister. Hey, look, is that her?'

It wasn't; this time it was an Indian girl, true, but not Isabelle. No comparison with Isabelle, though her chances were increased by the fact of being Indian as, it was rumoured, this year Miss Guyana would be Indian. Last year she had been coloured, the year before black, and it was a well-known public secret that blacks, coloured and Indian girls – with the occasional Chinese, Portuguese, and white girl, and various mixtures of the above, popped in-between for good measure – took it in turn to hold the crown. Rose McGuire was the black front runner, but this year the odds were for an Indian girl; and of all the Indian girls, Isabelle was the best. Everyone said so. Russell would say it too. No question. Russell liked girls. Russell liked beautiful girls. Rita had to admit it now, and had to admit she resented the fact. She had considered Russell above the fray. Now she had to admit he was, after all, a common-or-garden male. Dammit. And here, at last, was Isabelle.

The audience went wild for Isabelle. Rita had known they would. Just as she knew, informed in advance by the empty resignation that had settled in her heart, that Russell, too, would go wild for Isabelle – on his own account, and because she was Rita's sister. Just as she knew that Isabelle would shine, and Isabelle would be a star, and Russell would be dazzled, and she, Rita, would fade. She knew it all.

The rest of the evening she watched the programme roll by as she had predicted. The ball-gown appearance went without a hitch, and again, Isabelle was the favourite.

It was almost over. All that was left was the interview: child's play.

The girls were interviewed on stage. But at the very first interview, a noticeable buzz of nervousness swept through the crowd. One of the judges, an African businessman who was quite a Name in Georgetown, seemed intent on bringing the girls down. Each of the five judges asked a question, the usual routine questions that had been asked each year. Mr D., however, asked questions on social issues, politics and world affairs. 'What would you do,' he asked the black beauty Russell had so admired, 'if you were President of the United States? What would be your chief concern?'

'World hunger,' the girl said, and went on to give a little speech about her concern for the starving masses, and how best, through saving in other areas, world hunger could be combatted.

The applause, which had, till now, been meagre, swelled again as Rose McGuire made her departure. None of the previous girls had spoken with such conviction or authority or intelligence. Rose had sounded slightly naïve, it was true; but she had spoken from the heart, and that had been obvious to all her listeners. Suddenly, Isabelle was in trouble. The interview carried a third of the points.

The interviews following Rose McGuire's were of the same calibre as the ones before her: not one stood out. And then it was Isabelle's turn.

Rita felt the hammering of her heart, and a prayer rose in her mind, not to God, but to Isabelle herself. Oh, little darling, little dear, poor little sister! Don't make a fool of yourself, oh please don't, say something bright and cheery but don't, don't, don't make one of your silly stupid empty-headed announcements!

But the moment Isabelle opened her mouth, Rita's heart sank. She had abandoned her normal voice, which was, on the whole, quite pleasant, and had adopted a supposedly erotic deep purr, and in that tone recited the routine answers she had practised time and again. And then came Mr D.'s question.

'Miss Maraj, imagine for a moment you were in an important position, a position in which many people looked up to you. What would be your first priority?'

Isabelle didn't answer for an eternal three seconds, three seconds in which Rita's heart drummed so loudly she looked at Russell to see if he could hear it. But Russell was staring, enthralled, at Isabelle.

Finally, Isabelle spoke. 'Oh, but didn't you know?' she minced. 'I already *have* an important position. I am an Indian princess, descended from a great family of maharajas. My dream is to return to India and take up my position as rightful heir to the fortune. I am sure that as a princess I will be in a unique position and that my subjects will adore me. This has been my dream for a long time and I am sure that as Miss Guyana I would enhance the royal title.'

Rita groaned aloud. She could almost *see* Isabelle's provocative lowering of long sweeping lashes at these last words, the coy sideways glance, the practised pout of red-stained lips, the delicate pushing back of hair and the sensual long-necked stretching designed to impress and attract.

Rita covered her face with her hands and bent her head in shame. 'Oh shit! The *idiot*!'

'What's the matter?'

'Oh Russell, she's *blown* it. What a *stupid* answer!'

'Yeah, well, it wasn't too inspired, but otherwise she's great, I mean, *whew*, what a woman! Come on, Rita, clap for her, we've got to let the judges know we want her!'

Speechless, Rita glared at Russell, but he was lost in the applause, clapping as if his life depended on it, drumming with his feet, and, now, along with almost half of the audience, chanting, 'Isa-belle! Isa-belle! Isa-belle!'

She grabbed his arm. 'Shut up, for goodness' sake!' she hissed furiously into the general hubbub that now broke out. First Isabelle, then the judges left the stage. Speculation turned to noise; Rita and Russell had almost to shout to hear each other, which didn't help Rita's rising irritation.

'Why? Rita, what the heck's wrong with you? It's your sister, goddammit, I thought you *wanted* me to support her! I mean, isn't that why we're here!'

'Yes, but you needn't make a fool of yourself! It's bad enough with *her* being the fool!'

'Come off it, Rita, I mean, get real! This is a beauty contest, not an intelligence test! If you ask me, the contest is between that tall black lady and Isabelle. It's pretty close, but she'll pull it off. Heck, it's just a bit of fun!'

'*Fun!* You mean a farce! You call it fun; well, let me give you the *facts*. I've been covering this event every year for the past five years and believe me, I know what goes on behind the scenes and there's no way you can call that *fun*! And this year I know even better because my silly little sister's in it up to her neck, and I'll tell you what it's all about: exploitation. Take a couple of girls whom nobody would notice if they didn't happen to have a few nice features. Put a lot of big glossy ideas into their heads. Stardom, fame, riches, adulation, marrying a film star. Since Shakira Baksh, *especially* marrying a film star . . . Now they all think they're going to get some Hollywood dreamboat. Or at least some rich white man with a bulging purse—'

Russell lurched back in his seat and raised his palms as if defending himself.

'Hey, hey hey, don't bite my head off! Can't a guy have a bit of fun without getting the whole feminist pitch stuffed down his throat? Don't forget it was *you* who brought me here in the first place! I mean, shit, it's your own sister! Why don't you believe in her!'

'*Believe* in her? Oh, I believe in her all right. Don't forget I grew up with her. I gave her her first bottle. I changed her nappies. I rocked her to sleep. I dried her tears when she fell and I put Band-Aids on her wounds. I—'

Rita stopped suddenly.

'Go on,' said Russell scathingly. 'You what?'

Rita had been about to say, 'I was as good as a mother to her.' The words had already risen as thought, preparing to be spoken, but before they could form as speech another thought had whipped forward to silence them. *And I let her run into a car.* She bit her lip and was silent.

Russell opened his mouth to speak but his words were drowned in a storm of applause. The glare he gave Rita was hostile; her return glance somewhat apologetic. They both turned back to the stage, where the master of ceremonies stood patting the air to calm the frenzied audience.

'Ladies and gentlemen. La—a-dies and gentlemen. May I have your attention please. Ladies and . . . Thank you. The judges have reached their decision!'

The applause was again deafening, and it was five minutes before the MC was allowed to continue. He launched into an introductory speech calculated to raise expectations and tension to fever pitch, before finally announcing: 'The second runner-up is . . .'

The silence lasted exactly five seconds, and was so complete Rita could distinctly hear her heartbeat.

'Camille Chang!'

The little quarter-Chinese girl walked forward, smiling and bowing, modestly received her bunch of flowers and placed herself on the lowest rung of the pedestal.

'The first runner-up is . . .'

Rita tried her best to be blasé about it all. Superior knowledge seethed inside her, as well as annoyance with Russell, and exasperation with Isabelle, and pique at herself for provoking the whole disaster. She closed her eyes and bit her lips and didn't know what she hoped for more. Should Isabelle win, or should she lose? Each alternative seemed worse than the other, each courted trouble. And finally, loyalty triumphed. *Let her win.*

The crowd was in a frenzy; no silence this time, but a wild whistling and clapping and calling of names.

The MC began again.

'The first runner-up is . . . Ladies and gentlemen, may I have your attention please? The first runner-up is . . .'

At last, silence. Into the silence he spoke the name.

'Miss Isabelle Maraj!'

The crowd's frenzy multiplied a thousandfold. Calls of boo vied with shrieks of triumph, piercing whistles with catcalls and drumming of feet. The MC turned to the side curtains, arms open as if to gather a graceful Isabelle to his bosom. But no Isabelle came.

The clamour died away as Isabelle's non-appearance became obvious to every last person in the room. The silence grew cloying. Oppressive. And, finally, mortifying; Rita buried her face in her hands and felt with all her heart for her sister. Oh, she knew why Isabelle stayed backstage. Isabelle – she knew with an instinct that in times of great need linked her to the younger girl, an instinct that relayed feelings from heart to heart with the resounding clarity of an open telephone line – Isabelle was weeping. Weeping so loud and so heart-wrenchingly she could not stand, much less walk on stage and receive a bunch of flowers she did not want and stand on a pedestal that was only second highest. Isabelle could not take it; Isabelle had flown so high in her dreams that this puncture would send her flailing to the floor.

Rita jumped to her feet. 'I have to go to her,' she said to Russell as she hurriedly stepped past him. She pushed her way down the row, stumbling over legs, not hearing the MC as he apologized for Isabelle's absence due to 'unforeseen circumstances', not listening as he prepared to announce the name of the new Miss Guyana. Just as she reached the door she heard, as if from a distance, the jubilant words *'Miss Rose McGuire!'* And in that moment before she closed the door she heard the tidal wave of applause greeting the new Queen.

THIRTY-FOUR

Bamboo Gardens

Isabelle's face was blotched and puffy, her lips hung down at the corners and her eyes, though no longer weeping, were blood-shot and circled with smeared mascara. When she saw Rita she threw herself at her and the sobbing began all over again. Rita encircled Isabelle with her arms and patted her back soothingly: the usual motions of restoring Isabelle's damaged ego to an upright position; but this time, she knew, it would take more than a hug and a few encouraging words. Isabelle was shattered.

Marilyn, hurrying up behind Isabelle, was, predictably, furious. 'Those judges have *definitely* been bribed!' she ranted. 'How could they! It was all a trick. Isabelle was by far the loveliest girl . . . everybody said so, the audience loved her, didn't you hear the applause! How could they even *think* . . .'

'Shut up! Just shut up!' cried Isabelle. 'You're just making it worse. I've never been so humiliated in my life – I wish I could just die. Oh, Rita, take me away from here, please, please take me away!'

They stood in a cramped passage halfway between the stage and the changing rooms, and passers-by, filing past between the entwined sisters and the wall, stared curiously and, having passed, turned to their friends, whispering and looking back. Meeting the eyes of a tall, ornately dressed black woman, Isabelle made a face and stuck out her tongue. The woman turned away hastily and disappeared.

Isabelle pulled away from Rita. 'That was Rose McGuire's aunty,' she said in disgust. 'They must all be simply *gloating*. Oh, I hate them, I hate them all, I wish I had never entered, I wish I was dead. Rita, please take me away!'

Rita agreed. She took Isabelle's hand and led her, Marilyn in their wake, through the throng to the foyer of the Pegasus, now crowded as the audience poured out of the ballroom. It was as if the three of them emitted an aura of tragedy which carved a way through the milling, chattering masses; as they walked, people fell silent and moved automatically aside with curious, sympathetic glances at Isabelle's bowed head. Isabelle was, of course, instantly recognizable in her red sequinned gown – overflowing emotion had not permitted a change into a more commonplace outfit – and they left in their wake an awed hush as eyes followed the vanquished favourite. Isabelle clung to Rita's arm.

'Rita, Rita, we should have hidden somewhere and waited till everyone's gone home. Oh, I could just *die*! Everyone's watching me! How will I ever live this down!'

'Nonsense!' scoffed Rita, taking a deep breath of fresh air as, finally, they emerged from the building. Marilyn hurried forward and took Isabelle's other arm.

'My poor darling!' she murmured. 'My poor little darling.'

They made their way towards the car park. A tall shadow emerged from the shadows and Rita shrank back, pulling Isabelle with her so that they almost stumbled.

'Oh, wow, I'm sorry, Rita, I didn't mean to scare you . . . I was looking for you, I just went to your car, thought you might have left, and—'

'Lord, Russell, you scared the hell out of me. I'm sorry, but . . .'

'You've got to take her away, I know, I kinda figured that . . .'

Russell paused, as if it were Rita's turn to say something; Rita, waiting for Russell to move out of the way, said nothing. Isabelle

sniffed and looked up at Russell. Russell returned her look, interested and sympathetic. He coughed, waiting for an introduction,
and when none came he took matters into his own hand.

'Hi, I'm Russell Chambers. Pleased to meet you. You were just
great. In my books you're the winner!' he said to Isabelle, and
his voice was soft and pleasant. Isabelle sniffed, pushed the hair
from her face, and straightened her shoulders. She granted Russell a weak, grateful and yet proud smile. She said nothing.

Russell moved aside, Rita, still holding Isabelle's hand, moved
forward. Marilyn, on passing Russell, flashed him one of her
most dazzling smiles and said, 'Are you a friend of Rita's?'

Russell fell into pace alongside Marilyn. 'Yes, Rita and me are
old pals – don't you remember, I used to live next door? She
brought me along to help root for Isabelle. We were planning on
taking Isabelle out to a celebration dinner at the Bamboo Gardens.
Tough luck, what happened back there.'

Walking in silence two paces ahead, Rita heard every word.
Russell's audacity amazed her. Celebration dinner? It was the
first she'd heard of it. Russell must have had that idea while
watching the show. Red signals began to go off in her head at
Marilyn's next words.

'Oh, but there's no reason to change all your plans, we
wouldn't *dream* of spoiling your evening, I mean, even if we
don't have anything to celebrate . . .' Raising her voice, she said,
'Isabelle, dear, are you feeling up to the Bamboo Gardens?'

Isabelle, turning slightly, said, 'Are you mad, Mummy? I'm a
mess and everybody will point at me.'

'Ridiculous. You just go home, have a nice shower to wash
away your disappointment, put on another dress and a new face,
and you'll be fine, just fine.' Lowering her voice again, Marilyn
continued, addressing Russell: 'It's not a good idea for her to stay
home tonight. She'll only brood and cry her eyes out. And it
would be so nice to have an admiring stranger around, giving
her ego a boost. You know what I mean.'

Rita could imagine, quite clearly, the coy wink Marilyn now
gave Russell through the darkness, and the smile of complicity.

Marilyn was as transparent as Isabelle. Rita rummaged in the depths of her handbag for her key. They had reached her car; she poked the key into the lock with an angry jerk, and swung open the door on the passenger side.

'Get in,' she snapped at Isabelle, and to herself, *Pull yourself together. You're angry still. Angry at Russell, that quarrel is still grating inside you.*

Isabelle slid into the car, Rita reached inside to open the back-door lock. She opened the back door and gestured for Marilyn to get in.

'So, Russell, goodnight. See you tomorrow?' she asked, making an extreme effort to calm her voice and speak in a friendly, reconciliatory way. 'I'm sorry about this whole thing,' she added as an afterthought. Russell looked helplessly at Marilyn, who rose to the occasion.

'Oh, but, Rita, didn't you understand? We're all going to the Bamboo Gardens for dinner. As a consolation prize for Isabelle, to cheer her up. She needs a change of scenery. If we go home she'll just be miserable, and as Russell's booked a table for dinner, it will do Isabelle a world of good to go out tonight of all nights.'

'I thought she said she doesn't want to. She doesn't want people to see her.'

'There's a private room at the Bamboo Gardens,' offered Russell. 'We can sit by ourselves. Nobody need see her. And anyway, she hasn't got anything to be ashamed of. She was just great, everyone will tell you that, she just had hard luck.'

'There! You see!' said Marilyn triumphantly. 'Russell, you're a fellow after my own heart. Just what Isabelle needs tonight. She had really set her heart on winning, you see, and she's so disappointed, she's shattered, and she needs to be told again and again how marvellous she is . . . That settles it. Get in, Russell, and move over, I'm coming too.'

THIRTY-FIVE

The Winner Is . . .

Dear Diary,

I'm tired of being nice, it doesn't pay. Isabelle got Russell. She got him with a snap of her fingers. All she had to do was lose the Miss Guyana contest, look up at him with devastated eyes, preen at his gallant compliments, smile secretly down into her lap and then look up, gaze at him adoringly, blink away her tears, turn on the dazzle. How can I compete with *that*? I'm just not made for this game. No man will ever want me. I haven't got what it takes, I can't give what they want. What *do* they want, for God's sake?

I trusted him, I gave my heart to him and just like that he turned and walked away, hypnotized by Isabelle. Ensnared by her! Yes, that's it. She wove a secret web, and he was gone. Snared like a fly in the web of a spider, drugged senseless by a magic potion. Did I say senseless? No, he wasn't senseless. On the contrary. All his senses were alive as anything, simply sizzling with heat. You could feel it miles away. She pressed the right buttons and turned him on. Dear Diary, that's what *all* men are all about. They can't resist it. Somehow I've always known it, that's why I stayed out of the fray — because I can't compete — but oh God oh God oh God I *loved* this one! I really loved him and *still do*.

I am hurt and I am angry, and I can't tell anyone but you. I can never be like that. What do I know about pulling switches and triggering reactions, waggling my behind and sending secret signals like a bitch in heat? Nothing! The language of mating is like Martian to me. I'll never learn it. And what's more, I don't *want* to learn it! Never never never! I just want to be *me!!!!!!!!!!!*

It was embarrassing just to sit there, watching the two of them at it, and Russell not even ashamed, not even having the good manners to show her that we're together. We aren't. Not after tonight, we aren't. We never were. It was all in my imagination. My dreams running away with me, painting out a pretty picture. And then tonight, like a bomb in the midst of those dreams.

So bloody romantic, up there in the Bamboo Gardens roof garden, on top of the world with only the stars above you, and all that silvery background music, and waiters with white gloves gliding here and there between the foliage. Marilyn enjoyed every moment; she knew very well that Russell was mine. No, he wasn't, he isn't. He's hers. He was hers for the taking and he's hers right now.

He danced with me for manners' sake, and he danced with Marilyn. Marilyn was charmed. But when he danced with Isabelle — they didn't stop. Just stood there swaying, sparks flying, my heart breaking. Dancing gave them the privacy they needed to talk, he whispering into her ear, she smiling up at him. Pressing herself into him.

So, dear Diary, what do I do now? Hurt is flooding up from the place that love lived. It is flooding me, and I am drowning in it. I hoped too much, I loved too much, and now if I weren't holding this pen in my hand and writing these words I'd be ... I'd be ... I don't know what I'd be but it would be something drastic like tearing out my hair or screaming out the window.

But I won't. NO, I WON'T! I will not drown in sorrow like the heroine of some cheap novel! I refuse! Look the facts in the face, Rita, and see what a farce it is.

From the moment he saw Isabelle he was sweating for her. Like a dog who'd got a whiff of a bitch in heat. Yes, go ahead, put it in the crassest terms, that will help. Good, a dog. That's Russell. Hungry.

Panting and drooling for a piece of meat! Remember his eyes as he watched her in her bathing suit? And you, mad with jealousy, sitting next to him and wishing it were YOU up there looking so good? Is that what you really want? Jealous of your sister! Jealous of Isabelle! Wishing yourself a body like hers, the ability of hers to press switches that turn intelligent men into panting dogs!

Can you respect this puppy of a man? And if you can't respect him can you love him? Look, he's gone and he wasn't ever worth your love. Not for a second or a nanosecond. You've been wasting your love; never do that again. Love is the most precious thing you have to give; remember that. Thank you for reminding me, dear Diary. Sometimes I feel that you are God: just talking to you cures me. I can pour my heart into you, lay my life at your feet, and your benevolent wisdom relieves me of my pain, removes my burden of sorrow, and I am free!

I look at my heart now, and it is free — no pain, no sorrow, no jealousy. Light and free! Russell? He was never worth it. Not then and not now. Isabelle? Poor little thing. Marilyn? Let her triumph; she thinks Isabelle's hooked herself a white man.

Dear Diary, you have cured me! It is three in the morning, and at last I can sleep. Tomorrow we're meeting Russell at the Pegasus pool. Fine with me. I am free.

Isabelle recovered remarkably quickly from the shock of not winning. The consolation prize was much better, much bigger: it had two legs and male organs, black hair and cobalt-blue adoring eyes; it had, as far as she could tell, a well-stocked bank account, and, most of all, it lived in the Golden Land, America.

Somehow, Rita concluded, Russell's wooing of Isabelle was all predestined. The groundwork had been laid more than a decade ago, when Isabelle had left her bicycle on the road just behind Russell's car and Russell had ruined it, forcing him to ring the Number Seven doorbell; not for her, but for Isabelle. It was like an omen.

Even then, he had admired her: pretty, pert and perky five-year-old Isabelle, trailing behind her big sister; running over in her ballet dress, twirling on tip-toe for him, little hands fluttering like butterflies around her.

'She's so cute,' Russell had said back then, laughing, and now she was *devastatingly* cute, and Russell was helpless. What was happening now was just an echo of the past.

THIRTY-SIX

On Tip-toe

Once more, Isabelle was twirling on tip-toe, this time for Rita alone. She wore a close-fitting black dress with spaghetti straps and a little flared skirt that stopped one inch below her crotch: an adult, X-rated version of a ballet dress. Rita lay back on her bed against a mountain of pillows, wishing Isabelle would disappear so she could get back to her book.

'Rita, I'm certain, I'm *really* certain, that tonight's the night, so I have to look my very best. I'm *positive* he's going to propose. The way things have been going the last few days . . .' she giggled. 'Why, we're practically *engaged*. He practically said so. "I want you near me for ever," he said. I mean, it's obvious, isn't it? And—'

'But you've only known him two weeks! How can he propose after two weeks!'

Isabelle giggled again. 'Haven't you ever heard of a whirlwind romance? A romance that simply takes your breath away? Well, this is one of those. I thought that only happened in novels or in the cinema! And besides, we haven't got that much time. He's only here for a month more, we have to get things decided before that and I'll need a trousseau . . . It's a good thing I got my passport before the contest because they take such ages to get processed. Isn't it funny? If I hadn't entered the contest I wouldn't have had my passport and I wouldn't even have met Russell, and it's because I *lost* it I practically flew into his arms! Oh, Rita, I'm so happy! He's so manly, so adult and mature, I feel so – so – protected in his arms, and the way he helped me after the contest when I was so depressed, and he's been such a support since then; why, I don't mind at *all* about losing any more, and . . .'

Rita closed her eyes, and, as far as she could, her ears. She'd heard it all before and it wasn't a story that gained profundity by retelling.

'. . . Rita, you're not *listening*! Answer me!'

'Sorry, I didn't hear the question.'

'I was asking you if it's better to accept at once, when he proposes, or if it would be in bad taste to be over-eager. Maybe I should play a bit hard-to-get, say I need time and all that, make him *anxious* about me.'

Rita yawned and turned away. 'Whatever you think.'

'You're some help, I must say. And you haven't said if my dress is OK . . .' She pulled at the hemline. 'You don't think it's too *short*, do you? Look . . .' She sat down on the chair opposite Rita and crossed her golden legs. 'Can you see my panty? Do you think it's too provocative? Or would he *like* it that way? And look' – springing to her feet and bending backwards and forwards – 'can you see it if I bend over?'

Rita peered over the top of her book. 'Well, if I want to see it I can, if I sort of *bend down* to look. If he doesn't want to see it he could keep his eyes discreetly up. Depends if he wants to or not.'

Isabelle looked worried. 'I'm sure he doesn't mind *himself*, it's just if other *men* can see it. Now look . . .' She raised her arms above her shoulders and turned, slow-dancing with an invisible partner. 'Can you see my panty *now*?'

'Yes, definitely.'

'Oh shit. What shall I *do*?'

'Wear a panty with frills on the backside. Like you used to do at ballet class.'

'Rita, where would I ever get . . . Oh, you beast, you're joking, you're laughing at me, I hate you! Why can't you be *serious*! Don't you know how important this is . . .'

Isabelle, almost in tears, ran from the room, slamming the door behind her. Rita sighed, puffed up her pillows, and read another two pages. The door flew open and Isabelle burst in again, still barefoot, in a diaphanous red dress, longer and fuller than the black one, carrying an armful of shoes, which she let fall to the floor. She twirled once for Rita's benefit, and bent over, presenting a black-laced bottom for Rita's inspection. 'This is much better, isn't it? But I don't know what earrings to wear. Maybe I'll borrow Mummy's diamond ones? Do you think she'll let me? They would look just gorgeous with this dress; and then I have to choose my *shoes*, so tell me . . .'

Rita glanced over at Isabelle, slapped shut her book, slammed it down on the pillow and swung her legs over the side of the bed.

'Look, Isabelle: you know perfectly well that I'm the wrong person to ask, because I don't give a bloody *damn* about how you look and I don't have a bloody *idea* what goes with what. As far as I'm concerned you can wrap yourself in the bathroom carpet. Go and ask Marilyn and leave me alone!'

'*Bitch!*' Isabelle stuck out her tongue, gathered her shoes back into her arms, and stormed out of the room.

Rita stuck out her own tongue at the door. '*Women!*' she said in scorn.

Isabelle, in her pink lace nightie, looked lost and forlorn. She sat on the edge of Rita's bed and dabbed at her eyes with a corner of the seersucker sheet. 'I just don't understand, Rita. He's leaving next week and he still hasn't proposed! I've been dropping hints right, left and centre and so has Mummy but he just doesn't react! It's as if he doesn't understand what I'm getting at – but he must! After all, he started it! He just couldn't get enough of me at the beginning, and he still can't, so why doesn't he show me he's serious?'

'Perhaps he wants to surprise you the night before he leaves.'

'Don't be ridiculous, he must know it wouldn't surprise me. I've practically asked him myself already and Marilyn almost put the words into his mouth the other day. I mean if he loves me – and he does love me! He does, he does! He told me so many times how much he loves me. He adores me. I can tell. The way he makes love to me – Rita, he's just so loving, so tender, and his hands . . .'

'Isabelle, I don't want to know all your private stuff.'

'Yes, but he *does* love me. You can't imagine the way he gazes into my eyes and tells me so. So he must want to marry me! He just can't get enough of me – he told me so many times. A hundred times. And I love him. I *told* him.'

'Well then, if that's so clear he must be waiting till the last night to propose. Keeping you guessing, you know.'

'I can't believe he would . . . I've been hinting so loudly. I need to know *now*.'

'Mark my words: the night before he leaves he'll present you with a huge engagement ring.'

'You really think so?'

'Of course. And then you can join him later in America.'

'Oh, Rita, if he doesn't marry me I'll die! I'll just *die*!'

Isabelle in her black lace nightie looked like an angel of vengeance. Distraught, she paced Rita's room, stopping now and then to stamp a little foot.

'You should have warned me, Rita. It wasn't *fair*. You knew all the time and you didn't warn me!'

'I didn't know. I swear I didn't.'

'He said he told you!'

'He told me he was *divorced*! He *definitely* said divorced.'

'Estranged! He's been estranged from his wife and now they're going to give it another go. But you knew, all the time you knew!'

'Isabelle – he definitely said he *had been* married and was now *divorced*. I remember distinctly. If he hadn't said that I wouldn't have . . . wouldn't have . . .'

'Wouldn't have *what*?'

'Never mind.'

'No, go on, tell me, wouldn't have what?'

'I said, never mind. Forget it.'

'Russ hinted . . . He said . . . You and he . . .'

Rita stood up angrily and walked to the door. 'I said, *forget it*. I don't want to talk about it.'

She walked out onto the upstairs landing. Isabelle flung herself out of the room behind her.

'Talk about *what*? About the two of you? Did you have him before me? And you knew all the time and still you fixed me up with him even though you knew he was married, almost as if you—'

Rita had reached the top of the stairs but now she swung around. 'What did you say?'

'I said, you had an affair with him, you had your fun, and then when you found out he was married you passed him onto me, because . . . because . . . I mean, you must have *known* he's just my type, you could *see* I was falling in love with him, in fact, it was love at first sight, he told me so when we were dancing, and all the time you knew all about him and you didn't say a word! Why did you even introduce us? It's so humiliating . . . I've been telling everyone that we're getting married and what will I say now? And—'

Rita snapped. She wore an old torn T-shirt and the bottom half of an ancient pair of shorty-pyjamas, the top half of which had disappeared into some far corner of the wardrobe. Her hair, for once, was loose, and billowed out around her head and floated beyond her shoulders in a magnificent black mane as wide as it was long. She was a head taller than Isabelle, a natural advantage she now exploited: Isabelle understood well the silent language of dominance and subordination. Rita grabbed her sister's wrists and drew her close, glaring down at her with a menace in her eyes from which the girl shrank. Rita pushed Isabelle backwards and the younger girl did not resist; she let herself be backed into the room till she felt the edge of the bed behind her bare knees. Rita gave her one last shove, and she fell onto the bed and sat there, knees drawn together, arms tightly folded, and silent, staring fearfully up at the big sister towering above her with an expression on her face she, Isabelle, had never seen in all her life.

'Listen to this, Isabelle. Just listen, once in your life, listen.' Rita paused to make sure Isabelle was listening, and, assured of attention, continued. 'I did *not* fix you up with Russell. Quite the opposite. I had no intention of playing Cupid when I brought him to the contest. Can you understand that? Can you believe that?' She waited for Isabelle's feeble nod before continuing.

'Can you for once in your life get it into your little brain that the world does not revolve around you? That you and your well-being are not the object and the goal of everybody else's actions? If you could just once *understand* that – not just understand that, but if you could really and truly *absorb* that wisdom and somehow *grow up* out of it, then your life would be a whole lot easier. The only reason you broke down when you didn't win that stupid contest is because you *believed* the myth that Isabelle Maraj had some obscure right to win, that Isabelle Maraj is somehow the centre of the universe, that Isabelle Maraj is going to get everything she wants: name, fame, fortune and rich white man. If you had just for a moment considered that every girl there wanted to win every bit as much as you did, that every single girl had feelings just like yours and as liable of getting hurt as yours, that only *one girl* could win and that every one of the losers – except you – had the good grace to smile at her misfortune and even go and congratulate Rose for winning, then . . . what was I saying? Oh yes – if only for one moment you stopped and looked at your stupid, petty, self-absorbed, vain *obsession* with yourself and what you want then you might find yourself a better person and a more likeable person and even maybe a *happier* person! You know, I used to blame myself for your failings, I used to think it's because your accident somehow

265

made you neurotic and hysterical or whatever and that's why I put up with a lot of your nonsense, because it was my fault you had that damn accident. But sometimes I think you're just a common bitch and that's it. Brain damage, my foot! There's something in you that makes you a bitch and something in me that makes me excuse and forgive you though you don't deserve it but one day you've got to *learn*, Isabelle! One day you've got to grow up and just . . . just . . .' Rita paused in her tirade to push the bush of hair back from her face. She was sweating, she felt as if a fire burned under her skin. Isabelle cowered against the headrest with arms hugging her knees.

'Just be a *human being*! Lord, is that such a difficult thing!'

Rita sat herself on the edge of the bed and leaned over towards Isabelle. 'And now let me tell *you* a secret. I wasn't going to tell you because I have my pride and it's not a particularly flattering thing to say about myself. But I was in love with Russell. The reason I brought him to the contest was not to fix him up with you but because I didn't want to spend even one night without him. So I invited him to come along – since I more or less had to go to it anyway – for your bloody sake. Now can you just for one little fraction of a second try an experiment. Try to put yourself into my skin. Try to feel how it is to be me, and being in love with a man for practically the first time in your life, and watching your little sister flaunt everything she's got and wiggle her hips and bat her eyelids at that man. And while you're being me consider this – I haven't been in love often, I'm not like you. This is just about the second or third time in my whole life. So being in love is a special condition with me. Hard to believe, but true. Maybe there's something wrong with me but that's the way it is. Whereas *you* fall in and out of love at the same rate you buy new dresses. Try to feel my feelings that night. Stop thinking about yourself, shut your eyes, and *feel*!'

Isabelle shrank back even more and simply stared at Rita with wide-open eyes. 'Rita, I . . .'

'Don't say that word! I'm tired of it. I, I, I, morning, noon, and night! Shut your eyes, I said!'

Isabelle clamped her eyes shut.

'OK, good. And now feel. You're me. Feel how I felt. Watching the two of you flirting away without a care in the world. *Feel* it!'

Isabelle nodded quickly, eyes still squeezed shut.

'Watch yourself making bedroom eyes at him. Teasing him. Turning him on. Deliberately turning him on!'

'I didn't know I didn't know I didn't *know*! I didn't want to hurt you! Truly I didn't know!' Isabelle was blubbering, her words emerging in incoherent bursts. She threw herself against Rita and sobbed heartbreakingly. But Rita thrust her away, held her shoulders and, looking straight into her eyes, continued.

'I know you didn't know, silly. How could you! As far as you're concerned, Rita has only one reason for existence, to revolve around Isabelle like a bloody satellite. But Rita has a life too, Rita has feelings and Rita can love. That's all I'm saying. I'm not blaming you for doing something you didn't know you were doing. I'm not even blaming *him* although his behaviour towards me is despicable, but it's my fault for falling for such a heel. Let's face it: Rita and Isabelle were both used – two naïve little Indian girls from the backwaters, inexperienced and hungry for love, falling for the tall white prince from America. He wiped his feet on us, gave us a good hard kick, and now he's gone and Isabelle and Rita can just disappear into a corner and lick their wounds. And if you don't mind, Rita wants to be left alone for a while.'

'But . . .'

'Didn't you hear?'

Isabelle gaped, opened her mouth to say something, thought better of it, and left the room.

Isabelle was still the best apologizer in the world. 'I'm sorry, I'm truly sorry,' she said. 'I never meant to hurt you.'

'It's all right. You couldn't know. He's the one who knew.'

'Still, I'll understand it if you hate me. I can't bear it when you hate me, Rita. I don't know how I'll ever make it up to you. Please don't hate me – you know how much I need you.'

Isabelle brought Rita glasses of juice, plates of shredded tangerine, and polished her car. But she couldn't heal the soreness.

Dear Diary,

I couldn't stand it at home. Isabelle moping around with hangdog eyes, gazing at me like a sheep before the slaughter. I took two weeks' holiday and cleared out. So now I'm here, on the Pomeroon.

Granny, as ever, welcomed me. But how she has aged! I haven't seen her for a year and I never realized how much one year can batter an aged body.

It's as if her skin's been stretched to its limits, then draped around a tiny skeleton, hanging too loosely, wilted and soft. Her hair is silver and long and stringy, and so sparse her scalp shows through. She wears it in a knot halfway down her back. Her eyes are too large for her wizened face; they're as black as creekwater, and as shining, with hidden depths I long to explore, for in them is the wisdom of the ages. Her energy seems the same, but she's slowed down. Now Aunty Doreen does almost all the work. Granny does the things she can do sitting, the peeling, scrubbing, chopping things.

I told her the whole story. And I told her something else, something that's been dawning on me for a very long time, over years, in fact, but made acute by Daddy's death, and pushed underground by this Miss Guyana thing.

I've had enough. I can't live here any more. Not in that house, not in this country. I still hear a rattling of faraway drums, only they've grown louder and their call is incessant. I have to go.

I just don't know where *to*. Not yet. Granny says to wait; the answer will come from within me. Granny says all our answers are to be found inside us. If only we learn to wait, and to listen to the silence.

When the world's noise recedes, she says, when the jabbering of thoughts dies down, our own soul shows the way forward. Our destiny is written in the deepest waters of the mind. Be still, she says, and listen.

Granny can still paddle a canoe. She took me up the creek to a place where the trees meet overhead and the creek's black water is as shiny as glass, a secret place where even the least thought is more jarring than the croaking of a frog. There she laid her paddle across her knee and let the canoe just drift.

'Listen!' Granny said. 'There is nothing to do and nowhere to go. Just be. Be what you are; what you truly are, not what you have made yourself to be. Be like this creek. When it is still and its surface unbroken it reflects the truth: see how the trees and your face and mine are reflected in it, as clearly as in a mirror! Be like the creek, like water, and you will know your way.'

Sitting there so still, her legs stretched out in the depths of the canoe, unmoving as one of the mangroves on the creek bank whose branches reach down into the water's depths. Granny is a part of nature. I look at her with something like awe. I shudder; I feel small, but in loving her I know I am as vast as she is, as vast as nature, and that her wisdom will also be mine; that it is her true bequest to me.

Perhaps such stillness is only possible in sleep. Perhaps that's why I dreamed last night: Daddy came to me. He was crying. 'Take me home,' he said. 'I can find no rest till I come home!'

'But you are home, Daddy!' I said to him. 'This is Number Seven. You're home!'

Daddy only shook his head. 'No, no, no. All the way home.' And he wept some more.

That was the entire dream. It woke me up; and when I awoke my cheeks too were wet, and I was filled with a great sadness, a nostalgia for something I did not yet know, something beyond my comprehension.

'Perhaps he meant India?' Granny said.

'India? Why India?' I asked.

'Your Daddy is Indian; his soul is rooted there. Perhaps it's the other side of your soul calling you home; perhaps something in you needs to know India.'

'I've often felt a stranger to myself,' I told her. 'Hanging here in the world, not knowing where I belong, to what culture, to what race. Without roots.'

'Yes. You don't know your roots,' Granny said. She spoke in

269

simple Creolese words, but I understood her perfectly, and I know what she meant, because I feel her words as truth.

'You have to know your roots to find healing. When you first came here you were broken, because you were completely rootless. Your mummy's spirit brought you here to be healed; she brought you back to *her* roots. But that healing is not yet finished: another part of you is still rootless, lost and sick. My work is finished, Rita, I can't heal you any more. That's why your Daddy's spirit came in the stillness of sleep. He came to you to call you back home.'

'But India is so far away!' Something in me was reluctant to leave her, to cut loose from the safety of this home. Perhaps it was a fear of what the future might hold.

'There's no such thing as distance. There's no such thing as time. No such thing as separation. Your ancestors live in you; they are calling you home. You've reached a dead end in your life — you have to cut loose, move on, find new horizons. Remember the diamonds I gave you: they are the key to your destiny. Sell them: they will open doors for you . . .' She closed her eyes. 'I can see more diamonds, waiting for you there. But these are different diamonds. More precious than them pebbles I gave you. Much more precious.'

As she always did, Granny came to Rita's bedside the night before she returned to Georgetown.

'I won't see you again,' she said. 'This is the last time.'

'Granny! No! Don't say that! I'll be back!'

'No,' said Granny. 'You won't.'

THIRTY-SEVEN

Persuasion

'You can't just go off and leave me!' Isabelle wept.

When, on her return from the Pomeroon, Rita announced her intention of leaving, Isabelle had followed her up to her room and now refused to leave. 'Take me with you, Rita! Please! What am I supposed to do in this God-forsaken place?'

'Take you with me? You must be joking. Go and get a job like everybody else.'

'What kind of a job do you expect me to get with those exam results? Cleaning, or what? What will I do here all by myself? With only Marilyn? I can't bear the thought, Rita. And you know I want to go to India. It was my idea to begin with anyway.'

'Your idea!'

'Yes, of course! Ever since that man came with that funny story. You know how I was upset because I wanted to go and see what the whole thing was about. That's why I said that stupid thing about being a princess – I've never been able to forget. Go on, please!'

'Do you think I want you tied to my ankles!'

'I won't bother you, I promise. Just take me to that palace he spoke about, and leave me there. I'll manage once I'm there, I promise. I won't be in your way. You can go wherever you want to after that, just let me travel with you!'

'Don't be ridiculous, Isabelle. You're not a princess and you never will be one. There aren't any Indian kingdoms any more.'

'Well, all right, but he spoke about a fortune to be inherited, didn't he? And why should we be discounted just because we're women – it's so unfair. And in this day and age! Why does it have to be a *male* heir?'

'So you think they're all waiting for you to turn up and claim it! Baloney!'

Nevertheless, Granny's words came to mind. What was that about precious diamonds, waiting for her in her father's home? Meanwhile, she had her own diamonds. They would buy her freedom, Granny had said, and she had been perfectly right. And then there was the golden heart on its chain around her neck. That would bring luck, Granny had said. Something about Granny's words was prophetic. It seemed to her that it was Granny sending her off on this trip, Granny giving her the means to escape, Granny who would guide her.

'But they didn't *find* a male heir, did they? There isn't one! That means they'll probably *have* to consider me. Us. I mean, they've got no choice, have they? We are the only Marajs left. Daddy said so.'

'Isabelle, you're at it again. You can't just turn up on somebody's doorstep saying you're after their fortune! They'll throw you out head first and you can't blame them! My goodness, be sensible! It's ridiculous, and it's mercenary. No, I won't.'

'But after all they started it – they're looking for someone, and why not me?'

'If they started it let them finish it. What you're thinking of is fortune-hunting at its most blatant. It makes me sick!'

'But, Rita, you can't just go rushing off to India! You just can't! And leaving me here! What will I do without you! And why India, of all places! You never wanted to go there before!'

'I've got my reasons.'

'And how can you afford it anyway? You can't even afford to

272

move out into a flat of your own, how can you afford a plane ticket all the way around the world?'

'I have my sources,' Rita said. 'And talking about affording it, what about you? You can't afford it either!'

'Oh, Mum'll give me the money. It's an investment – she'll understand.'

'Don't be ridiculous. She might if she had the money but she doesn't. Daddy left so much debt behind she'll be paying it off for the rest of her life. She doesn't have a penny any more.'

'Oh, but she does.'

'She does?'

'Mum sold Prabudial to Hudson-what's it, a Canadian company that's been badgering them for a year. For a small fortune! Mum's rich again. She's been talking of sending me to modelling school in England but this is much better. I'll talk her into it.'

Rita's first reaction was outrage. 'She sold Prabudial? She sold that wonderful pristine rainforest to those *vultures*?'

Isabelle shrugged. 'She needed the money. And she'll give me some of it, if it's a matter of securing my future. Please take me, Rita. This is the chance of a lifetime for me. My last chance, probably. You can't just turn away and leave me here! I promise I won't get in your way. Just take me with you, that's all I'm asking. Please! And then you'll be rid of me for ever! I promise!'

Rita was silent.

'Rita! I don't know what will become of me if you leave me here. I'll probably go to the dogs, I'm so unhappy! Deep inside, I'm really miserable. I try to present a pretty face to the world but deep inside, Rita, I'm broken. And there's no future for me here. I know it. I'm not asking all that much of you. In fact, it's the last thing I'll ever ask of you, I promise. Please don't let me down, Rita. *Not again.*'

When Isabelle said 'Not again' Rita looked up and straight into her eyes. There was no mistaking it: Isabelle had known exactly what she was alluding to. The implication was patent. And for once, every one of Isabelle's arguments was accurate. Rita sighed, and threw up her hands. There was no escaping the past. She had not yet atoned.

Part Four

THIRTY-EIGHT

Twelve Mouths to Feed

I've always known that Amma and Appa weren't my real parents. But I was their real daughter. They were love and kindness itself and though they had five children of their own I always belonged to them.

But I've also always known about Him. Always, as far back as I can remember, there he was, the man who was supposed to be my real father, but who for me was more like a god, up in the heaven somewhere along with Indra and all the other celestial beings, occasionally deigning to descend to us and bless me with his presence. He came seldom; the last time I was only about eight, but I never forgot – each visit stayed with me for ever. At those times I was truly tongue-tied – I could hardly speak a word to him, and answered his fond questions with a yes or a no or even just a shrug of my shoulders, turning my face away so as not to meet his eyes, for I could not bear the way they seemed to see all the way through me, right down to the bottom of my being, and I would tingle with happiness. And when he left again the tingling would stay with me for a long time so I hardly felt like a human child until normal life seeped through me once again and called me back to earth. What I am saying is I really worshipped that man, and I didn't think of him as a father but as my saviour, even as a small child. Yes, I worshipped him; whereas what I felt for Amma and Appa was merely love – but love is enough for any normal child, isn't it?

We lived in a big house in Gingee. At least, for me it was a big house, though I have since seen really grand homes and ours was a hovel in comparison. But for Gingee it was certainly large. I had seen the homes of other children in my class, you see, and ours seemed so much grander though now I can only laugh at such innocence. I mean, I *would* laugh if I could, if I had not forgotten how to laugh. Our home, in fact, was just a gathering of rooms all leading into each other, and mats laid out where we slept – inside in winter, outside in summer – and some shelves where we kept our clothes and utensils. That's all, though we did have electric lights and a radio, which blared filmi music all day long; Amma liked filmi music, and she sang along with the radio.

So we had comforts, and our home in Gingee was no hovel either – for I have seen real hovels. Oh, I have seen the very worst kind of places where people actually live, holes in hell. Seen them, and lived in them. Just thinking of those places my heart beats faster and I feel the panic rising in me like vomit, panic that is trapped inside me and can never leave the body, like vomit that lurches up but falls back down again. I would give anything to be able to vomit but I cannot. It is trapped in me for ever and when I pray it is for healing from that sickness in me.

Anyway, the span between a hovel and a palace is extremely wide, and I would say our home in Gingee was somewhere in the middle. But looking back I think of it as paradise. And I would exchange all the palaces in the world and all of paradise to go back there, or never to have left. But my destiny said otherwise.

Appa was headmaster of the English Medium School and so he was highly respected, and so were we children. I was the same age as Prema, his middle daughter, who was also my very best friend; there were also two elder sons and two younger daughters, and we were all so happy! We lived in a quiet area and when we had finished our schoolwork and our household chores we children could play in the street outside our door as much as we wanted, because there was not much traffic, not like in the busier areas of town where the whole street would be filled with all kinds of vehicles with stinking exhaust fumes as well as rickshaws which would appear out of nowhere and pounce on you if you tried to cross the street. I used to be terrified of streets like that and always grabbed somebody's hand when we went anywhere in the town, either my big brother's or Amma's or if there was nobody big, then my sister Prema's. But of course now I know that that street was really nothing more than a quiet lane; because now I have seen the world and I know the terrors the world holds are worse than any terror you could possibly imagine, even in hell. I have read about hell, and the demons that live there, but I can assure you, what I have seen on earth itself is a million times worse. That is the truth. And because I was happy with Amma and Appa and Prema and the others I can compare, and so I can say my childhood was pure heaven. That is how it seems to me now.

Appa was one of the kindest men I ever met. He wore large thick glasses and he would peer at you over the top of them and smile. He could also be strict, of course, as a headmaster you have to be very strict. Sometimes he even flogged some of the naughtier children, but only the boys, never the girls. But then girls are never naughty. Why then is it always the girls who get the worst punishments? I would rather have been flogged a million times than endure the punishments I had to take later, because of being a girl. But you wanted to know about my childhood.

Looking back I cannot see much of the details. I see this house with a large veranda at the front, where Amma used to sit cleaning rice or stringing beans and things like that, because she liked to see who was passing by and sometimes have a little chat with the other ladies who lived on that street. Amma was just as kind as Appa. I cannot believe I was so fortunate to have parents like them, even though they weren't my real parents. When I think of them and that time before my twelfth birthday tears come to my eyes because it is so rare, I know that now, and when I close my eyes I can see Amma's beautiful face and those eyes brimming with love.

I am sure there were unpleasant things in Gingee as well, but I don't remember them because they are nothing. I only remember the good things, I mean how good Amma and Appa were to me; it is as if my life back then, the life I lived from day to day, was nothing more than a film passing before my eyes, insubstantial pictures of no lasting value, so there's no use at all in describing them to you. The important thing was the feeling I had, we all had, the feeling of being embedded in this wonderful cushion of love where nothing could touch you and nothing could hurt you. I suppose that is the essence of my childhood, not the individual events that followed each other in a chain – because those things pass away. What remains at all times is the thing behind it . . . the screen of my being, you could say, over which those pictures passed; because that is what stayed with me all of the time thereafter, that is what really kept me alive when everything else was dying, crumbling into a dark abyss and swallowing up my soul. Because I was able to say to myself, if the events of my childhood are nothing more than passing pictures, then so is this horror. Remain as what you are, I told myself again and again, and don't be affected by the pictures. Remain as you are. Remain as you are. Only that is the truth. Everything else is a passing picture.

That is the secret of my survival. I don't mean my physical survival, for my body, though badly injured, was never even near death – though often it felt that way, and often I prayed it could be dead, and I know that one day it will be dead. I mean the survival of my soul, which has been so much in jeopardy this last year or so. Yet it has survived and though it has suffered many wounds still it is whole, and it will always be whole, for ever and ever, because it is bedded in wholeness.

I told you I don't remember the unpleasant things; well, that's not quite true. I do remember when Appa got sick shortly after my eleventh birthday. To this day I don't know what sickness

280

he had, just that it was very serious and very short, in fact so short we hardly had time to get used to him lying in his bed and sweating, so weak he could hardly even smile at us, and then all of a sudden he was dead.

Of course Appa's death was the very worst thing that happened in my whole childhood, because it put an abrupt end to that childhood. The death itself was terrible enough and we were all plunged into the blackest grief; if you can imagine a dark mist where you cannot even see your hand in front of you, well, that is how we all felt, because we had all loved Appa so much and now he was gone. But we had to get used to life without Appa and it seemed to me that it would just be life minus Appa, I mean just Amma and the rest of us, but it was not to be that way. Now I am older I know why: it is because Appa had been the one to earn the money on which we all lived. I had been used to seeing Amma cooking food daily for us and I never realized it was Appa who earned the money to buy that food, and also to buy our school uniforms and books and all the other things which as a child I just took for granted. But now I know all these things have to be bought with money: clothes and soap and kerosene oil and dahl, and somebody has to earn that money. Well, Amma had to look after us, and what was she to do? She couldn't go and work as headmaster in Appa's place, could she? And so the normal thing happened, which was that Appa's younger brother inherited us all, as well as the house.

Appa's brother was also a schoolteacher, but that was where the similarity between them ended, because Appa's brother was not kind but very cruel. That's how it seemed to me. Appa's brother lived on the other side of Gingee. His was a much smaller house than ours, and we could not possibly all move there, so what happened is that Appa's brother brought his whole family and moved into our big house. I think he would have liked the house very much if it weren't for its content, which was us; but he had to take the house *and* its content. I think there was some law about that, or some duty he had to fulfil towards his brother. So now we all lived together with Appa's brother, Appa's brother's wife and Appa's brother's daughters. There were three of them. And all of a sudden our big house seemed much smaller, though it was the same size, just much fuller now, especially because Appa's three daughters were all quite young and very noisy and took up a lot of space for themselves. In fact, Appa's brother and his family took over most of the house for themselves, and left the seven of us – Amma and we six children – to live in one room all together.

I never liked Appa's brother or his wife, not even before all the terrible things happened. I suppose that's only natural, because he also did not like me. He didn't like any of us but he didn't like me most of all, because he said I was an extra mouth to feed, and not his flesh and blood, and such things. He once had an argument with Amma about it. I don't remember the words exactly, and anyway I was too young to understand, but I do remember Amma pleading with him and saying these words, 'But he sends money for her support!' And I knew then that she was speaking about Him, that god I had only met about three times. There was a lot of talk about money in those days, but I didn't understand it. How could I? Only now I understand the meaning of money, and how a human life and human happiness weighs nothing against money. I only remember things that were repeated often, like the two words 'twelve mouths' which it seemed to my eleven-year-old mind the axis upon which our whole life turned: 'twelve mouths to feed', Appa's brother would complain all of the time, and 'I have to cook for twelve mouths!' Appa's brother's wife nagged. Or almost as often as the 'twelve mouths' there were the 'seven extra mouths', meaning us: Amma and her children. I even used to dream about those seven extra mouths, gaping open and floating by without heads and bodies while Amma placed a tiny spoonful of food in each one, after which the mouth would snap shut. That is what we were for them: open mouths they were supposed to fill. You won't believe this, but even though they complained so much and hated me so especially I never once dreamed I could ever be separated from Amma, because Amma was a part of me. I just didn't think such a thing was possible, and I didn't really listen to all the negotiations on the matter; all I remember is that Amma often pleaded with them, sometimes weeping, and often when we were supposed to be asleep I would hear them shouting at poor Amma, and she pleading back. And Amma took me in her arms often and held me close and wept, but still I did not know what was going to happen. If I had had even an inkling, you can be sure I would have run away, though where could I have gone, eleven years of age and no knowledge of the world?

As it was, Amma tried to rescue me. One night she woke me up and pressed a finger to my lips, wrapped me in a blanket and guided me through the darkness of the garden and out into the street. It must have been very late at night because the street was quite empty, Amma had both hands on my shoulders and almost pushed me along, and though I was not fully awake and though she did not speak I felt the urgency in her manner and hurried as best I could, sometimes tripping on the edge of the blanket dangling around my hastening feet, sometimes stumbling on one of the many potholes we crossed. We walked for a long time but soon I had an idea where we were going to, and I was right – she was taking me to her sister's home. Her sister, my aunt, seemed to know we were coming because the moment Amma touched her shoulder – she was sleeping on the back veranda, just as we had been – she sprang to her feet like an uncoiling spring, and ushered me into the house. It was all so stealthy, so secret! I felt so scared because I knew that they themselves were scared, though I couldn't tell what of. Nobody had yet told me anything of what was really going on though I knew it was all about money. Now that I am older I know that Amma was not very clever to take me to her sister's, because of course that was the first place Appa's brother looked for me next day when he found I was gone. And early in the morning he appeared and so did Amma, and there was a big quarrel between the three of them, Amma, Appa's brother and Amma's sister. I didn't know what it was really about at the time, I was so confused, but I heard bits and pieces of the things they shouted at each other: Amma pleading with Appa's brother to let me stay with her sister, and her sister saying it was quite all right for me to live there, it wouldn't cost anything, and then Appa's nasty remark, that neither would I earn anything. That last remark I remember most of all because of the nasty way he said it. Nasty things stay in a person's mind as well as kind things; they are like thorns sticking in there and even if you try to pull them out they edge themselves in deeper. So I never forgot those words of Appa's brother, that I would not earn anything, and that was the first time I realized that I had to earn my living from now on.

That same day Appa's brother took me on a bus to Madras. I don't remember much of the bus drive because I was so terrified about leaving Amma and my brothers and sisters, especially Prema, and of course my home which was now actually Appa's brother's home. But still I missed it so badly I cried all the way to Madras, which is why I didn't look out the window much. And I didn't want to go to Madras at all, though of course everybody wants to go to Madras; the way people always used to talk about Madras I used to think it must be a kind of paradise, and if somebody had been to Madras it was a very special thing. I had friends at my school who had been to Madras and everybody treated them like kings and queens afterwards, and they strutted around telling about all the marvellous things in Madras, things the rest of us had never seen and never would see. And now it was my turn to see all these things but I wasn't happy about it at all, because all I could see was Amma's weeping face when Appa's brother tore me out of her arms.

I told you already that I was to see bigger houses than our own house in Gingee. Well, the place he took me to was the first of those big houses. It seemed to me then to be a palace, though now I have seen yet bigger ones. So you see, everything in life is relative. Happiness is relative and so is suffering. People complain about this and that, and they think their sorrows insurmountable and unbearable, yet if I could have exchanged just one little moment of my own burdens for a whole lifetime of those little trivial things some people call problems, oh, I would have rushed to do so! But that was to come later. Reaching this big house, which was also very beautiful inside, was the beginning.

I still don't know how Appa's brother heard about these people, and that they wanted a maid, and I don't know why they took me and not a girl from Madras; perhaps they knew I would have nowhere to run, if running ever came into my head? Anyway, Appa's brother handed me over to them and I heard some talk about wages, and how Appa was to have them sent to him every week. All that was not my business, it seemed.

Living with those people I began for the first time to wonder about the nature of cruelty. Why do some people choose to be cruel, when they could just as well be kind, and happier? I can tell by their faces that cruel people are not happy. Have you ever looked into the eyes of a cruel person? I have, and they are all muddy and twisted inside, and their mouths are ugly slits, and when they are being cruel I can see so clearly how terrible will be their fate. Cruelty is like a heavy ball thrown up into the sky: once it reaches a certain height, it changes course and falls with terrible speed and will hit the very thrower – perhaps not in this life, but in the next. Was I, then, a cruel person in my last life, that I should be the recipient in this? I do not know. Only God has his eye on such matters, and who are we to question him?

But I am straying away from my story. I will return. Appa's brother left me with those cruel people. It was a man and his wife. Their names were Sri and Srimati Ramcharran. And I was to be their servant.

But instead I was their slave. You may think that now I was living in this grand house it can't have been so bad, but you know, even if you live in the grandest of places, if you are treated like a beast of burden the pain is unbearable. That lady beat me for the slightest misdemeanour, or what in her eyes was a misdemeanour. For instance, if I polished a mirror, and she found one fingerprint on it, she would beat me with the leather belt she kept hanging on a hook especially for this purpose. The house was certainly magnificent and well furnished – they had real tables and chairs, Western-style, and it was the first time I had ever seen a home furnished this way. And carpets everywhere, and beds, and several electrical machines. I didn't know how to operate these machines at first, as a matter of fact they terrified me. That mixer for instance, the first time I used it Srimati had given me a bowl with some kind of mixture in it and she only told me to place the bowl under the beaters of the mixer and switch on the button but when I did so the bowl woke up and started dancing in wild circles, and when I grabbed it in panic the yellow slop inside started to dance and flew out all over the kitchen. She whipped me for that, of course. The vacuum cleaner wasn't much better, it was much stronger than me and pulled me in several directions at once, it seemed. But I won't complain about those machines, they can't help being what they are, they do not have a soul and they were not trying deliberately to hurt me. Srimati was.

In Appa's English school Teacher taught us that rhyme 'Sticks and stones can break my bones but words can never hurt me'. Well, it's not true. I may not be very old but in my whole life it's always been the feeling of being worthless to other people that hurts most of all. Yes, I have had my share of blows, but it is the words, and even the unspoken things, the looks of people who think of me as nothing and less than nothing, that is the worst kind of hurt in the world. I was hurt this way by Appa's brother and then by that lady and that man. But they hurt my body too, each one in a different way.

Look at my arms: do you see these marks, like the rungs of a ladder marching up and down? Those are from her. When I had done something wrong – it was always little things, so little I can't even remember – she would stick a fork into the flame on the gas stove, leave it there till the prongs were red hot, and then press them against my arm. And the more I screamed the more prongs I got. Now I mention forks, I remember the first of my crimes, which was not knowing how to use knives and forks, for of course at home we always ate with our fingers. But when I started to do so there – they gave me a bowl of rice with some thin sambar on it, that first evening, and I took it into a corner and sat on the floor to eat, a far corner where I wouldn't disturb anybody – that's when she scolded me the first time, calling me a stupid pig. She said I had to learn proper manners and must sit at the table, so I did, but then I put my fingers in the rice and made a ball of it and that's when she laughed that horrible mocking laugh which she always laughs before getting really angry, and she said to him, just look at this nasty little pig, how she eats! So I had to use a knife and fork, which I had never done before. I didn't know how to use them and by mistake I put the rice on the knife and lifted it to my mouth and she lashed out and slapped it away, scattering the rice on the floor. That's not how we eat in this house! she screamed. So I had to put the rice on a fork, which seemed silly, surely the grains would fall through the prongs? Seeing the fork must have given her the idea of torturing me this way, because that was the first time it happened. It is hard to believe that people can treat others this way but it is true, here are the marks to prove it.

But I am not complaining, I'm just telling you because you asked.

So with that lady I had to do all sorts of things in a different way, and I learned a lot about Western ways, though of course they were Indian. But they said Western ways were better and I had to do things so and not so.

I haven't told you about the children yet. She had two and though I have always loved small children I must say that those two were hard to love, for they were as nasty as their parents. They took such great pleasure in hurting me whenever they could; but in sneaky sly ways, especially that little girl. She was even worse than the little boy, if you can believe that. She would walk behind me quite innocently, but in passing kick me from behind, or pull my hair, or pinch me. Little things, to be sure, but still they hurt.

The man hurt me in a different way but excuse me for not talking about that, not telling you the details. Even after all this time and much worse things I am filled with shame at the very thought. I'll just tell you that it started soon after I came to live with them and it always happened when she was not at home, perhaps she had taken her children to her sister's or some such thing; she went visiting often, leaving me at home, locked up in the house which had heavy padlocks at the doors and bars at all the windows. That man would come home now and then and do dirty things to me. That's when I learned about the Demon that lives in every man. But as I said before, it is all relative. Now I can almost laugh at the things that man did. But back then they were no laughing matter. But I won't tell you. I don't want you to feel shame for me. The details don't matter.

So I will leave that man and his Demon and move on to the next chapter in my story. Back then I would not have believed things could get worse but of course they did, as you know. It's no consolation to say that that man and his wife got their just punishment.

I never knew what really happened, I only know that one day in the early morning hours the dogs barked and the chain on the garden gate rattled and somebody shouted loud enough to wake the street. I jumped to my feet and looked out of my little barred window; I couldn't see much but certainly three or four people were at the gate, shouting to be admitted. I heard the man and the lady, they were up, and whispering hastily with one another: it seemed they decided not to open the gate, at least no one went out to do so, and the shouting only grew louder. Somebody brought one of those cone-shaped things people shout into . . . Yes, a megaphone. And then I understood. Police, open! they were shouting. Still no one opened, yet the next thing I knew one of them had cut through the chain – I didn't know it at the time, of course, but I saw the cut chain later – and the three policemen were marching down the drive. The dogs charged at them. They were on long chains, long enough to reach the path and jump up at any stranger coming along. The first police simply shot them, both dogs! And then they were at the door, banging away and the lady finally let them in; I suppose she knew they'd break down the door if she didn't. The man had disappeared. He had hidden himself but they marched through the house, even coming into my little chamber off the kitchen, looking for him, and finally they found him, I don't know where, and hauled him off in handcuffs. It seems he had done something very wrong, something to do with money; I forget the word they used, something beginning with F, I think ... What? Yes, you're right, fraud. That's what it was. Well, I stood at my little barred window and watched, and my heart soared when I saw them dragging that man, handcuffed to the wrists of two policemen, up the garden. The woman was bawling and screaming and running behind them all the way to the garden gate, but they ignored her, they pushed her away. I was at the window, of course, peeping through the darkness, and when she came back inside I crept back to my mat and lay down, anxious to keep out of her way because I knew that in that foul temper she would knock me to the ground and unload her venom on me. But she wasn't thinking of me at all. I heard her wake the children, shouting at them to get up and get dressed, quick march. I heard her shouting on the telephone; she called for a taxi, and she called some more people telling them the story, and she called her sister, I suppose, because she said, We're coming right away.

And then the house was silent. Now, all this time – I had been living there about a year – I had always been on the alert, determined to escape at the first chance, but that chance had never come. Always she locked me in when she left the house, and as all the windows were barred it was just as if I was locked in a prison. I had the run of that huge house, for sure, but there was no way out of it.

Now again I was locked in. The first thing I did, of course, was check the door – which was locked, and I wasn't surprised at that. But my wits were about me, sharpened by excitement. The man and the lady each had a bundle of keys, but I knew the man had been wearing his white pyjamas, crumpled and baggy, when they took him away. He surely hadn't taken his keys with him. Had *she* thought to take his keys as well as hers? That was the question. I crept into their bedroom to search. I don't know why I was so stealthy, there was nothing to be afraid of, they were both gone, after all! And the children too! I suppose it was force of habit, and my heart was pounding so heavily you would think it was a terribly dangerous situation, but it wasn't – it was so easy! For of course his work trousers were laid across a chair, and his briefcase lay on the seat of that chair, and when I opened it there were the keys. I only had to reach for them.

I thought it better to pack a few things. I had the plastic bag Appa's brother had given me, and I stuffed it with a few bits of clothing. Then I went into the kitchen and filled myself a bottle of water, and wrapped some cooked food, the remains of yesterday's lunch, and a bunch of bananas, and two oranges. And then I was out of the door and down the garden path. The dogs were dead, and the gate was open, and freedom was all mine.

The night was dark as pitch, and the silent streets lit only by an occasional streetlamp, islands of light along an endless black passage. I hastened from light-island to light-island, frightened by the blackness in between them. I walked, not knowing where to go. The plastic bag dangled at my calves, heavy in my hands. I shifted it back and forth from right to left hand several times and finally I stopped and ate all the bananas, right there in the middle of the pavement. Then it was lighter.

The morning was also lighter. How long had I been walking? I couldn't tell. I couldn't even tell in what direction, for I had never been in the streets of Madras before, except the day Appa's brother brought me here a year ago. Sometimes I turned a corner; I did so when a street seemed wider than the one I was on, hoping in that way somehow to be led nearer to my goal. That I knew, of course. The bus station. Where else could I go, but back to Amma?

I longed for Amma but I prayed to Him, the long man in ochre who was my father whom I hadn't seen for years. I don't know why I still thought of him but I did, though he had abandoned me – what else could I think, seeing he hadn't come back for five years? Five years is an eternity in the mind of a child – enough to

290

erase every last trace of him, but still he loomed large somewhere behind the moving tableau of pictures that formed my life, somewhere behind all the pain and the suffering, the loneliness and the anguish, I felt he was there, waiting in the shadows, waiting to rescue me, and that's why I prayed to him, because as I said he was like God to me. Whereas Amma was *that*, Amma, my mother, and I longed to be in her arms again, it was like a physical thirst and that dark morning I hurried onward not knowing where I was going, trusting somehow my footsteps would lead me instinctively back to her.

By following sounds and signs of life – the claxon of a rickshaw, the vague hum of traffic coming from the centre – I found myself in a very wide street, and that's when for the first time I saw a woman. She was carrying a bundle on her head and seemed in as much of a hurry as I, on the other side of the road, and going in the right direction, as I thought. I would never speak to a man, for men carry demons in them, as I knew now, except for Appa and Him. So I crossed the road and hurried along at her side.

'Where is the bus station?' I asked her.

She glanced down at me without changing her stride. 'It's a long way,' she said. 'Are you going to walk there?'

'Yes.'

'Well, it's not a good thing for young girls to be on the streets on their own without company. Be careful. Just keep going straight ahead – you'll have to ask someone else again later, it's too difficult to explain from here. It will take you an hour to walk there, maybe longer. Are you a stranger here?'

'Yes.'

'Where are your parents?'

That lady was very curious and I didn't really feel like answering her questions but I was so grateful that somebody was interested in me after all that long time with those awful people that I answered readily. In fact, once I started talking I felt I could open my heart and pour out my whole story in her lap. But all I said now was, 'My father is dead, my mother and brothers and sisters are all in Gingee.'

'Oh, you're from Gingee, are you? Well, then you can save yourself a lot of trouble. My cousin has relatives in Gingee. I've never been there myself but I know the bus to Gingee. It passes down Mount Road, you'll have to go there – I've just come from there. Just keep on going in that direction, you'll see it when you get there because it's so busy. And then you ask someone what number bus, and then you look for a bus stop and wait there for a bus with that number.'

My heart gave a huge leap when I heard these words, and I smiled for the first time in a very long time, thanked her and hurried in the direction she had pointed to – she was going in the opposite direction.

Well, I found Mount Road and what a place that was! So full of traffic, though it was still early morning. I was quite dazed. Where should I go? Left, right, cross the street? Which way was home? And a bus stop? Which bus? Who would help me? Well, somebody would have to help me so I stopped in front of a lady who was rushing along the pavement, but she was in too much of a hurry to waste time on the likes of me – don't forget, I'd been wandering the streets since long before dawn and hadn't washed or combed my hair before leaving and all my clothes were old and faded, and a bit too small for me, so I suppose I looked bedraggled. This lady was well dressed and she carried a handbag over her shoulder, and when I asked her the way to the bus stop she looked vexed and shrugged and waved her hand, then she pushed me aside and hurried on to some important matter. After that I didn't have the courage to stop anyone else so I just kept walking, and then I saw it: a bus stop. And there were lots of people lined up there waiting, so I didn't feel bad about asking one of the ladies if the bus to Gingee stopped here.

'The bus *from* Gingee,' she said, and added, 'To Gingee you'll have to cross the street. Be careful you don't get knocked down!' And she was right, I had to be very careful because crossing that street was worse than crossing a river full of alligators! You need a raft to cross such a river, and even then it's dangerous; the raft I chose was a group of other people also waiting to cross at a place where the street had striped markings and when they walked I walked, and even then the cars that stopped for us nosed right up to us, nudging impatiently into our midst to make us hurry, which we did.

I found the right bus stop and even got on the bus but would you believe it, after only two minutes I had to get off again! Because a man came around selling tickets and of course I had no money.

Money! I hadn't given it a thought. That's how simple-minded I used to be, because as everyone knows, money is everything! Money is more than a life, that's what I know now, but for my ignorance then I was tossed off the bus that would have carried me to safety. I could have had those few rupees – nothing easier! Those people had had money all over the house – money for paying the dhobi, for buying coconuts or paying the milk-wallah and such things. There was no shortage of loose change! Or I could have taken something from the house to sell, if I had thought of such matters, but, you see, I am not used to stealing. I never stole anything in my life, not even a rose for my hair. Nothing. So I did not think to steal anything before leaving the house, but now I would do so a hundred times, a million times – too much honesty is a bad thing! Just a little dishonesty would have saved me! But how could I know! All is Destiny.

So, not having the money for the bus, and having nothing to sell, what was I to do? I begged.

At first I walked along the line waiting for the next bus and asked the women for some money. I didn't talk to the men. I told them I needed money for the bus to Gingee. The first three ladies turned their heads away and gave nothing. Then a lady gave me one rupee, and so did the man behind her, who heard my tale. Well, at first it shamed me to beg, because of course it is not my way, not at all – we were a good respectable family! But desperation dissolved all my shame and made me bold! I changed my way of asking as I went along the line; if at first I had been shy and fearful when asking, keeping my eyes lowered bashfully, the way Amma had taught me was fitting for a young girl my age, I grew bold, and I looked those women in the face as I asked, and put a plea into my voice, and a look into my eye that was hard to resist, that made them feel ashamed not to give, rather than making me feel ashamed myself. After all, my need was great, and true! And then I realized that men were also giving, though I hadn't asked them directly, and by the time the first bus came I had seven rupees, imagine, and I felt so happy!

Well, that went on for half an hour – or longer, who knows? – quite safely. By now I felt no compunction at all about asking even the men for money. And I even *looked* at them. Now, I was a well-brought-up girl and everyone knows it is wrong to look a man straight into the eye, but that was what I was doing, so perhaps it is all my fault. I've thought about this again and again since then and I feel it was my loss of modesty that caused everything else. I noticed that when I asked men they looked at me with great interest, and seemed quite willing to give me a rupee, whereas the women looked away when I asked, and if they gave they did so without looking at me, their heads slightly averted. It was the men who looked, but I swear it was not an over-endowment of wantonness that inspired my behaviour, it was simply desperation, the crying in my heart for Amma, the longing for her arms. I would do anything to get back there, even look men in the eye, if it made them give me money! For the sooner I had the money the quicker I would return home. One man even gave me five rupees!

But I needed twenty-seven. I received the coins they gave me in my right hand, raising my hand to my forehead with each coin in gratitude. I collected the coins in my left hand, and whenever I could no longer hold the coins I put a handful into the bag I held slung around my elbow. Twice I stopped, moved to the side of the pavement, knelt down, emptied that bag and counted the coins carefully. The second time I had reached twenty-three rupees. I needed four more, only four! The joy at knowing my goal was near must have shown openly on my face, indeed, I know I was smiling as I got up and walked back to the waiting line, and I felt a security that all people would be generous and caring and giving, and that is how I approached them, and indeed the first man gave me a two-rupee coin. It was just after this generous gift, for which I thanked with an especially broad smile, that the woman who was to cause my downfall spoke to me. She was standing right behind that man, and had heard my story, that I was going back to my mother in Gingee and needed the money for the fare.

'Why didn't your mother send you the money, beti?' asked this woman. She wore a dark green sari and she had a face that was wrinkled around the mouth, and protruding teeth, and a gold stud in her nose. She carried a bag like my own in one hand, as well as a tiffin carrier. She smiled kindly as she asked, and so I told her.

'My mother does not know I am coming home, Aunty, I was working as a servant up to now and I have decided to go home.'

The woman looked a little worried at these words. 'But if your mother sent you to be a servant, surely she expects you to obey, and work hard, and augment the family income, and only return home when she sends for you?'

I had been smiling up to now but when she spoke these words the smile vanished from my lips. 'Well, my mother did not want me to come to Madras, Aunty, she will be glad to have me back, truly! It is my uncle who sent me!'

Whenever I remember this woman I realize that it was just after these words that everything took place – all the decisions were made, my fate sealed: because she was silent for a moment, looking at me, as if making a quick calculation and formulating a plan in her mind, before she spoke again. Did I imagine that her eyes looked at me differently now, cagey somehow, as if already she was seeing in her mind's eye my face, grubby and tearstained, behind those Bombay bars, my hands gripping the hard cold iron while my knuckles turned white; as if she saw all that in the split second before she spoke again, as if she saw my destiny as it was laid out for me, and recognized herself as the instrument who would bring this destiny about? And if she was but an instrument of Destiny, how can I place the blame on her? Perhaps I have done some evil in my past life, and this was the moment when all the constellations came together, focusing on this one point in time and space, saying, Now. So what is all this talk of *I should have taken money from that house* or *I should not have listened to her*? Is there any way of knowing? No. Only looking back there can be recriminations – but futile they are, for they change nothing. That second came and went, and all was decided for me, and I could do no more than play along, and that is what I did.

When she spoke her voice too had changed subtly. It was kinder now, cajoling, and I was so starved of kindness and so hungry for attention that of course I smiled up at her and I know she saw the sadness in my eyes! How could she not! Because all along I had been fooling myself and in that moment I had to admit it. Of course Amma wanted me back! *But what about Uncle!* That was what had been whispering at the back of my mind all the time but I had not listened to it because all I was thinking all the time was Amma, Amma, Amma. Amma would save me, Amma would help! Amma would not send me back! Well, *she* wouldn't but Uncle would, and that's exactly what I realized in that moment and that's what that kind lady saw. Well, I thought she was kind because back then I couldn't read people's hearts and couldn't tell the difference between a smile that is a movement of the lips, and a smile that shines through the eyes, and hers didn't.

'It is my uncle who sent me!' The moment I spoke the words all the fear and doubt at the back of my mind pushed forward. I could feel them in my eyes! And so could she. She knew – and made up her mind.

My doubt and her decision: they met in that moment, and I was hers.

'Come, child, come speak with me,' she said in that low kind voice, and drew me aside. 'You look so sad. What has happened? Is there trouble at home? Why did your uncle send you?'

I thought she cared – how could I not! So empty I was, so broken inside, so starving for love! I was so accustomed to abuse – months and months of it – that everything in my soul cried out for a kind word, and who was I to discern the deceit behind the smile! I was filled with feeling at that moment, for I was so near to my goal, having collected almost my entire fare home, and now to realize that it would never work, that I had no home: Uncle would send me away again, maybe further! The despair welled up in me and I poured out my story, and she listened as no one had cared to listen in all the time gone by, and my gratitude bent low like a heavy monsoon cloud, longing to burst but unable to do so. I had forgotten how to cry!

'Beti, don't worry, you are safe with me; I will look after you. See, if you go home your uncle will beat you for running away, you know that, don't you?'

I looked at her, full of sadness and trust, and whispered, 'Yes,' because she was right.

'He will beat you and look for another place for you, a place perhaps much further away than Madras, somewhere where you can never run away again. There are bad places for young girls, did you know that?'

Truly, I did not know at the time – bad places for girls? Wasn't where I'd been bad? So I whispered, 'Yes,' and she smiled even more kindly.

'It's quite true,' she said. 'So you'd better not go back to your native place. I don't like the sound of this uncle of yours. He is trying to get rid of you, because now he has to bear the burden of the whole family, and you are only a useless girl he has to feed, and not his own daughter. Perhaps he will get rid of all your brothers and sisters in this way.'

I interrupted her now because it was important for me to tell her that they weren't really my brothers and sisters, and that seemed to make her happy, because she smiled and patted my shoulder.

'You see, you are not even his flesh and blood! An adopted child, and a girl at that! Who is there to claim you and stand up for your rights? Nobody! And don't you know girls cost money? How will he afford dowry for you, and if you do not marry you will be a burden on him all your life. So this is what we are going to do. You come with me to my home – I was going to visit somebody on that bus but I won't go now, your troubles are more important. You come with me and I will help you. I will find work for you. There are good jobs to be had where you can earn good money, and wear nice clothes and look pretty. You are a very pretty little girl, you know, your skin is soft and fair and such fine dark eyes you have! You should not be working as a servant.'

By this time we were walking, she holding my upper arm and guiding me. It was quite a long walk to her home, which was a small cottage on a street that had not been swept for some time. When we got there it was already lunchtime. That lady spread a mat for us to sit on on the veranda and brought me an aluminium plate from the kitchen and one for herself, and a jug of water and two glasses, and opened her tiffin carrier. It was full of food, rice and sambar, beans, chutney and rassam, but she didn't eat much, she simply sat on the floor across from me – she didn't sit on the mat but on the bare floor – watching.

After taking food she told me I should have a sleep. 'You are tired, I can see,' she said. 'And I have to make a telephone call, about your job. Just lie down here and take some rest, I won't be long. A friend of mine around the corner has a telephone. I'll be back in half an hour.'

When I woke up I could see I had slept for a very long time because the sun was beginning to cast long shadows. I sat up, the sleep still heavy in my bones, weariness clinging to my heart. I got up to find a place to relieve myself and when I entered the middle room she was there, sitting on the floor, cleaning some dahl. When I came in she looked up and smiled, and she seemed to know what I wanted for she waved her hand towards another door and when I went outside I found the toilet. I came back and she gestured for me to sit down. She had a handful of dahl on a plate which she shook gently from time to time, and as she spoke to me her fingers moved about picking out the little stones which she flicked on to the floor.

'Unfortunately the job I had in mind for you in Madras did not work out. They already have a girl,' she said. 'So I telephoned my husband in Bombay. My husband works sometimes in Bombay, sometimes in Madras, it is a sad life for a devoted wife but who am I to complain? Jobs are very scarce in Madras and if you want a good job you must be prepared to shift. My husband says he can help you, to send you to him in Bombay and he will take care of everything. He's a very good man and he knows a lot of people there, and he will find appropriate work for you, don't worry.'

Now I had heard of Bombay occasionally but all I knew of it was that it was a very very big place and hardly anybody from Gingee had been there, and I knew it was far away so I must have looked scared.

'Don't be frightened,' she said. 'He will take care of you. He said to put you on the next train, and he knows that such a long journey can be extremely confusing for a young girl, so he has asked me to find an escort for you, and I have done so. His aunt will accompany you, a very nice lady. I have already spoken to her and she has kindly offered to make the journey with you so that you will feel quite comfortable and at ease. You will leave tonight.'

'Tonight?' My consternation made my voice loud which was impolite, so she frowned.

'Don't you want a good job as soon as possible? Then you must not be complaining but jump at the opportunity. I thought I had made it clear to you how extremely difficult it is to find work these days and I thought you would be happy to seize the chance to shift there right away, especially as my husband's aunt has so kindly offered to drop her affairs and accompany you. Don't tell me you are ungrateful for such kindness – or shall I go and telephone my husband, saying the girl doesn't want to come, she prefers to return to her uncle?'

'No, no, please don't, I'm very sorry, Aunty, truly I'm so grateful and I really want to go to Bombay for work . . . I was just, I was just . . .'

I couldn't finish speaking then because I'm not accustomed to lying and of course it was all a lie! Everything in all my soul cried out for Amma and home but how could I hope to go back there! The door was closed and I knew it, and this lady was so kind and generous I didn't want to appear ungrateful, so I lied. But Bombay! So far away! How would I ever get from there back to Gingee, when the time was right!

Could she read thoughts? It seemed so, because right then she said: 'I know that most of all you want to go back to your native place but without money that is a hopeless dream. In Bombay you will earn good money. Save as much as you can, and when you go home your uncle will welcome you with open arms and a loving heart. See, you can stay in my husband's aunt's home in Bombay, she is kind enough to let you stay there for free if you don't mind sleeping on the veranda. All you need to spend money on is your food, which is not costly – my husband's eldest brother owns a shop with various foodstuffs and he can supply your needs for a good price. So don't worry about your Amma – soon you will wrap her in your arms, when you have worked in Bombay for some months, and saved your money, and returned home to Gingee.

'But enough talking now – it's time to go to the station. We will walk to the corner and get a rickshaw from there – it's quite a distance and we should get there early since we don't have a reservation. Come, beti, let's go.'

So that's how I came to Bombay.

Part Five

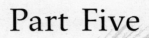

THIRTY-NINE

Visitors

Rani pulled impatiently at the bell-rope. The big brass bell swung back and forth several times, clanging out an impatient summons. Only seconds later three golden maidens, each clad in a long gathered skirt and matching blouse of evidently the finest silk hurried through the curtain that separated the Surya Hall from the Corridor of Mirrors.

'Hukam?' said the eldest of the three, placing her palms together, lowering her eyes, and bending forward from the waist.

Rani's finger traced a languid bow and pointed upward, to one of the two television screens fitted into the ornate woodwork arch at the entrance to her cubicle. On one of the screens flickered the coloured pictures of a new video film Lakshmi had brought the day before. A ravishing apple-cheeked heroine mouthed the words to a soundless song: Rani had pressed the mute button on the remote control. The other screen was black and white, and it was to this screen that Rani now pointed. The three girls' gaze followed the finger and they looked at the screen themselves, rather nonplussed for it showed nothing but the closed front gate.

'Yes, hukam?' said the first girl.

Rani's hand sank to the carved sandalwood table at her side, and her fingers closed around the remote control. She pressed a button, and with a thwack the television screen turned blank. The three girls looked at one another, more nonplussed than ever, for Rani hardly ever turned off the video. From dawn till dusk the moving pictures flickered; occasionally, during conversation or to issue a command, the film was mute for a short space of time, after which Rani would press the rewind button to replay what she had missed. Two or three times a week Lakshmi would sally forth into the town to Bisheswar Video Rentals and return with a bagful of new films, which Rani would consume without break over the next several days. None of the girls could remember a time when the screen went blank.

Rani, preparing paan, took her time. She rolled the ingredients into a green betel leaf and only then, looking up but not at the girls, her gaze fixed on some tiny point of greenish light between the carvings of the sandalwood screen, some minute piece of sunlit garden, she said, 'Some visitors are coming. Who are they?'

'Visitors, hukam?'

'Two of them. They were granted admission several minutes ago. I could not tell if they were male or female. They had the gait and the heads of females but the lower regions of males as far as I could tell. Go and ask Lakshmi what they are.' She flicked a hand in dismissal and popped the paan into her mouth.

'Very well, hukam.' The three maidens, still bowed at the waist with palms together, moved backwards with a rustling of silk until they vanished into the Corridor of Mirrors. The curtain of carved beads fell behind them with a clattering of wood on wood.

Chewing paan, Rani adjusted her back cushion, lifted a knee with both hands to relieve a cramp, grunted as she let the knee fall into place. A finger pressed *rewind*. The mute and buxom beauty rushed backwards across the screen, halted suddenly at another punch of Rani's finger, and burst into fervent song.

Lakshmi was sixty-six. Her legendary beauty had matured like quality silk. Her skin, nourished with rich oils and kept resilient by daily massage, held the patina of old gold. Not a wrinkle blemished her complexion; to her demanding mistress she had managed to smile through all the years of service, and not just with her lips but with her heart, so that her outer beauty remained undistorted by the inner ugliness of a disgruntled soul: Lakshmi had kept her dignity. She had gained weight, of course, and the folds of her sari now enclosed a solid form, thickset but without flab, and still shapely, curving in and out as befitting a woman in the ripeness of years.

Somewhat flustered as she plunged through the bead curtain, she quickly collected her wits and approached Rani in quietude, gliding up with folded palms, a winning smile and humble mien.

'Hukam, I was just on my way here when I was told of your summons. Hukam, there are two—'

Rani, lowering the volume, said: 'Are they male or female?'

'Female, hukam.'

'Why are they wearing male clothing?'

'They are foreigners, hukam, they know no better.'

Rani considered this in silence, chewing her paan. A gleam of heightened interest flickered in her eyes. She pressed the mute button and spoke: 'What have they come here for?'

'That is what I was coming to tell you, hukam. You see, they claim to be relatives from South America. Dilip Hanoman spoke to one of them apparently some time ago when you sent him to look for family members abroad. There were no males but there were these two females.'

'Let them come then. You are quite certain they are female?'

'Yes, hukam, quite certain.'

'Nevertheless please check.'

'Certainly, hukam, I will do so.'

'And let them dress as females before they come.'

'Very well, hukam.'

'Please go now.'

'Yes, hukam.'

They came in ill-fitting saris but Rani could tell, nevertheless, that they were indeed female. The taller of the two was also the darker and less interesting. Her hair was the worst of it: horribly crinkled, drawn back and twisted into a clumsy plait falling over one shoulder. The sari was certainly draped properly, Lakshmi must have supervised that part of it, but she had no carriage and the loose end drooped forward inelegantly, sliding from her shoulder no less than three times in the half-minute it took to approach. Each time she flung it back in an unladylike gesture of impatience. And her strides were too long as she approached: she walked like a man.

Not so the other one, and Rani leaned forward slightly the better to observe the smaller of the two. She too was obviously inexperienced in the wearing of a sari, but her carriage was exquisite, her head held high with uptilted chin, her left hand raised and resting tenderly on shoulder. Her face was simply delectable: the large, wide-apart eyes; the full bow of the lips; the gold-tinted skin, its texture flawless like the skin of an unblemished Himalayan peach. The hair was full and silky, black as coal and shiny as satin, and even though most of it hung down her back, probably carefully plaited by Lakshmi and adorned with flowers, Rani knew instinctively that, let loose, it would be long and glorious, curving at the shoulders as in synchrony with the girl's perfect body. Rani leaned forward as much as her thick waist would allow, to peer at the girl. She reminded her of someone – who? She grappled a moment with the remote control and for the second time that day the screen went blank as another picture rose in her mind: herself, at the age of fifteen, naked, draped along the low wall surrounding the mosaic fountain in the Purdah Hall of her father's court, lovingly massaged by her favourite handmaidens, at a time when all was well with the world and she was a bride-to-be, betrothed to the young Maharajah Ranjit. Before the end of that perfect world. Rani's eyes narrowed; the girl, feeling her appraisal, smiled. She smiled so charmingly that Rani's last defences dropped and she smiled back, showing stubs of teeth red from betel-nut. A hearty chuckle rose from deep within her. She raised a hand and pointed at the girl, then twirled her finger in a circle.

The girl understood instantaneously; she turned on the spot, slowly, arms wide open, tripping lightly on tip-toe as she had been taught, showing off the long hair clasped with a bouquet of fresh jasmine at the nape of her neck, and tumbling down the middle of her back, just like Rani's once did, in better times. Lakshmi leaned forward and whispered, 'Her name is Belle, hukam.' She pronounced it Belle-eh.

'What? Belly?' Rani cackled at her own joke, but the cackles turned into a cough and Lakshmi hastened to clap her on the back, helping her to lean forward as much as possible. Caught up in coughing, Rani could only gesture awkwardly in the direction of the sandalwood table. Lakshmi reached for the gold-plated spittoon and held it at Rani's lips. Rani hawked and spat a wad of phlegm mixed with bright red spittle into the bowl, Lakshmi covered it with a lace-edged handkerchief, produced a second handkerchief to wipe Rani's lips with, and normality was restored.

'Come here, Belly,' Rani said, signalling to the smaller of the two girls.

Kneeling at Rani's side and unseen by her mistress, Lakshmi gestured emphatically for Belle, who understood; she fell to her knees, placed her palms together in namaste, then bowed low to touch her forehead to the carpet at Rani's feet. Lakshmi's eyes blazed as she turned her gaze to the second girl, standing stiffly in the background. Sternly Lakshmi pointed to the space next to Belle and mouthed the easily deciphered command, *'Get down!'*

The tall, ungainly girl tripped on the hem of her sari as she stepped forward and stumbled to the ground; she looked up anxiously at Lakshmi, who pointed even more adamantly to the floor. The girl bowed and touched her forehead to the carpet, as Belle had done before her.

'This other one's name is Reetha, hukam,' said Lakshmi.

'Reetha and Belly . . . Belly is not an auspicious name, it is too vulgar for public use. I will think of a new name for the little one, but I personally will call her Belly. It is my own little joke.'

The girl she called Belly opened her mouth as if in protest, but Lakshmi shook her head vigorously and placed a finger on her lips. The girl's mouth closed, her words unspoken, like a fish. Lakshmi closed her eyes, smiled, and nodded in appreciation.

'And they come from South Africa, you say?' Rani strained her neck as far as it would go to look up at Lakshmi.

'South America, hukam.'

'South Africa, South America, it's all the same, what do I care!' said Rani dismissively. 'Why are they making this long journey to India?'

'They say they are looking for their relatives, hukam. Their father died some months back and they are orphans in the world so they are coming here seeking refuge. You are all the family they have left in the world.'

'Why are you speaking for them? Haven't they got tongues in their heads? Let the little one speak. She is my favourite. I have decided her name will be Balwantie, which is more auspicious than Belly. Still, when I am in a humorous frame of mind I shall call her Belly. Come here, Balwantie, sit on this cushion next to me so I can see you better, and tell me your story. Let me touch you. My, what lovely skin! Lovely, lovely. Just like mine used to be. And this hair, soft like silk. Eyes like black diamonds! Treasure your beauty, deary, it is your most precious possession! If you are indeed our relatives, and this you must prove to me, then this is your home and I am your grandmother. Family is the one thing I have too little of, and which money cannot buy! You may call me Dadi. It will be a delight to have fresh young blood and beauty in the Purdah Mahal once more. You will find a home here and I personally will ensure your well-being and see to it that you are pampered as well you should, with such beauty . . . I will tell you stories of my youth, so you may know how it should be. As you may know I was a princess and once I was every bit as lovely as you, child, betrothed to the Prince Maharajah . . . when I was seventeen . . .'

Unseen by Rani, unseen by Lakshmi, Belle poked Rita, kneeling at her side. Rita looked down surreptitiously. Belle showed her a fist, with its thumb turned up.

FORTY

Purdah

'You see!' said Isabelle. 'I knew it. I'm in the running.'

Rita sniffed, and didn't answer.

'What's the matter? Don't tell me your scruples have started up again!'

Rita opened the suitcase on her bed and took out a pile of T-shirts. Walking over to the wardrobe, she glanced at Isabelle and said, 'Do you know where we are, Isabelle?'

'Of course, in Mahapradesh. Why?'

'No, I mean, d'you realize what this building is? Where we are right now? This house?'

'It's the palace. Isn't it fantastic? Did you see those mosaic walls, and all those mirrors? I think the frames are real gold! And the floors, they're marble, and—'

'Did you hear what she called this place?'

'No, what?'

'The Purdah Mahal.'

'Well? So what? Sounds like Taj Mahal!' Isabelle giggled happily.

'Mahal means palace, I know that from my tourist guide. And d'you know what Purdah means?'

'No, what? You're the walking dictionary, not me.'

'Purdah is the women's quarters; it's where the women in these old-fashioned Indian homes have to live and move and have their being. They aren't allowed to talk to men or even see men, they're sort of women's prisons. Did you notice on the way up here: only women! Not a single man! And did you see that wooden screen that sectioned off the back of Rani's hall? And look at the shutters at the windows – look how dark it is in here, the only sunlight falls through those carvings! Come, look through here!'

Rita walked over to the window and tried to open the ornately carved wooden shutters. She couldn't; they were fixed irremovably to the window frame. The best she could do was peer through the carvings to the busy courtyard below, where, for the first time in what seemed ages, she saw men. Workers, obviously: men unloading a bullock cart; others carrying bulging sacks into a side building; two sentries on either side of a high gate; a circle of men, sitting on the sand and drinking tea.

The room they had been assigned was longer than it was wide, and at both of the two narrow ends there were windows. Obviously it spanned the width of the Purdah Palace, so Rita walked over to the windows at the other end, which were also shuttered. These windows looked over a magnificent view: peering out between the curve of a raised elephant's trunk Rita saw an exquisitely manicured emerald lawn stretching out to meet flowerbeds that could have come straight out of an Indian version of *Better Homes and Gardens*. In the distance two half-naked gardeners could be seen working the soil – the only humans in sight. Silence rested over the scene; silence filled the room. A musty, stifling silence.

Isabelle, at Rita's side at the window, looked up at her sister. 'You mean . . . you mean a sort of – a harem?'

'Well, no. I suppose a harem's something different, that's where a man keeps his concubines or whatever. I've never really gone into it. But you know, here in the East the women are kept separately. They aren't supposed to leave the home at all. And I think that's what she expects of us!'

'Oh, Rita, don't be silly. Why, this country is teeming with women, they're all over the place, in the streets and everywhere. We saw them!'

'Yes, but this is supposed to be a royal family, and that's where they had these purdah quarters. I guess they want to be certain the women are virtuous. And you know what I think? I think Rani'll expect that of you. Even if she does accept you as her heiress, she'll want you to live here in purdah.'

Isabelle's eyes opened wide and her hands flew involuntarily to circle her neck. 'No! Rita, I can't do that! Live here in this palace, day in day out, waiting till she dies! That could take *for ever*!'

'I warned you – legacy-hunters always pay a price. But look at her – sitting there on her fat backside and served day and night by bowing nymphs! If you want to crawl into her ass, that's your lookout, but me, I'm getting out as fast as I can! One night here at the most and tomorrow I'm off. You'd better make up your mind quickly what you want.'

'But, Rita, where'll I *go*! You can't just disappear and leave me here, and the least we can do is stick around to find out for sure which way the wind blows! We don't know a thing yet – I want to talk to that Mr Hanoman.'

'Didn't you get it? Why did they take us to that Lakshmi instead of to Mr Hanoman? She said he's out – can we believe her? I think he's very well here but somewhere else. Did you see that other huge building, next to this one? I bet that's full of men and Mr Hanoman's in there. I mean, just look at the size of this place, somebody has to run it, for goodness' sake, and that fat Rani, sitting there at her television, she doesn't look as if she runs a thing. I bet she's just a figurehead of some sort. She's crafty, though. She probably lets the men run things, but makes all the final decisions. I don't trust her. And did you see those sentries? They've got guns! People can't just go in and out as they please – you saw those gates!'

'You're not trying to scare me, are you?'

'Just telling you to keep your eyes open. And advising you to get out while you can.'

311

FORTY-ONE

Women

Rani was bored. It was a new film, but each new film, it seemed to her now, was simply a new variation on the last. She pulled the bell once, which was the signal for Lakshmi. She rolled a betel-leaf with her favourite spices and chewed impatiently in the minute's time it took for Lakshmi to hustle in.

'You called, hukam? Shall I change the film? Did you not like that one?'

'Film, bah. The girls. Are they resting now?'

'Yes, hukam. I think they were very tired, they have been travelling day and night for several days. I showed them their chamber and they must be sleeping comfortably now.'

Rani nodded. She punched the mute button and leaned forward. 'And what do you think?'

'The little one is very lovely, hukam, most delightful, but she has no manners and no culture. She is somewhat vulgar.'

Rani waved a hand dismissively. 'Ugh! Manners, culture, those are things that can be learned. It is the raw material which counts. Hers is flawless. She is extremely promising. I want her.'

'But, hukam, she has no inkling of our ways. She is from a barbarian culture, I understood that in five minutes. The big one is even worse. She has no natural grace like the little one. She is a water-buffalo in comparison.'

'Forget the big one, she is of no account. The little one is just what I have been waiting for all this time. She is exactly the right one. But I have to know some things first. The big one has contaminated blood, this is obvious in her hair. Please find out if the little one is pure. Point one. Point two is this: the big one may look clumsy but she is the cleverer of the two. The little one is brainless. The big one sees everything and might try to interfere. I think we should get rid of her. Send her away; you may give her some money if she has none. And provide an escort for her.'

'Very well, hukam, but if I may be so forward, I would like to know what plans you have for the little one.'

Rani cackled with laughter, forgetting again that laughing and coughing are twin sisters that, for her at least, cannot bear to be separated. Her face turned red and she almost choked, ejecting bits of half-chewed betel on to Lakshmi's cheek as she leaned forward to help her mistress. Lakshmi did not stop to clean her face; she raised the gold-plated cup of medicine to Rani's lips and held it patiently while her mistress struggled to sip between the coughs. A final rasping signalled that the phlegm was about to emerge, and it was time for the spittoon. That, too, Lakshmi held at Rani's lips.

'You must not laugh, hukam. It is very bad for your health,' she said finally, and only then reached into her bosom for her own private handkerchief and wiped the shreds of red chewed betel from her face. 'You should not laugh,' she repeated. 'Now please tell me what plans you are making for the little one.'

Rani obeyed; she did not laugh again.

The table was long, oval, of thick golden wood, and very low. So low that the girls, sitting cross-legged on cushions at one end of the oval, could not get their knees beneath it but had to lean forward to reach their plates. It was big enough to seat thirty, and there were only the two of them dining, but it was laid to feed a dozen; covered dishes of stainless steel, of all sizes, were presented to Rita and Isabelle by a deferential Lakshmi, who would lift each one, remove the cover, pass it under their noses, and tell them the name of the contents as if introducing them to a series of important personages, before lovingly spooning a generous portion on to their stainless-steel plates. The girls protested, made denying gestures over their plates, tried even to push the serving hand away, but Lakshmi would not be defied; she piled it on, smiling, and saying, 'Come, come, eat, eat,' and other edifying phrases of encouragement.

When the meal was over, the gorged girls were taken on a sightseeing tour of the palace. The ground floor, they found, was divided into two halves separated by the Corridor of Mirrors, a wide passage decorated, as its name declared, with gold-framed mirrors. The bare floor was of a fine mosaic in shades of pale blue; it began at a wide door leading into the entrance courtyard, and led to another wide door at its opposite end, which opened onto the garden. Rani's hall was to the left of the Corridor of Mirrors. To the right was another door which led into a large, long room filled with women: at least eight (Rita estimated in a quick glance) young women and girls, sitting in groups, chatting, playing, entertaining each other. Two sat on the carpet just before them, playing what seemed to be an Indian version of Monopoly. Two or three others were gathered in one corner of the room, around an older woman who read to them from a book; the reader raised her voice to emphasize a point, and stopped suddenly, and the listening women all broke into peals of laughter, some of them raising delicate hands to cover their mouths. One woman plaited another's hair. Two others sat together, sewing and chatting. They were all beautiful, and they were all idle; yet behind their various occupations of leisure was a certain tenseness, the seeming relaxation of a cat pretending to sleep, but in fact waiting for a mouse to emerge from its hole. They are all waiting, Rita thought; waiting for what? They had entered silently and it took a moment for their presence to register, but then one of the Monopoly-playing girls spotted them and jumped to her feet, followed by all the others; an awesome hush settled over the loose assembly as Rita, Isabelle and Lakshmi stood in the doorway, the centre of attention, all eyes fixed upon them, taking them in, weighing, comparing. They are staring at Isabelle, Rita thought, not at me.

'The handmaidens,' Lakshmi said curtly, gesturing for them to be reseated, and without further explanation turned on her heel and led the two girls back into the Corridor of Mirrors. At the far end a wide staircase led up to the first floor.

Isabelle took hold of Rita's arm and pulled her back. 'Do you see? D'you realize what *that* was? It *was* a harem. Rani's a lesbian, and those are her women! And . . . and she must want *me* now too!'

'You wanted to come, you'll have to handle it!' Rita hissed into her ear, and hurried behind Lakshmi up the stairs.

The girls had already seen part of the upstairs quarters: their room, and the huge bathroom next to it, and a dressing room. A wide corridor ran through the middle of the upper storey, interspersed with doors.

'Are those other bedrooms?' Isabelle asked conversationally, but Lakshmi merely shrugged. Rita and Isabelle exchanged a glance, and followed their silent guide. She led them to a very large room at the far end of the upper storey. The floor was of pink mottled marble, lain with ornately patterned, deep-pile carpets. The wall at their back with the door through which they had entered was of an enormous mosaic showing a garden scene with the avatar Krishna playing his flute, three gopis, a riverbed, a full moon, and two dancing peacocks. This room, Rita calculated, was at the opposite end of the building to their bedroom; like theirs, it was oblong, with windows at both ends, shielded with carved wooden screens. The big difference to their room, though, was the wall facing the mosaic: for this one was a huge marble screen. Standing at this screen, Rita peered between the fretwork and saw a courtyard, not like the busy workaday courtyard at the front of the building, but rather a courtyard fit for a king.

It didn't take much imagination to see it filled with richly clothed monarchs, princes, statesmen, and their attendants in full livery: there was the raised dais at the opposite end, in full view of the screen, where the king would sit; there were the low marble steps leading up to that dais. There were the fountains at either side, fountains from which no water spouted, but fountains nevertheless. At the back of the dais stood black stone statues of Hindu deities, for the most part full-bosomed four-armed goddesses holding lotuses. To her right she looked down on two enormous stone elephants, facing each other with raised trunks touching as if in greeting, forming an archway closed off from the main courtyard by huge wooden doors, themselves ornately carved. Rita saw in her mind's eye those doors swing open, a turbaned sentry at each side, and the procession enter: the monarch and his councillors, filling the courtyard; she could see the musicians on that platform at the side, tuning their instruments, she could actually *hear* the melancholic echoing twang of a sitar and the distant drumming of a tabla, far away and now nearer, louder, keeping time with the beat of her heart; it *was* her heart, beating, thudding, racing. She clutched at the screen, her fingers tightening between the spaces, while her head filled with space and the colour of light and the sweet fragrance of incense, intoxicating, dizzying. She felt herself swaying, falling . . .

'This is where we women would gather and watch the royal sessions through the jalis,' said a voice beside her, and immediately Rita was jolted back into the real world. 'Those were the days. Then, the palace was alive. It is now so empty, so still, so dead . . . There are no more men. No royal men, I mean, no prince, no Maharajah. Those days are all gone. The magic has gone.'

'What was it like – then?' Rita asked, realizing that Lakshmi's reserve, for the time being at least, had been broken by a wave of nostalgia. This is the time, she thought, glancing at Isabelle, this is the time to get her to speak, to tell us.

'What it was like? Oh, it was magnificent! Nobody alive today can imagine the glory of those days! I was just a young girl then, but I remember so well standing exactly here and looking down on Maharaj Sanjay sitting there on his royal cushions. We could see him so well from here! We couldn't hear a thing, of course, but why should we? We were only women; for us it was the excitement of seeing, of watching from our lofty hideaway while the men conducted their business. My mistress was not much older than I, she was a young bride, just married and so full of hope for the future! Who would ever imagine that her husband, the prince, would die so young, leaving her a pregnant widow! And after that . . . we did not realize – nobody ever told us – we could not guess . . .' She stopped suddenly, as if reluctant to leave that magic world and talk of things that should never have happened.

'What happened?' Rita whispered, so as not to break the spell.

'Betrayal,' said Lakshmi, her voice raised and trembling with emotion. 'Betrayed by the British Raj, those statesmen we had always been loyal to. Sold out! We had no choice! We had to merge; we were given no alternative! We had to destroy ourselves in order to survive – but how! All titles taken; no more land, no more subjects. What could the Regent Maharani do? She was only a woman, and when all over Royal India even the most powerful of kings, even the most ancient of royal families were destroying themselves and merging, what could she do? Nothing. It is all Destiny. It is God's will and we have to accept it.'

'And what happened when—' Rita began, then stopped, for a deafening peal rang out like the phantom voice of a wrathful electronic God. Lakshmi placed a stalling hand on Rita's arm.

'I have to go,' she said. 'My mistress is summoning me. I'll show you the way to your room; come with me.'

FORTY-TWO

Wild Designs

Rita, standing at the front window of their room, looked down through the carvings at the front gate. They were firmly shut and locked, she could see even from here, with two huge bolts and one thick chain, each with a heavy padlock hanging from it. There was a small door set in the middle of the left gate, through which she had yesterday negotiated with one of the sentries for almost fifteen minutes, before he had been persuaded to send for Lakshmi; there had followed a further fifteen minutes of bargaining before Lakshmi had been satisfied that they were, indeed, relatives of Rani, before the door had reluctantly swung open to let them in. Now, Rita realized, it might be as difficult to leave the place as it had been to enter, or even more so.

This little self-contained world, with its padlocked gates and turbaned sentries, its obese matriarch and her private harem, its ghost of a monarchy, purdah screens and marble floors – it was exactly the antidote to the slump she had fallen into since venturing from home. It was a world of closed doors, each of which was aching to be opened, and opened by Rita, and she alone; it was her world too: she could as legitimately lay claim to it as she could to the rickety house on the Akinawa Creek where Granny plucked bora beans and sorted rice and fed the chickens. *That* was the predictable, pedestrian world of everyday-the-same, centring on keeping the body alive and working, nourished and safe. *This* was a universe beyond the physical and the logical and the known; the purdah screens and the turbaned sentries, all these symbols of imprisonment, were keys to a flight of spirit spurred on by the need to discover.

Disquietude gnawed at her being. Stay, or go? She was intrigued, and repulsed, both simultaneously. Among all the vague uncertainties of their situation only one thing seemed definite: that Rani was the centre, and in her all answers could be found.

Isabelle sat at a long low vanity table of glistening honey-coloured wood, brushing her hair. When Lakshmi rushed off they had returned to their room to await further developments; Isabelle had changed clothes and refreshed her make-up and, as Lakshmi did not reappear, finally unpacked as if in preparation for a longer stay.

Rita had sat on the bed writing her diary, paced the room inspecting the furnishings, then got up to stand at the window. Finally she turned to face Isabelle.

'So, Isabelle, have you made up your mind?'

Isabelle stopped admiring herself in the mirror and frowned. 'Rita, please don't be a spoilsport! The fun's just beginning. I thought you wanted to experience India? Well, this is India, our ancestral home! You can't just run away ... It's my chance, the chance I've been waiting for. I really have the feeling it'll work out! But, Rita, pleeeeeease ... I beg you, I fall on my knees and beseech you, never leave me alone with Rani!'

Rita giggled. 'Poof, what can she do! I mean, d'you really think she could *rape* you? She's so fat, how's she ever going to catch you if you run away? Throw herself on you or what? Or ...'

She stopped giggling, thought for a moment, and started again. 'Or she could have you chained, of course, while she does the

319

dirty deed. What d'you think, Isabelle? Or maybe she'll try to get you to fall in love with her. Oh, Rani, Rani, my darling, *you* are the one I've been dreaming of all my life!'

In spite of herself Isabelle chuckled. 'Well, OK, it's a bit far-fetched. I suppose.'

Rita became serious. 'Whatever you do, keep your head on your shoulders. I don't trust her any more than you do and I just know she's up to something.'

'Your famous sixth sense.'

'And Lakshmi eats out of her hands. There's only one way to get any information in this place. Those ladies in that room – I bet they're full of gossip. That's where I'm going. Maybe they'll tell us what's going on.'

She walked to the door, where she paused and turned. 'Coming?'

Isabelle stood up and followed.

Descending the marble staircase they passed a woman on hands and knees, polishing the minutely carved wooden banister supports. She was an older woman, poorly dressed; her skin was very dark and wrinkled, and as they walked by she cringed and pressed herself against the banisters, like a dog fearing a kick from a cruel master. Here and there they had seen similar women: one pushing a wide-bottomed broom, around which a cloth was wrapped, slowly across the mosaic floor in the Corridor of Mirrors. Another carefully brushing the fringed border of the upstairs hall carpet. Other women, standing at the well in the front court, filling pails of water and lugging them into the building, presumably to the kitchen. All these women were dark-skinned, they all wore purple cotton saris, more or less faded, and their every cringing movement, every cagey glance spoke of servitude.

Rita knocked on the handmaidens' door, and then, not waiting for a summons, slowly turned the knob and pushed the door open. What happened next took place so quickly that for several moments Rita was completely dazed. She was aware only of a swirl of rainbow colours, rustling silk skirts and shawls; hands reaching out to pull her in; smiling faces next to hers; the heady mingling of fragrances, coconut oil, jasmine and rose, interspersed with white trails of incense; all superimposed on an all-encompassing yet indefinable essence of *femaleness*, closing in around her. And all this was accompanied by excited chattering, heightened by squeals and giggles and exclamations of welcome. She shook away her daze with a vigorous backwards jerk of her head and an involuntary raising of hands, as if to push away the pandemonium of silk and sounds and smells. 'No! Wait! Stop!' she cried. The hands drew back, chatter stopped and Rita looked around her.

She and Isabelle were sitting on a plush carpet; the handmaidens surrounded them, sitting and kneeling now in silence, encircling the newcomers and staring at them with unabashed curiosity. One impetuous girl reached out as if she could not help herself, to touch a black silk coil of Isabelle's hair.

Isabelle smiled. That was the signal; as if that smile was the invitation, the handmaidens edged closer in a new and even more ecstatic outbreak of babble. Slender brown arms encircled by rows of clattering bangles reached out again to touch. Isabelle, it was obvious, was the main object of interest, her classic beauty casting its spell as ever. Among outcries of transparent admiration the maidens examined her polished gold skin, her full hair, her soft slim hands, her tiny bare feet, her smoothly ovaled fingernails, the arch of her eyebrows, the bow of her lips, ignoring Rita for the time being. Then one of the girls touched Rita's plait and commented on it in an incomprehensible language. Pitiful eyes turned then to Rita; hands stroked the uncontrollable frizz along her hairline, and the accompanying voices were commiserating, kind, empathizing with Rita for Nature's unjust error. Behind her back, somebody pulled at her plait; it felt as if that someone was about to unplait it, so Rita swung around and grabbed it protectively, pulling it over her shoulder and guarding it with both hands.

'Does anyone here speak English?' she asked loudly, a fully

understandable question which elicited not an answer but peals of laughter and hands raised to mouths to stifle giggles.

But then one girl at the very back raised a hesitant hand. 'I speaky English,' she said.

'Good,' said Rita. 'Now, can you answer some questions for us?'

'Pleez?'

'Answer questions? Tell us something?'

'Yes, yes. Telling something, I telling something,' said the girl, opening her lips in a charming smile.

'OK. First of all, what is your name?'

That the girl understood immediately. 'My name is Saraswati,' she said in carefully enunciated words, as if she had repeated them hundreds of times before.

'OK, Saraswati, listen. My name is Rita.' She pointed to herself. 'My sister's name is Isabelle. Is-a-belle.' She pointed to Isabelle. Those were words universally understood. 'My name is Rita,' said all the girls in chorus, pointing first to Rita, and then to Isabelle. 'My name is Is-a-belle.'

'My name is Sita!' cried one of the girls in triumph, followed by shouts of, 'My name is Premawati!' 'My name is Jasoda!' 'My name is Rukmini!'

When all the introductions had been made Rita turned once more to Saraswati. 'Saraswati, I want you to help us,' she said.

'Helpus?' Saraswati frowned as she tried to figure out the meaning of Rita's words. 'Not understanding.'

'We're not going to get very far this way!' said Rita to Isabelle. 'Seems like we'll have to ask Lakshmi after all.'

Saraswati understood that. 'No, no, no Lakshmi,' she said, shaking her head vigorously, and at the word 'Lakshmi' the hand-maidens began to murmur and mutter among themselves. One of them began a complicated conversation with Saraswati about Lakshmi, and Rita was forced to intervene.

'Let's talk about Rani,' she said to Saraswati. 'What does Rani want? What do you all do here all day? So many beautiful ladies? Does Rani like beautiful ladies?'

Saraswati understood perfectly this time, and was proud to show off her comprehension. 'Yes, yes, Rani liking. Rani liking plenty beautiful lady. Plenty plenty beautiful lady keeping here this room, this beautiful lady, this beautiful lady . . .' She pointed one by one to her companions. '. . . Rani liking Jaya, Rani liking Indira!'

'See, I told you!' Rita turned to Isabelle again, who all this time had not spoken a word. 'She likes women, and you're the next.'

'Rani liking Isabelle?' she asked Saraswati, pointing to Isabelle.

Again, the combination of 'Rani' and 'Isabelle' in one sentence was universally understood. Cries of wonderment broke out, 'Aaahs' and 'Ooohs', energetic noddings of heads, lascivious smiles, suggestive flutterings of eyelids, whispers that were clearly lewd followed by shame-faced giggling.

'See?' said Rita to Isabelle, who, still silent, merely nodded her head glumly. 'Next thing you know you'll be one of these handmaidens. Forget about being Rani's heiress. She's looking for a new lover: lucky you! *Now* do you feel like staying here?'

'I still think I—'

'*What's going on here?*'

The stentorian voice put an immediate silence to the babble.

Rita looked behind her and saw what she had, somehow, expected: Lakshmi striding resolutely towards them all. Involuntarily, she too felt like shrinking into the corner, as guilty as a schoolgirl caught scribbling notes in class (*Rita Maraj! Stand up!*)

But why? What have I done? Why shouldn't we visit the handmaidens? Yet Rita instinctively knew that the handmaidens and their function here was just one of the secrets this house jealously harboured; that it was strictly forbidden for them to go around trying to uncover those secrets on their own.

'What are you two doing here?' Lakshmi barked unkindly. 'I've been looking for you all over the place. You are not to go

323

prowling around on your own, is that the mannerly thing to do in a strange house? You are to leave these girls alone. Do not visit them again, they only get overexcited and forget their duties. Please come with me now, Rani is asking for you.'

FORTY-THREE

A Plan of Seduction

The girls sat cross-legged on the carpet before Rani. The video was mute. Rani was silent, chewing. She leaned against the backrest of the divan and rested her eyes through half-closed lids on Isabelle. Her knees lay wide apart, propped by fat cushions. On the ledge above her head three sticks of incense waved thin white tendrils of fragrance, spreading into filigree lacework, dissolving into an invisible sponge that soaked up space. Rita repressed a cough.

The silence was dense, but not complete, for it was carved by the rhythm of Rani's breathing, a faint rasping squeak like chalk on a distant blackboard. Almost, it seemed, Rani slept. Almost. If it were not for those unblinking half-closed eyes, that unmoving gaze resting on Isabelle, enfolding her as if in a net of gauze.

Isabelle wrested her eyes from Rani to glance anxiously at Rita. This is ridiculous, Rita thought, it is going on too long. Someone must say something. I must speak, break this stupid ban. Who does she think she is, this Rani?

She cleared her throat and opened her mouth to speak but just then Rani stirred, lowered her arms, reached for a thigh and raised it. Immediately Lakshmi leaped catlike forward from the shadows and pushed, pulled and puffed at the cushions, adjusting Rani's legs into a more comfortable position. Rani grunted now and again during this operation, her expression of blunt disinterest broken by flickers of pain as creaking knee-joints were gently straightened and massaged, and reluctant limbs tenderly realigned and lovingly laid across cushions.

That done, Rani switched off the video and spoke.

'I have been considering the situation and I think the time is auspicious. Balwantie is very beautiful; she would make Kamal the perfect wife.'

Isabelle's bottom jaw fell open; she leaned forward slightly in order to speak but Rani continued almost in the same breath. Isabelle listened, twisting a corner of her sari in her fingers.

'Kamal is not here at present and I must tell you from the beginning that he is not kindly disposed towards a second marriage. That is the reason I have been casting around for an alternative heir. Kamal has become a monk. He has thrown off all worldly ambitions and taken up the life of a mendicant. Last time he was here he renounced the fortune and told me he would be donating it to charity. He is wearing the ochre robe of a sannyasin. He has settled somewhere in some hermitage with his guru who is the one encouraging him. It is a female guru. She has her eyes on the fortune and will trick him into giving it all away to her, under the pretext of donating it to charity. She has got her claws into him and will not let him go and Kamal is too blinded to know what is going on. He is completely brainwashed by that woman. She has him dancing attention on her day and night. I found all this out because I sent my spies up to investigate. This is what they found out. They are living in some ashram in the Himalayas. She is an old lady nearly sixty and this is what she is doing to my grandson. This woman is a complete fraud, turning the boy's head. He has completely lost his senses to take up with such a one. I am thoroughly disgusted at the situation. We have sent him notice that I am going to disinherit him but he has not reacted. There is only one way to lure a fellow like that and that is *Woman*. You are going to be that woman, Belly. You are suitable in every way.' The voice was slow and soporific, seeming to come from a great distance, each word deliberately spoken. Her hands reached for the betel-nut dish, and while speaking she calmly ladled out tiny spoonfuls of this spice and that, placing them in the middle of the leaf in minute heaps. Finally she folded the leaf around the mixture and held it poised before her lips, waiting for the appropriate moment.

'The saint Sri Ramakrishna said that man has two weaknesses: Woman and Gold. Gold has not worked in this case so we will try Woman. When he sees you he will be captivated – what man would not be! But we cannot leave everything to chance. You need schooling. You must learn how to lure a man so that he has no choice but to be your slave. You will be stronger than this guru of his and bring him back home where he belongs. That is my plan.'

Rani stopped speaking with her mouth open, tossed in the green packet and chewed, her jaw working vigorously to grind it into red pulp. She kept her eyes on Isabelle.

'Yes, but . . .' Isabelle began, which was the cue for Rani to continue.

'There are advantages on both sides. Your advantage is of course obvious. Who are you and where do you come from? A little nobody, orphaned, without fortune and without family except for me; unmarried – your only fortune is your beauty, but even with that you have failed to find a rich husband. What I am offering you is a rich husband *and* your ancestry. Without ancestry a human being is worth nothing. So that is what I am offering you. The other one over there' – Rani gestured vaguely in the direction of Rita – 'she can be your chaperone. For obviously you will have to go and seek him out since he is not coming here . . . Any questions?'

So abruptly did she stop speaking that Rita, for several moments, felt as if she were skidding to a slow stop on a muddy field in a violent hockey match, tumbling and stumbling to the ground. Isabelle, for her part, simply stared at Rani, inanity written across her features. Rani waited, chewing her cud.

'Well?' she barked.

'I . . . I don't understand . . .' Isabelle stuttered.

'Think about it. You are dismissed.' Rani yawned audibly, reached for the remote control, and punched a button. Plump flamboyant lovers caught up in a boisterous quarrel sprang into animation on the screen above, the chubby-cheeked woman screaming at the mustachioed man in a loud and alien tongue. Rani turned her full attention to the drama captured in the overhead box.

There was nothing, in fact, to be said. Rita glanced from Isabelle to Lakshmi, who gestured obliquely, furiously and unequivocally to *get out*. The girls scrambled ungainly to their feet and backed away. Suddenly, though, Rani swung her head around, caught Rita's eyes, and raised a stout finger to point at her.

'You, Reetha, I want you to remain for a few words. The little one can go and meet you later. Sit down.'

Furious at herself for obeying, yet unable to extract herself from Rani's all-encompassing command, Rita simply stood there, glaring. Rani glared back; it was a battle of wills. Rita felt, behind her, Isabelle hesitate, and sensed more than saw Lakshmi pull her away and shove her out into the Corridor of Mirrors. She was alone with Rani; the glaring contest seemed unending. Rani scowled and chewed, Rita simply stared.

And then the spell was broken. The folds of fat enclosing Rani's features relaxed, the lips curved upwards, a chuckle escaped, the hand reached out and punched a button, the onscreen lovers' tiff extinguished with a cutting *thwut*.

'All right, darling, come and sit down. You and I must discuss things.' Rani stretched out a hand as if inviting Rita to come and join her on the divan. Her smile was warm and embracing, her tone conciliatory, conspiratorial. After a short battle of conscience, Rita, for lack of alternatives, let herself be disarmed.

FORTY-FOUR

A Man Like Any Other Man

Again, the silence. Silence is the most potent form of power, Rita thought, waiting for Rani to break it. Whoever speaks first is the loser. That much is clear. Well, OK, I'll win the last round, let her have this one. Speak first, but make your position clear.

'Isabelle can't marry your grandson. That's ridiculous.'

Rani cackled so long and thoroughly that her entire body trembled with mirth. 'You ask her,' she said finally. 'Ask her and see. That Belly knows what she wants and I know what Belly wants: a wealthy husband. My Kamal is perfect for her.'

'A *monk* . . .'

'A rich monk. A man. Under those ochre robes Kamal is a man like any other and susceptible – like any man – when it comes to a woman with charms. Did he not once fall for the blonde charms of a foreigner? What happened once can happen again, but this time according to my wishes. This Belly has her charms, she must learn to ensnare Kamal in them. That is all that is necessary; nature will do the rest. Man will rise, monk will sink. Wait and see, darling.'

What was all this *darling* business? It was as if Rani had shifted into a completely new gear; whereas Rita had been certain of the matriarch's disapproval and dislike up to now, suddenly she was being treated as a guest of honour. Obviously, it was a tactic: Rani must consider her cooperation vital to the plan.

'She hasn't even seen him . . . How can she . . .'

'Seeing is not necessary beforehand. She must decide on what she wants and then she will attain it. Men are weak in this respect, unable to resist. Woman will bring down the mightiest man. Shall I tell you a story to illuminate this point?'

No, Rita wanted to say, but it came out as *yes*; Rani adjusted her knees, punched a cushion to lean her elbow on, reached to a lower shelf on the table beside her and lifted a heavy book to her knees. Several bookmarks of thin leather divided the pages of the book, and Rani searched for a while before nodding, smiling and opening the book wide on the shelf provided by her massive right thigh.

'This is the story of the Asura brothers Sunda and Upasunda,' she began. 'It's a true story, which happened long long ago. Come nearer, darling, so I don't have to talk too loud. It hurts my throat.'

What was it about Rani that made people obey her against their own will? Whatever it was, Rita had fallen prey to it; she found herself scraping her bottom nearer. Rani cackled at these efforts and threw her a cushion. 'Here, this will make you more comfortable, darling. Now listen carefully, and learn.

'These two brothers of the demon kingdom were famous in all the three worlds. They shared all they had: their kingdom, their wealth, their house, their treasures, their weapons. They were inseparable, invincible, and feared neither man, god nor demon. Everything about them was identical, including the desire to conquer the entire earth. They underwent holy consecration and performed severe austerities, fasting, staying awake permanently, standing on the tips of their toes, keeping their arms held aloft, fixing their gaze on the tips of their noses without blinking, and in this way attained minds as hard as steel. The mountain on which they lived grew hot through the power of their mortification and began to belch smoke, so that the gods feared and tried to obstruct them. They sent precious gems and glittering ornaments to tempt the Asura brothers away from their austerities, but such was their power that nothing could induce them to break their vows. The gods sent visions of their mother, sisters, wives, children and kinsfolk being attacked by terrible monsters and shrieking in terror, "Save me," but the Asuras neither blinked nor moved a finger. Finally the Grandfather of all the worlds appeared before them, saying, "Your austerities force me to grant you a boon. What shall it be?"

'The Asuras stood before the Grandfather with folded hands and said: "If we have pleased you, then we beg for the boon of immortality!"

'"Ask whatever you want, and I shall grant it. But immortality I can grant no mortal. That is beyond even my powers. Ask for something else."

'"Then let us be safe from all creatures, man, god or Asura. Let none be able to kill us, except we ourselves."

'"Granted," said the Grandfather, and disappeared.

'In possession of this tremendous boon the Asuras put into motion their design to conquer all the three worlds. They sent armies swarming over the earth in all directions; they vanquished all lands, leaving scorched earth and oily black skies behind them, but picking out a few select items for their later pleasure. Having conquered earth they began to lay waste to the Asuras in the underworld. Having subjugated the Asuras they ascended to the heavens and defeated all the gods, cowed the divine singers and dancers known as Apsaras, bringing them under their sway, leaving behind them a poisonous, stinking ooze. Moon, sun, planets, stars and constellations grew dim and sickly grey at the sight, and the universe was a most loathsome place. Now the divine Seers living beyond the three worlds witnessed this massacre and convened before the Grandfather.

'"Grandfather," they said, "now see what you have done. You have granted them this boon, that none may kill them except they themselves, and this is the result. The three worlds are in chaos, sun, moon and stars swirling in disarray. An ocean of blood covers the earth, the gods are in bondage, the Asuras enslaved. See this, and do what you have to do."

'The Grandfather looked down and saw what had happened; he pondered for a while; then summoned his Divine Architect, Maya, and told him what to do. Maya gathered together all the most beautiful things in all the spheres, moulded them together, and created thus a divine woman of most celestial loveliness, whose equal in beauty could be found nowhere in Time. No part of her was anything less than perfect, and wherever she went she carried with her the amorous glances of her beholders. The Grandfather named her Tilottama, and said to her: "I grant you the ultimate power. Go to these Asura brothers and seduce them."

'The two Asuras, having conquered the three worlds and being in possession of the entire universe, had by now repaired to a mountain paradise they had left untouched specifically for their own pleasure. There they gave themselves up to a life of delight with all the most beautiful things of the world at their disposal: women, gems, gold and silver, food, perfumes, drink. Like immortals, they roamed this lovely place at will, taking their gratification as they fancied, and the strength acquired by their austerities thus grew weak. Women waited on them with food and drink, music and dance, and they lacked nothing. Then Tilottama appeared before them in a single sheer cloth. Both brothers saw her at once, and both were seized with passionate desire. Their drink-bloodied eyes devoured her; they leaped to their feet and both ran to her and seized her. Maddened by drink and lust, they glared at each other with crazed hate.

'"Move over, she is mine!" said one. "Fie on thee! She's for me!" said the other. With horrible blood-curdling cries of "She's mine! Me! Me! Me!", they sprang at each other's throats and tore at each other's flesh with clawed nails. Raising their grisly clubs they bashed each other in frenzy till, covered in blood, both lay dead, fulfilling the boon that they could meet death only at their own hands. Tilottama laughed and wandered through the three worlds, touching all that was ugly and giving it back its life and beauty, and the Grandfather was very pleased.

'You see, darling? That is the power of a woman over a man. Man is but an infant when it comes to Woman: just a hint of her sweetness and all intelligence departs and descends to his loins. A woman like your sister knows this instinctively – her will and her wiles are channelled into cultivating this ability; she derives her satisfaction from bringing man to fall. It is the power of the shakti utilized to activate animal instinct. Do I not know this myself from my own experience as a lovely young woman! Oh yes.' She cackled and coughed. From nowhere Lakshmi slid forward holding out the spittoon, collecting Rani's phlegm, wiping her mouth and covering the spittoon with the lace hanky.

Rani continued. 'I can tell at a glance your sister is well experienced in this animal play. Is that not so? Her body is impure, correct?'

Rita nodded, understanding Rani's meaning but not knowing what to say.

Rani smiled in complacency. 'I knew it. I can smell these things.' She wrinkled her nose and sniffed, as if truly an unpleasant odour was drifting past her nostrils.

'That is a bad thing and a good thing. It is a good thing because it means she will not be unduly modest when the time comes to put her abilities into play; she will need an inner brazenness tempered by an outward docility. A woman of your sister's instincts will understand how to do that, these things come naturally to such a one. But it is a bad thing because Kamal too will be able to smell it and shy away from her; he is a man of heightened sensibilities and will not fall prey as easily as most men. So we have to think, you and I. You are of a superior intelligence; in you the shakti has not been turned to base instincts but refined into higher mental ability. So you must be your sister's guide and mentor. As you have always been.'

Rani delivered this speech, as always, slowly and deliberately, each word pronounced with cool precision, as if dissecting a butterfly and pinning it up on display. Her eyes were dark holes sunk into the wad of flesh padding her face, cryptic caves in whose depth pinholes of light glimmered, seeing all, digesting all, sucking in the world and letting nothing out. Below them, thin lips moved, enunciating words so preposterous in meaning that Rita, under other circumstances, would have worked herself into a lather of rage and lashed back with equal eloquence.

But not now. Now she only stared, biting her lip, and swallowed audibly. Logically, Rita knew that *she* was in the right, that she, and not Rani, had reason, discernment and common sense on her side. That Rani's logic was preposterous, her scheme outlandish. It was all unthinkable. An out-of-space, out-of-time fantasy, a science-fiction soap opera, and it was happening to her, or rather to Isabelle.

'It won't work,' Rita said finally. 'It can't. You don't understand. Isabelle is not like you, not really Indian. Where we grew up we do things differently. We just don't marry that way, by order, we don't marry people we don't know and don't love. You have to take into consideration . . .'

Rising panic inside her overcame awe and lent her eloquence, releasing a tumbling torrent of words, as rapid and passionate as Rani's had been slow and impassive. Rani merely observed, as if from a great distance, a silent core of omnipotence enclosed by mounds of flesh.

'Isabelle had no idea,' Rita said. 'She thought, we thought, well, when you summoned us Isabelle thought it was *her* you wanted. She wouldn't have come just to marry a stranger. Isabelle's a modern girl, she'd never agree to . . . she wouldn't ever consent to such a marriage, don't you see? We may be Indians but over there where we come from we don't marry that way any more – we choose our partners and Isabelle thought in coming here . . .'

'She thought she'd be able to inherit a vast fortune, and not do anything to earn it? Is that what Belly thought?'

The words were so near to the truth that Rita was silenced.

'And what did you come for? Just to accompany her? Or are you seeking a fortune too?'

'Look – we didn't come here with any particular plan in mind,' Rita said. 'I came to discover India – our father died a short time ago and I just wanted to come and travel around, get to know the country and the culture. Isabelle persuaded me to bring her along. She was curious about you, after you sent that Mr Hanoman to look for an heir. We were *both* curious – after all, this is our ancestral home!'

Rani's voice was low now, almost a purr. 'A nice pair of fortune-hunters you are, aren't you? Thought you'd come and find your rich grandma, your poor old rich grandma, and curry her favour before she dies, did you? Isn't that what you thought? Be truthful now. I can tell if you lie, you know.'

This could only happen in India, Rita thought, and felt a stab of repulsion so intense she would have jumped to her feet and fled – if there were not half the globe between here and the once-familiar world of mundane, predictable and safe events. And yet, in the context of Rani's world this plan was perfectly normal, perfectly sane. An arranged marriage – nothing unusual, and highly laudable. An arranged marriage between distant cousins – even more normal, even more laudable. An arranged marriage between distant cousins in a wealthy and once-royal family – standard procedure in a society where myth saturates reality.

Involuntarily, Rita began to laugh. She couldn't help it and she tried to hide it, so it came out as a sort of burp pressed back by her hand. A close up of her sister's face in the role of virgin-Indian-bride came to mind, the residues of old relationships gone awry resting as a patina – invisible to the senses, discernible only to an astute mind – on the flawless honey skin, her eyes lowered not in modesty, but so the bridegroom couldn't see the smudges of bygone passion lurking in their recesses.

Rani wasn't fooled. 'Why are you laughing?'

Rita gulped. 'It's just . . .' She smothered a giggle. 'You'll never get her to . . .' She bit her lip. 'You won't fool him, what's his name. He'll know! Men know things like that . . . Isabelle can't act to save her life; she'll never fool him, even if she were to marry him, and she won't – the whole idea is ridiculous, impossible!'

'Pah!' Rani spat the word and reached for the spittoon, into which she emphasized her disdain by shooting a gob of greenish-yellow phlegm. 'Don't underestimate your sister; all men are fools when it comes to women. A well-considered bat of a long eyelash – do you know how that affects a man? No, you don't – how could you, you have never had to cultivate such arts. No wonder you are still unmarried! You talk of choosing husbands – how to achieve that without the arts? Who would look at you? A charmless creature – I have to be truthful, you know, it's for your own good, don't be hurt. Men don't like women like you though you're not bad looking, except for that hair. You have no *intrigue*. Men love that about women. They like to be ensnared, conquered by artifice, by sweet female devices. Didn't your mother teach you these things? Don't think that just because our marriages are arranged we don't need feminine tricks. Oh no, we must be constantly on the alert because other women are there lurking in wait to lure our husbands into their beds, so a wife must be as skilled as a prostitute to keep her man for herself – don't I know it! Otherwise he will stray, he will take a mistress or a concubine or even a second wife, and who wants that? So we must be clever at all times. And your sister is ideal material. She will learn, I can see that. I am going to move her into the harem immediately.'

Rita knew better than to argue. Rani's conviction was of the unequivocal sort – nothing, no argument, no appeal to impartiality, would ever change her mind on certain issues, and this was one of them. Rani's opinion, to Rani, was a fact of life and no one, least of all Rita, would ever alter that. Rita could accept this. She could bow to reality. She could even smile as if in agreement, bobbing her head in acquiescence, rise to her feet, place her hands together in a namaste of farewell, and step backwards out of the great woman's presence.

It was time to have a word with Isabelle.

FORTY-FIVE

Fishing for a Monk

Isabelle had spent the rest of the morning surrounded by three harem ladies, who were giving her her first lessons in the arts she would need to change the inaccessible Kamal from a monk to a willing bridegroom.

They had taken off all her clothes – almost all, for Isabelle had balked at the removal of her panties. They had seated her on the marble steps leading up to a crumbling out-of-use fountain, where Isabelle, giggling, imagined dozens of sleek brown naked women draping themselves in suggestive positions up and down the low stairs and around the two stone lions at either side, and allowed herself to be pampered. As they rubbed scented oil into her skin their touch was soft, they murmured foreign words and hummed wordless songs, they smiled at Isabelle, coaxing a response from her, admiration in their eyes such as she had never known from other females. Someone slipped behind her, massaged her shoulders, placed two hands gently over her ears and delicately inclined her head backwards, so that it lay on the softness of somebody's thigh; fingers light as feathers kneaded the fine skin around her eyes. She closed them, and let herself sink into the lap of luxury, soaking in the deliciousness of touch, scent, sound.

Into this exquisite scene of sensorial indulgence, into this balmy atmosphere of honeyed pleasure burst Rita – it was a shock for all, including Rita.

'What on earth are you doing!' she cried the moment she realized that Isabelle was the near-naked nymph at the centre of attention. 'Come here at once and – No, put on your clothes first! Come on, get dressed. Are you crazy, or what!'

Even to herself, it sounded like a banshee cry, raw and primitive; it put her at an immediate disadvantage, she being the disturber of the peace, and having to defend herself.

Languidly Isabelle sat up; the three girls around her drew back into non-interfering poses, as in a carefully synchronized ballet.

'What's the matter?' she said peevishly.

Rita stalked forward, feeling clumsy and uncouth before the bevy of nymphlike maidens – another disadvantage, but she didn't care. 'Come on, get up, get up from there, don't be ridiculous! Come on, get your clothes on, and come with me!'

Rita's utter contempt of the situation, her indifference to the rawness of her approach lent her a certain authority, and Isabelle found herself obeying, but with a pout.

'You always spoil everything,' she said, slipping into the purple silk shalwar set aside for her on a velvet cushion.

'Who's spoiling what?' said Rita cryptically. Ignoring the three other girls she stared at Isabelle with such intense disdain that the girl turned her back as if in shame. She tied the cord of the shalwar, picked up the kameez, shook it open and slipped it over her head. She arranged the dupatta over her shoulder, patting it into place.

'Isn't this lovely,' she began in a conciliatory tone, gesturing downwards to her outfit. 'I was speaking to Lakshmi and I told her we don't feel comfortable in saris, and so she sent for these things, ten for me and five for you. I think they're much nicer, and so comfortable.' She raised her hands from behind her neck so that the hair bounced upwards and fell into its customary full, black curtain.

'You're so *cheap*, Isabelle.'

338

'And you're a prude, you always were. Why can't I . . . oh, Rita, you haven't seen it yet, the photograph! Come!'

The little spat already forgotten, Isabelle grabbed Rita's hand and pulled her through a series of doors and corridors, into the Corridor of Mirrors and up the flight of stairs. Once inside their bedroom she hurried over to the dressing table and picked up a framed photo standing there.

The frame was of a dark wood, ornately carved in a pattern of flowers and leaves. The photo it held was of a young man, an Indian; he stood against a background of blurred heads, faces and profiles; his own face was straight on, and smiling. He looked highly pleased with something, his eyes seemed to sparkle with mirth. His teeth were dazzling white, the nose a little thin, the lips slightly full even in the bow of their smile. The black hair was neatly parted to one side, and so well combed the tooth-marks of the comb were visible. He wore a white shirt and a tie; a strap, probably of leather, dented one shoulder, as if he carried a shoulder-bag unseen in the photo, which stopped a hand-width under the knot of the striped tie.

'That's Kamal,' said Isabelle, her voice high with excitement. 'And I'm to marry him. In this photo he's just off to America, to university, some really high-class school! It was taken about eighteen years ago so I suppose he's much older now but isn't he handsome, Rita? Think of it, and I'm to marry him! Isn't he fantastic! And rich too, and a prince!'

Rita merely glanced at the photo. She took it from Isabelle's hand and replaced it on the dressing-table.

'He's not a prince, Isabelle, get that into your little mind. This family is as royal as ours is – they're all fooling themselves and they've got you fooled too. Rani's not a queen and this fellow's not a prince and you're not going to be a princess. Stop dreaming! You're living in a fairy-tale!'

Isabelle stamped and reached for the photo again. 'I . . .'

'We've got to talk, Isabelle, we've got to talk. You've got to snap out of this madness. Can't you see it's madness! You can't just agree to marry this fellow, just like that! Are you out of your mind?'

'Of course I can, why not? I think it's a perfect way of getting married, having somebody really important and attractive chosen for you, and rich! Look at all the trouble Mummy went to to catch somebody and look what happened: nothing! What kind of a future have I got stuck away in the back of beyond? Rita, I want to get out and I'm not going to let you stop me. I'm going to marry him – I am!'

'And I used to think I was the dreamer! You must have lost your mind. You don't even know him! What's a photo! Twenty years ago, you said. So what if he looked nice then – how old was he? Eighteen? Nineteen? So now he's thirty-six! Old! Really old! As far as you know he's a fat slob like that Rani – and he's a monk anyway, he's given up women, he doesn't even want to get married, yet they're still all planning this wedding for him! You've all of you lost your minds.'

'No, Rita, you just don't understand – arranged marriages are perfectly normal here, and so what if he's a monk? That makes it much easier. All I have to do is turn on the charm and I've got him, just like that!' She snapped her fingers. 'Those monks, they've just suppressed everything. He'll be a pushover. I've just got to get him so attracted to me he can't resist, and then of course I'll insist on marriage before he can have me. And I don't believe he's fat and ugly. They would know, surely. I've been talking to Lakshmi, Rita, and it's really exciting. I've heard his whole story. Shall I tell you?'

Rita rolled her eyes. 'I suppose if you don't tell me now you'll be pestering me for days. Better get it over with. OK, so who is this marvellous Kamal?'

'Well, you know he's Rani's grandson. She raised him when his parents were killed. At first she tried to keep him away from a normal life, he used to be a wild boy and she was worried he'd get into trouble or get killed or something. I think she was very protective, because her son got killed so she wanted to keep this boy alive. She tried not to let him out of her sight, but it didn't work – he kept running away, and when he got bigger he wanted to go to school and made such a fuss she finally had to let him go. And then he wanted to go abroad to college – that was another shock but she had to let him go, he insisted. So he went to America! To some famous university. He became an engineer. And then he came home and brought some American woman with him and wanted to marry her, but of course Rani wouldn't allow it. She threatened to disinherit him – but he didn't care! He disappeared – vanished into thin air for years and years. Rani was terribly worried, she thought he was dead, just like she always feared.'

'But he wasn't – obviously.'

'No, of course not. Just angry. But Rani couldn't know that. She just sat here worrying and worrying, and preparing the palace for the day he would come home. To lure him back! But he never came. So she simply had to find out if he were alive, or if he had married this American woman anyway. Because if he had . . .'

'What if he had?'

'She would have disinherited him. She didn't want any American princess for him, and half-breed great-grandchildren. So she sent out spies to find him.'

'How could she possibly find him? India's so huge. I don't believe any spy could find anybody in this country – not if that person really wanted to hide. This country is absolute chaos!'

'Well, the thing is, normally she wouldn't have been able to find him – she'd have searched much earlier if she had had a hope of doing so. But a letter came from America, from that woman's parents. They were looking for him because their daughter had died and there was a baby and they wanted custody. They had information Rani didn't have about where he had been working and living and somehow they traced him to Rishikesh, in the Himalayas, where he was living with this woman guru. He was a monk by that time.'

'But he was living with this woman guru – you mean . . .'

Isabelle knew what Rita was thinking. 'No, no, it wasn't that . . . he really was a monk. There were lots of monks in that ashram and he was one of them. Rani used to send someone every couple of months to check on him. And then suddenly he disappeared again. Into thin air. Poof – gone. Rani went frantic. She was terrified he'd gone to live in a cave in the Himalayas, or something like that.'

'And the baby?'

Isabelle shrugged. 'What do I know about the baby? I didn't ask. I wanted to hear Kamal's story, not some baby's. Anyway, he was gone for years! Then, out of the blue, he wrote. He had left the ashram and gone to Saudi Arabia and was working on some oil project. As an engineer. I tell you! First a monk, then an oil engineer. He said he'd renounced his fortune – he wasn't interested in it. That terrified her all the more. She thought he meant he was going to give it to his guru. That's when she started thinking about an alternative heir. And then suddenly, out of the blue, he was back in India. He turned up here about six months ago. In plain clothes. And they all thought he'd given up his monkdom or whatever you call it, because of having been in Saudia Arabia and all that. But he said no, he was just a monk in plain clothes, and they were all so happy, because they didn't really believe him, they thought he just didn't want to admit he was breaking his vows. Rani actually went to the trouble of preparing comfortable rooms for him, and a harem. All these women – she got them for him, to lure him back into the fold! But he didn't seem interested. And then he began asking around about money and stuff, how much he could call his own, how much he could get his hands on right now and so on – and she panicked. She was certain the guru was pressuring him. You know what these people are like, always after money. That was when she dug up all those old documents about somebody wandering off to Guyana. So then she tried to find male heirs. She thought there'd be dozens of them.'

'And she ended up with us!'

'Yep. And if her plan works out she's going to have her cake and eat it too. She wants to use me to lure Kamal back into the fold. She's certain that if I play my part well I can hook him. And then everybody's happy. Kamal, me, Rani. Happy ending!'

'And they all lived happily ever after. Isabelle, you're a fool.'

'You're just jealous. Go on, admit it – I bet if it was you getting to marry Kamal you'd jump at it!'

'Me! In a hundred years maybe!'

'That's how long you're going to wait to get married anyway, the way you carry on. Talk about fairy-tales – you're the one waiting for some shining knight on a white stallion to appear. Look at the way you behaved about Russell – mooning around for months just because it wasn't the love of a lifetime. Me, at least I get over a broken heart. Men just aren't worth it, they come and go. If I'm going to be choosy it's going to be the right kind of choosiness. And you have to admit, this is the best catch yet!'

'If Rani could hear you now . . .'

'Well, she can't, and anyway, she knows very well that he's a good catch for me – I'm just a little piece of bait for her. She wants her Kamal back, and she's using me to get him. What's so terrible about that, since it's all to my advantage anyway? And this Kamal certainly sounds interesting – I could do worse!'

'Where's he now, anyway?'

'In Bombay. When Rani wouldn't give him any information about money he began writing to the bank himself and they got his address from the bank.'

'What's he doing in Bombay? Of all places?'

'Don't ask me. But Rani wants me to go there and – well, make him notice me. Make him see what he's missing.'

'And I'm supposed to hold your hand and help you execute this little plan, or what?'

'Well, what other plans do you have anyway?'

Rita had taken up her customary position at the front window, staring down at the life in the courtyard below. A bullock cart laden with strapped-down goats was at this moment ambling through the open gates. Rita watched as it creaked to a halt in the middle of the courtyard and two half-naked boys began to unload it. She turned slowly around and faced her sister. She had asked herself the very same question, even before she'd heard of Rani's matrimonial hopes. She'd turned the question over, and found her own answers.

'Isabelle, you forget I came here with a purpose. And my purpose isn't *you* and getting you married. I want to see India, and I'm going to see India if it's the last thing I do, whether you like it or not, whether you go fishing for Kamal or not. I said I'd bring you here and I did that. Now it's up to you. I can't let my life revolve around you. I've got to move on – I can't wait to move on. All this here is just an episode. OK, it's interesting and I might create a nice little story on exotic India or the Maharajas for the *Guardian*. But there's more to being in India than seeing you properly married. Ever since I set foot in this country I've felt a sort of excitement, a sort of a thrill – like there's something waiting around the next corner, the surprise of my life, some fantastic secret about to be revealed. I just don't know what it is, dammit!

'That's why I dropped everything – my job, my security, my home – and came here. I feel as if I'm on a quest – for something intangible, something I can't identify, but I know it's there. The quest for myself; for my place in life. I'm fed up of being put into slots and being told what I have to do. I hate making plans and following some beaten track. I know I'm a misfit; I always was one and always will be one but maybe there's something good in that. Maybe I wasn't meant to fit in. I've got to find my own way, and I can only do that by being free of plans and goals and just flinging myself into life. I couldn't do that back home. Now I can. And that's what I'm going to do.

'I long to be out there, outside those gates, discovering what there is to be discovered, throwing myself into life, seeing what the moment brings. And all you talk about is marriage.'

Rita had spoken slowly, in sentences that seemed half finished, using words that seemed hopelessly inadequate. It was the nearest she'd ever come to describing the rattle of the far-away drummer to another human; a rattle that had grown louder and more insistent with every passing moment, with every breath almost, a rattle that had grown into a roar, yet was silent; and it was welling up inside, choking her, like a swelling, pulsing wave of nostalgia – yes, that was the word, *nostalgia*; not a nostalgia of memory, however, one of anticipation. But anticipation of what? What's the opposite of memory? Not hopes, not dreams; nothing so concrete, nothing so vague: no, the opposite is knowledge undefined yet true and whole, unproved because unprovable, arising as a flame of insight, with her, her being, vast and free of thought, as its medium.

How to share it with Isabelle? Not possible. Isabelle's world was another, a world held together with simple understandable laws and tenets of behaviour, swaddling bands of normality in which talk of silent drummers would be the babble of a madwoman. Such talk would make no sense to an Isabelle.

'Travel through India!' Isabelle's tone was superior, scoffing. 'Rita, come on. Don't be a spoilsport. I mean, you talk of seeing what comes – that's just it! The whole idea is so exciting, meeting this Kamal and getting around him, trying to win him! Oh, Rita! Please stay with me, help me through – just till I succeed, then you can go off looking for your adventure. *Please!*'

Rita's sense of responsibility towards her sister was inviolable. It was there, installed in her heart from that first moment when the new-born baby had been placed in her hands with the injunction to 'feed it', and made irrevocable on the day Isabelle lay bleeding on the road outside Bookers through Rita's fault.

'Well . . .'

Isabelle, feeling Rita's hesitation, wasted no time in taking advantage of it. She replaced the photo on the dressing table and moved over to take her sister in her arms. 'Pleeease . . . I'm so alone in this, Rita, and I might make some terrible mistake. I really need your help! We're so far away from home and I haven't got anybody but you . . . Don't you see, this is MY big adventure. I simply have to go through with it but I need you at my side, at least until everything falls into place. I don't want to be alone with Rani and that Lakshmi. Please!'

'And if things go wrong? If you don't catch him, if he doesn't want to marry you, if you don't like him? What then?'

'Then I'll do whatever you want, I promise. Travel through India or to Timbuktu, or go home, whatever you like, I promise.'

'You know, you really are a little gold-digger, Isabelle. I never thought you'd consent to an arranged marriage. Never.'

'Why not? Mummy has been trying to do it all along, hasn't she? She just never found somebody of Kamal's calibre. And I like the challenge of it all. Charming a monk into marriage – what a task!'

'Good luck. Rather you than me.'

FORTY-SIX

Female Arts

Rani decided that Isabelle needed no more than a month to learn her arts. She was given over into the care of Koswilla, a woman brought in from outside to reign over the harem ladies and to teach Isabelle what Lakshmi called the Female Arts. A special interpreter was engaged for her. What went on behind closed doors was Isabelle's and anybody's secret.

'You smell as if they poured a bottle of perfume over you,' Rita commented, wrinkling her nose and waving her hand before her face. 'And you look like a high-class whore.'

Isabelle, draped in silk, shrugged complacently. 'What of it? I want to get my man, don't I? I've got to make the most of myself. That's what Koswilla told me. She's my own personal teacher, and she told me things – such things! I never would have thought ... There's a real art to being a woman, and most people don't have any idea, not the slightest. Marilyn's lessons were nursery school; this is the real thing – X-rated! Koswilla says when she's finished with me I can get any man I want. *Any* man! And keep him, too. It's simply a matter of making oneself irresistible. Charming him without letting him know he's been charmed. Getting under his skin, finding the place inside him where he's vulnerable, and overwhelming him there. That's the whore part of it – a subtle whore, that's what Koswilla said. As subtle as a breath of air: it's a mental thing. It's a matter of knowing your power to seduce, being absolutely secure in it; and doing it in secret, in the mind, while at the same time maintaining an air of absolute innocence and purity, and letting him believe *he's* doing the seducing. Men like being the conqueror, you know. That's all part of it. You've got to let him think he's conquering you, that he's the master, and all the time you've got him in the palm of your hand.'

Isabelle threw her head back and laughed, and even after only one day of Koswilla's tutelage Rita could see the difference, or rather, sense the difference. It wasn't just the overpowering perfume, the kajal outlining her eyes in upswept black, the lips gleaming red, the elaborately coiffed hair. Those were the superficial hints at an inner transformation, or the beginning of such a transformation – as if Isabelle had finally found her footing in herself, discovered the source of a secret power, and determined to use it. Rita saw the change, and shuddered, for Isabelle's eyes no longer held the insecurity of a baby sister. Rita felt herself dislodged from the pedestal of authority that had, till now, been hers by right. And what had till now been a silly game of 'catch yourself a husband' took on an alarming, even dangerous, seriousness. Koswilla, it seemed, was not joking. And neither was Isabelle. And least of all, Rani.

'Rani says we both need lessons in Hinduism,' Isabelle continued. 'At least, I do, and you can come too if you want to. There's some pundit going to teach us. And I also have yoga lessons and you can join in. Koswilla says it will help me gain mental strength. Koswilla thinks we Westerners are absolute morons, we don't know a thing about the mind and what power we can have if we cultivate it. She says Freud – I didn't even know who Freud is, but she knew and she explained it to me! – didn't have the slightest idea about how the mind works, and anything he was right about, the Indians knew thousands of years before him. She's going to teach me all kinds of mantras to achieve certain aims – she's going to make me invincible! It's absolutely amazing! In fact, I'm wondering if I still want this Kamal. If I have all these powers, then surely I can get a better man? Maybe some film star.'

'You'd have to meet him first before you can try your tricks, wouldn't you?'

'Yes, but even meeting him is all a result of mental power. I'll be able to do anything I want, Rita, just anything! All I have to do is put my goal into my head and empower that goal – it's certain to fulfil itself. It's a sort of spiritual *law*, only most people don't know about it.'

'I always thought yoga was about harmony and peace and such things,' said Rita mildly.

'Some kinds of yoga, yes. But there's also Tantra Yoga and that's the kind I'm going to be learning, and also Hatha Yoga which will make my body supple, and Rani thinks you can join me in that, she says it wouldn't hurt you. I mean you could learn the Tantra too, but I don't know if that would interest you . . .'

'It wouldn't,' said Rita quickly.

'A shame.' Isabelle glanced at her sister in pity. 'I mean, Rita, someday you might need to know all those secrets; like, for instance, if you fall in love with somebody and he's not interested, or he likes someone else. I mean, it's happened before, hasn't it? And if you knew those secrets—'

'Blah, blah, blah. If a man doesn't want me for myself then too bad. I wouldn't be caught dead behaving like a whore.'

'A woman has to be a saint on the outside and a whore in the inside. That's the way to get and keep a man. Koswilla says—'

'Koswilla, Koswilla, Koswilla. Koswilla says: stand on your head. And Isabelle dives to the floor and waves her legs at the world. Yelp yelp. Where have we landed.'

'Ten minutes headstand a day, keeps all your wrinkles away. That's what she said. I'd try it if I were you, Rita, you're getting old. Soon you'll be thirty.'

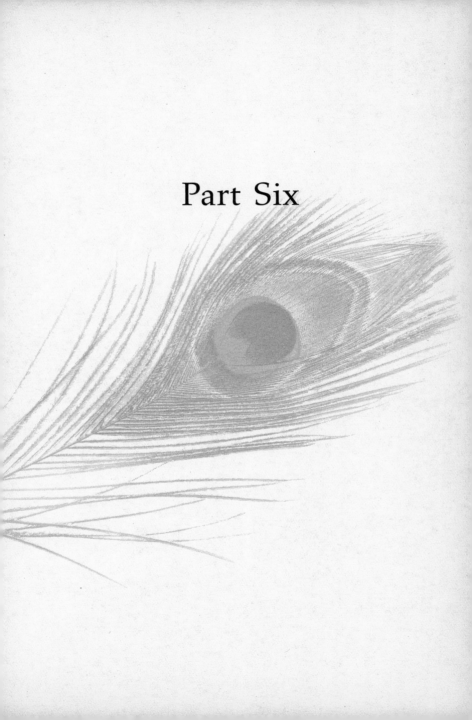

Part Six

FORTY-SEVEN

Bombay

If there is a hell on earth — not counting war, earthquakes, volcano eruptions, plane crashes and other natural and unnatural catastrophes — then it must be Bombay.

Rita stopped writing and looked up, gazing into the distance. She absentmindedly clicked the tip of her ballpoint pen in and out, biting her lip, searching for a starting point. They had arrived by plane just the day before; they had taken a taxi to their hotel — the best in all the city, compliments of Rani. They had taken lunch in luxury, and ventured out, first on foot, and then by taxi. After half an hour Isabelle had complained of a headache; Rita had sent her back to the hotel, and left the taxi to wander the streets on her own. She had stepped onto the pavement, and looked up. *That* was the starting point. She bent over her diary and began to write, remembering.

The moment Rita left the security of the taxi and set foot on that pavement the city simply gobbled her up. What a city! A hulking gargoyle of a city, monstrously ugly, wearing nothing but a black patina of filth. She had no idea where she was, and it didn't matter; it was a street like a million other streets. She walked for a while, every step a new assault to her senses, an offensive medley of sound and smell and sight that made her cringe backwards, into herself, into the safety of an inner refuge. Bombay roared on around her, oblivious to her presence and her shock. It sucked her into the stinking, churning mess of its bowels. Revolt lashed back from inside her: how can anyone live here! Why aren't they all stark staring mad! How can anyone make sense of this chaos!

So she wandered the streets, turning into this back alley and that, ignoring her own aversion, recording, memorizing, making inner notes, standing back from the chaos and the scum as a neutral, dispassionate observer. The professional; interested but unaffected. Bombay left her no choice: it was hell on earth, but it would make a hell of a good story.

Tomorrow, first thing, we go to find Kamal. Isabelle really believes Rani's drivel about her being a princess and him a prince! It's exactly what she's dreamed of all her life: a fairy-tale come true — for her. For me, a waste of time. I suppose I've got to 'do' Bombay anyway — it's a good starting point for any writing and there's more than enough to write about, but Isabelle's a chain around my ankles. I couldn't wish for anything better than love at first sight between her and Kamal. He cries 'Eureka' and tears away his monk's robe or whatever it is they wear, marries her and they all live happily ever after in Rani's Mahal. Fat chance. It's not going to work, and then I've got to find some way to send Isabelle back home. No way I'll have her traipsing behind me all the way through India for a year, yelping at every hotel that doesn't have room service and throwing a fit at every cockroach to cross her path. I shouldn't have let her come. I should have resisted her in a thousand ways for a thousand years. Now I've got her hanging on, and till I get her married off that's the way it's going to be. Hell's bells. My fault and nobody else's.

Tomorrow is her Big Day.

The sign on the gate read 'Ananda Nagar' in washed-out red paint. It was a crumbling grey building a stone's throw from the sea, protected from the street by a man-high hibiscus hedge. A forbidding metal gate, bars pointing skywards in rusty spikes, delayed their entry by some five minutes, as a thick chain bound the two wings together, tied in a complex knot that had to be unravelled.

'How welcoming,' grumbled Isabelle as Rita worked on the chain. 'Why people can't have a simple latch on their gates is beyond me.'

'Shut up, and save your breath for Kamal. You're the one who's going to have to explain what we're doing here.'

'I'm not explaining anything. I've got Rani's letter.'

'So what're you going to do? Push it into his hands, and then start batting your eyelashes and pouting your lips, or what? I don't know where you've found the nerve to barge in on him. I bet this isn't even the Indian way of doing it. There must be some subtler method of arranging a marriage.'

'It's subtle enough. As far as Kamal knows, we're just long-lost cousins here in Bombay for a spot of sightseeing. All he's supposed to do is show us around a bit, take us to the sights, and explain everything. The rest is up to me. In fact, it's she who insists I have to be subtle about it.'

'Rani doesn't know the meaning of subtlety. I bet she laid it on thick in that letter. What a beautiful girl you are, and what a pity you're unmarried, and so on. Anyway, here we go.'

The last piece of chain fell from her hands and she pushed at the gate, which swung open easily. When they had entered Rita turned, closed the gate and laid the chain lightly around the bars. 'Just in case he chases us out waving a sword over his head. You never can tell.'

'Ha ha ha.'

They walked towards the house on a once-sandy path which, judging by the ratio of greenery to sand, hadn't been weeded for several weeks, if not months. Rita lowered her voice to a fierce whisper. 'And remember, leave me out of this. This is *your* mission. I'm just here as supporting actress. Don't think you can force me into doing any persuasion work or anything like that.

This fellow's supposed to be a monk and if he doesn't want to marry it's his business. It's so embarrassing, us turning up on his doorstep with our two long empty hands. Like two lumps of salt. And if he so much as hints he doesn't want us here I'm off, and if you want to hang around . . .'

'Rita, stop nagging me. All you've been doing since we left Rani is nag nag nag. It's all you've been doing since we came to India. Why can't you just be open-minded and support me instead of constantly trying to put the brakes on my plans? As if I was still a baby or something.'

'A baby you're not, not with all the make-up plastered over your face.'

Rita was exaggerating, of course. True, Isabelle had spent at least two hours preparing herself for this first crucial visit – not counting a long session at the hotel hairdressers. She had leaned into the mirror, applying the various cremes and colours, and she had done so with a steady hand, a sure touch, and an inborn sense of style. The result was obvious even as they left the hotel, walking through the spacious hotel lobby to their limousine. Heads had turned – male heads as well as female. Isabelle had managed to perform the impossible – to invisibly improve on nature, to enhance beauty through sleight of hand so inconspicuous it appeared as nature's own perfect art. Just looking at her, walking beside her, Rita had felt her own artlessness was flawed. Isabelle radiated something akin to royalty, whereas she, beside her sister, was royalty's shadow. A shadow whose face, though not unpleasant, wore not even a trace of lipstick; whose hair, though shining, had not been styled; whose clothes, though costly, were not of silk; whose gait, though steady, lacked elegance. Rita looked ordinary and felt ordinary. Isabelle looked and felt extraordinary. Extraordinariness had been Isabelle's destiny since the day of her birth.

A few yards down the drive a man stepped into their path. He wore a khaki uniform and Rita judged him to be some sort of a guard. And though she had determined Isabelle as spokesman she knew that, in this case, she was the one to deal with the situation.

'Good morning,' she began. 'We'd like to see Mr Kamal Maharaj.'

The guard shrugged and said something in an Indian language.

Rita shrugged too, shook her head, and said, 'Mr Kamal, Mr Kamal,' and pointed at the house.

The man spoke again, and among the words Rita could make out the name 'Kamal'. She pointed to the house again, and said, 'Please go and get him,' knowing she wouldn't be understood literally. She turned to Isabelle.

'Show him the letter,' she said. Isabelle raised the flap of her handbag and removed the long white envelope Rani had given her. She gave it to Rita, who in turn handed it to the guard, with the words. 'You give.'

The man took the envelope, turned it over, inspected the name written on the front of it, looked threateningly at Rita and said something which she interpreted as 'Stay here, don't move, or I'll shoot.' He turned away, walked up the steps leading to the front door, and disappeared.

Taking his warning literally, Rita waited with Isabelle, using the time to inspect her surroundings. The house before them was more in the category of villa – large and rambling, built of stone that must once have been red, since this was the colour that here and there showed through the layer of black mould growing up the walls, enclosing the building in a patina of neglect and dereliction.

'Ugh, what a place,' said Isabelle, 'it looks haunted. And to think he's got a fortune!'

'It reminds me a bit of Number Seven,' Rita mused.

'Number Seven! Not a bit! Number Seven isn't a dump!'

'But it used to be, before you were born. Funny, how it comes back to me now. It was so long ago – Number Seven was practically falling to pieces. I loved it back then – I must have been about six or so and I thought it was the most beautiful place in the world. Then Marilyn renovated it. It was never the same again.'

'Thank goodness!'

'What I mean is, this house has the same aura, the same feeling of *history*. It must once have been really fantastic. Can't you just see elegant people going in and out! Maybe they couldn't afford to keep it up and it ended up like this, but you can still see it's got character – just like Number Seven. That's what I mean. The garden too – it hasn't been looked after for years, but once it must have been a paradise, and could be again if somebody took the trouble. I don't know – somehow I like the place.'

'It's creepy,' said Isabelle. She stepped closer to her sister.

'Yes,' Rita agreed. 'But so was Number Seven. That's what made it so interesting. Just look at the windows – like black holes.'

Wooden shutters hung from all the windows, awry where a hinge was broken, the paint peeling away, almost all with one or more louvres missing. Looking up, Rita thought she saw a face at one of the windows, but she couldn't be sure – her uncertainty sent a shiver up her spine. She grabbed Isabelle's hand.

'Did you see that?'

'What?'

'A face looking out. At that window, up there. At the corner.' Rita pointed.

'Don't, Rita, you're giving me the creeps! I'm not going to stay here, that's for sure.'

'Where will you stay, then?'

'At the hotel.'

'Don't be silly, we can't afford it. Rani gave us money for three days, that's it.'

'I'll write to Rani and tell her to send some more money. She doesn't expect us to live *here*. I'm sure of that.'

'Maybe it's OK inside.'

'Maybe it's worse inside.'

'Anyway, Isabelle, we're here and you're the one who wanted to come. There's no running away. We're in this thing up to our necks.'

'Who said anything about living in a dump?'

'Who knows, it might be interesting.'

'Interesting, my ass.'

'Look, there's that guard again.'

He was standing at the top of the entrance stairs, gesturing for them to come. They did so, climbing the wide, crumbling stone staircase. The guard stood in an open doorway, telling them something in his language and emphasizing his words with gestures.

They followed him into the house, stepping over a threshold, a line across the floorboards where darkness sliced through the sunlight. Rita felt a cloak of musty gloom close in and wrap itself around her, cool and dismal. After the glare she could see only blackness. Seconds later her eyes had adjusted and she made out a wooden staircase against the wall of a long, narrow lobby. Several doors left and right suggested that the lobby cut the house into two halves. The doors, the walls, the staircase, the floor: all was of unadorned wood, not a carpet under their feet, no pictures on the walls, and the paint so old it peeled. A faint background smell, pungent and familiar, told Rita that somewhere wood-ants were at work, building their underground tunnels, hollowing out the boards.

She gathered these impressions in a matter of seconds, following the guard along the corridor to the last door on the right. He knocked curtly, called something, and gestured to them to follow, all simultaneously. Rita felt Isabelle's hand, cold and clammy, take hold of hers as she entered the room.

It was a large kitchen, sparsely equipped. A two-burner kerosene stove stood on a stone counter along one side, and an old green refrigerator, patched with rust in the shape of a giraffe, rattled noisily beside a dirty-paned window. There were lines of shelves with cooking utensils below and above the counter, and foodstuffs – large jars of rice and dahl, smaller jars containing spices, a battered pot of limes – stood on shelves on the other side of the refrigerator. A line of half-green tomatoes basked in the sun on a windowsill, above the dripping tap of a rusty sink. A branch of bananas hung from the ceiling.

In the middle of the kitchen stood an oblong table with two straight-backed chairs. Against another wall was a planked bed-frame, like a long, low table. At the foot end of it sat a woman, cross-legged; she was stringing beans. She looked up as they entered, and smiled. Rani's letter for Kamal lay unopened on the wood beside the beans. At the other end of the bed-frame lay a heap of sundry articles: a pile of folded towels, a basket of onions, two coconuts, several chilli-peppers and, somewhat incongruously, a battered alarm clock and a rusty saw.

The woman was stout, in her mid-forties. She wore a faded red threadbare sari, and under it a blouse, which looked painfully tight, pinched in at the waist (where a tyre of fat bulged out) and at the sleeves. Her smile was warm, welcoming, echoed by her eyes. She spoke, but in that foreign language. Rita had no idea what it was – it didn't sound anything like the language they had heard at Rani's. It might be Hindi, she thought, but that was no use to her.

She shrugged and spread her hands, showing that she didn't understand. 'Don't you speak English?' she asked. The woman shrugged.

'We're looking for Kamal. Mr Kamal.' Rita pointed at the letter, then at Isabelle. 'My sister.'

'Ah, seester, seester,' said the woman, and her smile broadened. 'Kamal seester!'

'No, not Kamal's sister, *my* sister. We want to see Mr Kamal. Is he here?'

The woman seemed to understand. She spoke several words, gesturing and pointing outside the house. She repeated some of the words, and Rita guessed at their meaning.

'He's not at home?'

But the woman did not understand. Rita could only surmise that this was the case: that Kamal was out; but when he would be back, if ever, could not be ascertained. The woman laid down her knife beside the heap of unstrung beans and, with some effort and deep breathing, rose from the bed-frame, talking all the while. She pulled out one of the chairs, dusted some crumbs from its seat with the end of her sari, and gestured for the girls to sit down. Immediately Isabelle took a seat. The woman pulled out the second chair, rattled it, verified that one of the legs was loose and would fall off at the slightest weight, pointed to this flaw so as to excuse her lack of seating arrangements, and cleared a place at the other end of the bed-frame. She placed the heap of cloths on the floor, the onions, the peppers and the coconuts on the table, the alarm clock on a shelf next to a jar of rice and the saw on the fridge. With a damp rag she wiped once over the bare planks, dried the area with the end of her sari, and gestured with her open palm for Rita to take a seat. She did so.

All this time the guard had been standing in the doorway, picking his teeth with his fingernail and watching silently. Now, hospitality established, the woman spoke brusquely to him and – a gesture for the benefit of the girls – shooed him away. The man shrugged, stepped backwards into the lobby, and closed the door.

The woman was still on her feet. She stood in the middle of the room, looking inordinately pleased with herself. She patted herself on her voluminous breast and said, 'Subhadhai, Sub-hadhai.'

Rita pointed to herself, saying 'Rita', then at Isabelle, repeating that name.

'Reeta, Eesabell,' said the woman, satisfied. 'Koppee? Koppee?'

It took a while before Rita could figure out that the woman was offering them coffee. She nodded and smiled, looked at Isabelle, who nodded too, then held up two fingers, for two cups. The woman busied herself with boiling water and coffee powder, which she served in two mugs with three biscuits each for Rita and Isabelle. Only then did she return to stringing beans. And all the while she talked.

After an hour – Subhadhai had finished stringing the beans and chopping the onions: she had placed a pot with rice and water on a kerosene flame; breakfast and the biscuits had been digested; the morning was drawing to an end, lunchtime loomed near, and Isabelle was fidgeting with the ends of her hair – Rita decided to find out if there was a chance of meeting Kamal today; whether he would be returning, and if so, when.

Her carefully worded, slowly enunciated questions to this end produced only a further waterfall of words. Rita interrupted: 'Kamal coming? Today?'

She gestured as she thought appropriate, moving her fingers like walking legs, patting the table to signify 'here'. She pointed to the alarm clock and spread her hands in an open question.

Subhadhai understood.

Excitedly she began to explain; Kamal, it seemed, was indeed coming. She pointed at the clock, at the cooking food, at her own mouth, she moved her fingers like walking legs, pointed again at the clock, and held up one finger.

'Ek, ek, ek,' she said.

'I think she means he's coming at one o'clock, for lunch,' Rita said to Isabelle.

FORTY-EIGHT

Silent Tears

At twelve o'clock Subhadhai suddenly stopped talking. She placed a finger over her lips and cocked her head, gazing into space. Rita, too, listened; and she heard. The sound was unmistakable; somewhere in the bowels of the house somebody was crying. Subhadhai nodded and stood up. At the doorway she hesitated, as if making a decision, and then she gestured for Rita and Isabelle to follow her. She led them into the lobby and up the creaking stairs. The crying was louder in the lobby, and grew louder still as they walked upstairs: the forlorn lament of a soul that has lost all hope of solace and every right to happiness.

On the second floor there was another lobby, but less gloomy than the one below, for it was lit by a large window at the front of the house. Subhadhai opened a door and entered a room. Rita and Isabelle followed.

The cryer was a girl, sitting on a sharpai, leaning against the wall with knees drawn up. She might have been twelve years old, or a year or two older, a year or two younger – it was hard to tell, for her body was tiny and emaciated, the body of a young child, whereas the expression on her face was ancient. Her hands lay limp, palms-up, on the mattress; her uptilted chin was half turned to one side, her lips trembled as she wept, her eyes were vacant. She sat immobile, weeping apparently not because of any specific cause but because that was all there was left to do in all the world and in all of life. She did not so much as turn her face to look at the newcomers.

Rita felt like an intruder into some intensely intimate experience, unwelcome and inopportune. She backed towards the open doorway, but Subhadhai took hold of her upper arm and stopped her. Isabelle stood staring, biting her lip.

Subhadhai walked over to the sharpai, taking Rita with her. She was speaking to the girl, and though the words were unknown Rita could tell they were words of comfort. The girl did not react. Letting go of Rita, Subhadhai sat on the edge of the sharpai in front of the girl and reached over to stroke her cheek. The girl showed no reaction, did not look at Subhadhai, did not pause in her weeping. Rita stood awkwardly watching, the urge to flee struggling with compassion and curiosity. She stayed.

She stood before an abyss of misery so deep and so dark it filled every space in that child's soul. Rita needed no explanation – she knew it. The blankness in those dull black eyes, the downward pull of the trembling lips, the wretched whimpers: all spoke of unimaginable woe, too awful for words. This child was lost.

Is grief contagious? It had to be, for an involuntary trembling took hold of Rita. She tried to control it, but couldn't; her hands shook, her heart raced, a feeling of dread spread through her entire being, the fear of being drowned and destroyed by whatever agony possessed this child. Again, the desire to flee – to turn her back and never return to this terrible place – took hold of her, to be immediately superseded by its opposite: compassion, love even, the need to enter into the jaws of despair, defy its power, deny its existence. The trembling stopped as suddenly as it had set in.

She too sat on the sharpai, in front of Subhadhai, directly before the girl's face.

Rita looked into eyes that saw nothing. Not even a flicker of acknowledgement. It did not matter. She leaned forward. She placed both hands on the girl's shoulders, drew her away from the wall. The child did not resist. She was passive, a rag doll. There seemed not a remnant of human will left in her. Rita spoke to her, knowing she would not be understood, but it did not matter.

'Who are you? What is the matter, why are you crying?' She had instinctively lowered her voice, softened its edges; knowing the words themselves could not be understood, she filled them with feeling, knowing that somewhere, deep inside this child's being, was someone who would receive that feeling and understand it. She spoke on a level of communication beyond thought, beyond speech, and superior to both. She knew the girl, whatever was still alive in the girl, would understand. She brushed a strand of hair away from the face, held the little head in both her hands, centred it so that the eyes were directly in front of her. The child wept on. The eyes stared, not seeing. Empty. Dead.

She is dead, Rita thought. Dead inside. But no. She can't be. If she were dead she would not cry. Somewhere, deep inside, there is a last spark of life. She has heard, she has understood.

Suddenly a door flew open; not the door into the corridor – which still stood open – but a second, leading to the next room. Looking up Rita saw another girl, this time older, perhaps fifteen or sixteen, standing on the threshold.

This new girl was entirely different. She looked first at Rita, then at Isabelle, then at Subhadhai. A short exchange of words took place between her and Subhadhai, and the gaze returned to Rita, acknowledging her with a curt nod. She walked to the window and stood there for a while, looking out, before turning swiftly, walking to the connecting door and leaving the room without speaking another word. The door closed gently behind her.

Rita's hold on the first girl's face had slackened, for she had looked up at the newcomer. In that moment the younger girl had slumped back against the wall, and so she remained, her whimpering the only sign of life.

'We'd better go,' said Rita to Isabelle, and stood up. Subhadhai indicated that she would stay, and the sisters left the room and returned to the kitchen.

'What on earth was all *that* about,' said Isabelle.

'I've no idea. But I can tell you one thing – I'm going to find out.'

At one thirty Kamal had not yet returned and Rita was having her first doubts – had she perhaps misunderstood Subhadhai? Perhaps this was the wrong address entirely – she could make absolutely no connection between the Kamal she had heard of in such detail from Rani and Lakshmi, this house, Subhadhai, and the girls upstairs.

They had eaten at twelve-thirty. Subhadhai had served them a simple but tasty meal of rice and vegetables on a stainless steel platter in the dining room across the lobby from the kitchen, a room bare of any furniture save a long wooden table with six chairs around it.

Subhadhai had taken up a tray of food for the girls upstairs, and then she herself had eaten in the kitchen. She had produced a magazine and a newspaper from somewhere in the house and they had spent an hour, or two, or three, catching up on Indian news. Subhadhai seemed to have lost interest in them; she had clattered around in the kitchen, gone up and down stairs a few times, cleared the table. The house was full of sounds; the crying had gradually subsided, but the background drone of a radio or a television set from upstairs was persistent. At one point Rita heard the clatter of the chain on the front gate and ran to the open window, expecting to see Kamal, but it was only a very dark old man in a turban. The waiting continued.

FORTY-NINE

Waiting for Kamal

When Rita again heard the chain it was almost two, and she had given up any expectation of ever meeting Kamal. She glanced out of the window more from boredom than for any other reason, for she had read *India Today* and *The Times of India* from beginning to end, and conversation with Isabelle had run dry.

What she saw this time, however, made her at once jump aside from the window so as not to be seen, and at the same time peer cautiously from the side. For this was Kamal. This had to be Kamal; she recognized him, not from the photo, but from the echo she felt inside her, as if constant thinking about him had left an indelible imprint on her mind, and on seeing the living man Kamal that imprint had responded with a flutter of recognition. The taller of the two men now walking towards the house, as if directly towards her, was definitely Kamal.

'Isabelle! Come quick! It's him!'

Almost before she had spoken the words Isabelle was there, at the other side of the window, peering out from behind the curtain with the same clandestine intention of seeing without being seen as Rita herself. Rita glanced at her sister, the lovely creature bending forward and gawking, mouth open, through a peephole between curtain and wall, and felt several things simultaneously.

First, she felt the indignity of it all. Why all this hiding and peeping, she told herself furiously, and stepped out into the middle of the window where the approaching Kamal could see her plainly if he chose to glance that way. Second, a stab. A stab in the heart region, a pain, calling attention to itself, demanding a response. But Rita would not respond. Defiant, she ignored the pain and stood there, her face grim, staring out at the man now no more than three metres away, now walking up the stairs to the front door, now hidden from view. He had not looked at the window, he had not seen her, and somehow she felt offended by this oversight, as if he had deliberately ignored her. And angry at herself for caring enough to be offended.

Without saying a word she returned to the table in the middle of the room, picked up one of the newspapers still lying there, and began to read again an article she had already read. Isabelle joined her.

'You see!' she said triumphantly. 'He's *not* fat and ugly! I told you he wouldn't be. He's gorgeous. He's just exactly what I imagined. Now all I have to do is—'

'Apply your tricks,' finished Rita.

'No need to be sarcastic. You always try to belittle me. I don't know why – but I suppose you're just jealous because—'

She stopped speaking for the door to the kitchen had opened and Kamal stood in the doorway. Rita, who during Isabelle's mini-tantrum had held the newspaper up high as a screen against her sister's nagging voice, now let her hands drop and looked up.

She had had a good look at Kamal through the window, of course, but this was the first time she was seeing him face on, and so close. And as Isabelle had said, he was, for her too, very attractive. It wasn't just his physical appearance. It was the very *substance* of him, something which could not be seen but which imparted itself to her through countless signals, imperceptible to the senses but immediately recognized by the drummer within, who all her life had doggedly beat a rhythm of his own and who now, as if activated by the entrance of this new individual into

368

its radius, suddenly went wild – ratatatatatatatat at a breakneck speed.

Kamal wore khaki cotton trousers and a nondescript, faded, striped cotton shirt. He was barefoot, like everyone else in the room. He was tall and straight-backed, golden-brown in colour. His face was angular, almost gaunt, his eyes under thick eyebrows deep-set and large, the look in them probing, severe even, and at the same time veiled, seeing all while revealing nothing. A short beard covered his chin, a moustache his upper lip. He was unsmiling. The overall expression was of distance and superiority. He was unapproachable. He had looked first at Rita but now, as she looked away and as Isabelle spoke, turned his attention to the younger, prettier of the two. That's as it should be, thought Rita bitterly. That's the way it always is. That's the way it has to be. That's nature.

'You must be Kamal,' said Isabelle brightly.

Kamal did not return her smile, and only vaguely raised his hands in a peremptory namaste. He took a step nearer to the table and glanced from Isabelle to Rita, back to Isabelle, then as if unable to decide between two equally bad options, looked at the letter he was holding in his hand. He laid it on the table.

'My grandmother sent you.'

Rita had told Isabelle to do the talking, but seeing that one's asinine grin decided to overcome her own discomfiture and explain.

'Yes. We're distant relatives, from Guyana, and Rani got us to come because . . . because . . .'

You fool, she said to herself. You only have to open your mouth and you give the game away. If you finish that sentence we might as well go home. And in that moment she hated herself, hated Isabelle, Rani, Kamal, this whole game of subterfuge and seduction in which she had voluntarily opted to play a part. It wasn't her way, not at all. The whole plan seemed to her conniving and lacking dignity. She had let herself be coaxed by Isabelle; but ever since entering this house, ever since meeting the mysterious girls upstairs, and especially, ever since seeing Kamal, doubts had come crowding in and now the best thing she felt she could do was run; put as much distance between her and the situation as possible. Run; but she couldn't. Something held her; she didn't want to stare at Kamal but she did; she tried looking away but she couldn't; she tried to think of something clever to say but for once words refused to oblige.

'Rani says she wants you to meet me, and she wants me to show you around Bombay. I don't know what she was thinking of; I haven't got the time for sightseeing; I'm not here on holiday, you know. If you want to make a city tour I can arrange something for you. Where are you staying?'

Rita was more put out than ever by his curt tone, his lack of warmth, and the barest attempt at hospitality. In fact, he was downright rude; he might at least, for the sake of politeness, have *pretended* some delight at meeting his distant cousins. She was offended; she was indignant; she was fascinated.

'Oh, we're at the Taj,' said Isabelle, as pert as ever. Isabelle, it seemed, had not noticed the nuances of hostility that so vexed Rita. For Isabelle, the game was still on. The smile she shone at Kamal was seduction pure: the tilt of her chin, the subtle fluttering of her eyelashes, the curl of her smile all suggested, 'Look at me, am I not lovely? Wouldn't you love to have me? You can, you know.'

If he responds he's a fool, thought Rita, and narrowed her eyes to watch his reaction. There was no denying the fact that, from the moment she had first seen him walking down the garden path, she had been captivated. There are people who, even before they have spoken a word, command attention and esteem. They have charisma. Kamal had it, and she was lamed by it, and silenced. But seeing Isabelle's crude tactics – Isabelle would never call them crude; for her it was a subtle sending out of secret messages which the other, being male, would be powerless to resist – made her wary.

Would he react, or not? Would he fall for Isabelle's wiles, or not? Her final estimation of Kamal depended entirely on this last test of his inner stature. If he were simply a male animal, and

370

nothing *but* a male animal, he would fall; he would let Isabelle wind her gossamer-thin threads of seduction around his soul and the aeons-old game of male–female interaction would begin. And his charisma would crumble. And it would happen in the next three moments. Rita watched and waited.

Kamal was looking at Isabelle. Isabelle, too, had her charisma. That's what this whole thing is about, thought Rita. Isabelle's charisma against Kamal's. Isabelle has been raised – and I myself have helped to raise her this way – in the expectation of admiration from others. She has an instinct for the art of attraction, and has burnished that raw instinct to a gloss. It was irresistible – Rita reflected on the turning heads as the two of them walked through the Taj lobby that morning, the covert glances of the men, the resentful gleam in the eyes of the women. Isabelle had walked with head held high, as if oblivious to her effect. She wasn't: she basked in admiration while managing to appear unaware of it. Admiration was the bulwark that propped her personality; attractiveness to men was the be-all and end-all of her life. Without their response she was a limp vine, a rose creeper fallen to the ground. At times Rita felt guilt at the severity of her judgement; she genuinely loved her sister, so why then this constant fault-finding? Could it be that she was, as Isabelle so often claimed, simply jealous? That she was, at heart, nothing but a spiteful bitch?

Right now, though, Rita was not concerned with self-analysis. She was watching Kamal and Isabelle looking at each other. Waiting for one or the other to collapse.

Kamal, it seemed to her, was at an immediate disadvantage; his charisma was not deliberate, as Isabelle's was. He did not *intend* to be charismatic, he simply *was*; it was not strategy but his nature. As such, he was vulnerable to Isabelle's manipulative charm.

Rita wanted Kamal to win. For his sake – and for her own.

Isabelle's chair was drawn back from the table, and she sat in a pose of sweet innocence and feminine submission. In spite of the mid-day heat she managed to look as fresh and delectable as a newly cut slice of watermelon. Her face tilted upwards at a most appealing angle, large brown eyes limpid with serenity, lips twitching slightly in a shy and vulnerable smile. *See – I am so lovely, inside and out. In me is the essence of delight*, was the silent message she now imparted.

Rita slumped inside. Isabelle had won already – she could see it in the puzzled look in Kamal's eyes; a look which seemed to reply to Isabelle's message: *Oh, I have seen, and I am bewildered. You have taken me completely by surprise, you lovely thing!*

In a gesture of capitulation and acquiescence to the inevitable, Rita folded the newspaper she had been reading and laid it on the table. The rustle of the pages seemed to distract Kamal, or maybe he was simply seizing the opportunity of distraction to collect his runaway emotions – Rita was sensitive to all such nuances of behaviour – and let his gaze wander from Isabelle's face to the paper. It seemed to rest there for some time, apparently inattentive.

Suddenly Kamal lunged forward with an exclamation of surprise, and grabbed the paper with both hands. He pointed to something and spoke some quick, sharp words in Hindi to the man at his right elbow, who moved nearer and peered forward to read. Then Kamal looked up, and from his eyes a light shone out, and he even appeared to smile – a thing he had not done since entering the room, a thing which seemed impossible, so deeply drawn into his features was the expression of solemn austerity that presumably was normal to him.

The two men exchanged several Hindi sentences; excitement buzzed between them. Action was in the air, Isabelle forgotten, Rita even more so. Kamal nodded curtly in their general direction – his gaze aimed somewhere in the region of the window – rolled the newspaper into a tight wedge, and turned to leave.

Rita refused to let that happen; they had waited for this man all morning, and she wasn't letting him escape so quickly – for escape, that was plain, was imminent. He was going to leave the house, not having been there even fifteen minutes, not having so much as glanced at the food waiting in the kitchen, not having had so much as a sip of water. He was a man driven – and something in that newspaper was driving him.

She jumped to her feet, and called out, 'Wait a minute!'

Kamal stopped and turned, his expression, on seeing her, vague, as if he couldn't remember ever having seen her before in his life, and was wondering what she was doing there in his home.

'Uh? What?' he said.

'What about us? We came all this way – we've been waiting all morning – Rani said . . .'

'Oh, oh yes, you want to do some sightseeing. I'll talk to Subhadhai, she'll phone a taxi service and get a taxi to take you around. She'll ask for an English-speaking driver – go with him, he'll show you everything.'

'No, but, well, we also wanted to talk to *you* . . . When will you be back?'

The question seemed to puzzle Kamal, as if he wasn't used to timing his projects. He looked impatiently at a battered watch on his wrist, then back at Rita. 'Look, I haven't much time for conversation. I don't know when I'll be back; make yourself at home here. I have to go. I might be back in the evening, around six or so, but I don't know. Maybe then. Maybe not.'

'But – can we stay here? Do you have room for us?'

'Room? Well, yes, of course, upstairs. I'll tell Subhadhai to prepare something for you. Be my guests. I'm sorry – I have to go. Subhadhai will take care of everything. Subhadhai!'

He called loudly as he left the room and Subhadhai came clattering down the stairs. Rita heard him speaking to her in Hindi, presumably giving her instructions concerning their entertainment, room and board. She heard receding steps, two pairs, a door creaking open and slamming shut. She heard the crunch of gravel as the men walked away towards the gate. She heard her own outdrawn breath, the hammer of her heart-drum. *Round one to Kamal!* it said.

The last thing Rita felt like doing was going on a sightseeing tour of Bombay. It was the hottest time of day, the time most Indians with the leisure to do so would lie down and take a nap. That was what she felt like doing most. Besides, Isabelle was fretting; after Kamal's hasty departure the sweet expression on her face had immediately changed into its opposite, like a surface of water, calm and reflective one moment, whipped into untidy ripples the next. 'The nerve of him!' she said. 'Rushing off like that! Who does he think he is? What on earth was he so excited about?'

'That's what I'd like to know!'

But Kamal had taken the newspaper with him. Rita resolved silently to buy another – some piece of news had galvanized Kamal into action, and a thorn of curiosity pricked Rita to find out what, exactly. In the few minutes she had known him many things had become clear to her. First: Kamal was no ordinary man, driven by no ordinary urges. The portrait she had painted of him in the colours supplied by Rani's tales had been of a weak, wavering fellow, caught first by a blonde American fortune-seeker, then by a female pseudo-saint; a dreamer, a romanticist, a visionary; a man who, confronted with a diva of Isabelle's stature, would undoubtedly fall.

On first meeting him, this portrait had evaporated, unable to stand comparison to the rock of assurance that was Kamal. Then Isabelle had turned on the full-strength charm and it had seemed a sure bet that Kamal, with the animal urge of every man, would react to the age-old silent signals at Isabelle's command.

There had been a moment of vacillation. And then a new force had catapulted Kamal out of the periphery of gilded lust. Something in the newspaper had ignited that force. Rita needed to know what.

'So what do we do now?' Isabelle whined. 'He didn't even speak a word to me, not a single word. He just rushes in and dashes off again like a wildman, after we came all this way! Does he expect us to hang around here waiting for him, or what?'

'No, he expects us to take a taxi and go sightseeing!'

'Sightseeing, my backside! You think I care two hoots for Bombay? This whole place is a stinking dump! You can go sightseeing alone if you want – *I'm* going back to the hotel. I'm tired and I've got a headache. And as for moving in here, forget it. I'm staying at the Taj till Kamal comes to his bloody senses.'

'Yes. Let's go back to the hotel, I desperately need a shower. The taxi should be here in a minute, let's go and wait for it outside.'

As they walked down the driveway Isabelle added, 'But I'm not giving up on Kamal; Rani said he might be difficult, and I'm prepared – it's a challenge!'

Rita shrugged. 'You can always try again this evening. Perhaps you should wear your hair *down* next time you meet him. Maybe he'd prefer that. And those earrings, Isabelle – I don't know if they really suit you.'

Isabelle reached anxiously for her dangling pendulum earrings. 'You really think so . . . Oh, *Rita*, you bloody bitch, you're always laughing at me.'

Rita, grinning, raised an arm to shield herself against Isabelle's petulant blows.

When Rita emerged from the shower Isabelle was fast asleep, curled up under the blankets in a cool darkened room. The air-conditioner hummed soothingly, and Rita yawned. She wouldn't mind a nap herself; but no. She had other plans. She quickly got dressed in a simple cotton shalwar kameez, wrote a short note for Isabelle saying she'd be back by six, and slipped out of the door.

Down in the lobby she took *The Times of India* from the stand and turned to the Bombay page, the page that had so galvanized Kamal.

She scanned the headlines, looking for something that could possibly have caught his attention, and because she didn't know what she was looking for found herself also reading the accompanying articles, and puzzling over their contents. Not knowing much about Kamal – she no longer trusted a word Rani had said about her grandson – it was almost impossible to figure out what, exactly, could propel him out into the streets, without even waiting for lunch.

She immediately ruled out the strike by medical students, now in its fifth day, and an incident at the Viddalayak temple the previous day, in which a garland vendor had been injured by a pilgrim. The planned demolition of a tenement in Bombay's outskirts seemed also unlikely. She wondered about the suicide of a politician's wife – did Kamal know her, perhaps? Impatiently her gaze wandered from headline to headline, rejecting, rejecting, rejecting. It was only at the second reading that something clicked. She read the item again – a small item, tucked away in the bottom left-hand corner. The headline itself was innocuous: *Injured Girl admitted to B. K. Shivnandan Hospital*. It was one of the articles that she had on first reading rejected as being completely irrelevant. But then, not knowing what exactly she was looking for, every article had seemed more or less irrelevant and she had gone back for a closer look.

What clicked this time was a memory. Recent, yet indelible in its intensity.

A fourteen-year-old prostitute was admitted to B. K. Shivnandan Hospital with several knife wounds and a broken arm, sustained during a fight between a pimp and a drunken customer in Kamathipura. The girl was in a state of extreme shock yesterday and unable to speak to investigators. However, other prostitutes from the same brothel revealed that she had been kidnapped in Chennai and sold into prostitution about a year ago. She was brought to the hospital bleeding from the knife wounds by a health worker from an NGO, who later filed a charge of trafficking with minors . . .

It was the words 'in extreme shock and unable to speak' that caused Rita to pause, and the memory to assert itself: here was an echo of something she had herself seen. *A girl in shock, and unable to speak*: the girl upstairs in Kamal's house.

It was a purely speculative connection – objectively speaking. Rita's suspicion, though, was not objective, not based on a study of the facts; not based on any rationale whatsoever. It was a simple click inside her brain, a drum-rattle within her, an intuitive certainty. She knew.

The taxi took an hour to get to the hospital, hindered by traffic jams at every corner. The streets were clogged, and by the time she arrived at the Shivnandan Hospital it was almost four. Convinced as she was that her hunch was right, she was equally convinced that she would miss Kamal, who surely would not hang around the hospital for hours. Certain that she had missed him, uncertain as to what she would say if she had *not* missed him and almost hoping she would, Rita made her way through the labyrinth of hospital corridors to the ward in which, according to the receptionist downstairs, the injured girl could be found.

The door to the ward stood open. Inside, several simple cots lined the two sides of a long room. All of the cots were occupied; the patients lay in various conditions of apathy or illness, some alone, others surrounded by family members. An elderly woman was being hand-fed by a younger woman; a middle-aged woman with oily, uncombed hair cried, alone, into a corner of the sheet. The ward, sparse and drab in its appointments, smelled of stale urine mixed with medicine and antiseptic, and a slowly rotating overhead fan did little to dilute the smell with fresh air from the open window. A slight nausea rose up in Rita. There was only one girl of the right age.

She hardly expected Kamal to be at the girl's bedside, and he wasn't; instead there was a young woman, wearing, rather than the obligatory sari or shalwar kameez, jeans and a T-shirt. She was light-skinned, but not European – the coffee colour of her complexion was natural, not a tan, and that thick black hair, swept back and up into a ponytail, and the bushy eyebrows over coal-black eyes, were definitely Indian.

The girl – for she was not much more than a girl, perhaps twenty-five, maybe younger – looked up at Rita's approach and smiled. 'Hi!' she said. 'Have you come to take over?'

'Take over?'

'Yes . . . didn't Kamal send you? He said he'd send someone

around this time.' She looked at her watch. 'I've got to go soon. Somebody has to stay with her – just in case they come to take her away.' She glanced at the inert figure on the cot beside her. Rita looked down.

The injured girl lay curled on the sheet, her face half-hidden in the crook of her left arm, which was encased in fresh plaster of Paris. Her left shoulder was thick with the padding of an elaborate bandage, which could be seen at the short sleeve and the neck of her white hospital nightdress. A threadbare sheet covered the embryonic curl of her body.

It took a few moments to establish that Rita had not been sent by Kamal; and that the young woman's name was Gita.

'Rita and Gita,' said Gita. 'Sounds good; rhymes even. So what did you come here for, if not to take over the next shift?'

'Well, I was looking for Kamal.'

'Oh, you won't find him here. He spends most of his time in Kamathipura. He's obsessed, that man. But you can't blame him.'

'Obsessed?'

'He's a man with a mission. And what a mission. Looking for a needle in a haystack.'

'And you? Are you his . . . ?' Rita stopped.

'His girlfriend, you mean? Me?' Gita chuckled wryly and pointed to her forehead. 'I'm not that crazy. No, I'm just helping out; just a friend in need. I've known him practically all my life – since I was about twelve or so. We went to the same boarding school in Kodaikanal, though I was many years behind him. However, my best friend's brother was his best friend and so I saw him quite often. We met again when I came to study medicine in Bombay; this is where my friend Rehana lives, and when I went to visit her this year there he was again – Kamal, I mean. I hadn't seen him for years and years. He got me involved in this thing – he has a talent for getting people involved. You can't help it. It's just all so terrible. And so hopeless.'

Rita moved forward and sat down on the edge of the girl's bed. The girl was sleeping the sleep of the dead, her back to her visitors. Rita glanced down at her, then smiled at Gita.

'He's certainly got me *interested*. And I don't have the vaguest idea what's going on. What's so terrible and hopeless? What's the needle in the haystack?'

'It's quite simple. He's looking for his daughter. She's been sold into prostitution, here in Bombay. And she's thirteen years old.'

Rita was speechless. She simply stared. And, suddenly, she understood. With a burden like that, how could Kamal be anything other than what he was: unapproachable, unsociable, walled up within himself?

Finally, she spoke. 'And this girl here, she – He was so excited when he read about her in the papers, did he think . . . Is she . . . ?'

Gita nodded. 'He thought this girl might be her, but she isn't. Still, he feels he's got to save this girl as well. That's just the way he is. His daughter came from Madras, you see, like this one. She was working there as a maid and then she suddenly disappeared. Into thin air.'

'How does he know she came to Bombay?'

'She wrote him a letter. Her abductors probably didn't know she could read and write – most of these village girls are illiterate. And somehow she got the letter posted – probably gave it to one of her kinder customers, and he sent it off for her.'

'Thirteen, my God.' Rita's mind reached back to the time when she was a teenager; to the happy-go-lucky days of teasing Archie Foot and falling in love with Russell Chambers, tearing around Georgetown on her brand-new bike, pigtails flying and no hands.

'Thirteen,' she repeated. 'That's just the worst . . .'

'Yes.'

Their eyes met; Gita's were moist with unspoken, unspeakable compassion. Looking into them Rita finally understood what drove Kamal. The thing, the terrible, horrible thing too appalling to be spoken out loud but which they all felt, all knew; which passed from soul to soul without need of words, because speaking it out loud would be to unleash it from the world of feeling into the world of intellect, to defuse it, lessen it, drain its poison, make it graspable to the mind; would be to make the unthinkable

thinkable: and that should never be. Yet it was there, its awfulness palpable. And it was contagious.

Rita's voice, when she spoke again, breaking the awful silence that had settled between them, was a whisper. 'And is he any nearer to finding her?'

Gita shook her head. Sadness was written into every contour of her face. 'No. How can he? There are about thirty thousand prostitutes here. Ten per cent are minors; and you can be sure the minors are kept hidden away, because they're illegal. Do you know what that world's like? It's an anthill – teeming with people. Brothels on top of brothels and behind brothels; stinking hellholes where you wouldn't even keep a dog, and he spends his time combing through them looking for this girl. But how can he find her? He doesn't even have a photo. He just goes and looks and asks. He's got friends, men friends, pretending to be customers and going from brothel to brothel every night – that's what he does himself. But no luck. The prostitutes? They gossip a lot among themselves, they try to help, they say there's a girl here and a girl there who might be the right one but it's never come to anything. And as for the brothel-owners, the pimps: if they know anything they send out warnings and quick as anything she disappears. How can he ever find her? If he does it'll be sheer luck, or God's grace. I suppose that's what he's counting on. And he might be lucky one day – there's such a fire in him that if there's a God then one day He's got to react.'

Again, a thick silence enveloped them. Rita felt the pounding of her heart; her mouth was dry and her hands wet. She wanted to reach out to Kamal, give him back his girl; her inability to do so numbed her. Pity was all she had to give and she instinctively knew that he abhorred pity.

'What about the girl's mother – Kamal's . . . wife?'

'She's dead. Died a long time ago, I think shortly after the baby's birth. Shazeed met her once – she was an American, a perfectly lovely woman. Kamal adored her. Shazeed says—'

'Who's Shazeed?'

'Shazeed's Kamal's friend, my best friend's big brother. My

fiancé, in fact. He's a doctor; he's also helping as much as he can.
I think you met him earlier today? He said—'

'Met him? No . . . I don't think . . . Oh, wait a minute, did he
come to Kamal's house? When I was there?'

'That's the one. He checks on those girls now and then, makes
sure they're all right.'

'And who are they? What are they doing there?'

'Girls Kamal has managed to rescue. The thing is, he can't stop
with his own daughter; the moment he finds some poor child
working in the trade he moves heaven and earth to get her out.
Ananda Nagar is a kind of a safe house where he keeps them till
they can be sent home. Or somewhere else.'

Rita breathed out audibly. 'My God. So that's why Kamal
was so unfriendly when we turned up with a letter from his
grandmother, asking him to take us sightseeing!'

'Who wouldn't be! But even to his friends, Kamal doesn't talk
about it. He's like a man possessed, locked up with his horror.
Since this happened nobody can reach him. Not even Shazeed.
And yet everybody wants to help. That's just the way he is. You
can't help it. The prostitutes adore him, they'd all die for him,
they're all looking out for Asha. But nobody has ever seen her.
Apparently.'

'How long has she been in the trade?'

'About a year now, probably. Kamal got that letter six months
ago, and he's been here for the last five months.'

'But what happened? You said she was working as a maid?
Why did he let her work as a maid? Surely . . . ?'

'The thing is, the girl wasn't living with him, she was with a
foster mother and then somehow she was sent to Madras to work
– I think the family hit on hard times or something. Kamal didn't
know anything about it.'

'Why was she with a foster mother?'

'Because her own mother, Kamal's wife, died soon after her
birth.'

'So why wasn't she with him, with her father?'

'Who really knows? Shazeed says after his wife's death he was incapable of doing anything for the baby. He had to get away; first he went to his guru in the Himalayas, then he went off to Saudi Arabia to work on an oil field – he's an engineer, you know – and he was there for some years. He drowned himself in work, so as to forget. Probably he was right. Asha was well settled with the foster mother and it wouldn't have made sense to take her out of a stable family. And as an Indian man it would probably never have occurred to him to raise her on his own. Raising children here is women's work. But it's all conjecture. Shazeed says he never talks about himself and what he feels, not since Caroline's death. At any rate, he came back to India, returned to his guru and became a monk, joining the ashram. Renounced the world – Woman and Gold, as they say here. A penniless monk. Though Shazeed says he's not as penniless as all that – heir to a fortune, I heard.'

'Yes. In fact, that's the reason I'm here. I mean, that's the reason we came to Bombay in the first place.'

And now it was Rita's turn to talk. Gita listened fascinated as Rita told her about the palace waiting for Kamal in Mahapradesh, of the distraught Rani wringing her hands at the loss of her beloved grandson, willing to move heaven and earth in the effort to lure him home. Talking to Gita was easy; it was as if they'd always known each other. She could be open, hold back nothing.

When Rita described Isabelle's plan of seduction Gita laughed, and Rita joined in.

'Poor girl, she never had a chance,' Gita said finally. 'Kamal hasn't looked at a woman since Caroline's death – that's more than thirteen years. He's just not interested. And it's genuine. The thing is, he's found something better than women, and that's what we ladies just have to accept, like it or not! He's got a trail of broken hearts behind him.'

The words hurt, yet still there was something Rita needed to know. 'Does that mean . . . I mean, did you . . . are you . . .'

'In love with him, you mean?' Rita nodded, and Gita laughed. 'No. That is . . . No. I had a crush on him once but I'm a realist, I gave it up pretty soon and settled on Shazeed, who's not only available but interested, very interested. We're getting married as soon as I get my degree. But his sister, Rehana, oh Lord. She's got it bad for Kamal. And no hope in the world. In the meantime she's learned to live with her broken heart. Just like you'll have to. Poor Rita!'

Gita's eyes narrowed; she looked keenly at Rita. Rita lowered her gaze, then raised it to meet Gita's. Gita chuckled wryly.

'It shows from miles away, you know. Those eyes of yours, positively smouldering when you speak his name! But don't worry, I'll keep the secret, and Kamal doesn't notice things like that. He'll be blithely oblivious of your adoration, but if you join in the search for Asha you'll win his heart for ever. I promise! And if that's enough for you, then welcome to the gang! But—'

She stopped in mid-sentence. Rita turned to follow her gaze, and there, just entering the room, was the object of the last hour's conversation. Gita's last words still echoing in her mind, Rita felt like fleeing. Smouldering eyes . . . If that was the effect of just speaking his name, what would they be like now! She kept them averted as he approached and greeted them. He was clearly amazed to find Rita there, but Gita claimed his attention with a waterfall of words, for which Rita was grateful – she herself was incapable of speech. She pretended to be preoccupied with a bird on a wire outside the window.

She was embarrassed, flustered and mortified. It was extremely inconvenient to feel this way; and to be in Kamal's presence, feeling this way. Paying attention only to the confusion inside her she did not hear what Gita and Kamal were saying, and it was only when Kamal spoke her name for the third time, and loudly, that she looked up.

'I'm sorry, I didn't get that, what did you say?' Her voice sounded perfectly normal, perfectly sensible, as if she had but imagined the storm that, only seconds previously, had set her mind slithering out of control. She took a long breath in and a long breath out – that helped.

'Gita suggested you help her bring Uma – this girl – to Ananda Nagar? And help her to settle in?' He looked at his watch. 'I have to go, or I wouldn't have asked. She might have to be carried – she's physically all right now, apart from the broken arm, but so apathetic, she might not want to walk. I'd help myself, but . . .'

'But he's a man, and shouldn't touch her,' Gita said. 'If you have the time, Rita?'

Rita looked at her own watch. 'Of course,' she said. 'But I can't stay too long. I promised my sister I'd be back in the hotel at six. She'll be worried if I'm too late.'

'Then let's get going,' Gita said.

'Goodbye, then, and thank you,' said Kamal. He turned to walk to the door. 'I'll get a nurse to bring a wheelchair.'

Just when Rita had grown accustomed to breathing calmly and behaving sanely in his presence, he was gone.

FIFTY

The Parting of Ways

Rita found Isabelle perched at a table in the hotel restaurant, a long neon-green drink on the table in front of her, facing two men sitting opposite her, bathing them in the glory of her most winsome smile.

Rita approached the trio and drew back a chair.

'Rita! Where did you run off to? Sightseeing?' Isabelle's voice dripped honey; the heat of this morning had dissolved. She propped herself up on one elbow, and, shading her eyes with a hand, said in her best Miss-Guyana-Contest-Interview enunciation, 'May I introduce you? Rita, this is Shankar and Ranjit. This is my sister Rita.'

The two young men half rose to shake her hand and flashed her dazzling but bored grins before turning their attention back to Isabelle. Rita scowled at them and said, 'Isabelle, we have to talk.'

'Well, go ahead, talk,' said Isabelle.

'No, I mean, talk seriously.' Throwing a menacing glare at Shankar and Ranjit: 'In private.'

Isabelle pulled down the corners of her mouth in a deprecating grimace. 'What a bore! What's the hurry?' She looked helplessly at the two men, as if expecting some sort of alternative suggestion to come from that direction. But the men weren't biting. Rita's presence was a bucket of cold water over the romantic episode; they stood up, bent low over Isabelle, kissed her hand, and sauntered off.

'Now look what you've done,' Isabelle said. 'You just turn up here, and they disappear. You always spoil the fun. You always—'

'Isabelle, we have to talk.'

'Yes, I know, you said so already.'

'Listen – I'm moving into Ananda Nagar. Tomorrow.'

'Oh. Wonderful. And what about me? You won't get me moving to that old dump, I can tell you.'

'That's what I figured for myself. But you can't stay in this hotel either.'

'Why not?'

'Because we can't afford it, that's why not.'

'But Rani can.'

'You can't just go on living here at Rani's expense. She sent you here for a purpose and it's not going to work out. I guarantee you that. Kamal's involved in charity in the Bombay slums. A sort of a social worker. There's no way he's going to look twice at you.'

On her way here Rita had made up her mind just how much to tell Isabelle of Kamal's life, and how little. Her version was the truth, but not the whole truth. She had made this decision almost simultaneously with her decision to bring Uma to Ananda Nagar. Her resolve had taken form and contour on the way to the house; helping to settle Uma in with Gita and Subhadhai had strengthened the feeling of belonging here, just here. But what to do with Isabelle? Isabelle would not be wanted at Ananda Nagar. And it was mutual: Isabelle would definitely not want Ananda Nagar. There were only two options open for her: back home to Marilyn, or to Rani. Isabelle could choose; and Rita felt she knew what that choice would be.

If Isabelle went to Rani she would have to tell her about Kamal's present activities, so this would be the story: Kamal was doing charity work in the Bombay slums, which was true, but only up to a point.

Isabelle pushed a lock of hair behind her ear. 'You mean there's no way I'm going to look twice at *him.*'

'Oh, come on, Isabelle. Let's talk sensibly. I only wanted to say that Rani's plan isn't going to work. So what do we do now? I mean, what do *you* do now? I've already made up my mind. I'm staying here, like I told you. And you—'

'Don't you dare say you're sending me back to Guyana!'

'Well, that's one alternative. You've got to go somewhere. You won't come to Ananda Nagar and anyway, I won't have time for you.'

'I don't need you. When will you stop babying me, Rita? When will you stop making plans for me and giving me advice? I can make up my own mind. I know what I want to do.'

'Well, what?'

The best way of dealing with Isabelle, Rita knew from long experience, was to let her believe she had made the decisions Rita had already thought out as best for her. By implying that Isabelle should go to Guyana Rita had practically ensured Isabelle's refusal to go home. There was only one other alternative. One place which fit Isabelle like a snug shoe.

'I want to go back to Rani. I liked it there. There's so much more I have to learn. And besides, when I tell Rani what Kamal is up to she'll have a fit and she'll like me all the more. She likes me already, but she still had all those hopes for Kamal. When I tell her how he lives, what he's doing . . . she'll be livid. And frightened. She'll be so afraid of dying and Kamal getting everything she'll be eager to accept me. I mean, she won't want to leave him a penny, will she, if he's going to squander it in the slums? And all she has is me.'

Rita sniffed. 'You're so bloody *mercenary*, Isabelle.'

'Don't use all your big words on me. I don't know what they mean and I don't care – but I know you're always wagging your finger at me! At any rate, I am *not* going home. No way. I finally got out and I'm staying out. I always knew Rani was my big opportunity, and she is, and even if it didn't work with Kamal I've still got a chance. She can really make me into somebody, into a princess! She really enjoys it! I think she's so bored with her life I'm like a breath of fresh air to her, a challenge!'

'Great minds think alike.'

'What? *Whose* great mind?'

'Never mind. That was meant ironically.'

'I don't think—'

'Look, Isabelle, if you want to go back to Rani, that's fine with me. I'll take you to the airport tomorrow morning. And then you're on your own.'

Accompanying Isabelle to the airport and getting her on to the right plane to Madras took the entire morning, and afterwards Rita was exhausted. Something debilitating seemed to lurk in the very atmosphere of this city, she reflected, a huge, invisible parasite that crouched malevolently in the shadows and nourished itself on her vital energy. She felt unclean, sticky; she would have enjoyed nothing better than a return to the Taj, a shower, a good meal, and a long deep sleep in a cool darkened room. But it was not to be. She had checked out of the hotel already and brought her own luggage and now it was straight on to Ananda Nagar.

Sleeping during the day always had the effect on Rita of a heavy drug, knocking her out for hours. It was five when she awoke. Here in Bombay the lethargy clung to her like a coarse skin; she lay awake under the slowly rotating ceiling fan, too lazy even to get up to pour herself a glass of cool water from the flask on the sideboard. The drawn blinds kept out the afternoon sun, and the gloom lent itself well to Rita's thoughtful mood. Now that she was here she was wondering why; nobody had asked her to come, Kamal least of all, and there seemed nothing she could do. Perhaps, she thought, I'd better just move on.

Far away, the telephone rang. Rita heard footsteps on the downstairs corridor and, a few seconds later, Subhadhai's voice calling her down. She pulled on a T-shirt and baggy cotton trousers and padded down the stairs. It was Gita.

'I'm glad you're there,' she said. 'I was hoping you'd stay. I wanted to talk to someone about my little plan but not Kamal, and not Shazeed. You know what men are like – they always think they know better. Even the nice ones. You ever noticed? It's automatic. When a woman makes a suggestion they only listen with half an ear; they're all nice and condescending, but they don't really take you seriously. It's what's been getting me so crazy in this hunt for Asha. I suppose it's some kind of cave-man instinct.'

Rita chuckled. 'I've noticed.'

'Good. Anyway, Kamal and Shazeed are great but they're men, they can't help their genetic programming. Those two are a team. For my plan I want my own team – another woman. You.'

'You have a plan?'

'Yes . . . I told you. And I suggested it to Kamal and Shazeed and they nodded and smiled and made the right noises, but d'you think they acted on it? No way. Obviously, since it comes from a woman, my suggestion makes no sense whatsoever.'

'Obviously. So what did you suggest?'

'It's the language aspect. Asha comes from Tamil Nadu. Mightn't it be possible that there's a particular Tamil mafia, and that all the Tamil girls enter through that port? It seems kind of obvious to me. A Tamil brothel, perhaps. Or, at least, a Tamil brothel-owner. Doesn't it make sense? Tell me. I want your unadulterated unbiased opinion.'

'It makes sense.'

'Well, why didn't the men follow *that* lead? It makes me so mad. "Yes, we can take that aspect into consideration too," Kamal said. But I bet they don't. They're concentrating on Asha's skin colour. She's fair, you know, unusually fair, because her mother was a blonde American. The men think they're going to get somewhere looking and asking for a young light-skinned girl. I mean, that makes sense too but my idea is *better*. So what I've been doing is this. You know I do voluntary work in the brothels—'

389

Rita chuckled. 'Well, Gita . . .'

'Um . . . don't take that too literally.'

'Then explain.'

'I do voluntary work for the Public Health Organization. I go twice a week and help with HIV tests, health checks and so on. And I've been gathering information. Asking if anybody speaks Tamil. I speak it myself, you see, fluently. Tamil and English are my native tongues – I'm from Tamil Nadu. So I ask, innocently enough: Do you know of Tamil sex workers? Tamil pimps? Tamil brothels? You'd be amazed at the list I've made.'

'So then you go and check the places on your list?'

'Exactly. It hasn't come to anything yet, but I'm persevering.'

'But how can *I* help? I don't speak a word of Tamil.'

'Yes, but you speak English.'

'So do you. And Kamal, and Shazeed.'

'And Asha. Not so many sex workers speak English. In fact, hardly any of them. So that's another lead.'

'Yes, but what can I do? How exactly do I fit in?'

'Well, I haven't figured that out exactly yet, but I'm certain the language track is the best one. Could you not come with me while I'm working, look around and ask questions in English? Didn't you ever play detective as a child?'

'Not really. *Explorer* was more my thing.'

'Detective, explorer, it's all the same. Come and explore with me. Will you?'

'Of course! You know, I've just been wondering what I could do and I had an idea as well. You see, I'm actually a journalist and when I came to India I thought I'd do some writing on the side: dig out some unusual stories, and peddle them back home. If I said I'm writing an article about prostitution in Bombay, would they let me interview people, ask questions?'

'It's not a bad idea, Rita, but they're not hungry for publicity. Still, it's worth a try. Who knows, you may get an exclusive after it's all over and we bring Asha home.'

'When do we start?'

'I'll come and pick you up tomorrow morning.'

'Where will we go to?'

'To Kamathipura. Into the heart of it all. Bombay's sleaziest red-light district. The place with all the cages.'

Rita replaced the receiver and turned to go upstairs. Kamal came out of the kitchen. She stopped, and their eyes met. He was the first to speak.

'Rita, are you hungry?'

Rita hadn't thought about it, and paused. Kamal spoke again.

'Because if you are, I thought you might like to come out for a meal. I know a nice little restaurant near Chowpatty Beach. If you want to.'

'I'd love to,' said Rita. For an instant Rita believed he was about to smile. But he didn't. She might have imagined it, but it seemed to her that a shadow slid between the two of them, that the gloomy corridor turned just a shade darker. Neither his lips smiled, nor his eyes. She nodded, and formed the word 'Yes' with her lips, for the dryness in her throat barred speech.

'I'll meet you down here in half an hour, then,' he said, and returned to the kitchen. Rita had wanted to get herself a glass of water. She thought better of it, turned and went back upstairs.

FIFTY-ONE

A Walk on the Beach

All through supper Kamal had been preoccupied. He did not speak a word, did not look at her even, except for a single glance while ordering their meal from an indifferent waiter, and his eyes, to her, seemed opaque and cold. Kamal, Rita understood by now, had an inner world into which he retreated at odd intervals. There he was alone with himself, cut off from physical reality, enclosed in another, interior, reality, a bubble hermetically sealed, impenetrable and unfathomable. This invitation to dinner might have been an opening into Kamal's world; she had hoped it would be so, seen it as the beginning of what could be friendship. Instead she found herself shut off, alone and lonely, knowing that any attempt to draw him out would be not only unwelcome but unforgivable. All she could do was wait. It would pass. The bubble would float off, leaving Kamal behind. A veil would lift from before his eyes, they would meet again. He would smile again; his lips first, but not his eyes. She would wait. Then one day, that smile would move up to his eyes. A curtain of frost would draw back, and behind it would be radiant warmth. She felt it; she knew it. She would be a part of something deeper, wider, grander than all that had gone before. She only had to wait. She knew this with all her instincts; but meanwhile her heart pined, fearing that he would never reach that place, that he would retreat for ever into the recesses of his mind and never re-emerge.

After the meal they walked out and down towards Marina Drive. The traffic seemed heavier than ever before, a thick river of metal indifferent to them both. Kamal tried to hail a taxi but was repeatedly ignored. In the distance, the Jewel Necklace, the row of lights along the Bombay waterfront, curved away in a spangled chain, like stars.

'Come,' said Kamal, and it was the first word he had spoken to her since they had first sat down to order their meals. It fell like the proverbial seed into fertile ground: warm, inviting, a promise and a prophecy that all was not lost, Kamal had returned, and he was aware of her presence. They walked to a traffic light; others were waiting at the zebra crossing and the pedestrian light turned green just as they arrived. Rita felt Kamal's hand close around her elbow: a gentle but firm grip instructing her to stop, turn, cross, not to lose herself in the crowd, to stay near, rely on him. A good feeling. Something so small and yet so great. A hand on her elbow: it felt like all the universe. Now they were on the other side, and the hand was gone, and with it a feeling of loss great as a hole where the universe had been.

Yet he was there, beside her, so near she could touch him by merely leaning a millimetre to the side, walking silently beside her. The hum of traffic receded into the background for his silence was greater, nearer, more palpable, and that was what she listened to.

'It's a beautiful night. Shall we go for a walk on the beach?'

More words, and another invitation, and since he could not see her face and her joy Rita immediately answered, 'Oh! Yes! I'd love to,' and she knew he would *hear* her joy – but didn't care.

A gentle warm breeze, a heartbeat and a presence next to her. Above her, the stars strewn carelessly across the indigo vastness of space. Kamal bent down and took off his sandals. Rita did the same. The sand felt warm and hard beneath her bare feet.

'I wish I could bring Asha here,' Kamal said. 'It's the best thing about Bombay. One day I will.'

For a moment Rita was stunned by the intimacy of his words; if he had laid an arm around her shoulders she would have been less surprised. It was the first time he had spoken of how he felt, or what he wished. It was a peephole into his inner world, a privilege, an honour. What could she offer to equal that?

'Asha's lucky to have you,' she said. 'She's so lucky. In spite of everything, she's lucky.'

'Lucky? To have me?' His voice was bitter. 'I'm the cause of all this. If I'd been a better father . . .'

Oh Lord, oh Lord, what have I done.

'I meant . . .'

'You meant to be nice. Comforting. Kind. You're a nice kind comforting woman and you'd never accuse me of neglect. Would you? No, of course you wouldn't. But you don't know. How could you? Everybody around me is just bleating on about what a dedicated father Asha has, searching for her day and night. Nobody knows.'

'I know a little bit. Gita told me—'

'Gita knows nothing. What she knows, she got from Shazeed and Shazeed knows nothing. Only I know. And Asha, and God. Shall I tell you?'

He had stopped walking and turned to face her. Rita stopped too, and looked up at him. In the darkness his face was hardly visible but his eyes seemed to burn with some fever which, Rita knew, had nothing to do with her. His eyes were filled with yearning and heartache so manifest Rita could not bear it; she let her own gaze sink.

'Yes,' she whispered. 'If you want to.'

'Do you want me to?'

'Yes. Oh yes.'

After that he was silent, silent so long she believed he had changed his mind. Because why should he tell her, her of all people, almost a stranger, someone he had known less than two days, who had walked into his life from across the globe and had no right, no right at all, to know, except the right given her by the licence of love. Because it was love. If this was not love that she felt for him, then what? She had known it was love all along but never dared to say so, never dared speak the word, never dared admit it to herself because to love is surely to need and she did not want to need this or any man she could not have.

There were others on the beach, and yet they were alone. To their left, the ugly beast Bombay brayed and wallowed and passed stinking wind, but here it was clean and quiet, the sea reaching out into the dark purity of night, reaching in as if to remind the city of an existence beyond itself, beyond pain and sorrow and urban barbarism. And Kamal at her side. Poised in the moment before speech, breathing in the space and timelessness of silence, gathering the silence into himself before bridging it with the words that would open his past to Rita.

'Where to begin?'

Rita said nothing; there was nothing to say. She walked beside him, slowly, to the rhythm of her breathing like a monk's apprentice, all of her senses wide open to the sea and the sky and the wind and his presence beside her. She waited. She was patient; time was open-ended, and filling it was his task, not hers, and she could wait just as she had waited all her life for this moment.

'With Caroline. I'll begin with Caroline.'

It didn't matter. Let him begin with Caroline.

'Caroline and I met in Cambridge. Not *the* Cambridge, England; Cambridge, Massachusetts. That's where she lived, that's where I studied. She, too. Her thing was anthropology. Caroline loved people; people fascinated her. India fascinated her – I suppose that's why she first approached me.'

He spoke softly, slowly, taking his time with each word, and very soon Rita realized he was reliving his life: he was not here, on the beach, with her; he was with Caroline, back in Cambridge, in the golden autumn woods of New England, the white winter forests. They were in a Tamil village in the scorching heat. He was not here on Chowpatty Beach, with her; he was there, far away, joined to that *other* by invisible threads that death and time could not sever.

'Caroline's death almost killed me. I was like a madman. She had been my whole life; I had lived for her and our future together. And as for the baby – I hardly noticed her in my grief. Don't misunderstand me – of course I loved her. The first time I held her in my arms was one of the happiest in my life. But when I was left alone with her – I couldn't. She didn't know me – she turned away from me right from the beginning, and I just couldn't deal with her. Remember, I was just a young man. I'd never had any dealings with young children before. How could I win her heart *and* deal with my own grief? I couldn't – I took the easy way out and left her with Sundari – Mrs Iyengar. If I'd been living with her before Caroline's death, if she had known me as her father, it would have been a different story; or if I'd been living under normal conditions, with a background, a life of my own, a loving mother who would have helped. You see, I've thought about this a lot since then, analysed my callousness a thousand times, tried to justify myself, excuse myself, but there is no justification, no excuse. As soon as Caroline was taken away to be buried I fled Gingee. I couldn't bear to be in that house where she had lived. Poor Asha – she only reminded me of her mother; I fled *her* too. Left her with Mrs Iyengar – after all, she was in good hands!

'Under the circumstances leaving her there was the best solution. What could I, a single working man, with no home, no family, do with a seven-month-old baby? And in India, where single fathers are simply not an issue!'

'But surely Rani would have—?'

'Rani? You're kidding! Accept my half-caste child?'

'I think she would have. I'm sure she would have.'

'The rift between Rani and me was too wide. Unbreachable. I'd cut away from her – permanently. There was no question of me going back there with hanging head and a half-caste baby.'

'But her American grandparents? Surely they'd have taken her in, now that Caroline was dead?'

Kamal chuckled mirthlessly. 'Sure, they would have. At first. They even set a lawyer on my trail. But there wasn't much they could do without my consent. Asha's an Indian citizen – not even *their* influence could change that and get her out of the country. And I wasn't going to let them have her because I knew that'd be the end of it for me – they'd never let me near her again, and I certainly didn't want her growing up with those ice-blocks. No, she definitely had it good with the Iyengars.'

He stopped speaking, and they walked for several minutes in silence. It was a comfortable silence, one in which Rita felt herself as warm and close to him as if his arm were around her. She wished it was; she glanced at him sideways, surreptitiously; her thoughts, she felt, must be loud enough to hear. But Kamal's arms hung loosely at his side, swinging gently to the rhythm of his walking, and his own thoughts were obviously more potent than her own because his face, even in profile and in the darkness, revealed nothing. He spoke as if to himself, as if she were not present, as if he were telling this story for his own benefit, and not for hers.

'But I'm getting ahead of myself. No – after Caroline's death Asha wasn't the problem, the problem was me. I had to deal with my grief. Confront the issue of death. We spend our lives hiding our faces from death, pretending it's never going to touch us, but I tell you, Rita, there is no one single issue of more moment in all the world. Death had taken that from me which was most precious – more precious than my own life. I had nothing left. I had Asha – but I was too empty myself to give her anything. Caroline had taken all the life I had; I was drained; I was so filled with grief I was afraid I'd contaminate the baby. But perhaps even that is only an excuse, or an attempt to excuse the inexcusable. Lovelessness is inexcusable, and I was loveless. I had nothing left to give.

'There is only one way to deal with such a loss, and that is religion. God. I ran to him; to Her, for God is for me not the Father but the Mother. That is the beauty of the Hindu religion: that God can take on any shape, any form, any image. God can be Father, Mother, Child, Friend, Master, because what counts is not the form of the beloved but the act of loving, or being loved by Him. *Her*.

'I went to find Swami Subramaniananda, but I found Ma. She had an ashram near Rishikesh in the Himalayas, near to Swami's ashram, and when I came to her I knew that I was at last at home. And if losing Caroline had any purpose whatsoever, it was that I should find Ma. Have you ever been in the presence of a human being, Rita, who has loved you completely, through to every fibre of your being? That was Ma. She saw everything, even before a word passed between us. She saw my pain, and healed it, and taught me how to truly love. I spent three years in that ashram; I won't, I can't tell you the details but I found healing there. All worldly ambitions dropped from me; I was free, and happy, and wanted nothing more than to live there, in the Himalayan foothills, forever, at Ma's side, in Ma's service. It was idyllic; I was happy, blissfully happy.'

'That's why you became a monk.'

Kamal glanced at her. 'Is that what they told you? Well, I suppose it's true. In a way. In my heart – but not officially. I never was one for the institutions of religion. But I did wear the saffron robes for a few years. I never told anyone directly I was a monk, it's what they all gathered. In Rani's case, it was good that way. It helped to make the break with her clean – at least as far as I was concerned. Let her believe I had taken sannyas; it would help her get on with her life, stop planning weddings for me and worrying about her will. I didn't want any of it. It seems, though, she never gave up hope of gathering me back into the fold.

'But I'm getting ahead of myself again. For the time being I was so at peace with myself I would have stayed in that ashram for ever. But Ma saw everything; she told me I was not finished with the world. Two matters were yet unresolved: I had to secure Asha's happiness, and make peace with Rani. I went to see Rani, to be reconciled with her, but it was impossible: she was like an enormous black spider reaching out to trap me in her gilded palace and suck the life out of me. I knew I could never live with her under one roof; I told her this, calmly and resolutely, and told her I would officially renounce the fortune she was hoarding for me, that she need not look for a bride for me. Like I said, the sannyas robe helped convince her I was serious.

'And Asha. I went to visit her. She was three at the time – a delightful little girl – but she wasn't mine. She stood there watching me, her thumb in her mouth, with these huge black eyes. I stayed to try and win her affection but she was already too much a part of the Iyengar family. The Iyengars loved and wanted her – she was like another daughter to them, and they had had two more children since, she was in an intact family, with brothers and sisters – how could I take her away? And to where? I had no life to offer her. But at least I could take care of her financially. I decided to get a job and send money to the Iyengars for her. I had not given them a single rupee up to then – I had nothing. But I would make up for that. I went to Bombay to my friend Shazeed to see if I could find work there, and Shazeed got me a very well-paying job – in Saudi Arabia. What did I care? I had no ties, no home. I went to Saudi Arabia, I earned a small fortune, helped the Iyengars move to a fine new house, helped with all the children, paid for them to go to the English Medium School in Gingee. I wanted the best for Asha. She would have the best education – in England, America. Whatever she wanted. There was more than enough – I was a rich man, and it wasn't inherited wealth, I had earned it all myself. I set up a trust fund for her. Asha learned English, she wore nice clothes, and yet I was careful not to spoil her with material wealth. The Iyengars had a good standard of living, and still retained their simplicity. They were deeply religious, and I knew she was being raised with sound values. It was the perfect solution, and I was relieved she could be there, and happy, not missing me. I thought of her a lot, but I never actually *missed* her – how can you miss someone you have never actually lived with? That's what I thought at the time but now I know it's not true because I do miss her, I've always missed her, but simply turned my back on the pain of missing her because it was easier for me that way, easier for everyone, and I didn't have to make any changes – what did I know about looking after a little girl? And so I gave them money – it was the least I could do, and giving to them eased my conscience. Those were the fat years.

'I spent five years in Saudi Arabia. I had earned enough to make sure that Asha would never know want, and to support the two of us in a simple life in India – perhaps near Gingee. That was the plan. But when I came to get Asha I knew it wouldn't work. My presence made her uncomfortable: she didn't speak a word, simply stared at me as if she was terrified. That hurt; but I knew it was only because she was happy with the Iyengars, and I was only a stranger to her, that it made her insecure, all this talk about me being her father. I felt awkward, an intruder.

'It was too late. She was much too attached to her foster family, *their* daughter, not mine; she didn't know me as a father, but as a stranger who appeared out of the blue and sat tongue-tied in front of her, not knowing how to approach her, not finding the words that would open her heart. I felt she was afraid of me even, relieved when I went – and I suppose that's what kept me away.

'I felt I was clinging too much to her and I made every effort to set her free, to truly let her belong to the Iyengars.

'So I left. I went back to Rishikesh, settled in Ma's ashram. Determined to lead a solitary life. I wrote to Asha regularly, but she never replied – I assumed she just wasn't interested. And yet she must have memorized my address. How else could she have written to me when she was in trouble?

'I was a terrible father – there's no excuse. I should have done something, found some way . . .'

'You couldn't have . . .' Rita stopped in mid-sentence. Kamal was not looking for comfort or solidarity. He was simply stating a fact. It was not for her to speak. She closed her lips, and waited for him to continue.

'Anyway, what's the use of recriminations? It happened, and it's my fault – nobody else is to blame. Now I can see my own selfishness – I should have fought for her love and affection, taken her away and made a life for us both, and none of this would ever have happened.' He was silent again, and when the silence lasted too long Rita said:

'What actually happened, then? How did Asha end up . . .'

'Out of the blue I got a letter from her. A desperate, heartbreaking letter, saying she was in Kamathipura, hinting at her situation, and begging me to rescue her. Her English wasn't very good and I hardly spoke a word of Tamil, of course. It was scribbled on a scrap of paper, but the envelope was new and the writing on it not hers. She must have known my address by heart because Sundari later told me she hadn't taken any of my letters with her when she went to Madras, and of course she hadn't been receiving the ones I'd been writing the year she was there – Iyengar's brother destroyed them. I literally dropped everything and went to Gingee and found out what had happened. When her stepfather died his brother took over the family and sent Asha to Madras to work as a servant – a not unusual development when a widow gets adopted by her brother-in-law, and he doesn't want to be burdened with extra mouths to feed. Sundari said she had written three times to let me know but her letters never arrived – it seems her brother-in-law had bribed the post-sorter at the post office to intercept all letters to Rishikesh. I don't suppose there were many of those. Naturally he didn't want her notifying me – he might lose the money I sent, and Asha's trust fund.

'How Asha got from Madras to Bombay is anybody's guess. I went to check on the family she'd been working with, to find out what they knew – at first I thought they must have sold her into prostitution. But it turned out she'd run away herself – the husband was in prison on some fraud charge, and the woman obviously didn't know a thing. Or perhaps she did know but wasn't telling. Whatever. And so I came here. Bought Ananda Nagar fairly cheaply and started the search for Asha. About five months ago.'

'It's like looking for a needle in a haystack,' Rita put in and for the umpteenth time regretted her words immediately. Why couldn't she keep her mouth shut? There simply weren't any words that could measure up to the wretchedness of Asha's situation and the hopelessness of Kamal's task. He certainly didn't need her to comment on the sheer futility of the search for one lost little girl in a labyrinthine network of hellholes, each one darker and more sinister than the next, overrun by thirty thousand of the city's most abject cast-offs. He didn't need her to nudge him over the edge of hope and into the waiting pool of despair.

Almost as if he had heard her thoughts Kamal said, 'It's like walking a tightrope; there's such a fine balance between hope and despair. Seen from a rational perspective it's utterly hopeless. I can't even be sure if Asha's still here and not been carted off to Pune or Delhi or Calcutta. Who knows? And yet . . .'

'And yet – what?' Rita whispered, afraid to tread on sensitive ground yet aching to know the measure of his faith.

'And yet I know. I feel her. I can almost hear her. There is something in me, a voice, an inner certainty that *she is here* and waiting. I have no proof, not the slightest clue; it's like a still, silent current deep inside calling me on and driving me forward and buoying me up, so fine it can't be seen or heard or measured. A scientist would say it's wishful thinking, I've been duped by an emotion all of my own making. It's a knowledge with no substance, and yet it's there, so real I would lay my life upon it. I know I must go on.'

This time Rita did not break the silence. What came to her was the gentle lapping of water against sand, the breath of breeze coming in from the sea, the hum of the city at her back – but hearing, the physical act of taking in sound, was at the periphery of her senses. Beyond hearing she could *feel* Kamal's words. Feel their content and the substance out of which they sprang, and know the truth of them.

And in that knowledge she felt strong; in sharing with her his secret source of strength Kamal had made her a part of him in a way that was deeper, more essential, more intimate than any physical act of union could ever be; he had reached out for her and drawn her into himself and now, despite the horror and the tragedy that surrounded them both, she was inexplicably happy, singing, flying, wheeling with joy.

But from Kamal there was only silence. As they stood on the street, Kamal reached out not for her hand but to hail a taxi. Rita's entire soul collapsed back into itself, a deflated balloon. His eyes glanced off her as a taxi stopped. His half-smile revealed nothing, he did not speak a word all the way home, wrapped in an interior monk's habit that kept her, mind, soul and body at arm's length.

Courteously, he opened her door for her, and paused as she walked by him, still expectant, still hoping. His eyebrows lifted slightly, his lips twitched. He was going to speak. No, he was silent; but still watching her. She entered the room, turned, looked at him, beseeching him to break the silence which was no longer companionable but terribly, terribly awkward.

'I don't know why I told you all that. I don't usually speak about it. Sorry I bothered you with the story,' he said. He turned and walked away.

FIFTY-TWO

Kamathipura

The Public Health Organization was housed in a tiny building off a side street in a seedy area of a city which seemed to consist exclusively of seedy areas. By the time she arrived Rita felt as if she had been driving for hours through a solid mass of blaring, stinking, metal-grime mélange. She had no idea where she was: she had lost every sense of direction, moved through one chasm of grey crumbling buildings after another, in and out of gridlock, through shanty towns and past high-rises of glass and steel. She crossed the squalid courtyard to the one clean building on one of its three sides, drawn by a large white board, on which, she saw as she drew nearer, the name of the organization, its opening hours, and the names of several doctors were written in large bold letters. Dr Gobin's name headed the list.

'Come on,' said Gita. 'We're early; but that's fine.'

Next to the board were large double doors of glass, their polished cleanness incongruous against the general background of shabbiness and grime. They walked in.

'I want you to meet Dr Gobin,' Gita said. 'He's fantastic – a pillar of strength. He's done so much for the women here. I already called him to ask if you can come along this morning. I told him you're a journalist.' She winked. 'So you'd better think about the article you're going to write.'

Dr Gobin sat behind a cluttered desk which almost filled the shoebox office. Along one of the walls was an examination table; the walls themselves were covered with posters, almost all of them AIDS information or warnings. A computer monitor and a telephone sat among the papers on the desk, and a tired overhead fan creaked its weary rotations.

Dr Gobin stood up as Rita entered. A tall, gaunt man with thinning hair and thick spectacles, he reached his hand across the desk, smiled earnestly, asked her to sit, and in the same breath, almost before he himself had sat down again, said, 'You are from the press? You want to write about us? Will the article be published in the West?'

'Yes,' said Rita, and stated her aim, omitting any reference to Kamal and Asha, and not mentioning that the article in question would be published not in England or America but in poor backwater Guyana, would be read by only a handful of people, and certainly would not generate the Western interest the doctor obviously hoped for.

'Gita said you want to go out into the brothels with the Mobile Clinic. You're very welcome.' With those words Dr Gobin dismissed Rita curtly, and she returned to the waiting area with Gita.

'So – I have to leave you for a while,' Gita said now. 'I'm going to do some work in the lab upstairs. Read this stuff – it'll give you background info.' She thrust a file into Rita's hands. 'You can sit in the waiting room. I won't be long.' Then Gita disappeared.

Rita took a seat among the patients and read. She turned the pages of the file, newspaper articles ten, fifteen, twenty years old, protected from wear in their plastic sheaths. She read tales of girl-children torn from their parents, girl-children sold by their parents, girl-children given by their parents to serve the Goddess Yellamma, and ending up in Bombay's stinking dens; tales of girl-children of the Nepalese Badi caste raised by their parents to a career of prostitution. Tales of torture and abuse and brutality, of little lives crushed and destroyed day after day after day, night after night after night. And as she read she heard a cry as silent as death but greater than the universe, lifting up from the bowels of hell and up to heaven, a cry of utter abandonment, utter torment, a scream of devastation too loud to be ignored, too silent to be heard, so heartbreaking it seemed her own heart would crumble there and then, her own voice join in that wail of agony – that she herself would be crushed by the weight of a barbarism so immense all humanity must break beneath it. And yet the world moved on, oblivious. There was dancing and singing and normal lives led; weddings and births celebrated; pleasure yachts and designer clothes and gourmet food and beauty contests and all in the very same world that held these bleeding hearts. Rita raised a hand to her forehead as if to push away the consciousness of it all. Here, in this room, reading these clippings, Asha's world became real to her. The words she now read became keys that opened that faraway land to her imagination, preparing her for the first faltering steps she was about to take within it. The horror of it slammed into her consciousness. Hell was just a few street corners away: and she was to be a passive bystander, a dispassionate tourist. Nausea rose like gall in her throat, bitter on her tongue. Her fingers trembled as she turned the pages. Her eyes filled with unshed tears.

I can't – and yet I have to.

'Kamathipura,' Gita announced. 'Here we are.' Dr Gobin's Mobile Clinic van came to a halt. Gita opened the sliding door and helped Rita out into the glaring sunlight. Rita blinked and looked around.

'We'll go on foot.'

'Is it – safe?'

Gita smiled reassuringly. 'Don't worry, nobody's going to abduct you. Come on. I'll just take you on a walking tour of some of the lanes to begin with. There are a couple of Tamil-speaking brothel-owners I'd like to locate, just to see where they are; we'll keep our eyes and ears open.'

She marched off. Rita ran to catch up.

She felt curious glances taking her in as she walked by. She felt awkward, embarrassed, and it was only Gita's confident, purposeful stride through the seemingly aimless bystanders that kept her from turning back. The narrow street was lined with ramshackle houses, their doors opening directly on to the small forecourts where people gathered. Women leaning against the doorjambs looked up as they walked past. One or two of them waved at Gita. Others sat on sharpais. Many looked as if they had just rolled out of bed, though it was already almost mid-day. Some, though, were heavily made up, their perfume pungent in the congested air. Indeed, the smell of Bombay seemed here more acrid than ever. Perhaps this was its source: here all its ingredients mingled in their essence – the tangible ones of cooking, spices, flowers, perfume, hair-oil, face-powder, incense, rotting fruit, drains, sewage, urine, vomit, sweat and semen, with the intangible ones of fear, loneliness, anguish, hate, hunger, malevolence, abuse, dread and horror. Mingled, coagulated, metamorphosed into that unique and pungent odour Rita had named Bombay-sweet-and-sour, seeped out like a crawling mist through the lanes and alleys of the city, creeping up the walls and through the windows and laying like a shroud over the entire city.

All of Rita's senses were operating now on crisis frequency. She could hardly think, for the impressions they gathered pelted themselves against her and screamed for attention, a jumble of sound, sight and smell colliding with her own unsorted feelings of disgust, dread, embarrassment and sheer horror. Once again, she wanted to turn and run, but they had gone too far by now.

Gita was talking as she walked, sometimes waving at a woman and smiling, sometimes stopping to explain some detail, but Rita hardly heard, merely nodded as if she had. Gita turned a corner; they walked down another lane. And another. They were lost in a labyrinth of hell. And yet it was all so harmless. Women, standing and sitting around, a few men – where was all the horror? Wasn't she being unnecessarily squeamish?

'Since the outbreak of AIDS business is bad for the women,'

Gita was saying. 'Still, health workers have managed to convince everyone to use condoms and things are improving. Though a lot of men are still convinced that sleeping with a virgin can cure them of AIDS. That's why young girls are in such demand. Look at that one!'

She pointed to a girl, sitting on the spreading lap of an older, fatter woman, on a sharpai, outside one of the doorways. The older woman was plaiting her hair. The girl wore a two-piece outfit of a shimmering artificial fabric. 'She looks like a schoolgirl, doesn't she? Bet she's not even thirteen!'

'Asha must be around that age.'

'Yes.'

'How could anyone – any man . . .'

'Don't ask me.'

They were silent for a while, and then Gita pointed up to the second storey of a row of buildings. Here, the windows were all barred.

'The cages,' Gita explained. 'The famous cages of Kamathipura. That's where they keep the youngest girls, the ones they've stolen, till they're broken in. In tiny cells, stinking and filthy. They can't escape; they're trapped. And after that, where can they go to? They belong to Kamathipura. Nobody else wants them.'

'It's like slavery!'

'It *is* slavery, no question. And who cares? A handful of people. Respectable people say it's a necessary evil. Decent middle-class women are even in favour of it – they think it protects them and their daughters. Allows them to move freely without fear. And somewhere in all this mess is Asha.'

As she walked through the narrow lanes of Kamathipura Rita felt a mounting panic as the atmosphere seeped deeper into her consciousness. Like glue, clammy, sordid, vile, clinging to her like a hungry leech. And, she realized, these are only the *streets*; I am only an onlooker; I am safe. Behind the crumbling, grey façades that lined those streets – *there* the horror took place. Day after day after day. Night after night after night. A thousand wretched voices silently cried out to her: she heard them. And somewhere in the cacophony of woe she could make out a single anguished strain – Asha's voice of innocence, calling in vain.

She knew the call was there. This one little girl, this one little voice out of thousands, tens of thousands, became for her the quintessence of Kamathipura's misery, Kamathipura's shame. She listened, and she heard; and in hearing she was nearer to Kamal than in any lovelorn fantasy. His pain was hers; what powered his heart, powered hers. She could feel, as clearly as if they were etched before her in granite, two strains: that of little Asha, crying out above the discord of the streets, and that of Kamal, casting his consciousness into the mess of Kamathipura like a net into a sewage pit, searching for a diamond in the darkness. She knew him. She knew him, because she could feel all he felt. She understood, too, what Gita had meant, that Kamal's intensity was infectious, that everyone he knew joined in the search. She had picked up that intensity, that need; and she too was, finally, with every fibre of her being, a part of it, and a part of him.

Again they walked in silence, slower now, and Rita gradually relaxed. The initial storm of emotion that had threatened to crush her receded. Once that happened she could look around, absorb her surroundings without being swamped by panic. That, she realized, was Gita's strength, and a precondition to effective work. In the silence between them Rita finally understood why she had been brought here. It had been a test; and she had passed it. There would be no more running away. She was a part of the search for Asha, and glad of it. She had a purpose, and an aim; and with that knowledge she felt something else, something akin to joy – for this was what she had been searching for all her life.

They had stopped walking. Gita was standing in front of a squalid grey building. Barred windows in its upper storey were flanked by ragged scraps of would-be curtains. Between the two narrow holes of windows hung a washing line sagging with the weight of a few nondescript pieces of clothing. A woman stood at the window, screaming down at another woman who sat cross-legged on a sharpai outside the doorway, nursing a baby and playing cards with a boy of about thirteen years, and yelling what sounded like abuse back at the woman above. Gita took Rita's hand. 'Shhh . . .' she said.

'What's the matter?'

Sensing their presence, the card-playing woman looked up, quickly assessed Gita and Rita as irrelevant, and returned to her card game and her screaming match. She pulled the baby away from her breast and laid it on the sharpai behind her, where it began to squall with rage. The boy had his back to them and did not look around. The door was open, offering a glimpse of a long black passage in whose depths blinked a string of red fairy-lights, perhaps framing a door, perhaps lighting the way upstairs.

'Come on,' said Gita, and pulled Rita onwards. When they were several houses further on Gita stopped again and looked back. There was a fruit-stand piled high with oranges between them and the brothel, not only blocking their own view but blocking the view of anyone who might think to watch them from the house.

'Try to memorize the place,' she said to Rita. 'The houses don't have numbers, so make a note of other landmarks. That Coca-Cola sign on the house next door, for instance. Got it? Think you could find the house again?'

Taken aback, Rita replied, 'Well – ah, I think so, but not the street. Why?'

'It could be the right one. Asha might be there.'

Rita frowned, glancing behind her at the house in question. 'You think so! But why? What did you see?'

'It's not what I saw; it's what I heard. There are several Tamil houses on this lane – all owned by one person, it seems. And that house there could be the one we're looking for. Those two women—'

'The ones arguing through the window? Yes, I saw them. They were pretty loud about it, too. Was that Tamil?'

'Yes. And they *might* have been talking about Asha.'

'What did they say?'

'They spoke of a girl, a young Tamil girl. The woman with the baby must have beaten her badly; she's bleeding on her back, the other woman said, and she won't be any good for a few days. That was the gist of it.'

'But why do you believe she's Asha?'

'Because of what the woman upstairs said; apparently, she's just visiting from Madras. It seems she brought the girl from there many months ago, but she hasn't been paid off yet, and she's furious about the delay. Of course, if the girl can't work she can't earn any money. The other woman, the woman downstairs, said she can pay her tomorrow because somebody is coming to buy the girl, somebody with cash. But the woman upstairs thinks they might not take her with those wounds. Rita: I'm *certain* they're talking about Asha! Certain hints; that she speaks English, and . . . we have to tell Kamal right away!'

Gita had turned and was walking on again, away from the house. Rita did not follow her; she stood where she was, and for the first time since entering Kamathipura that morning her thoughts were entirely clear. She nodded, once, then hurried after Gita and grabbed her, so that she stopped.

'No, Gita. Let's not tell him. We'll go after this ourselves, and only tell him when we're certain.'

'But *why*? Surely . . . Oh. Yes. I see . . . You're right. In case it's a mistake.'

'Exactly. I just want to be absolutely *certain* before we tell him anything. Kamal has followed so many false leads. If this turns out to be another one we'll just look like idiots. I want to actually *find* Asha before we go back to Kamal! You said he and Shazeed didn't take you seriously – well, I have the same feeling, that he doesn't take *me* seriously, either. It's the story of my life and I'm sick of it! I don't want to be just an observer of this, Gita, I want to *do* something. I *need* to do something. This place makes me nauseous, just the thought of it – just the thought of that girl . . . I want to find her! I want to get her out! Gosh, I want to get them *all* out, every last girl and every woman too who isn't there of her own free will! I feel like just rushing into all these houses with a sword and . . . and . . . Oh, I'm so angry, Gita! How dare they do that to these girls? How dare they! I could just, just . . .'

Tears of rage and frustration gathered in her eyes. She took a deep breath and continued, her tone milder.

'Let's *show* Kamal, Gita. Your theory about the Tamil houses is sound, and it looks as if we're on to something. And even if it's not Asha they're talking about, oh, the *idea* of it, of them beating that girl, and selling her, and . . . and . . .'

Indignation rose once more and seethed within her, breaking off the words in mid-sentence. She shook her head in bitterness and glared at Gita, pleading silently for understanding.

Gita did understand. 'I know what you mean. I know. But, Rita, be sensible. I've worked here for a few months now and that gives me a better perspective on the whole situation. It's the first time you've been here and naturally you're shocked, but—'

'But that's just *it*, Gita! It's all routine to you, but this is my very first time and that's exactly the right moment to act, when the shock is alive and burning. It's like dynamite! I have to use it now!'

Gita reached out and patted her on the shoulder, as if to calm her. 'Rita. I know exactly how you feel, and I know that you're doing this for Kamal. Maybe you think it's the only way to attract his attention, or that if you find Asha his mind will be free again and—'

But Rita flung the soothing hand away angrily. 'Don't say that! Don't you *get* it! I'm not doing this for Kamal! I don't care about winning Kamal's approval or love or whatever you think it is I'm trying to do! I just *hate* it when people are so condescending! All my life . . .' She stopped for a moment to gather her indignation and fling it at Gita. 'All my life I've been held back from doing what I *knew* was right. Right for *me*, what I *had* to do. People have always told me no, no, it's just not the done thing. My stepmother. She told me I was a ragamuffin and wouldn't let me keep animals. My boss. He called me a loose cannon and made me into a nice tame women's page chatterbox. My bloody sister who sees me as a private lady-in-waiting. Always this tut-tutting: Rita has such *strange* ideas. Rita's such a *dreamer*. Rita wants to save the world. Rita's unrealistic. She's so *quirky*. Smiling knowingly when they said it. Well, I'm sick and tired of it. For once in my life, Gita, I'm going to do what my feelings tell me to and neither you nor anybody else can stop me!'

'But you can't just rush in there! At least wait and—'

'No. Now. Immediately. Come on. I don't want to waste a single minute.'

'Yes, but—'

'No buts, Gita. If you want to come, follow me. If not, go home. I can do it alone. I don't care. But you might come in useful as a translator, since I don't speak a word of the bloody language!'

She turned and strode in the direction of the house. Gita followed, almost running to keep up. 'But, Rita, what are you planning to *do*?'

Rita glanced at her. 'I haven't planned anything. I'm just playing it by ear.'

'But we must make a plan . . .'

'I never work with plans. I listen to what my instinct says. For every moment there's a right response but you can only know the right response when that moment comes. So let's just go back and see what happens.'

'Rita, *stop*, for goodness' sake. Let's talk this through!' Gita's hand was on Rita's upper arm, holding her back. Rita stopped, and turned to face her.

'There's nothing to talk through, Gita. I *know* it's right to go back *now*. Don't ask me how I know, I just *know*. I know we haven't got a moment to waste. I'm sorry if I sounded belligerent. No, I'm not sorry. I *am* belligerent. Right now I'm so furious I could kill someone. And I'm going in there with all my fury and if Asha's there I'll find her, and if it's not Asha I don't care, there's a little girl in there who's been beaten and who's going to be sold and whoever she is, I want her! So are you coming, or not?'

The two women faced each other in silence, the street din clattering and swirling around them as a tide rushes around a rock, the rock being Rita's doggedness that held her steadfast. In Gita's eyes she saw indecision, then fear, then doubt. She kept her gaze steady and strong, and under it Gita's vacillation gave way to resolve until her eyes were a mirror of Rita's own, reflecting an intrepid fervour that would stay its course like a river heading for the sea.

'OK. I'm coming,' said Gita.

FIFTY-THREE

Fools Rush In

The woman on the sharpai looked up. Rita met her gaze steadily, nodded in greeting, and turned to Gita. 'OK, translate, Gita. Tell her that I'm a journalist, that I'm writing an article for a foreign magazine. Tell her I'm doing research on prostitution and would like to talk to her and visit this brothel.'

Gita spoke. Rita could not understand a word, but she gathered that at first there was a decision made as to what language the woman would prefer to speak, and that the language they decided on was strange to Rita's ears, and thus probably Tamil.

'She says she's not interested,' Gita said after a few sentences. 'I thought she wouldn't be. The last thing these people want is publicity, especially not in a foreign magazine. It's when the foreigners start talking about us that the authorities start paying attention. Perhaps, Rita—'

'Tell her I'll pay her well, and I guarantee her anonymity. I don't have a camera, and I'll change her name in the article. She has nothing to lose, and a lot to gain. See if you can bargain with her. Offer her whatever she wants, within reason.'

'What's within reason?'

'Let me check. I changed some money yesterday. Just a

moment.' Rita reached for her bag and opened her purse. She counted the hundred-rupee notes and looked up. 'Offer her two hundred rupees. If she wants to bargain you can go up a few hundred. Eight hundred's the limit; that's all I've got.'

Gita, Rita could tell, was a hard bargainer, but so was the woman, who sent away the boy and gathered up the cards before getting down to what was obviously hard business. Finally, Gita said, 'She wants two hundred for the interview alone, one-fifty more for a guided tour of the brothel, and one hundred for every girl you speak to. That means for the eight hundred limit you can speak to four girls. I'm sorry, I couldn't do any better than that.'

'It'll have to do.'

'She wants us to go inside for the interview, she doesn't want to be seen talking to strangers outside here, and she has to cook.'

The woman got up from the sharpai, taking her time to do so, as if moving caused her much pain. Once she was standing she rearranged her sari, tucking in various corners and ends, hawked and spat into the gutter, screamed at a skinny dog that had ventured under the sharpai foraging for grains of cooked rice, and then gestured to the two women to enter the house.

Just inside the doorway was a small square area which was obviously the kitchen; there was a one-burner kerosene stove on the concrete floor, and glass jars, bottles, battered aluminium pots and various other cooking utensils against the wall and on shelves. A large onion stood on a wooden tablet next to a sharp knife, ready to be peeled and sliced.

Muttering disagreeably to herself, the thin woman edged past Rita and squatted on the floor. She bundled the skirt of her sari between her knees and began preparations for cooking: lighting the stove, pouring water into a pot, placing the pot on the burner, peeling the onion. All the while she and Gita talked spiritedly; from her tone Rita gathered she wasn't pleased about the intrusion.

Finally Gita turned to Rita and said, 'She's ready to talk; sit down.'

Rita looked around for a chair, but there wasn't one. The woman gestured silently, impatiently to a rolled-up straw mat, which Gita unrolled and spread on the floor for Rita to sit on. She herself sat on the bare concrete floor. A cockroach scurried across the floor and disappeared among the cooking paraphernalia. There was a sharp, rancid smell of something spoilt. Fruit flies hovered above a rotting bunch of bananas.

Rita opened with standard questions, beginning with the woman's own personal history. Gita translated her questions into Tamil and the woman's answers back into English.

'How long has she been here?'

'Since she was fifteen.'

'How did she enter this trade?'

'She came here through the devadasi system. Her parents dedicated her to the Goddess Yellamma – she was sold to various individuals and finally to a brothel in Kamathipura. She has worked in several brothels and worked her way up to be in charge of this one.'

'What do you mean, "in charge"? You mean she's the madam, or what?'

'No . . . she's not the brothel-owner. The brothel-owner is a man who comes once a day to check on things, collect money and so on. She is just the senior sex-worker here.'

Rita asked several more questions concerning the woman's past, which were reluctantly answered. Rita began to close in on her subject.

'How many girls are working under her?'

Again, that suspicious, ill-tempered glare. The woman gave a long and detailed answer, which Gita translated simply with: 'Fourteen.'

'Do they stay in this brothel a long time, or do they move on?'

Again a long answer, and a short translation.

'Some are like this, some are like that. That was the gist of it.'

Displeased, Rita frowned. 'How many clients do they have per night?'

The woman spoke, and Gita translated: 'Any number.'

'How much do the clients pay?'

'Sometimes twenty rupees, sometimes thirty. It depends on the girl.'

'Are any of the girls HIV positive?'

'They are all clean. Perfectly clean.'

'How old are the girls?'

'They are all ages.'

'Are they all Tamil girls?'

'Most of them. They are sent through a business partner in Chennai.'

'Are any of them minors?'

The woman hesitated before answering this question. Then she spoke sharply and Gita translated: 'No. The youngest is twenty-one.'

'She's lying, of course. Tell her I will pay double to speak to a girl under sixteen.'

A particularly long and extremely hot exchange followed. The woman stopped what she was doing and used her hands to demonstrate her rage at the impertinent proposal; but she was obviously tempted. Gita held her ground; Rita had to admire her for the calm, unflurried way she presented her case, and, though she couldn't understand a word spoken, felt the authority and confidence with which Gita made her point. Her support was essential; Rita had not been bluffing when she had told Gita either to come or to go home earlier, but still, she knew very well that she could never have managed this on her own. She felt a wave of gratitude towards Gita for putting aside her doubts and plunging in against her own judgement.

With another furious glare at Rita the woman finally gave in. She stood up, leaned forward into the blackness of a corridor leading off from the kitchen, and called out. An answering call could be heard from upstairs, followed by the dull pound of bare feet on wood.

Gita grinned. 'Money always speaks. But I didn't double the price. I added fifty rupees to every minor you get to interview.'

The woman had disappeared into the darkness, still muttering. From the depths of the building emerged various muffled sounds: steps on a staircase, a curtain snapped back along its runners, someone speaking in sharp tones. Gita reached out and took Rita's hand.

'I'm glad you came, Rita. Sorry I tried to talk you out of it. You just took me by surprise. But where do you go from here? Are you just going to take the girl by the hand and run? You said you didn't care if it wasn't Asha, but what if it isn't, and Asha is still up there somewhere?'

'The tour of the brothel,' Rita said. 'That's what I'm counting on most.'

'But even if you *do* find Asha, what then?'

Rita shrugged. 'I told you. I'm playing it by ear.'

'Promise me you won't be reckless though, Rita. I know this woman seems harmless enough but don't forget there's a whole mafia behind this business, and there's a lot of money in the game. It could get dangerous.'

'Nothing risked, nothing gained,' Rita replied, then smiled reassuringly. 'Don't worry, my head's still screwed on tightly. But if—'

The kitchen suddenly darkened, the pool of sunlight coming in from the open doorway filled by a hulking shadow. Rita looked up, and saw a huge, well-dressed man in brown trousers and a white shirt, wearing an ostentatious gold watch and a gold chain around his neck. He was barefoot. He glared at them, and shouted a two-syllable word into the building.

The woman re-emerged from the darkness. Fury had left her face, to be replaced by fear. Her eyes blinked quickly as she plunged into some long explanation, but the man interrupted her, spoke sharply, pulled at the waistband of his trousers, and left as quickly as he had come. Sunlight swarmed in through the emptied doorway.

'Who was that?' Rita asked.

'It was a moneylender. He came to get a repayment but she couldn't pay him. The moneylenders have all the power here;

they ask for a hundred per cent interest. They're the ruin of the brothels. That, and AIDS. She told him to return in an hour. She must be relying on the money you're about to pay her.'

'So I'm helping to run this business, am I? How lovely. Ask her about the girl.'

Gita said something to the woman, who cast Rita a particularly poisonous glance before turning back to the dark interior of the house. She yelled something. From deep inside there came a reply. The yells echoed back and forth for a while until finally a young girl appeared in the doorway. The woman spoke sharply to her and she stepped over the threshold and stood in front of Rita.

'She can sit down,' Rita said, and patted the mat next to her. Gita spoke and the girl sat down in the corridor's threshold.

'How old are you?' Rita asked, but before the girl could reply, the older woman barked and Gita translated.

'Twenty-one.'

'Do you believe her, Gita? She looks older than sixteen, for certain.'

Gita shrugged. 'It's hard to tell. She could be anything between sixteen and twenty-one. Only one thing's sure – she's not Asha.'

'How can you tell?'

'Too old, definitely. And besides, she's just not fair enough. That's Asha's most distinguishing hallmark, you know – fair skin. Caroline was a blonde American; and it shows. For an Indian, Asha's very fair. True, she's got black hair, but her skin is what Indians call "wheatish". It's not very common and very much in demand. That's probably why she was abducted in the first place. She must have fetched a high price.'

Rita's mouth formed a round O. She nodded, and turned back to the girl. 'How did she end up in this profession?'

'She says she was abducted from her village in Tamil Nadu. She was promised a film role in Bombay and believed the man. She came with him here voluntarily and then was sold to a brothel.'

'Why doesn't she go home?'

'She can't go home. Her parents would be ashamed of her and people in the village would drive her away. She has to stay here.'

'Would she like to do another kind of work?'

The girl shrugged.

'She says, what else can she do? She doesn't know any other kind of work. There are no jobs anyway. There is no point looking for another job because she will not get one. Her destiny is to do this work. It is all God's will. Who is she to hanker after another life?'

The woman had returned to her place on the floor and was silently chopping the onion, chut-chut-chut, hammering the knife furiously, expertly against the silvery ball. A row of paper-thin slices fell to the chopping board.

'Is that the way they all think?' Rita asked. 'So utterly hopeless? Resigned to their fate? Why can't they just – run away?'

'Run away to what? You heard what she said – she can't go back home.'

The girl began to speak again but suddenly the woman started yelling. The girl cowered into the darkness of the corridor. A torrent of sharp, loud, hot words rained like gunfire upon her, and the woman dropped the knife and gesticulated wildly with her hands, pointing at the girl, at Rita, slapping the heel of one hand into the palm of the other, her face distorted with anger. Her eyes seemed to withdraw into black holes beneath overhanging brows, and her lips drew back from uneven, yellow teeth in a snarl vicious enough to conjure fear in any hero's heart.

Then, as suddenly as she had begun her yelling, the woman fell silent and picked up the knife again, viciously peeling another onion.

Rita stood up.

'What now?'

'We're not getting anywhere. I want the tour of the brothel. Now. Otherwise we go and she only gets paid half. She's trying to cheat. I'm not paying extra for that girl, she's too old . . . I want Asha.'

Rita turned to the girl and namasted in dismissal. She disappeared into the corridor. Before Gita could translate or the woman get to her feet – an obviously painful undertaking – Rita, too, had disappeared into the brothel's bowels.

FIFTY-FOUR

Where Angels Fear to Tread

The corridor was so dark Rita was forced to slow down. She didn't want to stop, so she groped until she felt the wall, cool and dank with what felt like slime. She shuddered, but moved on until she stumbled against something like a plank at ankle level; but by now the blackness had lightened to grey and she could see the shadowed outline of a steep staircase. Behind her there were voices: the woman's shout of anger and Gita's cry to come back. She ignored both, groped for a banister, found it, and felt with one foot for the steps.

Asha, or whoever the girl was, would be upstairs, of that much she was certain. The building was narrow but tall – perhaps four storeys high – and the woman had shouted from one of the upper storeys. She would just keep going until she found what she was looking for. Rita felt not a trace of fear. The woman in charge was a pushover – she could hardly even get to her feet without a struggle, and she, Rita, was strong, and fired by an uncurbed resolve.

The staircase was, in effect, nothing more than an appropriately adjusted ladder, fitted to slant snugly against the wall and upgraded with a precarious banister. She reached the first landing and edged herself along a dimly lit corridor little more than two feet across, and interrupted by several narrow doorways, some open, some curtained. Glancing through the open doorways Rita saw tiny cubicles, each one about the length of a human being and the breadth of a human being with an arm stretched out. A cot occupied half of the space, on which lay filthy mattresses and crumpled sheets. There was a rat-like scurrying at the far end of the corridor and Rita glimpsed the shadow of a human being disappearing into a cubicle and heard the *ratch* of a quickly drawn curtain, which still shivered as Rita passed it seconds later.

At the end of the corridor was another flight of stairs. She climbed it; but by this time Gita and the woman had reached the top of the first flight. Rita peered over the banisters; the woman, it seemed, was hurrying as fast as she could, half limping, half running in pursuit, Gita behind her, unable to pass, too polite to push her aside and scramble forward. Gita was still calling her 'Don'ts' and 'Come backs'.

'Don't be stupid, Rita! You can't just rush in like that. Come back! Don't be a fool. Don't . . .' But Rita had heard it all before, and the time for obedience was over.

She reached the second landing, where she stopped for a moment to draw breath and, literally, sniff the air. The smell was acrid, an alloy of rancid body fluids and other unidentifiable rotting waste. Rita felt her mind like an open satellite dish, receiving signals imperceptible to the senses: thoughts and feelings, heartbeats and heartaches, and a never-ending, silent wail of terror. She continued up to the third storey. This corridor was identical to the two beneath it, except that the cubicles here had doors, and all the doors were shut – and bolted, with heavy steel padlocks hanging from the bolts. A triumphant crash of inner drumming told her she had arrived. She stopped and waited.

The woman came panting up the steps, bent almost double with the effort of hurrying. Her face was a distorted mask of rage; she burst into a torrent of words. Rita could not understand a syllable, and Gita wasn't translating, so she simply stood her ground and waited for the woman to finish. Gita was still protesting.

'Rita, you can't just—'

'I can,' said Rita, and then, because the woman had stopped for breath, added, 'Tell her to open these doors, one by one.' She pointed to the bunch of keys dangling from a knot at the end of her sari. 'Those are the keys. They were the first thing I noticed about her. Tell her to open this door.' She tapped at the first door.

'Rita, what's got into you today?'

'It's all right, Gita, don't worry, I'm only a bit mad, you'll get used to it.' Rita laughed. 'Back to my old self. I was always a bit *deviant*, you know. It's much more fun. Have you translated? Because I'm going to take those keys off this old witch if she doesn't open the door. A bit of arm-twisting might be in order!'

The woman opened her mouth as if to speak, thought the better of it, scowled and fumbled with the knot in her sari, muttering and uttering what could only be foul curses. She held the bunch of keys up nearer to the naked bulb (to which clung peeling shreds of red paint) that hung from the ceiling and cast a dim glow through the corridor.

The door creaked back into the cubicle. Rita heard a loud gasp; she peered inside. She made out some movement on the cot, but it was too dark to make out more than shadows.

'Isn't there a light in here?'

Still muttering crossly, the woman reached up and groped along the upper edge of the doorframe. A switch must have been hidden there, because a bulb sticking out from the wall inside the cubicle lit up. Now Rita could see the inhabitant of the cubicle. It was a girl, whose age she judged to be ten or eleven. She cowered at the back of her cot, a ragged sheet drawn up to her chin. She stared at them both from above clenched hands and the terror in her eyes was like a dagger in Rita's heart.

Her skin was dark – almost black.

'Oh Lord.' It was an exclamation of horror and a prayer combined. Rita felt a prick of tears in her eyes; she wanted to rush in and gather the child into her arms and run. Instead, she turned to Gita.

'Ask her if she speaks Tamil,' she said. Gita did so, and though the girl did not answer the hungry, agonized plea in her eyes and the slight motion of her head showed that she understood, that she recognized a friend.

'Tell her not to be afraid,' Rita said. 'Tell her we have to go now but we'll be back. Tell her it's going to be all right. Tell her . . .' But she could not speak, for the words could not get past the lump in her throat. She smiled with what she hoped was reassurance, and gestured to the woman to move on.

There was no padlock on the next door. Opening it, Rita found the cubicle to be empty, and the next one. Of the ten cubicles, in fact, only four were occupied – each with a pubescent girl, though none so young as the girl in the first one.

'These are holding cells for the new girls,' Gita whispered. 'For the youngest ones. These are the cages. It would be unusual for Asha still to be held in one after all this time – but she's undoubtedly very valuable to them . . .'

'Funny, up to now I always imagined they were in *real* cages, as in a zoo.'

'The rooms that face the street do have bars across the window. But *this* here – imagine, when we go, the lights are out. The girls are in complete darkness, day and night.'

'Come, let's go on. There are some more rooms upstairs. I keep hoping we'll find Asha. And fearing we'll find Asha.'

They still whispered, as if there was someone to hear, as if, if they spoke aloud, the horror that cowered tamely in the shadows would be unleashed and break over them in a pandemonium of demonic screams and crazed carnage.

'Barbaric,' said Rita.

'Rita . . .' Gita began. 'You said you didn't care if it was Asha or another girl. You said . . .'

'You mean I should have taken that first girl? The youngest one? That was my first instinct. But, Gita! It was Asha who brought me here. I hear her. I feel her. Don't ask me how, but I know she's here. And I have to find her. We can come back later. Send Kamal, the police, and get the others out. But it's Asha I need to find now.'

She led the way along the uppermost corridor. At first, it seemed her instinct had led her falsely, for the doors here, though bolted, were not padlocked, and looking into the first three Rita saw they were empty.

But from the last door's latch hung a thick, rusty padlock.

Without waiting to be told the woman came forward, the right key already in her hand, and opened it. The padlock snapped, the door creaked as Rita pushed it open. There was no need to switch on the light, for this cubicle, being the end room, had a barred window, although its glass was so grimy the sun filtered through only faintly. But enough for Rita to make out the slight figure half lying, half sitting on the cot beside her, head and shoulders leaning against the wall. Enough for her to see that it was a child with pale, pale skin.

FIFTY-FIVE

Caged

Was this Asha? Surely it must be, her colouring confirmed it. The girl's face was so pale, so motionless, Rita thought she was looking at a corpse, and her first instinct was to touch the face to feel if it was cold. She reached towards the sunken cheek, but the girl moved sharply aside, raising her hands as if to ward Rita off, and the eyes, eyes that had been open and staring like the eyes of a corpse only seconds ago, widened in terror. Rita drew back her hand, and sat down at the foot end of the mattress which was hard and smelled of stale urine. She glanced around her. Two or three threadbare, slightly torn and very grubby sheets lay in limp, untidy lumps near the girl's feet, as if she had kicked them away. Rita moved them aside to make room for herself – they were slightly damp, and they, too, smelled of urine. But then the whole cubicle reeked of excretion. In the corner was a rusty potty covered with a folded newspaper, across which two flies marched, and above which several more flies circled. The stench came mainly from that source. The walls had probably once been bright green but were encrusted with grey, mottled fungus, which emitted an odour of its own. Rita's breathing automatically became shallow. She wished she could open the window, but even from here she could see it was nailed shut. There were slats in the boards above the window which supplied the only fresh air. She felt like pushing her nose up through the slats, gasping for oxygen. Instead, she turned back to Asha, and smiled.

'Asha? It's all right, I'm a friend; don't be afraid.'

At the name the terrified eyes suddenly seemed to focus in recognition, and the brow above them creased with a frown of puzzlement. Rita reached out to take a hand, but this too the girl pulled away. She wriggled into a sitting position, cowering against the head end of the mattress, knees drawn up close to her chest, hugging her legs.

Rita looked at Gita, who had entered the cubicle and was kneeling on the ground next to the mattress.

'It's her, isn't it, Gita? But she's in a terrible state. She's responded to her name, but she's afraid, she doesn't trust me.'

She turned back to Asha. 'Asha! We know who you are, we've been looking for you and we want to get you out of here. I know you understand English. Get up now, and come! We're leaving. We'll help you. Come on . . .' She was halfway to her feet when a loud crash made her swing around. The door to the cubicle had been slammed shut; she heard the rasp of the bolt as it crashed into its slot. The clatter of keys and the click of the padlock snapping shut followed, and the vile cackle of their jailer.

The woman shouted something obviously very rude at them from beyond the door, after which there was silence.

Gita was instantly on her feet, hammering on the door. 'Now look what you've done!'

'One of us should have waited outside,' was all Rita said. 'It was a bit stupid for both of us to come in.'

'You mean it was stupid of me to come in after you,' said Gita. 'You, after all, simply rushed in. Like fools where angels fear to tread.'

'OK, OK, we both rushed in and didn't think. No point quarrelling about it now. We're locked in, and that's that. But at least we found Asha.'

'What a fine thing, to have found Asha. Now we're all three going to be prostitutes.'

'Are you being sarcastic?'

'And are you really the fool you seem to be right now? Don't you realize that we're prisoners? Don't you know what they do with women prisoners here? We're in Kamathipura, for goodness' sake!' Gita's voice was shrill. 'You don't think they'll let us run free after this clever trick of yours, do you? Rita, I thought you were sensible when we first met but—'

'Calm down, Gita, just calm down. Look, we can't do anything right now. We can't get out. All we can do is wait till either Witch Hazel or her malevolent puppeteer returns, and *then* I'll think what to do, depending on what they do and what comes to me in the moment. You're panicking because you don't know what's going to happen. I'm *not* panicking because I believe I'll know what to do when the time comes. Can't you just trust me? Why don't you just sit down, for a start, instead of pacing up and down like a caged animal?'

'You're just too naïve to realize the danger we're in!' Gita shrieked.

'Since we can't do anything else right now,' Rita continued, 'I think we should try to get Asha to trust us instead of panicking. You may be dismayed, but I'm *glad* we're here. I'm glad we found Asha.'

Rita turned back to Asha and now addressed her instead of Gita, who, dumbfounded by Rita's reaction to their predicament, dropped scowling to the floor.

'You understand what we're saying, don't you, Asha? You speak English. I know you do. But even if you don't want to speak you can listen and if you agree you nod your head, and if you disagree you shake it. OK?'

Rita waited for Asha to nod, but the girl simply did not react. She sat there, staring straight ahead as ever. Though the sheer terror with which she had greeted Rita's first overtures had fled, and the spark of animation she had shown on hearing her name, her expression still reflected trepidation and distrust. Rita noticed a tightening of the grasp that held her legs hugged tightly to her body. Watching her, for the first time Rita took in Asha's physical appearance. And for the first time she acknowledged Asha's almost ethereal beauty, which managed to shine through in spite of the veneer of abject misery that coated her both physically and mentally. The girl was the personification of distress, and yet instead of distorting her features that distress itself seemed somehow uplifted by resting on this girl; it glowed with a pain so exquisite and poignant Rita could feel it almost physically, echoed in her own heart. The eyes were of a midnight black, eloquent in their very lifelessness. Her features had a symmetrical swing; her skin, so fair for an Indian, was translucent; her cheekbones were too prominent. Her clothing was ragged and dirty; her hair unkempt. Yet all of this seemed to accentuate her beauty rather than diminish it.

'That hag!' said Rita. 'The poor child is a bundle of raw nerves. Listen, Asha! We're your friends. We came here to rescue you, and we will. Your father has been looking for you for a long time and we're going to bring you back to him.'

Rita couldn't be sure, but she thought she saw a flicker of something in the staring eyes at the words 'your father'. Hope? Longing? Or simply the absence of terror, a drawing back of shadows? Whatever it was, Rita was encouraged, and continued.

'My name is Rita, this is Gita. You can trust us. You needn't be afraid. We know all about you. We know they stole you from your mother. We know your mother's name – Sundari Iyengar. We know you wrote a letter to your father; he got your letter and he came here right away to look for you. He loves you very much and wants to get you out. That's why we came. You want to be free, don't you? We know you've been treated badly. But we're your friends. Believe me.'

'Save your breath,' Gita said sourly. 'She's not listening. I don't think she can even hear you. She's catatonic. Who wouldn't be, after what she's been through!'

'She's listening, all right. I know it. She understands every word.'

'If you believe that then either you really are naïve, or you've got a sixth sense. She's like a statue.'

'That's what you think. Asha, you're listening, aren't you? You know I'm talking to you?'

'It would be more useful if you gave some thought as to how we can escape from here.'

Rita, who had been smiling with what she hoped was reassurance at Asha, turned back to Gita. Her tone now was belligerent.

'Gita, I'm sorry I got you into this mess, truly sorry, but right now Asha comes first. I want to talk to her. I want to see if she's got wounds on her back and how bad they are. I want to get her to trust me, dammit! And if you keep dousing me with cold water it's not going to work! So can you just *shut up*!'

FIFTY-SIX

Sleepless

It was the longest day in Rita's life. The minutes ticked by as if they were days. She and Gita, having argued over the same ground time and time again, shared long silences. Asha huddled in her corner; now and again she fell asleep, her head lolling to one side, her body leaning abjectly against the wall. Even in her sleep she shifted several times, as if unable to find a comfortable position. Rita remembered her wounded back, and wished she could look at it, wished she had the means to clean and dress it, since she did not for one minute believe that it had been treated. But Asha would not let Rita touch her.

Again and again she spoke to the girl. She spoke about her life before coming to India, about her family, her dreams. Asha seemed to hear nothing, but still Rita talked.

She had grown used to the stench by now; occasionally she had gone to the window to sniff the fresh air that seeped in through the wooden slats. She looked through the windowpane, but it was so smudged that not much could be seen except the vague outline of the opposite building, an almost black tenement with barred windows just like this one. Rita inspected the window more closely, to see if there was any chance of opening it, but it was nailed tightly shut, and the bars outside it were obviously solid, so that even if she broke a pane of glass there could be no escape that way; nor would shouting down to the street be of any use, for who would hear them? And who would care?

After they had been imprisoned for about three hours they heard footsteps outside and the clatter of keys. She and Gita both jumped to attention, signalling to each other to be quiet. A male voice called out something.

'He said, don't try any tricks, he's armed,' said Gita, and the corners of her mouth drooped in disappointment. They had considered flinging open the door as soon as the latch was opened, but the door was in an awkward position, making it impossible for any surprise attack from within. Now, it opened only about six inches, and a blackened aluminium pot was pushed through the opening at floor level – Rita got a glimpse of a tiny hand, the hand of a child, pushing it in, the fingers flicking it forward, and quickly jerking back to safety. The door was slammed shut again, the latch rasped, the lock snapped.

The pot contained rice soaked in a yellowish liquid. There were neither plates nor cutlery. By now Rita was ravenous, but she could not eat, and neither could Gita. She forced herself to take three mouthfuls – scooping up the rice with her fingers – before giving up and turning away in disgust.

'We should eat, though,' said Gita. 'We don't know when our next meal will be.'

'I can't,' said Rita. She passed the pot to Asha, who ignored it as she ignored everything else.

'I think she'll have to be hand fed.' Rita formed a ball of rice with her fingers and put it to the girl's lips. Half of the rice fell away, the other half she pushed into the mouth which, to her surprise, relaxed enough to open and receive the food.

'She's eating,' said Rita almost joyously. It was the first physical contact she had been able to make with the girl, the first touch that had not been rejected. She tried a second time, and a third, and with every attempt Asha seemed hungrier and more alive, finally actively chewing. When the pot was half empty the feeding stopped, since Asha refused to take more. But Rita felt elated. She had cut through the wall of apathy; she was on the way.

But Rita's calmness was flittering away with every passing minute. She had always been well prepared to deal with the unexpected turns her life might take; her calmness could normally maintain itself through any emergency. It was the *nothing happening* that tore at the fabric of her patience, however, the endless waiting with no sign that it would ever end. Her conversations with Gita went around in circles, more banal even than the silences they broke; her ears constantly strained to pick up noises from beyond the door. Occasionally she heard voices or footsteps from the bowels of the house but they never came up to this floor. Her sense of frustration was like a rising tide of boiling water within her; she wanted to get up; move around; stretch her limbs aching from so much sitting. Occasionally she did; but the cubicle was too small to bring any relief and every time she simply flung herself back to the mattress. Gita was obviously having the same problems. Only Asha seemed resigned to this infinity of waiting, or rather, she didn't wait at all, but simply existed, as if her mind had lost the capacity to move forward into the future, to expect and hope for change.

Night fell, and the darkness was complete except for the dim glowing of the windowpane, like a rectangle of blotting paper picking up whatever faint light the streetlamps below emitted.

Asha was asleep again, huddled against the wall, and Rita took the liberty of touching her again, helping her down into a lying position and covering her with one of the torn sheets. Asha did not awake. Rita longed to partly undress her, to check her wounds; she longed to stroke her hair. If there was one thought that made this predicament bearable it was the thought of Asha. She may have been impulsive, reckless, headstrong, giddy – but she had been *right*. She had found Asha.

Asha was the only one of the three privileged enough to sleep prone. Rita and Gita had to lean against the wall or against each other – though there was little sleep to be had. The night seemed even more endless than the day; the sounds filtering in from the street, muffled though they were, helped keep Rita awake. The street had been quiet during the day; now, at night, it seemed to wake up and the mélange of loudspeaker music, raucous laughter, shouting and a thousand other noises conspired to ensure she could not escape from her carousel of thoughts for even half an hour at a time.

It must have been long past midnight when she was abruptly shaken out of a restless nap. The lightbulb glared overhead; there were voices in the cubicle, loud male voices, and, as she saw on rubbing the sleep from her eyes, the men to go with them.

The woman was there too, chattering loudly and coarsely, pointing and glaring at her. Gita was awake too, and Asha's eyes were open.

The woman bent over and snatched Rita's shoulder bag, which was lying on the floor. She opened it, found the purse, and took out all the paper money. She threw the bag back on to the floor, counted and folded the hundred-rupee notes, and stuck the wad into the neckline of her blouse.

One of the men was speaking to Gita; Gita was nodding. When she turned to Rita her eyes had a new hope in them.

'They're letting us go, Rita! Asha has been sold, they're taking her away, and they don't want us! I suppose we're too independent for their liking. Anyway, you and I can go!'

The immediate effect of her words took every one of them by surprise.

Asha, who till now had been lying apathetically on the mattress, shot up into a sitting position and flung herself against Rita; she looked up at Rita with wide, terrified eyes; she said nothing, but her grip on Rita's arms was like a vice – Rita would never have guessed the girl had such strength. Rita put her arms around the emaciated little body. She laid one hand protectively on the matted, dirty hair. She looked at Gita.

'I can't go, Gita. I have to stay with Asha. Tell them that.'

FIFTY-SEVEN

Playing the Heroine

Gita, true to character, tried to argue Rita out of it. Rita was mad, she was stupid, she was ridiculous. What she said made no sense. She was putting herself in danger, not helping Asha. Asha could be better helped by informing Kamal and having him search for her, now that they had a lead. She could do more for Asha by going home, now, and making a formal report to the police. She could inform the press, make a scandal out of it; the police would have to act. The woman would be arrested; she'd have to talk. The house would be raided. Asha would be found – officially. There was no need to play the heroine. It was pointless to play the heroine. This was not an action movie. It was real life and these people meant business. Her very life would be in danger. She'd be made a prostitute herself. They'd take her with them and separate her from Asha anyway. You couldn't trust them. She was a fool. An idiot. A child.

Round and round went the arguments. Rita's rejoinders were curt and to the point. She could not leave Asha. She had to finish what she started.

'I can't help it, Gita. I know you can't understand it. But I have to stay with Asha. I just have to. I can't explain why. I just know I have to. That's all.' And she tightened her arms around the girl and felt the little trembling body and knew that she was right.

'Is it because of Kamal? Are you doing this for Kamal? To impress him?'

'Gita, believe me. I haven't given Kamal a single thought in the last twenty-four hours. I know you don't believe me, but it's true. I'm not doing it for Kamal. I'm doing it for her. And for me. Because I have to.'

'I hope you don't expect me to be as heroic and selfless as you!' Gita sounded angry now.

'No, I don't, Gita. You're the sensible one and you should do the sensible thing. Go to Kamal and tell him what's happened and set everything in motion the way you just told me. I don't know why they want to let us go, to be honest, after we saw all these children in here! It's strange!'

'Oh, you think they care? They're safe enough. Bet you if the police ever make a raid they won't find a single minor – these men are only letting us go because they've got everybody bribed.'

'Anyway, Gita, you go and do what you can. I'm staying, and there's nothing you can say that can change that.'

This was better. Things were finally *happening*, and as always at such times Rita's entire being rose up in full regalia, all flags flying, decked out in audacity and fervency. She was elated; Asha was hers to fight for!

'It's all right, Asha, I won't leave you!' she whispered, lowering her voice and her head so that Asha's ear was near her lips. 'I'll stay with you and look after you.'

Imperceptibly the child's head nodded, the arms around her tightened. The trembling seemed to lessen, as if Asha had absorbed some of Rita's own sangfroid.

Gita, meanwhile, had given in and repeated Rita's decision, in Hindi, to the men. Now they were conversing among themselves; arguing, it seemed.

'One of them is for it, one is against it,' Gita said. 'They can't pay for you.'

'Tell them it's buy one, get one free,' said Rita carelessly.

'Rita, are you out of your mind? You can't joke about something like this!'

'Well, if they were going to let me go anyway, what difference does it make? Look, tell them I'm the only one who can make her eat. She trusts me. She'll listen to me. She's just a nervous wreck otherwise. I'll take care of her. They need me.'

Gita translated, and after a few minutes of heated debate both men seemed to be in agreement.

'Seems you convinced them. I think these are just middlemen, Rita, and they want to sell her on to some high-class pimp, and they need her to be more – complaisant. They think you could be useful.'

'That's what I thought.'

'But it's highly unusual. They never met anybody like you before.'

'I never met anybody like me before either,' said Rita. 'That's the problem most people have with me. They'll get used to it.'

'Rita, you're mad.'

'I know. I've been told that before.'

'What if . . .'

'Don't worry about me. I can look after myself.'

'Mad! Absolutely mad!'

Rita grinned. 'It feels good, though! Life is so boring if you're sane!'

Gita's eyes misted over. 'I don't want to leave you, Rita. I feel so bad about it . . .'

'Gita, one mad person is enough. I told you – you have to go home and raise hell. That's *your* role.'

'I don't think it'll do any good, Rita. They wouldn't let me go if they were afraid of a raid. I'm so . . .' But she was being pushed out of the cubicle. She turned once more to Rita. 'Be careful, Rita. Don't do anything silly. Please take care . . .'

'I can't promise anything; I always seem to do silly things. All you can do is pray, Gita. Pray that it turns out OK.'

'I'll be praying. I promise.' They were marching along the upper corridor now, Rita's arm around Asha's tiny waist, squeezed together between the banisters and the wall, Asha limping, Rita being pushed from behind, made to hurry. She felt as light as air, as if her thoughts had spun away on a flight of their own through the spheres. At the stairs they had to part company; Rita gently pushed Asha forward. The girl gave her a fleeting, beseeching look. Rita smiled comfortingly.

'Go on down. I'll be right behind you.'

They reached the front door. They were out in the street, Asha clinging to Rita's arm. Rita felt a tight grip on her other arm; one of the men had taken hold of her and was urging her forward, up the lane. She saw that Asha was being held by the other man. She looked over her shoulder; Gita was following a few paces behind them. When their gazes met Gita gestured to show how helpless she was. Rita tried an encouraging grin.

'It's all right, Gita. Don't worry. I'll be fine. I can take care of us both,' she called.

The street was half deserted. A few women in bright saris stood in an occasional doorway. Late male stragglers made their way to the end of the lane, where the main thoroughfare, in daytime a roaring, fuming chaos of motor vehicles, lay quiet and forsaken. A black car crouched at the roadside. Its back door opened silently at their approach, as if at the hand of a ghost. Rita and Asha were pushed inside; Rita threw one last glance behind her; Gita was watching, standing forlornly behind the car, and Rita waved. 'Take care, Rita!' Gita called, but then the car door slammed and they were enclosed in the black, musty interior. There was a third man already waiting in the driver's seat, reeking of some heavy men's perfume and smiling in a manner that made Rita cringe and draw back in disgust. One of the men from the brothel had sidled into the back seat beside her and now held her arms firmly to her side while the man in the driver's seat tied a blindfold tightly around her eyes. Rita sensed more than saw that

Asha, too, was blindfolded, that the last of the men had climbed into the car and was now sitting next to the driver. The door slammed. The motor coughed once, twice, then relaxed into a quiet purring. They drove off.

FIFTY-EIGHT

Into the Night

It seemed they had been driving for about two hours. But it could have been one hour, and it could have been three. Rita had dozed off now and then, only to be startled into wakefulness by a dream or a memory or a sound, then to drift back into sleep. Sometimes when she was awake she heard the men talking; sometimes she heard nothing but the hum of the engine. When she woke up for the last time the car had stopped and she felt fresh air on her cheeks and heard raised male voices. She was pushed out of the car. She could feel the bite of loose gravel beneath her bare feet, hear its scrunch as she was pushed forward to walk. The tight hold on her arm did not relax for a fraction of a second. She walked up a short flight of low stairs. She knew it the moment they entered the house, for the air's texture changed into the compressed, still solidity of an enclosed space, and under her feet she felt the coolness of stone tiles. She could barely hear Asha's feet padding behind her own. The voices around her were loud and rude, the grip on her arm tight and uncompromising.

They reached the top of the stairs and then there was a woman's voice, speaking three or four sharp words, and uncouth hands tugged at the blindfold's knot at the back of her head, and pulled away the strip of cloth that had bound her eyes. Rita blinked at the harsh light, then looked around. As she had sensed, she was standing on the landing of a house; two of the people standing around her she recognized, for they were the men from the brothel. With them was a woman. She felt the brush of Asha's fingers, and knew the girl was searching for her hand, and her fingers groped till she found the frail little hand and closed protectively around it. She did not look at Asha for the woman was staring at her with such intensity she could not look away.

The woman was anything between thirty and fifty. She wore a faded beauty with the dignity of a queen, though she was not dressed to fit that role. She had obviously been roused from her bed, for she wore a long neck-to-ankle cylinder of a nightgown in pink seersucker, slightly gathered around a buttoned bib that rose above a generously loose bosom. She had skin the colour of dark honey, high cheekbones and long heavy-lidded eyes which seemed to have slid slightly lower into her cheeks than was originally intended. Her hair hung in a long plait over her right shoulder. She wore several gold rings on her fingers and a small gold stud on the flare of her nostril. She was speaking to one of the men, but her gaze flitted now and again from Rita to Asha, summing them up with cunning expertise. Rita felt like a collector's doll being offered for sale.

The woman was obviously unprepared for their coming; she was also obviously of higher rank than both of the men who had brought Rita and Asha. She was arguing with them, but Rita, of course, could not understand a word. Finally the woman addressed her directly. She shrugged. One of the men spoke, and she understood the one word English. The woman addressed her again.

'You speak English?' Rita nodded. Asha neither nodded nor spoke. The girl was edging behind her, trying to hide. The hand in her own trembled like a small captured bird. The woman addressed Asha now; she reached for her, gripped her by the upper arm, and pulled her out from behind Rita.

'Let me look at you,' she said, and turned Asha around, forcing her to let go of Rita's hand. 'Do you speak English too?'

Asha did not answer. The woman spoke to the man who appeared to be the senior, the taller, darker, bulkier of the two.

There followed a long conversation, in which the man spoke the most, the woman merely shaking her head and saying 'a-cha, a-cha' at intervals. Then the woman took over. Finally they seemed to have reached a sort of agreement, for the tone of voice changed; it became friendly, almost. The man and his crony turned and clattered down the stairs. The woman gestured for the girls to follow her, and led them a short way down the corridor and through a door. They were in a fairly large room, sparsely furnished with a double bed, a chest-of-drawers, and a wardrobe; frugal, but, compared to the room they had just left, a queen's chamber, for it was clean, the bed had a sparkling white sheet, and both the windows were open, though barred by wrought-iron patterned grids.

'It's late,' the woman said to Rita. 'You should get in the bed and sleep now and we'll talk in the morning. I heard that one' – she flicked her thumb towards Asha – 'doesn't speak. Well, she'll have to start. I'm kind but I don't stand for any nonsense. Don't give me any trouble and I won't give you any. Are you hungry? Shall I bring you some food? There's water in the jug over there.' Another flick of her thumb, this time towards the flask and two glasses on a tray. 'Look, I'm tired and I have to go and finish the business with those men so I'm leaving now. I'll talk to you in the morning. You'll find nightdresses in the top drawer.' She pointed to the chest-of-drawers.

She was gone, and Rita's reply, that indeed she was hungry, they were both hungry, and could she have something to eat, died on her lips. They key turned in the lock.

Rita sighed and, assuming there would be a breakfast within a few hours, first helped a passive Asha out of her sari and into one of the nightdresses the woman had indicated. While doing so she had the perfect opportunity to see, for the first time, the three bloodied welts across the thin back.

The vicious witch, Rita thought angrily. People like her ought to be publicly flogged. One of the wounds seemed to be infected;

it ought to be dressed properly but Rita knew she could not bring their caretaker back. Tomorrow would have to do.

Rita then pulled on the other nightdress. It was white, starched and ironed, and smelled strongly of washing powder. Whatever the future held, at least their conditions had drastically improved since yesterday. She touched the golden heart locket at her sternum. Granny, she thought. Mummy, Daddy. Be with me through all this.

It was three a.m. when she glanced at her watch before turning off the light. She walked to the bed where Asha had lain down and now, as far as Rita could gather, was already fast asleep. A minute later Rita, too, was sunk in sleep.

FIFTY-NINE

Sold

Rita awoke to the sound of a key turning, and sat up, still groggy but immediately aware as soon as she saw the woman of last night crossing the room. Behind her followed a maid with a tray, on which were some slices of toast, butter and jam, as well as cups, plates, and a steaming pot. The delicious aroma of coffee drifted in Rita's direction, stimulating the accumulated hunger of the previous day. The maid set the tray down on the table and silently left the room. The woman stayed.

'All right. Take food. I want to have a few words with you. What is your name?'

Rita told her. She sat down at the table and poured herself a cup of coffee. Asha was still asleep. Let her sleep as long as she can, Rita thought.

'And the girl's?'

When Rita told her Asha's name the woman said, 'Is it true she doesn't speak? Why not?'

'I'm sure you know already,' Rita said.

'Don't be rude,' said the woman sharply. 'I told you: don't give me any trouble and I won't give you any trouble. I only know she is speechless, I was told this by our friends last night.'

'They're not my friends,' Rita said, then stopped herself. She did not want to provoke the woman more than necessary. Though she looked exhausted rather than cruel, there was a no-nonsense severity in the eyes which warned Rita not to push it too far.

'She's had a shock,' Rita said, 'and hasn't recovered yet. Can you blame her?'

'Pah! She'll just have to put armour around herself and get on with it. It's survival of the fittest in this trade. This girl – your sister? – doesn't look as if she'll last for long.'

'Not the way she's been whipped, she won't!' Rita retorted. 'I need something to dress her back with, she's wounded, dripping pus.'

'What?' cried the woman, and hurried over to the bedside where Asha still lay in deep sleep. Not worried about waking the girl, she turned her over on to her stomach and pulled at the nightie till her back was bare. She inspected the weals, running her fingers lightly along them.

'Those scoundrels! They never said . . . Well, anyway, she's very beautiful and with a bit of care she will get more beautiful, fill out and so on. A doctor is coming today to look at both of you. But first you have to be bathed and deloused. Both of you stink to high heaven. This is a respectable house, not like that place you came from. We never beat our girls here. If a girl is so recalcitrant she needs to be beaten she is simply passed on to such houses where beatings take place; Mr Rajgopal doesn't stand for any corporal punishment in his houses. He believes in treating the girls kindly, then they will work willingly, for they know they are in a good position. You are very lucky to come here.'

'I'm not a whore,' Rita protested loudly. 'I just came to look after Asha!'

'She's your sister?' the woman asked again. 'Whatever she is, I paid for you both and you both belong to me – that is, to Mr Rajgopal. I'm only his procurer really, I have nothing to do with you – what do I care? I only make sure he gets good quality for price. He trusts me completely you see. I'm good at my job. But it's only a job. Mr Rajgopal is kind though, or at least as kind as

447

any man. I've seen much worse but not many better. Thank your deity you were brought here. But in fact you only have your sister to thank – she is much fairer than you, and much more beautiful, or I would not have paid that price. She was wasted in Kamathipura. A girl like this needs special care and now she will get it – they don't call me Devaki the Blameless for nothing! I would never have bought you but your sister now . . . Perhaps she needs you to start with? Maybe you can help her find her tongue. Mind you, if she doesn't find it within the week it's out she goes, back to Kamathipura, and you with her – head first! We can't have speechless girls here. It's good you speak English, I can do with some girls speaking English. You sound educated as well, that's a good thing. I can get you some excellent escort work. But your sister now, she's the real prize. You don't realize how . . .'

Devaki chattered on as if she hadn't noticed that Rita had stopped eating long ago, and was only fiddling with her food. She had stopped listening too, ever since the words: 'I paid for you both.'

It couldn't be. It just couldn't be. It wasn't possible that she had been sold. She had *volunteered* to come with Asha, for good-ness' sake. She had been set free; she could have gone but had insisted on coming. She knew for a fact that the men had not bought her. She could have left at any time before getting into the car with Asha. She had not been bought; so how then could she have been sold?

But perhaps such logic did not exist in this business.

Slowly, slowly, it dawned on Rita that at some point during the drive between the house in Kamathipura and this house she had changed status. She had been transformed from the self-determined, free individual she thought she was into a com-modity, a marketable ware to be bought and sold at the whim of strangers. And once more Gita was perfectly right: she had rushed in like a fool, where angels fear to tread. She now belonged to Devaki.

SIXTY

Proving Innocence

Up until this point Rita had known no fear. It was as if she had worn an armour of invulnerability, which was the underside of the dauntlessness and artlessness with which she lived her life. She tried to speak, but the words would not come. Devaki, on the other hand, was still talking away, her back to the girls, while sorting the clothing in one of the drawers into two piles.

'These are some of the best shalwars you can find in Bombay; I think you would look good in a rich emerald green. Your sister would look beautiful in any colour, any style. How come she looks so different from you? You don't look at all like sisters. Look, I have found something suitable for you. I want you both to wash your hair now. Afterwards I will put some ointment on it to get rid of the lice. The best thing is shaving off all the hair but that is too extreme in this case. I am putting you in charge of the girl, she doesn't seem capable of bathing herself. The bathroom is through that door. Here's a nice red shalwar for her, but don't get dressed properly until after the lice treatment.'

'Devaki, listen.' Rita had found her voice, and though it seemed, to her, to be little more than a croak, it was determined. 'I told you – I'm not a whore! I stayed with this girl voluntarily in order to look after her. I don't know what's going on but I'm glad you speak English and maybe you can explain to me—'

'I have no time for explanations! It's quite simple. I work for Mr Rajgopal and he will want to have a look at you this afternoon to consider where he will place you. I shall advise him. There are several options but I would strongly suggest that you behave and look your best for him because then you will have a good life in a very good house. You'd better explain to this girl that she should start speaking soon. If she speaks English, that talent, together with her beauty, will mean she can look forward to an excellent career. As for you, you're not bad looking but you don't have her class – I know of a good place for you but you can't expect luxury. I'll have to separate you, of course. Now look . . . No, don't interrupt me. I haven't much time, I have to see to some other girls upstairs. You get her bathed and put on your nighties again for delousing. I am sending a maid with the bottle. You just massage it into the hair and leave it there for ten minutes. It's a special ointment we import from Germany, very efficacious; all the lice and nits are gone afterwards, it's a devil's liquid. When you have done that you are to wash it out properly again, then dry your hair and hers and get dressed. I'll be back in an hour to see how things are. I want you looking lovely for Mr Rajgopal, it's all to your advantage. If I were you I would persuade her to speak now. He has a bad temper sometimes and if he thinks she is being stubborn he might just send her into one of the cheap houses back in Kamathipura. You don't want that. You've been there, you know what the houses are like. Both of you could have a better life but you have to behave sensibly. Then all will be well. So I have to go now. Do what I said and get yourselves cleaned up. You'll have to wake her, she can't sleep all day. I'll be back in an hour.'

When Devaki had left the room Rita walked to the window and looked out; she was trying to assess their chances of escape. Her heart sank as she saw that the house was in the middle of a garden, and that garden was surrounded by a high fence of wire netting. There was an iron gate obviously very securely locked, and two sentries in khaki uniforms sat on metal folding chairs just inside the gate to the side of the gravel driveway, smoking and chatting. Though they weren't very alert at the moment, Rita could tell at a glance that they would be armed, and that they would be vigilant should she ever manage to leave the house. From this window, at least, there was no escape. It was firmly barred.

Her panic on realizing that she had, in Devaki's eyes at least, been sold into prostitution had settled into a quiet dread and stimulated a wary, high frequency of thought. She had plunged into this predicament without thinking, following only her instinct. The moment Asha had clung to her in fear she had known she could not leave the girl to the wolves. There had been no premeditation to her actions, and this was the first time she had to consider the situation and ponder how to react.

Since there could be no physical escape for the moment it seemed to Rita prudent to do as Devaki said. It did not seem as if she and Asha were expected to begin work immediately; in that case going along with Devaki was a play for time. Sooner or later a situation would turn up which would make flight possible; until then it would be best to keep Devaki's guard down. And as far as flight was concerned, she would play it by ear. That was Rita's strength: she would wait for the right moment, trusting that at that moment the right means of escape would present itself. More than that she could not do. And anyway, she was dying for a shower.

Her mind firmly made up, she walked over to the bed, gently placed her hand on Asha's shoulder and shook it. 'Asha,' she said softly. 'Wake up.'

Her head was still tingling from the delousing liquid. The instructions on the bottle had been in German, but she had done what Devaki said and doused first Asha's then her own hair generously, left the liquid to soak in, and then washed it out. In Asha's rinse water there had been several dead lice, in her own none, but it had felt good to know that if any had been hiding there, they were now well and truly wiped out. Nothing could survive that devil's brew. And she had to admit it – the emerald shalwar kameez suited her well. Asha looked simply radiant – if one did not look at her eyes. She wore crimson silk, the kameez embroidered all the way up a front seam, with a pattern of tiny mirrors sewn into the neckline. She looked like a princess.

Asha had submitted willingly to Rita's handling of her. On awakening, she had followed the bathing, shampooing and delousing routine without a word. Afterwards she had allowed herself to be fed, and had drunk from the cup held to her lips. She had stepped into the shalwar Rita had held out for her, right foot, left foot, holding on to Rita's shoulders for balance, allowed the drawstring to be tied; she had raised her arms and let Rita pull the kameez over her head and fasten the hooks and eyes at the shoulder. Her hair had been blow-dried and brushed, so that it fell in a thick black curtain halfway down her back. Now she sat in the chair with her hands in her lap and stared at the wall, and her eyes, large almond eyes that should be like brilliant black sequins shining with spirit, were dead. And all of Rita's efforts to catch those eyes and fan a little spark into them simply failed, like flies hitting against a pane of glass and falling stunned.

Rita tried to keep up a lively, cheerful banter. 'Asha, I think it's going to be all right. We're much better off here, and if I keep my wits about me I'm sure we'll be able to get out soon. Don't worry. I'm taking you back to your daddy, Asha! And look how clean it is here, and we get fed properly. I think your luck has turned, Asha. But I don't know how long it will take. We have to meet the owner of this place in a while, and somehow impress him. I don't want to push you, you can take your own time, but it would be much better if you would speak a word or two – just to keep him from shunting us back into Kamathipura. I'm sure you can do that. Say good morning, and try to smile. Just to let him know you speak English; it's a play for time because I don't know when and I don't know how I'm going to get us out, but I will. That's a promise!'

But all Asha did was stare, and her lips did not so much as twitch.

Rita was beginning to despair of ever coaxing a reaction from Asha when once again the key turned in the lock and Devaki entered, followed by the same maid who had brought their breakfast.

'Oh, you look lovely! Very lovely, both of you! Who would have guessed it – though I certainly knew that beneath all the grime there were two little jewels hiding! Mr Rajgopal will be extremely pleased with you – this girl is simply delightful. She has a very rare beauty! I can imagine he might even want her for his exclusive escort service – but she would have to be speaking perfectly by then. Have you persuaded her to speak?'

'Not yet,' Rita admitted, 'but I'm sure I will.'

Everything in her was rebelling against the role she knew it was necessary to play. She wanted to lash out at Devaki as she had once lashed out against Marilyn; to dig at her eyes, scratch at her face, bite and kick her before taking flight; but she knew she had only one hand, and had to play it carefully. The time would come; and the means would not be violent ones, but wily ones. She had lost the battle with Marilyn. She would not lose this battle, even if it meant, for a while, playing the mild meek pussycat while a tiger crouched within, waiting to attack . . . But no. There would be no attack. The situation called for cunning.

Devaki impatiently beckoned the maid forward and said something to her in another language.

'What you both need is some jewellery. I will have some costume jewellery sent up. What's that?' She reached out and fingered the heart around Rita's neck. 'It's not terribly pretty, it looks old. You'll have to take it off. It's not worth much, is it?' Her eyes narrowed.

'No, it's only gold-plated, not solid. It's an heirloom, you see. It hasn't any commercial value.'

'Well, if it is of any value at all I would take it off and hide it if I were you – that's my tip. Because Mr Rajgopal will want it – you need to pay him back the price he paid for you, you know.'

'Do you think I could buy my freedom with it? And Asha's?'

'With that?' Devaki laughed. 'It might be worth a few thousand rupees but that is peanuts to Mr Rajgopal. I know a little about jewellery and I can tell he won't be impressed – it's certainly not enough to offset the amount he intends to make with you. If you like, you can give it to me. I will keep it for you.'

'Why should I trust you?'

'Oh, I am very trustworthy. Don't think because I am working in this trade I am a thief. You won't find a more honest person than me working in the trade. In fact, I am a very decent woman, my origins are extremely respectable. I used to be a maid for a very high-class English lady. I have a good education, my parents sent me to an English Medium School! And I am a very kind woman; I have never hit any girl working for me in all my life. I only happened into this trade through bad luck.'

Rita had realized that if there was anything Devaki liked doing, it was talking. The woman seemed under a compulsion to talk, talk, talk, and Rita realized that the more she kept her talking, the more information she would get out of her, and the better she would be able to figure out an escape.

'What happened?' she asked boldly.

'Well, it was that dastardly son of the Englishwoman, James was his name. Very good looking! I was a young woman of eighteen at the time, very impressionable. He coaxed me into acting against my conscience – I was a very innocent girl, what did I know of the ways of men? What could I do to repulse the advances of a young Englishman? He was younger than me, fifteen, sixteen. Well, all went well for a time but what did I know about the facts of life? Before I knew it I was expecting a child and that woman threw me out. What could I do? I could not return to my village – what a disgrace for my parents! I found a Catholic home where I could stay till my daughter was born. They wanted me to give her up for adoption but I would never do that – give up my own flesh and blood! Never. So I put her in the orphanage and went to look for work. Well, what work could I find after that disgrace – me, a woman on her own in such a big city? I was a fallen woman, and I fell still further – how could I not? What a terrible life I was forced to lead! But the worst of it was losing my daughter. Ay! Those nuns found out what I was doing and wouldn't let me near her. They wanted me to sign some papers to take her away from me permanently – in fact they stole her from me! But I wasn't doing that! And when she was six I stole her back.'

Devaki opened a plastic box. It was brimful of hair-styling apparatus: brushes, combs, ribbons, grips, everything one could possibly need.

'I shall make this hair really beautiful,' she said. 'You won't believe what magic my hands can perform!'

'So how old is your daughter now?' Rita prompted. She might have been able to work out the approximate age but always avoided any kind of arithmetic, and anyway, she had to keep the woman chatting.

'About the age of this girl, or a year or two older,' said Devaki. 'Perhaps not as lovely but to a mother her daughter is always beautiful! She is fair too, of course – her father was an Englishman, after all. This girl is also half-breed, I suspect. You must tell me her story one of these days, when you are fully a member of the family. I like to hear all your stories – I am like your mother, I really care about my girls.'

'If you really cared about them you'd let them go. You wouldn't be doing this at all!'

'But my girls are happy! I can tell you're new at this trade – any girl who's lived for a time in Kamathipura would give her eyes to work for me! You are very ungrateful. I can tell this girl here thinks differently – she can appreciate the difference.' Devaki was now vigorously brushing Asha's hair, and obviously taking great pleasure in it.

'But would you let your own daughter work like this? If she's Asha's age, do you also have her doing this kind of work?'

The woman glanced at Rita and scowled. 'Of course she isn't working like this! Don't even suggest it! That's one of the reasons I used all my cunning to advance in my profession, so I could move out of that place I was living in and find a more respectable lodging for me and my daughter. But rents are so expensive in Bombay – all I have is a small room and it's quite near Kamathipura. She goes to a normal school. I would never let her work this way – of course not. Though I have had several offers for her.

'My daughter is very lovely. She is also educated, and in a year's time she will have finished school.'

'What will she do then?'

'Well, I have to try and find a proper husband for her but it is difficult – I want her to marry decently but how can I prevent the boy's parents from finding out what I do for a living? That is my great sorrow. It is hard enough raising a child alone, but finding a husband for a daughter is near to impossible for a single mother and especially trying for me. But everybody has their dreams.'

Devaki twisted a strand of Asha's hair into a long curl and clipped it to the top of her head. She picked up a second strand and did the same, till only one strand was left. This she began to plait with quick, deft fingers. Every now and then she stopped to push the bangles up her arm. Why doesn't she just take them off, Rita wondered vaguely, since they all keep falling down anyway?

'What is your dream?' she asked.

'My dream? Well, I don't usually tell this to my girls but between you and me, for my daughter's sake it would be necessary to start all over again, in some other city where I can be anonymous. Lucknow: that is my dream! My native village is in the vicinity of Lucknow and I know the city well. A nice clean little flat for me and my daughter. It doesn't have to be big, but respectable. I don't even mind working as a housekeeper for some rich family – I would not earn as much as I do here but I would make good contacts that way. My daughter could also find work as a maid – I would train her myself. But hairdressing is my real dream. I have a gift for hair-styling. I would like to style the hair of brides – I'm sure I could make a business out of it! And my final dream is to see my daughter as a bride herself, and style her hair for her own wedding! But it is only a dream. How can I start anew? I am trying to save every paise I have but life is costly here – money just fritters away and I am struggling even to survive. How can I save anything? You see, we all have our problems, and everyone's problem is a mountain to that person, so you shouldn't complain. Now please don't talk to me any more, I have to concentrate. When I'm finished you will see why.'

And Rita did see why. Asha's hair, when finished, was truly fit for a bride: smooth and sleek around her face, and at the back a sculpture of interwoven plaits which managed to be sophisticated and simple at once, every strand placed in exactly the right position, not a single hair out of place.

Pleased with herself, Devaki pushed the bangles up her arms again and turned to Rita with a smile. 'See! That's how Mr Rajgopal likes hair to be styled. Now it's your turn.'

The mysterious Mr Rajgopal came after lunch, and his visit was short and businesslike. He was a medium-sized, stocky man in a white shirt and silk tie who looked more like a banker than the boss of a chain of brothels, and his perusal of the girls was formal and impersonal. He had them stand before him, walk a few paces, and turn around; then he exchanged a few words in English with Rita – an interview for a job, Rita thought, and though I definitely do not want this job, I'd better act as if I do. So she answered his questions politely and accurately. He seemed to be giving her a sort of intelligence test – perhaps he was testing her general knowledge and her ability to carry on a reasonably intelligent conversation? Then it was Asha's turn.

'How old are you?' Mr Rajgopal said.

Asha, who looked the picture of loveliness, kept her head bent to the ground.

Devaki looked anxiously at Rita as if beseeching her for help.

'Answer me, girl!' Mr Rajgopal's voice contained a hint of impatience. Asha kept her silence.

'You said she speaks English,' said Mr Rajgopal accusingly to Devaki.

'Yes, yes, she does. It's just that she has a problem right now. She was treated badly, you see, and is still afraid to speak.'

'Well, if she's just a body she will have to go back where she came from,' said Mr Rajgopal. 'I could use this one's brains in her body—' In mid-sentence he stopped speaking English and he and Devaki had a long conversation, at times heated, in their own language.

Finally Mr Rajgopal left, without a further word to or even a glance at the girls. Ten minutes later Devaki returned. Her face was lined with worry.

'He isn't satisfied,' she said. 'If she doesn't speak he can't use her. He says he will give her a week. He wants you to work on her and persuade her to speak normally. If not, she will be sent back. He wants to keep you though. You will go to another house in Bombay at the end of that week, and either she comes with you, and the two of you can stay together, or she is sent back. So it's up to you. Now take off those good clothes and put them away – the doctor is coming in an hour's time. You have to take an AIDS test as well. Until the results come out you will have to take precautions. But Mr Rajgopal has kindly given you a week's holiday in advance – isn't it kind of him! Luckily Mr Rajgopal didn't see her wounds; but by the time she starts work they will be healed. So I am leaving you now. You must use all your influence to get her to speak. Otherwise she will go back to some hell-hole. For you, it is different. You will go to another house like this, nice and clean. Though the woman in charge there is not as friendly as I am – rather bad-tempered, in fact I have told her again and again not to be, but she can't change her ways. I will be sorry to lose you, I like you, but Mr Rajgopal is the boss and the boss makes the decisions. I am only his employee.'

'Asha,' Rita whispered when they were alone. 'You heard, you understood, I know you did. I'm going to get us out of here, sooner or later, but I don't know if I can manage it in a week. After a week they will separate us if you're not speaking, and if they do that it's over. I'll never find you again. So please, dear, please try hard to speak! Even if it's only a few words . . . just to let him know you can and will do so. I'm not rushing you. I know it will come in its own time.'

Two days later Asha still hadn't said a word.

'Asha, darling, can't you even look at me, and smile? Just to show me you understood, and will make the effort? You don't want to go back to Kamathipura, do you?' There was a slight pressure on the hand Rita was holding. But no smile. No flicker of acknowledgement in the eyes. No word.

'Asha, I haven't tried to pressure you. I know you need time to recover; I know it's been terrible but this is your only chance. You don't want to go back there, do you? Who knows where he'll send you to? He's perfectly ruthless but he's a hundred times better than anything you'll ever experience in Kamathipura. Please, please, please make the effort! He's coming tomorrow to interview you again. Please speak to him! It's your last, your very last chance! Come, speak to me now. Tell me something. A word – just a word! Let me know you've understood, and will try to save yourself! Oh Asha! Please!'

Rita fell to her knees, bent her head over Asha's lap, and wept real tears. Holding the girl's hands between her own, she pleaded for just a flicker of recognition. But nothing came.

'Has she spoken?' Devaki walked across the room and slammed the plastic box on the table. She already knew the answer. The girls were bathed and beautifully dressed as a week previously, Rita this time in a lemon-coloured shalwar kameez, Asha in a rich royal blue.

Rita shook her head glumly. 'No. She hasn't said a word.'

'Well, Mr Rajgopal will be here in an hour and she'd better speak then, or she's in trouble. I thought you'd have some influence on her. How could you fail? She's a very bad girl. We should have used other methods to get her to speak – but I told you, I never flog my girls. Well, she'll have to learn her lesson. She won't get a chance like this again.' She turned to Asha. 'I know you understand what I'm saying, girl. If you fail the test you'll be back in some rat-infested hole by tonight! I'm going to have to bring you there personally! What a waste – such beauty!'

Devaki's annoyance revealed itself in the roughness with which she styled Asha's hair – more than once the girl winced when Devaki pulled a little too hard, stuck in a pin a little too sharply. But she held her silence.

The key turned in the lock. One last time Rita took Asha's hand and whispered in her ear. 'Asha, please. It's for your own good. Otherwise they'll separate us. You don't want to be separated from me, do you? I know you don't. They'll tear you away from me. It's not like last week, when I could persuade them to take me along with you. This time it's really serious.'

Asha's fingers moved. Rita knew she understood. She still had not spoken a word, but there was still Mr Rajgopal's test. She would speak now. She had to. There was no other way.

The door opened, Mr Rajgopal entered, followed by Devaki.

Mr Rajgopal was curt and to the point. He did not waste time with preliminaries. 'So. What is your name?'

Asha hung her head. Mr Rajgopal looked at Rita and raised his eyebrows. 'You have failed? She won't even answer that one simple question?'

'Ask her again,' Rita pleaded. 'I'm sure she will . . .'

'What is your name, girl?'

No answer.

'Very well. I'm giving you one last chance. It's a simple question, I expect a simple answer. Your name. What – is – your – name?'

Asha continued to hang her head. Rita held her breath, waiting for the word that would bring salvation. She felt the girl's fingers quiver in her own; she knew Asha was dying of fear. But it was as if she had, literally, lost her tongue. There was no answer.

Mr Rajgopal accepted defeat with grace. 'Very well.' He looked at his watch. 'Devaki, I have a meeting. I am sending the car back for you. Bring her to Baboolal's place. The other girl you can take with you, you know where she's going to. That's it – it's a waste, but I can't have insubordination. Perhaps in a year's time she'll be punished enough and she'll want to speak to save herself. I have to go now. Come with me.'

Without looking at the girls again he left the room. Rita felt like screaming at Asha. Instead, she turned to her and took her in her arms. The little body was trembling all over, as with an ague. She seemed to be crying, tearlessly, silently. Most of all, silently.

SIXTY-ONE

Back to Kamathipura . . .

The car slid through the open gates and out into the street. The inside of Rita's mouth was dry, her heart pounding so heavily she could feel it like footsteps echoing in an empty house. Her very breath seemed to have stopped. Asha, next to her on the back seat, had taken her hand and was gripping it for dear life. Asha knew exactly what was going on – of that there could be no mistake. *Why* had she not spoken? Surely it couldn't be so difficult, no matter what trauma she was going through, simply to say her name? Rita could only think with terror of the future. There could be no doubt that the house they were leaving was one of the best kept and most humane in this trade in the whole of Bombay, and that Devaki's insistence that she was among the kindest of madams was true. In fact, Rita had grown almost fond of Devaki during the past week, and dreaded moving to another house. She would escape, she had no doubt as to that – but when, and how? And most importantly, she had lost Asha. Asha would disappear again into the bog of Kamathipura, and would never again – Rita was certain of this – resurface.

Devaki, sitting on the back seat next to a very stiff Asha, leaned forward to address Rita. 'She's a very stupid girl,' she said. 'She could so easily have saved herself. I never saw such folly in my whole life. But what to do? I am sorry for her though. I am quite fond of her – she reminds me so much of my own daughter. I feel for her as if it was my own daughter I am taking to Kamathipura.'

'Devaki, if you care for her even a little, why don't you just stop the car and let her out? You can say she escaped somehow – I'll stay with you and help make up a story. Please – just let her out, not me. I can look after myself.'

'What! And lose my job?' Devaki was astonished at the suggestion. 'One thing about me – I am reliable! And I need this job. I may not be saving much, but still my bank account is growing a little every month. Do you think I would sacrifice my future and my daughter's future for a stranger!'

She pushed the bangles up her arm and adjusted the dupatta of her sari. She turned away from the girls; Rita could see her fumbling with her shoulder and saw that she had removed a safety pin and was about to pin the dupatta back into place.

And she knew the moment had come. The moment she had been waiting for all this week, but which had never arisen because, in that heavily guarded house, the risk would have been too great – and she could not trust Devaki in that situation. She knew this moment had been given to her on a platter – she and Asha, virtually alone with Devaki, no armed guards, just a driver who, as far as she could see, did not have a gun or any other weapon.

'Devaki,' she said. 'Could I borrow that pin? Just for a moment?'

'This pin? What do you need a pin for?'

'I'll show you in a moment.' Rita had already reached behind her neck for the clasp of her locket, fumbling with her thumb-nail to open it. Devaki, mostly out of curiosity – for what could she be wanting with a harmless safety pin? – had turned again to look behind her. With the point of the safety pin Rita pressed into the heart of the bottommost flower in the tiny chain of flowers around the golden heart. The heart opened like a book; its inside was hollow. Rita tipped it upside down on the palm of her hand, and held out her hand to Devaki.

'Here. I will buy our freedom. Freedom for all of us.'

On her hand was a tiny, sparkling jewel. Rita was sure the driver could not speak English, but nevertheless she lowered her voice and spoke in low, coaxing tones to Devaki.

'It's real. It's mine – my grandmother gave it to me. I had it polished back home and brought it along on this trip just in case. I've had it valued: it's worth a small fortune; it'll go a long way in India. It's yours – if you let us go. We can all get out of this car right now and walk away from Mr Rajgopal for ever. You can go to Lucknow, start again with your daughter. All you have to do is stop the car.'

'You've had this with you all this time? A real diamond?' Devaki's voice was hushed, awed.

'Yes. I would have offered it to you before but I couldn't be sure – there were so many guards in that house, they would never have let us out! I wanted to be alone with you. Now there's only the driver – what can he do?'

Devaki did not answer. She reached out her forefinger, as if to touch the diamond, but Rita withdrew her hand quickly, closing her fingers over it. Her heart was beating furiously. She knew the risk – which was why she had not acted before. If she had offered Devaki the diamond back in the house, what guarantee would there have been that she would not have simply taken the stone and left the girls in their predicament? Rita had not wanted to take the risk. Now there was also a risk. Devaki could still take the diamond, and command the driver to drop Asha off at Kamathipura – and that would be the end.

'I'll give it to you when we're all three out in the street,' Rita said, her fist closed tightly over the gem. 'Not before.'

Devaki did not hesitate one moment more. She spoke a few words to the driver, who bobbed his head in acquiescence.

'The doors lock automatically,' she said. 'He has to unlock them for you. I told him we are going for a meal at a restaurant at the next corner. He's a stupid man, and I'm his superior – he will obey me, though it's an unusual request. But he knows I don't fool around. So he'll let you out. But how do I know you won't just run away with the diamond and leave me with nothing?'

'Because you were kind to us. You can trust me – you know you can. You let us out of the car, and I will give you the diamond. You have to trust me.'

The car stopped in front of a restaurant. There was a click as the locks were released. Rita opened her door, and she and Asha stepped out onto the pavement. Devaki's door opened too, and she climbed out to stand beside them.

'Now we all walk calmly towards the restaurant. He'll have to drive away, he's going to park somewhere nearby and I told him to pick us up in half an hour. When he comes he won't find anybody!' Devaki could hardly hide her mirth at this thought; she placed a hand over her mouth to suppress a giggle. 'He's very faithful to Mr Rajgopal but he has to obey me. Come on, let's go. Walk in front of me as if I'm the boss!'

They made their way towards the restaurant; the car slid past them.

'All right. He's gone. Now – the diamond!' Devaki proffered her hand. Rita held her closed fist above it, opened her fingers, and let the diamond fall into Devaki's palm.

'Thank you. I like you girls! I wish you all the best. I hope she recovers. I would not like to think of her back in Kamathipura. I am not a beast, you know. I too am a victim. My life has not been easy; I only tried to make the best of it and I hope I do not treat people too badly.'

'I like you too, Devaki!' said Rita. 'I think the trade is losing a little piece of humanity today. But I wish you well. And your daughter.'

They namasted; then, simultaneously, they turned around. Devaki walked in one direction, Rita took Asha's hand and walked in another.

She had no idea where she was. Traffic snorted and screeched around her, exhaust fumes belched, the pavement was filled with a stream of humanity which parted at their coming and closed again behind them. She decided to take a taxi. Devaki had given

465

her back her little shoulder bag; she rummaged inside it. The brothel-keeper in Kamathipura had taken all her money except for a few stray coins. She counted them: three rupees: That would come nowhere near to paying for a taxi, but once at Ananda Nagar she could get Kamal to pay the driver, or Subhadhai. She stopped to hail a taxi, but they were too near the corner and there was no room for one to stop.

They walked on. It was unlikely that she was anywhere near Ananda Nagar, she realized. It would most likely take at least an hour to get there by taxi. She was bursting with happiness; she wanted to shout from the rooftops that she was free, and Asha too. She felt like dancing in the street. She wanted to tell Kamal; she could hardly wait to tell Kamal. She had to tell Kamal; now, right now!

'Come,' she said to Asha, and led her to one of the shops lining the pavement. It was a bakery; behind the counter was a man, bent over a newspaper spread open on the countertop, reading.

'Good afternoon,' said Rita. The man looked up. 'Can I use your telephone?' The man stared at her blankly, uncomprehendingly.

'Telephone, telephone,' said Rita, and made the appropriate gestures. The man bobbed his head and gestured towards an old black telephone behind the counter, at the back of the shop. Rita rummaged in her bag and found her little black address book. She opened it at Kamal's name and dialled the number.

She could hardly breathe as she heard the telephone ringing at the other end. It seemed to ring interminably. Somebody had to be home; please let somebody be home! What if it was Subhadhai? She wouldn't understand; but surely she would recognize Rita's voice? Perhaps she could get hold of Kamal, wherever he was, and . . . Rita jumped: there was a click on the line as somebody picked up the phone.

'Hello?' said a woman's voice.

'Hel— *Isabelle*!'

'Rita! Rita, is it you? Is it really you? Oh my God, where are you? Are you free? What—?'

'Isabelle, I'm free, and so's Asha, we're coming in a taxi! But what are you doing there?'

'I came back to Bombay as soon as I heard,' said Isabelle, almost sobbing with relief. 'Oh, Rita, I was so *worried*! I rang once just to say hello and Kamal told me and I came right away, we've been so *terrified*! And Rita, oh, I can hardly speak, I . . .'

'Look, don't worry, I'm on my way. We can talk when I get there. You'll have to pay for the taxi when we arrive. See you in an hour or so!'

Rita replaced the receiver, thanked the man, and laid the coins she had on the counter. He bobbed his head again and returned to his newspaper. Rita and Asha went out into the sunlight to find a taxi home.

It took nearly two hours to reach Ananda Nagar; Asha had fallen asleep and Rita had to shake her awake as she recognized the landmarks that told her they were almost there. They turned the last corner into the street. Rita saw a familiar figure standing outside the gates: Isabelle, who had apparently come out to wait for her.

The taxi stopped on the opposite side of the road. Rita opened the door and got out, and helped Asha out. Isabelle must have seen her immediately, because her cry of greeting was so loud Rita heard it even above the roar of traffic. Isabelle was waving wildly, almost jumping in excitement.

Rita waved back. Isabelle, it seemed, could not wait. She plunged out into the street.

'*Isabelle!*' Rita screamed. 'Look out!'

The screech of brakes seemed to last an eternity; it ended with a silence a fraction of a second too long, followed by a terrified scream, the scream swallowed by a thunderous crash and the smashing of glass . . . and more silence. An endless silence.

Then another scream; Rita seemed far away, wondering who it was who was screaming, till she realized it was she herself, and she was running through the traffic herself. Two cars, their bonnets smashed into each other, blocked her path. She had to get around them. She did not dare to; afraid of what she would see. Afraid of what she was not hearing – afraid of Isabelle's scream which was no more.

A woman's body, lying motionless on the street.

A pool of blood.

Isabelle.

More silence. Crowds gathering; people talking without speaking; flapping soundless goldfish mouths.

A mind like space.

A young girl staring.

A young woman with the heartbeat of a drummer gone mad, drumming in the vacuum of a space called Isabelle.

Above the commotion two pairs of eyes met.

Kamal had heard the pandemonium on the street and come out to see what had happened. Even before he saw the accident he saw Asha, standing still as a statue on the opposite pavement. His heart missed a beat; then he raised a hand, telling her to stay where she was.

He had pictured the moment he would first see her over and over again. Every day, every night, every minute for the last six months. The moment had finally come. Kamal, not even aware of the drama taking place in the street before him, not seeing the body and the blood, not hearing the screams and the loud chattering voices, walked through the stalling traffic as if in a dream, his arms held open to gather her to himself, the way it had always been in his imagination.

He walked toward her, smiling, with arms that would soon close around her.

Asha stared at him. Her eyes widened with panic; she shrank away.

SIXTY-TWO

Yellow Shoes

'Miss Maraj?'

Rita jumped, spilling her coffee. She looked up at the nurse. 'Yes?'

'Your sister has opened her eyes.' The nurse was smiling appropriately, brown eyes soft in a plump round face. 'Would you like to come with me?'

The puddle of coffee spread across the white Formica table surface, reached the edge and slipped over. Suddenly it seemed to Rita she had all the time in the world. After waiting here or at Isabelle's bedside for twenty-four hours the opening of eyes now seemed strangely irrelevant. Just as her own tiredness was irrelevant. Just as the whole world out there, beyond the walls of Dr Khan senior's private clinic was irrelevant. It was all irrelevant. Isabelle was going to die. She gestured wearily at the coffee, now dripping in quick time to the floor.

'I should mop this up . . .'

'Oh, just leave that. The maid will get it. Come along.'

Rita nodded and followed the nurse up the stairs to the private ward where Isabelle was to spend her last hours on earth.

Isabelle had not given in easily. In the hours Rita had sat

watching by her side, she had struggled for expression. Sometimes her lips had moved, and mumbled phrases and dislocated words had given Rita cause to hope that consciousness was near.

'The coach. Let me come too! Please!' Isabelle had said in an ancient, creaking voice, and Rita cringed, remembering how she had denied Isabelle a ride in Jaws of Death. Now she would personally drive Isabelle around the world in a white coach with six horses, if she would recover.

Then, 'I don't like those. I like the yellow ones.' That spoken loudly, petulantly, the old Isabelle.

'I'm bound to win. I *have* to.' That whispered, barely audible. A reference to the beauty contest?

'Shoes.'

'*Pas de deux. Pas de deux.*'

'Shoes,' again, and again. 'Shoes.'

Then, suddenly, and very clearly, 'Santa Claus. It's all Rita's fault. Wicked, wicked Rita!'

That was when Rita had left Isabelle's bedside, to find her comfort in coffee. Guilt, a whole new mountain of it, would be Isabelle's legacy to her if and when she died. The spectre of that guilt lurked in every shadow of the deserted canteen, lit only by a naked bulb courted by two dozen fluttering moths.

Now, Isabelle's head was wrapped in a bandage, framing a face so fragile, vulnerable, Rita's eyes misted over. She sat on the chair next to Isabelle's head, took the hand groping for her, and leaned over. Isabelle's eyes were transparent. They searched Rita's as if trying to find some harbour, a place to rest. They were no longer blank screens but soft and yielding pools. For the first time in their lives, Rita and Isabelle met each other.

'Rita . . .' It was little more than a croak.

'Don't talk, darling, it'll only hurt. Just be still.'

Isabelle struggled, as if trying to raise herself up on her elbows. 'I have to . . . Rita, I'm going to die.'

'No, you're not. You're not going to die. Isabelle, you have to fight and you'll live. Don't say those things. And, Isabelle, Marilyn's coming! She's on a plane right now. She'll be here tomorrow.'

'Don't let her come. Let me just die.'

'You're *not* dying!'

'But I am. I know it. I nearly . . . went already. But I have to . . . tell you. I'm so glad you're free. I came back . . . to tell you.'

'Yes, yes, Isabelle, you already told me. But I don't believe you. I know you're going to live, I just know it.'

Isabelle tried to shake her head but the pain of doing so caused her to wince. 'No. I must tell you . . . I remember now. The *shoes*! Oh, Rita, forgive me!'

'There's nothing to forgive.'

The fingers around her hand tightened in impatience. The voice was little more than a whisper. Rita had to bend low to understand.

'Yes. There is. It wasn't your fault. I made you believe it was your fault but it wasn't. Marilyn made me say it was your fault but it wasn't.'

Isabelle's eyes were still locked into her own. Their eloquence was devastating.

'I don't understand.' Rita's voice matched Isabelle's, also a whisper, barely audible. 'What do you mean, Isabelle?'

'The accident, my head . . . it wasn't your fault. Marilyn took me away to try on some yellow shoes . . . You didn't notice. And then . . . Then she met Mrs . . . I forgot who. A friend. And started to chat and forgot about me . . . I heard Santa's bell . . . and left her to find Santa . . . and then . . .'

Isabelle's eyes seemed to grope within Rita's soul, searching for rejection, accusation, condemnation . . . and forgiveness.

'Marilyn told me never to tell you about the shoes. Never, never, never, she told me. She . . . threatened me. If you say you were with me I'll leave you and go away and never come back, she said. Rita, I was so afraid, I did what she said. And she said it so many times that finally I believed her and I thought it was your fault though somewhere inside me I knew it wasn't, it was hers. And I knew I was awful but you were so good to me when I was awful. You forgave me everything because you thought it was your fault when I was bad . . . It was so easy to get my way

471

with you after that! . . . And then I got tummy-aches, headaches
– the pains were real, I promise! Terrible pain. Like a punishment.
Because I knew . . . I'd forgotten but somewhere inside me I knew
and I remember everything now.'

The last words were almost gasped. Exhausted, Isabelle closed
her eyes. The hand around Rita's relaxed. The words shot through
Rita: she's dying! She shook her sister's arm as gently and as
fiercely as she could.

'Isabelle! Isabelle don't go!'

Isabelle's eyes opened. The lips moved. The eyes closed. '. . . so
tired . . .'

'Isabelle, you can't go! It's all right, I don't care what happened,
I love you! You were only a child! *Isabelle!*'

Again the eyes flickered open. '. . . had to tell you. Glad.
Couldn't go . . .'

'Isabelle! Don't go!'

'. . . without telling you.'

Rita wanted to call again but the words choked her and she
could only shake her head in anguish. It was palpable . . . Isabelle
was drifting away. Rita closed her own eyes.

'Rita!'

The voice was startlingly loud, no longer a whisper. Clear and
precise.

'This is the moment, Rita, this is the most important moment
. . . Everything leads up to this moment. Everything has to be
put right before this moment. It's all about that. Nothing else.
Putting things right. I couldn't go . . . as a bitch.'

There were no more words. The eyes never opened again.

SIXTY-THREE

Kamal's Farewell

Kamal came home late that night. Rita had been listening for him; she had expected him much earlier and had stayed up late but he hadn't come and now it was past midnight and she had not slept a wink. She heard the creaking of the gate as he entered, low voices as he spoke a few words to the guard and then the door opening. She was halfway down the stairs before he looked up and saw her. She was barefoot, and wore a long yellow cotton nightdress. Her hair was dishevelled from all the tossing and turning but she had not waited to make herself presentable.

Kamal stopped when he saw her and they stood for several moments not speaking, because in the silence everything was said and there were no words to bridge the gap.

Kamal was the first to speak. 'I'm sorry, Rita. About Isabelle.'

Rita shrugged and looked away. She knew he was sorry; he'd said so on the telephone.

'But you've got Asha back,' said Rita, and she couldn't keep the bitterness out of her voice. For she had lost Asha *and* Isabelle.

'Yes, and no!'

'What d'you mean, no? You've got her back. You got what you wanted, didn't you?'

'Yes, and I wanted to say thank you for all you've done. Ever since Gita came back that night – was it only a week ago? – and told me, that you'd actually volunteered to go with Asha, I've been marvelling about you. It's been a terrible week, worse than the six months before this, because there wasn't just Asha to worry about, there was you. So, from the bottom of my heart, thank you.'

'Don't mention it. But you shouldn't be thanking me. I did it for Asha, not for you. I couldn't let her be taken away again.'

'I know – but still I have to thank you.'

'Well, anyway, you've got her back and you can start your new life together.'

'No.'

'What do you mean, no?' Rita said again.

'Asha doesn't want me. She doesn't need me. I realized that right from the beginning. She's had enough of men . . . she won't even let me touch her! She won't speak to me!'

'Oh, that,' said Rita, shrugging. 'She'll recover, don't worry. You have to win her trust. It might take time, but you'll win through in the end. Just like I won through. But she won't talk to me, either. That'll take longer, I suppose. Just be patient, and persevere. I think you should take her away; go to some nice place in the country. Or the beach, a place where she can recover slowly.'

'No. That's not what she needs. It's not me she needs at all. It's her mother.'

'Her mother?' *Caroline?* Rita started, then relaxed. 'Oh. You mean her Indian mother.'

'Yes. First thing is to get her to Sundari as soon as possible. Get her home. I'm sending her tomorrow. It's where she wants to be, where she belongs.'

'You're sending her away?'

'Yes. I've been stupid. So stupid. Only thinking of myself. I thought once we rescued her I could make up for the past. Be a

474

father, give her back everything she never had. Make up to her for the years of neglect. But it's not to be that way. I knew it the moment I saw her. There's no way I can turn back the clock. All I can do is make some arrangement for Sundari to have her own house and Asha to return there and live a normal family life again. As far as possible. She doesn't know me. Who am I to her? Why should she want me?'

'But she wrote to *you* when she was in trouble!'

'Yes, but only because she realized her mother wasn't getting her letters. Or couldn't help her. I was a last resort – the only other person she could turn to. It didn't mean anything. Nothing personal, I mean. And now she's safe again the only one who can really help her is her mother. So that's the next step: Sundari's got to have her own home and Asha will be with her. And as for me . . . I'll go back to being an absentee father. It's the only way she knows me. I send the money, write the letters. That's all she expects of me.'

'And . . . and you . . . ?'

'You see,' Kamal said. 'I have to go.'

Kamal took her hand, squeezed it, and then let it go. Rita let him; it hung limp through it all. His eyes met hers again. 'Rita, I . . . Come, let's go in the kitchen and sit down. We have to talk.'

They sat opposite each other at the table and above their heads yet another naked bulb burned – Rita felt like a prisoner being interviewed in the visitors' room, not like a woman in touching distance from her beloved. She was cold. She shivered. Something was wrong, badly wrong, but she didn't know what and she couldn't mend it.

'Go . . . where? And why?' Rita asked. She could hardly bring out the words. Her throat was dry. She drew back her hands, which had been resting on the bare scrubbed wood of the kitchen table: they were suddenly cold. She placed them under her armpits and hugged herself, her crossed arms a shield against whatever it was Kamal was about to disclose.

'Rita. Don't think I don't know . . . I don't feel. I do . . . very much. I want . . . but what I want is irrelevant. I don't know if I can make you understand. You see, years ago, shortly after Caroline's death, I made a decision never to remarry, to devote my mind to the spiritual. That is the life for me, the only life. But I made that decision too soon . . . I had not finished with life. I had made mistakes, and I had to correct them. We can't progress till we have put right what we've done wrong. But I made more mistakes and more, and it was Asha who had to pay for them, not me. These last months, searching for her, I did my best to put things right for her but I know they can never be perfectly right again because she has been through hell and nothing can eradicate that. All this time I've been thinking: once she's found I will be her father and make it up to her. No more running away. For I felt that perhaps God had been an excuse, an escape from facing up to certain issues in my life. But when she saw me she shrank away and I knew that she feared me because I am a man. The only way she knows me as a father is as a father who has abandoned her, allowed her to end up in hell. How can she ever trust me? The life I was thinking of building up with her can never be. She belongs with her mother. And so my task is over. I've done my duty. Things here have come to an end. I've donated this house to the Public Health Organization and Dr Gobin – you met him, I think, a very dedicated man – is going to turn it into a real home for the girls he rescues, so it's all come to some long-term good. And as for me . . . I can continue on my path. The search for Asha brought me down to earth. But now that she's free, so am I.'

'But . . .' Rita couldn't help it. She had to butt in like an emotional little schoolgirl full of needs and wants and selfish ends. What she wanted seemed so small, so petty, compared to his grand vision. She herself was small and petty. Kamal's eyes, trained on her, glowed with a zeal whose source she could not see, could not feel, could not even imagine, but which, she knew, was mightier than her and against which she was helpless. Her confidence sagged and became a clawing, helpless creature throwing itself against a wall of glass. Kamal turned away.

'Oh. Well, in that case, I can continue my own journey.' Rita couldn't keep the bitterness out of her voice. Just seeing him again had brought up a whole jumble of feelings she preferred not to explore right now. His words seemed clear enough. He would send Asha home and get on with his life; she would have to get on with hers. There was something welling up in her that she couldn't identify and didn't want to face; it was big and round and terribly painful and made her eyes smart, so she looked away. She was a fool; she was a baby.

Take me with you! Rita cried in her heart. *Don't you see, that's what I want, what I've longed for all my life. It's been like an abyss inside and what I've found with you would fill it! A bigger, fuller, more perfect love! Show me the way, Kamal! Take me with you wherever you go! You never gave us a chance – now that Asha is back we can get to know each other under a different star, without tragedy hanging over us . . . Let us at least try . . .* But her lips remained silent, and she looked away so he would not see her tell-tale eyes.

For a moment he wavered, opening a keyhole into his soul and Rita saw and felt and understood and knew – he loved her, but would not let it be. There was a wall of glass between him and her, and she was as alone as she had ever been. More so than ever.

Kamal stood up. 'I am going back to Ma tomorrow,' he said. 'I've given Shazeed instructions concerning Asha and he will take her down to the South to reunite her with her mother tomorrow. And make some arrangement for them to live together. Gita is going with him; she's hoping you'll go too, since you know Asha the best. But of course, we don't want to impose on you any longer – not after all you've done . . .'

'You're going off just like that? Leaving others to take care of Asha? Leaving me here with my grief?' Rita had blurted out the words before she could stop herself. They simply tumbled out, as did the next words, words that were heavy with sorrow. 'I feel so – alone! I've nobody! I . . .'

Kamal was kind but hard as steel. 'I know. That's why I

suggested you go with Gita. Believe me, Rita, that's the best and quickest way to recover from your grief. Asha still needs you. Go with her!'

He turned away.

But what do I need? Rita wanted to scream behind him. But the words remained unspoken.

SIXTY-FOUR

Coming Home

For the want of an alternative, Rita accompanied Asha on the flight to Madras. At first, Rita had been reluctant to make the trip. But then, she asked herself, what else is there for me to do? Where do I start picking up the pieces of my life? And so she had gone too. She was still aching with grief for Isabelle. This was one way to deal with that.

Early that same morning she had met Marilyn at the airport, a frenzied, hysterical Marilyn who wanted nothing to do with her, who refused any help she could offer, and who had no other aim than to claim Isabelle's body and have it shipped home. It was Kamal who offered his support, who delayed his journey to the North in order to help Marilyn through the maze of officialese concerning Isabelle's post-mortem arrangements; and Kamal's help she accepted. Rita (according to Marilyn) was, once again, responsible for Isabelle's accident, and this time for Isabelle's death.

Shazeed had gone ahead to Gingee to bring Asha's mother to the airport, to arrange for the family's economic independence, and generally to sever all ties with her brother-in-law.

They left the airport building at Madras and walked along the wall of waving, shouting, jostling Indians leaning against the barricade which formed their path to the car park. Rita had her arm around Asha's shoulder; Asha walked slowly, as if slightly dazed, her head lowered, her sari draped around her head.

There was no sign of Shazeed. Then: 'There they are,' said Rita, pointing, for there was Shazeed with a pretty, plump, fiftyish woman in a pink sari coming towards them across the tarmac. She gently pushed Asha forward and stepped back herself.

The woman in the pink sari opened her arms and Asha ran forward the last few steps and pressed her little body against her. The arms closed around her. Rita turned away.

EPILOGUE

Dear Kamal,

I hope you don't mind me writing to you; I hate to barge into your life again but I still felt I should let you know how things turned out. I suppose Shazeed told you parts of this already but anyway, I'll start from the beginning.

As you instructed, Shazeed bought a house in Gingee for Asha and the family was reunited. However, things didn't turn out as well as you expected. First of all, that uncle of hers spread the word of where she had been the last year and the whole community turned against her. People began throwing stones at the house and the other children – her brothers and sisters – were shunned at school. And Asha herself, of course, was shunned wherever she went. She was not allowed to attend school.

And then the AIDS test came in and Asha is HIV positive. The health authorities panicked: no question of discretion. They wanted to take Asha and place her in some sort of quarantine. Shazeed came back from Bombay and made a big fuss so at least we prevented that.

But I'm sorry to say Sundari could not cope with the situation and I understand why. She has her other children to think of and she is quite ignorant of AIDS and is terrified the others might get it, and what with the harassment they had been going through she simply couldn't manage. She was torn apart. I have been living with them all this time so I know it all.

You see, Asha didn't want me to leave. She just wouldn't let me go. She held onto my hand when I tried to go and then she actually spoke – can you imagine, her first words! 'Please stay with me,' she said. I suppose she felt insecure about returning to her family and I had been taking care of her and trying to be kind to her all the way down so she sort of latched onto me. So I decided to stay, just till she got used to her mother.

But when things didn't work out I realized we had to leave. I know you won't mind the family staying on in Asha's home, but we, she and I, had to go. Where would we go to? Well, there seemed only one other place possible, and that was – to Rani.

I didn't ask you beforehand because I know how you feel about Rani, and I know you wouldn't have wanted that. But where else could we go? And, you know, somehow, Rani and I get on very well together. Somehow, she always respected me. And so I simply brought Asha here.

Rani is her grandmother; she is Rani's nearest relation, after you. I know for a fact how Rani hungers for an heir – and Asha is her heir. Not that I brought Asha here as a legacy-hunter – I went through that with Isabelle – but simply because I know, behind all her bluff and her bluster, Rani is as starved for love as anyone else in this world. And Asha needs love, the love of a grandmother. Rani is doing her best – if one shows one is not intimidated by her, not afraid of her, she can even be quite funny.

She has had two heart attacks in the past month.

We are in Mahapradesh right now and it is going well. We are staying in the old chowkidar's cottage, at the edge of the rose garden. Bombay is a universe away. Every morning the two peacocks and their hens come for breakfast and Asha feeds them puffed rice. Before dawn, she picks flowers and sits on the veranda making garlands for the shrine.

I haven't told Rani about her adventure in Bombay. Why should I? How will she ever find out? Rani's unpredictable and I don't know how she'd react, but for the time being she adores Asha. She has even forgiven her for her American blood – fair skin seems to open all sorts of doors in India. Asha is, of course, very beautiful. Recently she has started to smile again. You have never seen her smiling, Kamal, but there is nothing like it in this world.

We visit Rani every day – enough to satisfy her, not enough for her to get possessive about Asha. Rani likes to read her stories – the *Ramayana*, the *Mahabharata*, all the old stories. Asha seems quite happy listening.

And what about me?

I'm going to stay with Asha. Rani has persuaded me to. At least for the time being. One day I want to finish my tour of India, to write about what I see; I've already started and I know that what I've got is good. But for the time being, I'm going to write a book based on Asha's experiences.

You see, Asha has started to talk. I'm writing it all down. The world must know about the children in Kamathipura. We must put an end to this horror!

Asha is telling me everything. Once she began to talk I saw how much good it did her; and now she's talking talking talking. She's started to heal.

I thought you might like to know some of the things told me, things that pertain to you.

Because you were wrong, very wrong. Asha did not reject you. She did not accuse you of neglect and she did not blame you for her fate. Never. Not once. That was all your own imagination – your own guilt, perhaps. No. It is quite a different thing.

Asha adores you. You are to her like a living god. She feels you are so far above her; too good, too pure for her. She feels dirty, full of shame. *I am nothing but a lump of mud*, she told me yesterday. *I could not let him touch me. I will dirty him too*

483

*if he touches me. I don't want him to see me – I must hide my
face from him! How can anyone love a filthy thing like me! No
wonder he has gone, after seeing me in my dirt.*

These are Asha's words, Kamal, not mine. How I hate to tell
you this, I hate to enter your pure and perfect world with all
this bad news but still I thought that you should know. She
has been rescued, but though she smiles, though she is going
through the motions of healing, she still has one huge wound
and that's the one inflicted by you, when you gave her back
to her mother instead of showing her you loved her. I cannot
say more.

I think, once more, you were running away.

Dear Diary,

What a day this has been!

After a sleepless night I decided I had to write a letter to Kamal;
I did so at four this morning. Everything came up again, all the love
and all the hurt and resentment. All the anger. I think I called him
every name in the book. The self-pity which carried him off to his
precious Ma just when Asha needed him the most; the self-
righteousness with which he decided she'd be better off with her
mother; oh, the conceit of him! While writing my anger knew no
bounds but still I managed to keep it to myself, for Asha's sake. I
didn't bother to accuse him; why let him think I'm in any way
personally affected? No, Rita's too proud for that. But it boiled in me
anyway and I wrote five angry letters and finally, when my anger
was spent, one very rational one. As soon as we had breakfasted I
went off to the post office. Absolutely seething.

Just as I left the gates a rickshaw drew up and I almost fell over
backwards when *guess who* stepped out.

What was I supposed to do? Pick up a rock and pelt him with
it? I wish I could say I was so furious I had him tarred and feathered
and sent packing. But of course, and this you know perfectly well, I
didn't.

I simply stood there, stiff as a statue, staring, the letter in my hand.

He stood on the street, looking at me, not moving. His eyes were grave and warm and spoke a language for which there are no words, words being too gross, too rough for all there is to be said. I understood. I spoke that same language. I always have; but there was nobody to speak it too, and I ached in my isolation, struggled for acknowledgement. People called me strange; didn't they know that *they* were strange? How could they not know that language, how could it not consume them as it did me? How could they not hear the drums? But I was the only one who spoke it. I have always been alone with this language.

The language of my heart came to me muddled, confused; I was a walking Tower of Babel. I carried it all my life, locked away inside me, interpreting it into the language of the world in order to perform in a manner acceptable to my fellow humans. I was forced to learn it in my heart; I perfected it in a space inside me no one could ever enter, singling out the one strain that would lead me here, to this one perfect instant.

I heard it as a gentle rhythm inside me, like a beating of drums but silent, summoned to a magnificent concert that no one could hear but me. I was an audience of one.

Now we were an audience of two. Alone in all the universe, and yet the universe was contained in us, in that perfect moment when all is said and done and a touch, a spoken word, would be superfluous, would spoil the flawless union of minds and hearts.

I threw away the letter.